# Praise for *These, Our Bodies, Possessed by Light*

'In her masterful debut, Dharini Bhaskar gives us a young woman hovering at a crossroads in her life – and before she chooses, she must first consider the lives and loves of the women who came before her and whose choices both bind her and set her free. With a poet's easy grace with language and a philosopher's comfort with ambiguity, she traces how each one of us contains multitudes – and shows us, in a way we can never forget, how family is both the greatest fact and fiction of all.' – **Chandrahas Choudhury**

'Dharini Bhaskar's writing has the muscles of light – in her first novel she takes us to places that we haven't seen before, places left invisible by life and literature. In this deeply moving novel, we encounter a family of women related by the inheritance of confusion – there were times I found my hand touching their names on the page, as if reaching out to hold them, to tell them that we were there, their relatives, waiting outside the novel. I think I understand the punctuations of my pain better after reading this book.' – **Sumana Roy**

'Dharini Bhaskar's first novel is a beautifully structured exploration of a Tamil family that comes to settle in Mumbai. Their world is presented through the experiences of five women: three sisters, their mother, and their grandmother. The action moves beyond Mumbai, to Delhi, Norway, and the US. The men in their lives arrive like magical driftwood, strike against them, drift away. Some manage to stay put. Weaving all of this into a dense emotional tapestry is an undercurrent of legend and mythology. A first book, a fine achievement, truly an auspicious beginning!' – **Gieve Patel**

'The novel jump-cuts from a village in South India with a large family to a pub in England and a photographer of overage retired ships. But the narrative is seamless and written with a verve and passion that could be the envy of other novelists. An unforgettable read, dotted with pensive moments and uncertainties.' – **Keki N. Daruwalla**

# These, Our Bodies, Possessed by Light

## DHARINI BHASKAR

First published in 2019 by Hachette India
(Registered name: Hachette Book Publishing India Pvt. Ltd)
An Hachette UK company
www.hachetteindia.com

1

ISBN 978-93-5195-281-7

Hachette Book Publishing India Pvt. Ltd
4th & 5th Floors, Corporate Centre,
Plot No. 94, Sector 44, Gurugram 122003, India

Typeset in Dante MT Std 11.5/16
by R Ajith Kumar, New Delhi

Printed and bound in India
by Manipal Technologies Limited, Manipal

*To Aayansh, the firstborn,*
*the light in my sky*

'What makes life life and not a simple story? Jagged bits moving never still, all along the wall.'
　　—*Anne Carson*

'You remember too much,' my mother said to me recently. 'Why hold on to all that?'
And I said, 'Where can I put it down?'
　　—*Anne Carson*

# Preface.

*Tell me about the dream where we pull the bodies out of the lake*
*and dress them in warm clothes again.*

This, the inheritance of a night – Neil's voice, his hand running over my own. 'You'll be there?'

An answer should come easy. 'Yes,' I ought to say. Yes, we'll meet. Maybe we'll live together.

Yet, even as Neil steps into a waiting taxi, retreats, his form a blur, I am reminded of a fact – one that's quick to fade away. In a week, my husband will return. In a week, he'll ring the doorbell, ardent and ship-soiled and wanting.

What to say as the husband approaches?

What to say to Neil?

Instead of recovering an explicit response, I dwell on a household's semi-stories. I see before me Mamma with postcards that can't be posted; Amamma stepping out of a gate, not turning back; Tasha–Ranja with selves that have vanished, dust to dust.

Every attempt at pinning down a reply evokes recollections of a family – Daddy, Rangaa, Janaki. I turn a rosary of names and half-names.

Maybe all of us are no more than Venn diagrams – our personal biographies and those of our relations colliding to create the teardrop of our selves. Maybe when we speak of genes, of the double helix of DNAs, of being heir to black eyes, idiosyncrasies, a voice, we also speak of coming into histories, reminiscences, a shared unconscious.

Maybe, to answer the most vital of questions – *you'll be there?* – I need to not only understand my past but also retrace the stories of those closest. I need the big picture, a frame of deep time, vast swathes of space marked Before-Daddy and After-.

Perhaps I should start at the beginning –

# Beginnings.

*How it was late, and no one could sleep,*

# 1.

This is how it begins – a girl of sixteen by the front porch. It's 1943, and she's pretty, the way those in 1943 would be, without wrinkles and sunspots, with hair, black and oiled, set into two ribboned plaits. She's plump – she *must* be – with flesh cushioning her elbows and knees and knuckles. She must also be without glasses, so her eyes peer at rimless objects and people – now at the man before her with a burgeoning rice-tummy.

'Sarojaa,' I hear him call – though I cannot associate her with the name, with anything apart from a made-up word, part Tamil, part babe-speak, *Amamma, Amamma*. I suppose she responds – it's what people do – though already she senses in the pit of her belly that things such as names don't mean very much. They change just like skin would – sag, turn colour, bruise, peel, shed – without permission, without warning.

It's mid-afternoon, and the sun smoulders in the south.

An hour ago, Sarojaa was in school, an outcast in a game that involved classmates, tight circles, and a chant that tediously went, in garbled English, *A-tisket, A-tasket*. Since she lacked the patience to break into a loop of bodies, clutch on to a pair of wrists, and repeat an all-too-simple rhyme, she did the next best thing – she devised a game of her own. It entailed sitting in a corner and studying the pure blue of the sky.

There was something about this girl that annoyed her classmates. Maybe it was her aloofness, that she did not implore them for an invite. Maybe it was that she could spot clouds – invisible, shape-changing clouds – denied to the rest. Maybe it was simply that in her dhavani, three inches too short, sixteen-year-old Sarojaa seemed startlingly complete. Her eyes – always wide, even when she laughed rambunctiously – led easily to the bridge of her nose; her nose dipped into a plump upper lip. So, if you glanced at Sarojaa even fleetingly, there was an inkling that each feature would hook up, connect. And astonishingly, this is one attribute that has endured.

I'm willing to believe that Sarojaa was not popular with the girls. I'm also willing to believe that she was secretly observed, even admired by the boys – that there were those who could look beyond her budding adolescence and delight in the evenness, the staggering unity of her features.

Venu – and I must call him this because I can't think of any other Tamil-sounding name – was naïve enough to believe in things beyond the body. He was young – eighteen, if we must arrive at a number – with a fascination for things of one piece. Which made him linger by the school enclosure and watch Sarojaa in conversation with the sky.

It's possible that Venu had seen her earlier – arguing fiercely with her younger brother, the only boy in her family of twelve girls, about the colour of a common housefly, or pouring a pitcher of milk into a puddle to see if it permanently changed colour, or scrutinizing painted nudes by a tamarind tree while her mother cracked down on an errant offspring. The truth is Venu might have been watching her for years now, vaguely aware of the details – the defiance, the daily mutinies – that contributed to Sarojaa's allness, that made her a creature unlike the other girls, unabashedly spirited, unabashedly whole.

So, the more Venu watched her, the more he yearned for her actual presence, for the joys of dialogue, for the thrills of jousting and repartee, and it is this impulse that finally made him bound to the neighbour's, scoop up a handful of wild flowers, and wait near the school gate for Sarojaa.

Rangaa was not one for flowers, partly because he was already a man. Such dainty gestures were not to be expected of him. At thirty, he carried the world's expectations on his shoulders, and being a dutiful, submissive doctor of Ayurveda, he felt obliged to fulfil them.

Life had not been easy for Rangaa. Orphaned at eight, employed as a doctor's compounder at eleven, married at eighteen, Rangaa's plunge into adulthood had been dizzying at best. But strangely, after the noise and clamour of a wedding, weeks had slipped into months with terrifying quietness, without incident. Twelve years had passed, and Rangaa had been unable to introduce a line of descendants, a brood of children to carry forward his name. It was incomprehensible, this failure. Night after night of uncomfortable, frantic coition with a woman who scarcely tolerated his body (the clumsiness of his mouth, the pudginess of his stomach, the stubbornness of his crotch) and who refused to disclose herself to him – she stayed hidden beneath her sari and a bed sheet that fully concealed her breasts – had produced nothing of value, not even sentiment.

Rangaa could endure many things – ninety-hour work weeks, obdurate patients, a reluctant spouse – but it was impossible for him to suffer the gibes of his neighbours, those with limber families that expanded at will, or the sympathy of friends and acquaintances inclined to ask the same question each time they chanced upon his shuffling figure: 'Good news yet, Anna? Good news?' Rangaa wanted to be the bearer of good news. He wanted desperately a clutch of burbling children somewhere in the background. He wanted runny noses and colic-ridden nights and the prospect of finding fault with a headstrong son. So intense was this desire that it interfered with his razor-sharp focus, made him take two wrong turns on the way to a patient's home, and reach a school enclosure. Inside, Sarojaa was seated – plump arms wrapped around plump knees pressed against a plump belly.

Rangaa noticed her – the keenness of her figure, its possibilities, its capacity to hold and sustain and nurture and yield. All at once, he sensed a spurt of anxiety, a quiver, a sudden palpitation that began somewhere in the nether regions of his brain and sped downward past his throat, his pounding heart, his belly, straight down to his bumbling loins. 'I must have her,' he decided and darted beyond the girl, the enclosure, the school gate, past a boy clutching a bouquet of wilting flowers.

Venu noticed Rangaa the way he would notice most things – distantly, as a smudge of light, rather than as a form with a sharp fringe of voracity. And it strikes me that this is where he erred. That had he been a more acute observer, trained in identifying the language of bodies – the firmness in Rangaa's eyes and the odd swiftness of his feet – he might have stopped the older man with a gesture, stalled his thoughts with a remark. But such things could not be expected of Venu. So Rangaa ran, unchecked and unopposed, through a narrow gully, across a waterless sewer, past a puddle still white with milk, beyond a tree hiding poorly produced nude paintings, to a house with a thatched roof and children pouring out of every door and window.

Now lithe with sweat, Rangaa stopped for the first time in minutes before a man slumped on a rocking chair, already overfull with two baby girls and rattles and laundered diapers. 'Good news yet, Anna? Good news?' the man must've asked, while his wife approached the doctor with the long list of ailments troubling those gobs of children – a stye in the baby's eye, a stutter that slowed down the infant's talk, the faulty vision of her son, the tiresome inquisitiveness of her oldest daughter.

At this point, I imagine, a mile away from that house infested with people and tetchy voices, the schoolgirls engaged in a game of rhymes decided to leave. And Sarojaa, reminded of matters beyond the sky, got up, dusted her dhavani, and rambled to the gate, where she saw floppy wild flowers (a splodge of purple and red), then a hand soaked with sweat, a body in an ironed shirt, a face framed by doubt. It's true that Venu, a mathematician by profession, doubted a good many things – the findings of Ramanujan, the stances of Aryabhata. But now, for the first time, he found himself doubting the familiar, the everyday, the stock capabilities of his body – the capacity of his legs to support his torso, the strength of his torso to bolster his head – so suddenly, by that school gate, the simple physics of existence seemed awfully complicated.

Sarojaa, meanwhile, never known to acknowledge the complications of existence, and always too quick for Venu, raised a pert chin and an eyebrow (with the kind of smoothness Venu envied) and asked, 'These flowers – they're for me?'

Venu gulped, shocked by her effrontery, or stood still, terrified that a rising tremor would compromise the unity of knuckle-and-wrist, or blinked and hoped that his stubby eyelashes would compensate for his overdry mouth. Or maybe, in a moment of acute bravery, the kind books and films are built on, he stood tall, rolled his tongue, and pieced together that perfect syllable – 'Yes.'

'Yes.'

And Sarojaa, at ease with affirmations, trained in the laws of high drama, laughed, grabbed the flowers, handed a satchel in exchange, and said in that voice I'm now used to, sharp like vessels clanging, 'What're you, there, standing like that for? Come.'

Venu followed on meek feet, stopped when he was told to, looked when she pointed skyward, spoke when she quizzed with a wagging finger, 'Cat got your tongue?'

'No. No.' The conversation wasn't quite the kind he had imagined – no room for logic, no space for the barter of coherent thoughts. Rather, words hopscotched from topic to topic, fact to belief. They spoke of birds and where they nested ('On sun rays,' said Sarojaa; 'As if!' said Venu); of mushrooms and the way they'd look upside down ('Like Viking ships,' said Sarojaa; 'Like upturned shrooms,' said Venu); of the sound of raindrops, the smell of sambhar, and the exact depth of the sea ('Whale-deep,' said Sarojaa; 'You're crazy!' said Venu).

It was crazy, for Venu had experienced nothing like this. His mind unspooled, his hands recovered the joys of motion. As he mulled over the number of homeless dogs in the neighbourhood, he felt his free arm stirring, moving upward, over, against – sensing Sarojaa's forefinger, its warm blush, its shiver, the way it coiled around his pinkie. Sarojaa, for her part, learnt of a new kind of touch, far removed from her brother's nudges, her mother's whops, her father's assertive clench – tender, barely present, yet enough to make each nerve tingle.

Rangaa knew nothing of this sensation. But he knew mortification, he knew anxiety. Which is why he was at the house, opening his mouth slow-fast, fast-slow like a goldfish, trying to piece together a sentence, subject-verb-predicate intact. Till what emerged was a non-sentence, the kind that is known to erupt during a decisive moment and shape lives. 'Your daughter, Sir, marry lovely I want to.'

The man slumped on the rocking chair opened his eyes wide, tried to sort out the hotchpotch of words and half-words. Then, showing the first signs of comprehension, he sat erect, studied the knots of bleary-eyed daughters, those in diapers, those in skirts they had outgrown, those learning the first of the letters, those squatting on their haunches, helping their mother scrub the courtyard, and one – that smudge in the far distance – who ruined family portraits, robbed milk, skulked by bushes like a rogue animal.

'Which daughter, Anna?'

Rangaa, probably stunned by the force of his incoherence, raised an arm, moved away from the squawking of girls with bags that needed mending and hair that needed combing and elbows that needed bandaging, and pointed a feeble finger that landed plumb on the figure of Sarojaa squabbling with Venu.

'You're such a coward!'

'No, I am not!'

'Then climb that mountain with me!'

Venu – too shy to accept her challenge and much too shy to flee – stood rooted to the spot. So Sarojaa snatched her satchel, threw away the flowers, swore to teach a lesson to her lily-livered sweetheart. 'Just you wait!' she shouted. 'You'll see!'

If Venu had been smarter, he'd have climbed on to a rooftop and announced, 'Sarojaa, you're beautiful.' If Venu had been quicker, he'd have clasped Sarojaa's hand, smelt her hair, peeked into her blouse, and located the lone vein weaving in-and-out-and-in, holding together her body, each of her features. If Venu had been –

But Venu wasn't.

I'd like to portray Venu as either clever or agile, perhaps even a little desperate, so he'd gain Rangaa's pluck, his ability to gabble, rush to the house and scream the doctor down. But integrity would demand that I leave Venu alone, an obscure figure under a tamarind tree, and make Rangaa – ponderous, unassuaged Rangaa; Rangaa with a belly as large as Asia – the lead actor.

Rangaa's finger now followed a muttering Sarojaa past the altar to nude paintings, another milky puddle, to the porch of a busy house. 'Her!' he disclosed in a moment of sudden lucidity, and the man on the rocking chair looked at his daughter, the most unreasonable girl in his flock, the one who scampered down trees, bruised her legs, produced bills worth fifteen annas. *Fifteen annas!*

'Her? Are you sure?'

And the mother, never one to be discreet, interrupted, 'Yes...are you sure? You have a wife, no, doctor?'

And Sarojaa, baffled Sarojaa, only now beginning to comprehend the enormity of the situation before her, its implications, yelled, 'What is this? Tell me, what is this? Chasing girls – '

The man on the rocking chair relinquished his seat, stood up, raised an autocratic hand. 'Quiet!' he shouted. 'Running up trees and after no-good boys! Is this what I taught you?'

'But I – '

'Will you or will you not do as I tell you?'

'Eh. Well. Perhaps.'

Ignoring the brazenness of Sarojaa's retort, the man turned to Rangaa and asked matter-of-factly, 'Anna, you want her?'

'Why – '

'Yes?'

'Yes.'

'Good.'

'Good?'

'Take Sarojaa right now.'

'What?'

'What?' I hear the question posed by two people – one flabbergasted by the turn of fortune, one beginning to break.

From here, everything unfolds in jump cuts. And it is this lightning-fast montage that we acknowledge as the beginning, and that we repeat during weddings and family gatherings, not entirely, but in bits and pieces, with amusement and wonder.

There is a bullock cart, a man seated in it, Rangaa. There is a bundle of gold jewellery and fresh clothes. There is a woman instructing the driver, 'The temple, third left, fifth right!' There is the sound of drums. There is my grandmother by the porch, looking at something or someone – a timid boy in the far distance – while my grandfather shouts in a triumphant voice, 'Sarojaa! Hello! Hello, hello!'

This is all we claim to know.

I should tell you, my household is obsessed with marriage. I should tell you, too, that it is quick to erase life's defining events outside of matrimony – the unrequited love stories, the short-lived affairs, the bodies claimed with rapture and curiosity.

It's what has made this family stick – the blessed art of forgetting.

## 2.

Amamma forgets.

Sometimes, when I close my eyes, I can see her, my grandmother, stark, almost real – loose flesh hanging by the hem of a blouse, breasts sagging like giant udders, bespectacled frog eyes moving, studying pieces of an old world. There are photographs on her lap, creased, in faded colours – Tasha, all of four, lying by a lawn with a pile of plums, knickers showing; Ranja, primly bibbed, dipping a spoon into a bowlful of pear purée; me –

'Who's this child?'

I start, partly because this is a description I'm unused to – 'child', with its overtones of lightly carried cheer – but also because Amamma's question reminds me that she has moved on, retreated. Her mind's clear like air.

'Amamma, it's Deeya – don't you know?'

'Who?'

'Deeya. Dee. Your pethi. Your granddaughter. My sister.'

'Her?'

'Yes. Her. Deeya.'

'Her?'

'Yes.'

It's hard to tell who is speaking. The voice in my head is shrill, somewhat petulant, so it could either be Ranja after scoring a B in a test or Tasha with a boyfriend who has lasted too long. But I can see – sharp as light – my grandmother poring over my body, poorly waxed calves to concave belly to –

'Too small.'

'What, Amamma?'

'Too small. Her breasts – ' Then flailing her arms, 'Really, she should do something about them.'

I open my eyes and observe the instant – it's splayed like something dying. There it is, Amamma's remark, my sudden awareness of my body and, with it, the desire to erase her words, replace them with kinder, softer, emptier ones.

So sometimes, when I'm angry, I wish to blame her, my mother's mother, for the things I've lurched towards, opted for – all the men – those who've come and refused to stay, those who have, and that boy, the lone boy, whose name I cannot remember.

'*Amma!* Don't you know Deeya?' My mother interrupts.

'What?'

'Natasha. Ranjana. Deeya.' My mother points to each of us.

'Oh. Deeya?'

'Of course. Deeya.'

'Well. Perhaps.'

I can picture my mother – hair coiled into a bun, a few strands of silver – turning around, walking, not waiting, as Amamma works out an impossible puzzle –

'My granddaughter?'

I don't know when it began, Amamma's descent into forgetfulness. What I do know is how I learnt of it.

Even now, I can see the sky, rosé red, liquid. My grandmother underneath it, full, in nine yards of silk. Her hair blows, wisps of pepper and salt, and her face stays pressed against a window. She is in a car, a black and yellow Ambassador, its meter running. I am beside her, young, twelve years, not older.

All at once, the driver says something. I hear every other word. 'Madam.' 'Kahaan?' 'Where?'

My grandmother says nothing, looks, keeps looking – oddly anxious – at the roads that fork, wind, loop, end altogether abruptly, or don't. Already her hands reveal a net of veins; her fingers trace them uneasily.

'Stop!' my grandmother shouts.

The driver swerves, the car screeches to a halt, but I don't attend to any of this. Instead, I watch Amamma, her hair still wind-tossed, her eyes large, bewildered, her mouth trembling with uncertainty. 'What's wrong?' I ask, but my grandmother will not answer. Rather, she's all verbs – *flings* open the door, *tumbles* out, *commands* the driver, 'Take her home,' and *inserts* cash, too much, into his pocket.

I recall the sky, still liquid red, my grandmother's escape, and my twelve-year-old annoyance at her total fickleness. I direct the driver home, not far at all – two lefts, a right – enter a building, stomp up the stairs, and ring the doorbell.

As I march into the house, Mamma looks past me. 'Where's Amma?' she asks. I shrug, careless, displaying the first signs of pettish adolescence.

'What does that mean?'

'Amamma dived out of the cab.'

'What? How come?'

'I don't know. She paid the driver and went.'

'Where did she go?'

'She didn't tell.'

'What?'

'I told you. She left. No explanation given.'

Mamma's forehead creases. She approaches the telephone. Stops.

'It's strange.'

'What is?'

'Strange. This slipping away.'

This is the day my family shares stories.

Each of us – Mamma, Tasha, Ranja, and I – holds clues to Amamma's retreat. We disclose them, these narratives, half-narratives; we speak of our first brush with her descent into forgetting.

Mamma begins. She tells us of a morning, a fortnight before the cab misadventure. She was cooking, making curries for a colony of office-goers. My grandmother was close, scrutinizing odds and ends like a ragpicker – lids, spoons, Ziploc bags, glass bottles. 'Want something, Amma?' my mother asked. But Amamma ignored her.

Then, all at once, it fell – crashed – a word. No, something quite else. Bare. 'Arghl,' Amamma hollered. Her face as bleak as her utterance.

Mamma stared. Her eyebrows, perfect arches, rose, then collapsed; her lower lip shivered. 'Amma?'

Ever since my grandmother had been whisked away in a bullock cart to a house with a kindly first wife and a stingy husband, she had been hoarding riches. Not huge amounts, no, but trifles – a rupee here, an anna elsewhere – bits and bobs once stolen from her husband's shirt pocket or his rolltop desk, now taken from Mamma's purse. These embezzled sums would be concealed in the kitchen – under the mortar, inside the cavernous bin for red chillies, by the emptied-out earthen water pot – and retrieved when the need arose to buy a brand-new sari, a cinema ticket or (the biggest extravagance of them all) a piece of local art. Amamma, as a rule, knew where her stash lay. Like a squirrel, she'd conceal her precious scraps, then ferret them out a while later.

A fortnight ago, my grandmother failed to locate her fortune. And Mamma guessed she was losing her mind.

Tasha is the next to speak. 'It was three weeks ago,' she says, 'early', light dribbling in, so the drawing room acquired definition. The sofa with cushions stacked like Lego blocks. The vase with a chapped lip. The photograph of a painting – swift lines, colour, the impression of a face, woman-child, with a mouth altogether fluent.

The painting. I should speak more of the painting, its known histories. It had been made by an emerging artist in Madras, A.P. Santhanaraj, and Amamma, still young, spied it by the grilled window of his house. 'This,' she said, 'this I want.'

It wasn't easy, the transaction. My grandmother was forced to round up all the cash in the chilli bin, a princely sum of thirty-nine rupees. Once the deal was clinched, she clung to it, this piece of art, cherished it, not for its value or its obvious sophistication, but because, I imagine, it reminded her of an old self, a time and a place almost lost – down the road with milky puddles, not far from a crammed house, by the side of a boy with shrivelled flowers.

Santhanaraj's painting eventually left Amamma's home. It happened, not by design, but by a turn of circumstance – a daughter to provide for, three granddaughters to support. By then, Santhanaraj had become an illustrious painter, the most influential name in the south, lauded for his engagement with space and form, fluid lines, rock faces. And Amamma, apprised of this, sold his work to an art collector for one lakh rupees. A day before delivering the artwork, my grandmother strode resolutely into a studio. She wanted a photograph of the painting. 'The mouth,' she pleaded, 'get the mouth.' The photographer tried, tried again. Failed.

The mediocre photograph now hangs on a wall in the house bought with the money Amamma made after winning what Mamma calls an 'art lottery'.

Each morning, after her bath, before her puja, Amamma would stand by the photograph, her hair wet, her eyes thought-filled. She'd talk to it, quiet, too quiet for us to hear, place a flower, a rich marigold, against the frame, and leave.

Tasha looks at us. 'Three weeks ago, Amamma stood near the painting. Tried to say something. Couldn't.'

'Amamma?' Tasha had whispered.

'S.'

'S?'

'Or I think – the artist. An R? An A.'

'I don't understand.'

'His name. It must start with an H. H?'

So Tasha knew.

She knows.

Ranja is about to speak –

But then the doorbell rings.

I hear the doorbell even now, shrill, insistent, ringing twice, thrice, four times. Mamma rushes to the door, returns. Amamma is half-hidden behind her. Her hair is slovenly, her sari is rumpled. But her feet – her feet are assured.

There are questions in the background that hang impatiently like chimes. 'Where were you? Why? What made you – ?' But Amamma cannot respond, will not talk, refuses to pause. Instead, she hurries, drawing room to bedroom – the one she and I share – crosses the shadow line, the chalk stroke that distinguishes her space from mine, draws out a carton, squats.

I've seen her with it before, the tattered cardboard carton. Her hands sink into its open flaps, her fingers sift through the contents. A black-and-white photograph, parents and twelve siblings, plaits and smiles, Amamma the sole exception, loose hair and a scowl altogether ferocious. A prescription, date intact, scribbled by the late husband Rangaa – '*1 November 1960. One tomato, two cashew nuts*' – known to make married women mothers. A brooch with a bird, procured during a self-sponsored trip abroad. A book of Titian paintings. A note. Finally. The note –

Its edges are worn with constant handling. Its margin displays a date: *31 October 1960*. Underneath, there's a sentence, smudged, in blue ink, each letter falling backward, each word precise: '*Meet me tomorrow at four in Chetpet*'. No period. No signature.

Amamma reads it, eyes vacant. 'Who wrote this?' her dulled mouth seems to ask.

And suddenly, I'm certain.

Amamma cannot remember.

*The Greeks call Lethe, deep in Hades, the river of oblivion. So potent are her waters that a mere drop can wipe away all recollection. Each evening, the departed – the living-dead and the deceased – huddle around her bank, heads bent low as though in reverence, and wet their throats. Within seconds, amnesia sweeps over their souls, and they're sundered from the lives they've fought for.*

*Aethalides is an exception. The young man has spent days by the mouth of Lethe, but the river has failed to overpower him. Her ripples cannot draw him away from his past; her waters cannot wash away his consciousness. Friends imagine this is because of an ancient boon or a curse; no doubt, Aethalides has been granted eternal memory.*

*The facts, though, are different, and they have to do with Aethalides's drift towards an island many years ago.*

*At that time, Aethalides had been under his captain Jason's command. As his ship approached the island of Lemnos, he saw rows of armoured women by the coast, brandishing swords and lances. The residents of Lemnos were convinced that the vessel held their enemies, the plundering Thracians.*

*As the swiftest herald ever born, Aethalides was ordered to deliver a message of peace and announce that he represented the Argonauts, harmless friends. Racing like the very wind, Aethalides appeared before the queen of Lemnos, the exquisite Hypsipyle. She was covered, livid head to toe, in a shell of bronze, flickering against the sea of her subjects. A glance in her direction and Aethalides was overcome with an emotion he was ill-equipped to define – part terror, part awe, part veneration, part bewilderment. He walked up to a wary Hypsipyle, assured her of his innocence, made extravagant promises – 'We'll stay here and help you. For however long. In whatever capacity you desire. Always.'*

*Hypsipyle smiled. She accepted the offer. And even as Aethalides learnt that the indefinable was love, she wooed a self-satisfied Jason.*

*Aethalides, stunned, refused to surrender hope. He waited for Hypsipyle to shift her ground, pined for her reciprocity, lingered as she romanced the beaming captain of the Argonauts.*

*He lingers still.*

*Not even the mighty Lethe can erase the memory of the one he treasures – of the queen by the shore, forbidding-beautiful, raging like a shaft of light.*

Amamma has been engulfed in the waters of Lethe –

Maybe amnesia rushes in when we acknowledge the demise of love.

Mamma.
Daddy.

*the horses running*
*until they forget that they are horses.*

# 1.

I'd like to make sense of Amamma's paling memory –

But such attempts are for later. Such attempts, I believe, can only be made once the surrounding facts are established.

Let's start with the fact of Mamma's birth.

My mother was born in a bungalow on McNichols Road, Madras, eighteen years into Amamma's association with my grandfather. Back then, the neighbourhood was a curious place to inhabit. It was anchored to the past and suspicious of anything newfangled. The outdoor faucets slunk behind private wells. The cycle-rickshaws hid behind the more assertive hand-pulled ones. The evening beverage-seller put away his ceramic cups; he drew out, instead, two steel utensils, poured filter coffee back and forth, davara to tumbler, tumbler to davara. Inside bungalows, wall paint was interrupted by old lime plaster; metal plates lost their sheen when confronted with plantain leaves.

If homes shape stances (as they sometimes do), my mother came to be a child of tradition. She wished to fit into bright, hand-stitched pavadai-chokhas, braid her hair into two plaits, cast a dot between her eyebrows. There are photographs of her seated with my grandfather, an array of god-prints in the background, a brass lamp in the vicinity; Mamma smiling.

Sometimes, I suppose I have coveted that – the ease of my mother's childhood and the ability she possessed to slip into a place's larger life.

Such conduct though did not impress Amamma. Having wrestled for a childhood of tree-top-rebellion and candy-shop-joy, my grandmother hoped to bless her child with cosy defiance. She did what she could to tempt her daughter. Steal her away from school. Sneak her into local buses. Drag her to new, defiant lands – Marina beach with fruit-sellers peeling-cutting-selling tart mangoes; Gemini Studio, renowned for its semi-nude mascot (and the throngs of children on the street squealing, *'Gemini Studio jetti avandha pochu'*, 'The mascots have lost their knickers'); MGR's house with the vendor outside, bugle in hand, announcing, 'Rita ice cream, one anna, ice cream.'

There are so many childhoods my mother could have had. Sometimes I attempt reimagining her as an unruly nine-year-old, learning paths the way kids do, the way my grandmother had, not through signs or maps or books, but by sliding down water pipes, clambering up walls or following files of ants and crickets and grasshoppers –

Let me stop. That life held no appeal for Mamma. She wanted, not the thrills associated with scraped knees, those little adventures, but the simple pleasure of housekeeping. My mother's childhood, consequently, despite Amamma's early efforts, must be located in the garden patch outside the bungalow, in the kitchen or by the ancient well.

With Amamma, my mother would willingly squat in the vegetable garden. She'd cut off the heads of carrots and plant them in tilled soil or bury onions, full, into the earth. She'd wait for the first flowerings – the yellow blossoms of okra or a bright cucumber bloom. She'd dig out potatoes, pick snap beans, and harvest the tender leaves of pea shoots.

For Mamma, the practice of food-finding and -making was intimately linked to the act of building stories. When my mother was little, Ammama, loath to cook but compelled to by an exacting husband, tried to make the process painless by involving Mamma. Mother and daughter would sit by the porch – Amamma with an arivan manai, a knife attached to a piece of wood, slicing okra; Mamma, close by, shelling groundnuts. Together, they'd imagine another life – as beings of static, minor celebrities, radio chefs. Ammama would whisper, 'Quick. We're being interviewed! Remember the recipe?'

And Mamma would respond hurriedly, 'Yes, yes, we're making puliyodarai.' Or seppankizhangu varuval. Or vatha kuzhambu.

Let's assume it's vatha kuzhambu – the only recipe I have learnt by rote.

'Right you are!' Amamma would announce.

'We have to – '

'Wait! Three, two, one. Ready, kutti? We're on air!'

Mamma would clear her throat. 'Good morning, ladies and gentlemen.' She'd pause, soak in the sound of applause. 'Thank you, thank you.' She'd smile. 'Today, two of Madras's most talented chefs will guide you with the recipe of a mouth-watering dish. Home-made vatha kuzhambu.'

Amamma would interrupt, 'It is simplicity itself.'

And Mamma would speak in her most adult voice, 'First, gather okra, fresh from the garden. Cut the vegetable into long, slender strips. Like this.'

'Like this. Did you know, kutti, roasted okra seeds were used as a substitute for coffee beans in America?'

'I know! You've told me. Three times already!'

'Have I? Well, I've begun repeating myself.'

Even as Mamma'd giggle, Ammama would collect a pallu-ful of cut okra, inch towards the kerosene stove, place an enormous pan on it. 'What happens next, kutti?'

'Pour oil, throw in mustard seeds. When the seeds sputter like firecrackers, add Bengal gram and curry leaves. Once they change colour, toss in the okra. Let all of it cook.'

'And once the okra is nearly cooked?'

'Oh, add salt, then sambhar powder.'

'Wonderful. And then?'

'Tamarind water!'

'Excellent. And then?'

'And then gobble it all down with rice.'

'How does it taste?'

'Oh, so yum.'

'It tickles your throat and teases your tongue, no?'

'Yes, yes.'

'Is it far too tangy?'

'No, of course not, it's perfect.'

'Okay, but let's imagine. What if it becomes much too sour?'

'Well, in that case, we add sweet potato!'

'Exactly. Sweet potato.'

'Yes.'

'Hmm. There's a story about the vegetable, kutti, that I read in a book many years ago. Would you like to hear it?'

'Yes!'

'Then listen. It's said that in a faraway place, many thousands of years ago, people would only eat fish and meat and chicken. There were no vegetables to pluck, no fruits, not even overripe berries. Paraparawa lived during this period, a young, hard-working lad.'

'Like me.'

'Like you, only a boy. And older. Eighteen or so.'

'That's *very* old.'

'Yes. Yes, I suppose it is. Now, one day, when Paraparawa went out to sea, he caught a plump fish. As it wriggled this way and that, left and right, it shed its scales and became a woman.'

'Oh!'

'Paraparawa was startled by this sea-creature's beauty, wanted to marry her. And as luck would have it, she agreed. Soon after, she stood by the edge of the coast and called out to her father. "Papa, I have news, I'm getting married," she shouted.'

'And?'

'And her father, the king of sea-creatures, a giant anaconda, slithered out of the depths of the ocean. He drew out his hands, blessed his child, and gifted her what seemed to be a hard, maroon, oddly shaped rock.'

'Bah!'

'The princess would agree. She was far from pleased. But before she could protest, her father bellowed like the very waves, "This is for the wedding feast. Bury it in the earth, my daughter. Drench it with rain. Bless it with your hands. And watch."'

'What happened?'

'Well, the princess placed the offering in the soil and watered it. A day passed, then two days, then three, the little rock sprouted baby rocks, and the baby rocks multiplied further. All under the earth.'

'Like magic!'

'The soil's magic, yes. "Gather and cook this offering, my daughter, and consume it," the father said. And as the princess tasted those boiled rocks, her eyes grew large. As large as yours. "Why, this has to be the most delicious thing," she said, "sweet and soft."'

'*That* tasty?' Mamma must have stretched her arms out wide.

'Tastier than even that. A day later, the princess married Paraparawa. There was a feast beyond compare, with bowlfuls of soft-sweet rocks, doused in oil, mixed with salt. Such plenty! And still there were many raw rocks left over.'

'Oh!'

'These remains, kutti, these were reunited with the earth. And that is how vegetables were born. And the first of them, the very first, and therefore the most beloved was – do you know what it was?'

'What, what?'

'Guess.'

'Don't confuse me. What?'

'The sweet potato, kutti.'

'Oh! That! That I knew!'

The faux radio show would end at this point. Mamma would ask for seppankizhangu varuval or vatha kuzhambu or puliyodarai, and Amamma would smile indulgently and feed her ravenous daughter.

There are so many kitchen stories my grandmother left my mother. Some strange, from faraway countries; some sourced from the jagged states of India. But what Mamma would remember most of all was Amamma's account of apples.

'Once, it's said, there were varieties of apples in house orchards, all beautifully named – Ziegler's Sweeting, Aaron Holt. Girls would sink their teeth into these fruits, men would carry them in their pockets. Then the old era slipped away. People got busy. Gardens no longer came with trees. There were markets to drive to instead, with long-lasting apples, each distinguished from the next by bruise resistance and shelf life. Names vanished. Hundreds of apples became extinct –'

Mamma thought about this as a child – the textures she had missed, the tastes she'd never know. The dry astringency of one apple. The nutty aftertaste of another. The bizarre cocktail of flavours, tart-sweet-bitter, of a third. So much lost to the tongue. Not just tastes, but pasts and histories and stories, of women plucking the tiniest of apples, no larger than half-annas, sweet-scented, and carrying them in their purses; of workmen hiding a special cider in the hollow of a tree; of children staring at the Baltimore Monstrous Pippin, one foot in diameter, four inches high. Such immensity.

Gone.

For a long time, these facts strummed in the far corners of Mamma's mind. Detached.

Then, one day, it happened. The surfacing. The coming together.

It was an ordinary apple that would rescue my mother from the edge.

# 2.

Mamma grew up. She breezed through school. She revelled in a quiet adolescence. She stumbled into a new decade, that of the 1980s.

1981 was a year of ends and beginnings. Bob Marley dead. Natalie Portman born. Lady Di married. And Mamma waiting for Amamma in the courtyard of a temple in Madras.

Mamma was twenty years old, maybe younger. Her skin was an even-toned brown, lustrous with youth and inexperience. Her hair was plaited, a string of jasmines pinned on, two clips to keep stray wisps secure. And her forehead carried a pottu, a meek dot in red. Mamma, I'm sure, was smiling – and this is what I find hard to picture – no grief lines along the corners of her mouth, no dark circles around her eyes, nothing to foreshadow the enormity of the troubles to come. Her smile must have been easy. As simple as the statement, 'Thank you, yes, I am very well.'

On that precise day, my mother had been exceptionally well. She had topped her exam in mathematics. She had options, even if she didn't know what they were precisely – perhaps a job revolving around accounts or statistics, it didn't matter very much. She was a girl in pursuit of marriage, and this is what she'd pray for to the gods in the temple, eagerly, with unreflective faith.

Unlike Mamma, Daddy did not come with easy faith. He rarely beseeched idols or frequented temples. But that day, if he found himself in the same courtyard as Mamma, it was because he was absconding from an older brother's wedding in the banquet hall next door.

Daddy was as small as Mamma, but in my mind he towers over

all of us. His eyes were set wide apart, obscured by a pair of bushy eyebrows – though if you looked closely at him, past the commotion of hair, you could spot his irises, a restless swirl of black. Even now, when I think of Daddy, I must picture his eyes – the ferment they held, the turbulence.

I suppose such turbulence was Daddy's chief inheritance. With a mother from the south and a father from the north, both tethered to the places of their childhood, both incapable of arriving at a permanent address, Daddy was constantly on the move, oscillating between two ends of a nation. From Cochin, the family shifted to Agra; from Agra, they marched, five boys in tow, to Bangalore; from Bangalore to Chandigarh; from there to Pondicherry and then to Bhopal. It was relentless, such yo-yoing, and through it all, the only constant was this – Daddy's father squandered his meagre income in gambling dens, while his mother, my Paati, strove desperately to save the money that came her way.

There are stories we hear – of how Paati would walk three miles to the inexpensive wholesale markets of each city; of how she'd buy potatoes, ten kilos at a go, and hitchhike rides back home; of how she'd spend her weekends sorting out the purchases, the soft from the firm, those that had sprouted from those that were unblemished, smooth. She'd perch a ladder against a craggy wall, hoist herself and each of her boys up to an attic, and wrap the potatoes in burlap. This vegetable (mixed with onions and garlic and green chillies) would be fed to the famished members of the household.

The life my father had come into wasn't easy. And he sought escape. He longed to break away from his father's recklessness, his mother's stinginess, and especially from the persistence of movement. Eventually, he succeeded.

It all began with charcoal, little chunks he'd pocket from the markets he'd be taken to. With these, he'd draw, not the most accomplished of pictures, no, but sincere ones, and those that possessed impossible stillness – stout fingers would refuse to beat drums; carousels would forget how to spin. I've heard of these sketches, these ominously quiet images, and even today I'm convinced that they possess more of Daddy, his soul, than of any of us – Tasha, Ranja or me.

Daddy sketched, and eventually, at the age of seventeen, shortly before commencing college, decided to leave home. He shifted to a city, too far from the Vindhyas to be considered south Indian, too distant from the Himalayas to be judged as 'northern'. In the indeterminate municipality of Bombay, he shared a paying guest accommodation with a friend from college, secured a degree in history, and taught drawing in a school.

In the afternoons, he'd wander down the roads of Kala Ghoda. Here, in Bombay's booming art district, he'd squat with pavement artists beneath trees and street lamps, observe them intently as they engaged with colour, make notes as they spoke. With time, he procured an easel, reams of canvas from a tailor, and oils and brushes. After school hours my father pursued what he called 'personal art'.

For three years, Daddy created paintings, not unlike the sketches he had drawn at ten. They froze rather than suggested movement – a stock-still hand would rest against a bedspread; a cloud, heavy with rain, wouldn't breathe; stars would refuse to swim. They were tragic, according to my grandmother. Happily, they brought my father some pocket money, small sums that helped pay for rare extravagances – vada pavs from Samovar, coffee-table books from Fountain.

Shortly after painting a flamingo, its orange wings stagnant (the inscribed date frozen – March 1981), Daddy found himself on a train to Madras for his brother's wedding. A day later, he was in a hall surveying a ceremony that did not interest him in the least. Soon enough, he was scuttling to the neighbouring temple courtyard – where he found Mamma alone, beflowered, smiling abstractedly.

Daddy made his way up to Mamma in his starched white bell-bottoms, tie-dyed cotton shirt, bright silver necklace, and faux leather belt – my dad was nothing if not hippie-fashionable. He even carried a jute satchel, the painting of the flamingo peeking through.

Mamma wasn't the kind of girl Daddy would have ordinarily fallen for, what with her adherence to custom, her piety, the timid pottu. But that day was far from ordinary. There were wedding guests who had asked my father about his age, his work, his prospective relationships, the half-hearted attempts his parents had been making at finding him a bride. There were girls, too many, who had taunted him with gestures and smiles and half-enunciated words. There was his own brother opening his hand and placing it unprotestingly against a woman's. So, suddenly, my father wanted that, *precisely* that, for himself. The ability to unclench his fist. Place it in somebody else's hand. Keep it steady, unwavering. If lifetimes are dictated by an instant's whim, this moment in 1981 shaped my father's sketchy future.

As Daddy inched towards Mamma, and Mamma glanced at him, her eyes sweeping over the length of his body, something odd happened. Mamma began to flounder. To judge, it's said, one must be able to slot. And my father, with his incongruities – his restless eyes and composed mouth, quiet bag and much too strident shirt – refused to be pigeonholed. So, robbed of her first and chief instinct – that of severe judgement – my mother found herself free-falling, plunging rapidly into an obscure space without names and markers, the space that artists term as love.

Daddy, very much an artist, sensed the approach of this new province and lurched forward.

'Warm day, yes?' I imagine he asked without conceding a greeting.

And Mamma, always matter-of-fact, is certain to have replied, 'Well, but it's warmer in May.'

'Yes. Exactly. May. That's what I meant. May, it's very hot. Now, it's March.'

'Yes. True. March.'

'Mid-March.'

'Yes.'

'Not quite the middle of March though.'

'No.'

Even Daddy could have rambled on only for so long. Eventually, he must have been compelled to pull together a sentence, ask, 'Tell me, what are you doing here?'

And Mamma, hesitant, must've replied, 'Waiting for Amma. She's expected soon.'

'Ah! You live close by perhaps?'

'Yes, two roads down. A five-minute walk.'

'Oh. I live elsewhere.'

'Elsewhere?'

'In Bombay. It's awfully far. And a lot less hot.'

'Oh! I've heard of it. Every road has an actor?'

'Yes. In a way. Well. No, actually.'

'No?'

'No, no.'

'Why! That's sad.'

Mamma's face even now wilts when she mouths words of sorrow. Back then, her dismay must have been all the more transparent. Her eyes must have drooped, her mouth must've sagged like an empty hammock. And Daddy, penitent, anxious to undo the damage done, must've said fast, too fast, 'I'm sorry, so sorry. Let me wait with you please? For your mother?'

And Mamma, willing, must have conceded, 'Okay. You can stay with me. Till she comes.'

Now, Daddy must have turned intrepid. 'Really? Only that long?'

Now, Mamma must have revealed, 'Well, after that we're busy. I've asked Amma to find me a husband here.'

So began the questions, all pertinent.

'A husband?'

'Yes.'

'Here?'

'Yes.'

'Wha – how?'

'That man, there? He decides.'

'That man?'

'Yes.'

'That? *Him*?'

By a large pillar in the temple courtyard, a portly man sat, clutching a sheaf of papers. Near him were women, throngs of them, their nose studs quivering with fear, their anklets chiming, full of questions. 'Does my daughter's chart match his?'

The joshiar – the astrologer – crinkled his tiny eyes, scrutinized the horoscopes in his hands, shook his head. 'No. No. These – these don't match.' A moment of anxious silence. 'But – '

A woman leaned forward, 'Yes?'

'But *this* horoscope – whose is it – your daughter's? It's in harmony with *that* one!'

'Yes?'

'A good boy, this Subbu. His father's a doctor. His mother donates to the temple.'

'What does Subbu do?'

'Engineer. Civil!'

'Oh!'

'The best match for your girl.'

A smile advanced, accepted. An address revealed. And a woman in the crowd, daughter in tow, marched out.

Daddy watched, mouth agape with incredulity. Watched as families jostled, weaving in and out of the marriage market. Watched as my grandmother entered the temple's gate with a horoscope. Watched as she took my mother's hand and led her towards the temple's sanctum sanctorum.

When a man watches long enough, watches rooted to a spot, it's said an idea crashes into him. Daddy, thus struck, reeled under the impact. He gasped, sputtered, darted pell-mell to the joshiar. 'I must talk to you,' he said. '*Now.* Alone. *Please.*'

The astrologer's eyes, mere slits, studied him – flared trousers, outsized jewellery, batik shirt – eccentric but doubtless moneyed. He excused himself, hobbled to a corner, rasped, 'You want to talk?'

Daddy, following him, nodded.

'What about?'

'I need your help. Please. To get a girl.'

The astrologer smiled, 'You have come to the right person, my boy. I know several. *Several.*'

'Several?'

'You hear right, my boy, I know – '

'No, no, you don't understand. There's one. Only. I *found* her.'

'Found? Yourself? This is very wrong. *Wrong.* Bad.'

As Daddy heard a squawk of disapprobation, his features buckled, slow, like a collapsing kite. The joshiar was flummoxed. In his career spanning thirty years, the astrologer had borne witness to a range of things – summer drought in the eyes of girls, fear smeared across a boy's forehead like ash. But never before had he seen sorrow assert itself this emphatically, undermine the skin, fold it over as though it were as insubstantial as paper.

The joshiar could not allow it. 'What do you want? Tell me. How am I to help?'

Daddy seemed to recover. 'Thank you. Really. There's a girl.'

'I get that, yes.'

'I will point her out, she's very beautiful.'

'Of course.'

'Or rather, I'll point out her mother when she approaches you.'

'Hmm. The girl has a name?'

'Yes. Yes, I *think* she does. But – I forgot to ask.'

'Really.'

'The girl's mother will give you a horoscope. Can you create one for me *please*, so it is aligned with that one?'

'What?'

'And speak of me highly. Say – good family, very good education, one brother is an engineer – this is true.'

'This – '

'I'm an artist. And I'm not from here – not entirely. Part Tamilian. Part Punjabi. But mention I'm better than a local boy. Okay? Convince the mother.'

'Hmm.'

'That is all.'

'*All*? This is not easy, my boy. No. Very difficult.'

'Please.'

'Will take lots of time. Plenty of thought.'

'I can give you seventy rupees. And a painting, too. My latest. I call it "The Tired Flamingo".'

'Two hundred and fifty rupees. And no painting required.'

'But – '

'Fixed price, my boy. Pay it or I'm very, very sorry.'

It was no small sum, two hundred and fifty rupees. But my father was blind to such concerns, to the sacrifices the deal he was about to strike would demand – loans from former friends, distress sales to art enthusiasts, another work post. All he was conscious of was the target before him – winning over Mamma, placating *her* mother.

So my father gave the joshiar a token sum of money, seventy rupees. It was all he had. He opened his satchel and handed over the painting. This was to act briefly as collateral. 'Deal,' Daddy said. And with that lone utterance, time shifted.

There was no turning back.

The joshiar tetchily rearranged himself by the pillar. The women bunched around him like overfull grapes. My grandmother, after sending her daughter home, squeezed her way in and presented a chart. 'Is there a match?' she asked uncomfortably.

Even as my father signalled from the distance, 'It's her, it's her, it's her,' the joshiar studied the sheet of paper, the intersection of lines and numbers.

'This is difficult.'

'I'm sorry?'

'The horoscope. It says, "The boy should have a *distinct* personality."'

'Distinct?'

'Yes, yes. Engineer, no, that does not sound good. Doctor, terrible, just terrible.'

'Oh.'

'Give me ten seconds. Let me go to my quarters. There must be other horoscopes.'

Twenty minutes later, the joshiar rolled back carrying a page of hand-drawn patterns. 'I found it,' he announced and added with raised eyebrows, 'This – *this* is a blessing.'

The astrologer guided Amamma through the horoscope. He described the boy it spoke of – good-looking, good-natured, 'everything, everything good'. He assured her of his antecedents – 'one brother is an engineer!'

Then he coughed. 'I should add this – '

'Yes?'

'The boy, he's an artist.'

Amamma's eyes glistened. '*Really?* That's – ' Then quick, nervous, like a bird, she sighed, 'Well, that's not good news.'

'Hmm. Maybe I should also add that he's not a complete Tamilian.'

'What?'

'See, the mother is. She's from the same state as ours. Same community. But the father is from Bihar. No, no, Punjab. Yes, Punjab.'

'Oh – '

'But the boy is a perfect match. Heaven-made. From the gods!'

'Oh.'

'Madam, let me give you a piece of advice. The boy, he is rare, good, just – '

'Yes. Could I see his work?'

'What?'

'His paintings? Something he has made. *Something.*'

The joshiar beamed with joy. 'Well, actually I *do* have a painting.' He trotted off, returned, announced, 'Here.'

Amamma barely noticed him now, the suety astrologer. Her hand reached for the rolled sheet of canvas. She opened it out. She studied the splash of orange, the bright flamingo, its wings unable to flap, its legs outstretched, inert. A bird denied flight. Yes, my grandmother knew something of that life.

Amamma ran her free hand through her hair, then hunched. She looked at the road rushing past the temple, hairpin narrow, disappearing. She imagined the house it hid away by a tree – one-storey high with peeling colour. She pictured the man within it, old, much too old, intractable.

Now, she could see herself telling him of the day's events, the afternoon's peculiar narrative. And just as plainly, she could see the man, arms extended, gathering facts, the bald essentials. 'No allegiance to medicine', 'no pedigree'. No.

'No. My husband won't agree.'

The story should have ended here.

But at this point, the astrologer becomes much more than a simple messenger. He transforms into a hero with agency. He plots. He asks my grandmother about her husband, if he is god-fearing. He urges her to bring him before the temple's idol. He tells her, 'I will take care of everything. *Everything.*'

Soon, Rangaa, my grandfather, my Thatha – swollen eyes, protruding nose, still pendulous belly – arrives. He pushes his way forward through the gathering. He approaches the joshiar. 'Is something the matter?' he asks in his most imposing voice.

'Well.'

'What is it?'

'I have a boy, a nice boy. He's perfect for your daughter. The horoscopes say so.'

'Good. What does he –'

'First, I must ask you, do you believe in the stars?'

Rangaa, conscious of the people around him, the scrutiny of eyes and ears, nods impatiently. 'Yes, yes, of course.'

'And you believe in this temple?'

'Certainly, I give it money.' (Here, a hint of pride.)

'And this god?' The joshiar points to the idol, once blue, festooned with ghee and ornaments.

'Naturally.'

'Then I have a proposal.'

The joshiar folds a sheet of paper right across the middle and tears it. He creates two chits. Each, he claims, holds one of two words – 'no'; 'yes'. He places these chits before the idol.

Then he speaks the way storytellers do, or magicians. He says the stars may steer the future, but the gods – the gods alone dictate. Let this god, the one we stand before, worship, invest in; let this one with the flute and the feather, three feet high; let Him decide. 'Should the boy I have chosen be Rangaa's daughter's husband?' he asks the idol. 'If yes, say so. If no, say so.'

Even as my father watches nervously, the astrologer shuffles the chits, throws them like a pair of loaded dice. He urges Rangaa to step forward, select one of them, and let the idol speak through him.

Propelled by the moment, the roar of people, the voice of the shrewd astrologer, Rangaa, far from protesting, agrees.

I can see his hands reaching out. I can hear a chit opening. I can see a word emerge, letter by perilous letter.

'Yes,' I can hear my grandfather announce.

And so – so it is.

After the manoeuvrings in the temple, a series of events follow, some known –

My grandfather's discovery of my father's antecedents; his shock and dismay; his attendant fear that if he rejects this boy he'll offend a higher power; his abrupt decision to agree 'if Lakshmi permits', if the boy earns well.

There are other events, near-simultaneous –

Amamma's meeting with my father (now suitably attired); his promise to provide handsomely for her daughter; his promise, too, to share with her his other works of art.

Mamma's sighting of Daddy soon after as a potential husband; her bewilderment ('Such a coincidence!'); her exhilaration ('I shall marry!').

But there are other things – secrets – acknowledged only later –

By my father to my mother – the invention of horoscopes, the dealmaking. Deceit.

By the joshiar to Daddy – the real words scribbled on those chits of paper, the absence of any kind of choice.

'Yes' read one chit all too clearly.

And 'yes' read the other.


There's a sentence behind 'The Tired Flamingo' in my mother's handwriting. Neat. A note to herself; a warning to her daughters. *If you cheat the gods, you will pay the price.*

# 3.

After his meeting with Amamma, my father made an abrupt decision. 'I'll become a scribe!' he informed my grandfather.

Rangaa was far from pleased. Medicine and engineering, now those were real professions. A *newshound* – what would the neighbours say?

Then, again, it had to be admitted – world-famous scribes fared better than small-town doctors. Earned more. Found wider acclaim.

'And, who knows, the boy could be the next Chockalingam!' Amamma reassured her anxious spouse.

So it came to be. Mamma and Daddy were bound by a date. 12 June 1982.

From this point, my parents began living their lives backward. Wedding date sealed, they started getting to know one another. Daddy would send thin blue aerogrammes embellished with ink and paint. When he'd feel sufficiently wealthy, he'd call – go to the nearest STD booth, slip in a coin, rotate the dial, and wait for a voice, Mamma's voice, near-far, far-near.

I can imagine the conversations. Daddy, enclosed in a cubicle, his hand half-covering the mouthpiece as though fending off potential eavesdroppers. Mamma in her room, cross-legged, twirling her hair, playing with her anklets, adjusting a pottu or arranging her pallu, hoping to convey this, these silent love signals, through the mess of wires.

Daddy: Vanaja?

Mamma (*nodding*): Yes. Karthik?

Daddy: Karthik. Yes, yes. How are you?

Mamma (*playing with her nose ring, her bangles, her necklace, taking five seconds, precious seconds, to soak in the syllables*): Karthik.

Daddy: Hello? Are you there?

Mamma (*smiling, delighting in his name*): Karthik.

Daddy: Yes, yes, it's me, it's me. I was asking, Vanaja –

Mamma (*interrupting*): Say it again.

Daddy: Can you hear me?

Mamma: My name. Say it.

Daddy: What? There must be something wrong with the phone. Vanaja, it's me, Karthik. Are you well?

Mamma (*smiling, giggling, tracing her name on a pillow; five more seconds*): Happy. Yes. You?

Daddy (*impatient, rolling his thoughts into a single sentence*): I'm well, and I've kept my promise, and I've got a new job as a reporter for the *Economic Express*, and I start tomorrow, tell your mother and father, and Shrikant, my roommate – I wrote to you about him, remember? – I informed him I'm moving out next year, and there is no milk.

Mamma (*listening for sound, little else, letting this one slide*): Milk.

Daddy (*not listening*): I meant to say – there was a story – I've ruined it, haven't I? This morning, when we were away, a cat slid in through our kitchen window, licked all the milk clean. We didn't know, of course. Shrikant thought I had been a glutton, and I thought Shrikant had been an inconsiderate boor – till the neighbour rang the bell, deposited a cat on our sofa, and said, 'Look after your cat, for god's sake. First you feed it, then you leave it at our door.' Now, we have a famished, thieving cat. And absolutely no milk.

Mamma (*holding a hand-held mirror, watching herself with her eyes, his eyes, the way her mouth moved when she said 'like'*): Like. Like – *cats*.

Daddy (*worrying he had offended her*): Don't get me wrong, I like them, too. I like cats. I really do. It's just that –

A beep.

The rest would be conveyed through aerogramme.

There are nights when I dream up my parents' conversations. But the letters – the letters I've seen. I've stolen them from my mother's room, read them under blankets with torchlight, reread them to learn each sentence by heart. I remember them still. The scent of decades-old paper. The tears where the folds once were. The faded blue of ink. The words.

*Vanna* my father called Mamma third letter onwards. *Dear Vanna.*


Dear Vanna,

I must begin this letter with an apology for the poor connection. I doubt you could hear me, and I suppose a lot got lost in phone static.

I write to you two days after starting work at the *Economic Express*. I like the office building which is unbelievably tall, and the terrace with a view of South Bombay's parks and skyscrapers and limitless sea. I spend my lunch break here, but mostly I'm at a desk that faces a wall littered with pie charts, and I'm surrounded by colleagues who speak of pie charts.

I make it sound dreary, don't I? I don't mean to, and perhaps, with time, once I rise from the position of a cub reporter, become familiar with economic terms, and get a cabin with a window, it will become simple. Maybe I'll ask for a corner on the terrace – I could work out of a tarpaulin-covered hut there.

I tried painting yesterday after I returned from work at one in the morning – a picture of you, as I recall you, with long hair and a red bindi. I rolled out some canvas, cut it, stretched it across a frame. But before I could dip my brushes in paint, I dozed off. The cat tripped over me four hours later, hissed, and I had to wake up and leave for my work desk.

Did I mention we adopted the cat? You told me you like the animal. Ever since, I've been seeing you in Moti's eyes and in her lithe walk. Shrikant looks after her for the most part, and we've had to purchase an extra litre of milk, not exactly cost-efficient, but otherwise it's been easy. Today she even purred as a sign of happiness.

Vanna, are you happy? Write to me. If the post is delayed, and even if it isn't, I will call you next week.

Yours,

Karthik


PS – Here's how I imagine you look today.

Beneath, on the blue sheet, a spray of red and green, bindi and gossamer silk.

Mamma, post-marriage, clipped her responses to Daddy's letters. Hers went on handmade paper, and her writing was in ballpoint, less swift than my father's, with sentences that halted awkwardly, words that paused. Karthik she always called him. Except here –

Dear Malai,

I tried sending a painting. So it's fair barter. But the colours don't match. The shapes are odd. I can't draw. But I can offer words. So here's one. Malai. Tamil for rain. Because that's what you remind me of. Your gaze darts. Seems to. All the time. Like rain.

Amma says that rain is a sorrowful thing. Malai, are you happy?

I am happy. Yes. I have started taking tuitions at home. I enjoy this. There are now three older girls for Economics. Twelve children overall for Maths. My class is expanding. The young ones pose questions. Yesterday, Padma asked, 'If $9 \times 3$ is 27, is $3 \times 9$ equal to 72?' I didn't know what to say.

I wish your office was as interesting. But it's a matter of time. The workspace will grow on you. As will the news stories you cover. Even pie charts. They will become tolerable. I actually like pie charts.

But I don't like cats. I said I did? You might have heard wrong. Anyway, I look forward to the call.

With best wishes,

Vanaja

PS – The picture of me was very nice. But show me the reports you file, too.

Ten days later, Daddy's aerogramme reached Mamma. It had a photocopied story stapled to it. Two hundred words, twelve full stops, no byline. 'Sensex down 38 points'. Mamma, I imagine, read and reread the news item with fingers-lips-eyes. So, when I stole the rookie article, evened out the folds, the ink sank, blurred, too blurred.

Daddy wrote in the aerogramme he had attached:

Dear Vanna,
I am trying to get used to my job and the skills it asks for.

I stand outside the BSE, and figures and percentages slither past. I try finding images within them. Sometimes I succeed. On other days, I rush past the stock exchange and run pell-mell to Kala Ghoda, Bombay's milling art hub. I sit by the pavements and observe painters at work. I long to dip my fingers into their palettes and smear colour on canvases.

But then I think of you, of how proud you will sound on the telephone if I file another story. 'Good article,' you'll say (won't you?), and your voice, the memory of it – it is enough. It leads me back to the BSE.

Vanna –

When I try making sense of my father, I see it clearly, perceive it – the slow distancing of a life once known.

In the silences of the night, before marriage, Daddy would watch Mamma in his mind's eye, her long hair unravelling like a kite's string, her mesh-like sari billowing, her pottu, that spot of red, smudging lightly. He'd observe her figure, the way it would swing, left, then right, up and away like a bubble, then towards him. He'd hear her, her voice –

And suddenly, it would happen. Even as the voice would open out, swell, gain in clarity and definition, the details of the past would lose consequence – the silence of stretched canvas, the lonely, altogether wordless sprint of a paintbrush.

My father, smitten by form and voice, transformed. Almost. He became a man of numbers.

By 12 June 1982, Daddy had filed more than a hundred reports, each growing in scope and ambition, each displaying his bourgeoning ease with an acquired set of words.

His eightieth news story, a few months before his marriage, was carried on the front page of the *Economic Express*, a byline in uppercase bold, a title in sans serif – 'The Story of Cement: The End of the Dark Ages'. Even while applauding the imminent liberalization of the cement sector, my father detailed the workings of the industry in an era of restraint – the payoffs under the table, the dirty bargaining, the sleazy racketeering.

For his acuity, Daddy won back thumps, an increment, a small award. But most of all, he won the admiration of his faraway lover. 'Great article,' Mamma said, and after that Daddy –

Daddy was ready to pitch a tarpaulin-covered hut outside the BSE.

So it was.

After committing to Mamma, talking on the telephone, exchanging more than fifty letters, swapping personal histories, falling in love – after leading this swift, rearward existence – Daddy was trussed to my all-too-willing mother, a husband to a wife.

# 4.

A wedding comes with an afterlife. It grows into either sorrow or joy.

I must ask – did my parents' marriage know happiness?

In the early months, I believe Mamma and Daddy's marriage did. I find confirmation in snapshots. There is a picture of Daddy in front of a sacred fire – his hand holding my mother's, his fingers mildly longer, as quiet as his paintings, as static. There's another of Daddy feeding Mamma a roundish sweet, a laddoo perhaps, winking as my mother bites off too much. There's a third, of them in an Ambassador, the doors flaunting two lopsided hearts, sellotaped red roses, gold glitter, a childish scrawl – *Just Married*.

I imagine my father leading Mamma through a new city, to a rented apartment in Malad – one bedroom, a balcony, a wee parlour – and following her as she studies every nook, the slim corridor, the low-hanging loft, the sun shelter. I see him nod indulgently as she asks, 'Do all the roads have actors?' ('Yes,' he must say, 'yes. Film City is our neighbour.') I spot him by her side, her chiffon pallu washing over his skin like fresh water, her hair coming undone, this time not in a vulnerable dream. No.

It must've been enticing, the newness, the sheer touchableness of that moment, the many moments that made the year. Mamma, young and willing. Daddy, flush with desire. They ought to have been in love.

They were in love.

Mamma, self-conscious, as early lovers must be, was a vision of care and exactness. Her pottu, perched between her eyebrows, matched the colour of her spotless sari. Her sari, silk, cotton or gauzy chiffon, danced like the bellows of an accordion. Her hair, the stuff

of song or poetry, was plaited, a string of jasmines pinned on. That
first year, Mamma's earlobes smelt of far-flung Madras gardens.

Never once during that short-lived period did Mamma cut her
nails, pluck out a white hair or scrub corns with pumice stones before
Daddy. These rituals, the cleansing and laving, the reaching out for
loveliness – Daddy was left out of such sacraments. Instead, my father
was invited to watch the dazzling woman before him, immaculate,
much like the being he had conjured up.

Daddy – and it must be said – loved the wife he had half-imagined.

As for Mamma, she appreciated the man my father was toiling to
become. Once a squanderer, a bungling artist, he had now morphed
into a senior reporter, an editor.

How much Mamma delighted in the details of this hireling's life
– the shuffling of shoes at the doorstep at 8 p.m., 9, 10.30, 11; the
scraping of a key in a keyhole; the slow entrance of her husband,
his collars limp with sweat, his hair greasy with the smoke and dust
and heat of a chug-chugging city. Here was a man who held a job,
brought home cheques, paid the bills, and scrimped and saved. Here
was a man relinquishing a life to raise somebody else's empire. Here
was a man consenting to a predictable life of purpose. To him, my
mother gave of her youth, her beauty.

Mamma – and it must be said – adored the everydayness of the
man she had dreamt up.

Over a period of four years, these spectres of longing created three
children. Ranjana, the first, the oldest, who even as a child flaunted a
kind of prissy charm – look at her bib, the way she holds a spoon, her
sage fondness for pear purée. Me, the oops-baby, the child squeezed
in-between. Natasha, the youngest, the most beloved.

In Sunday family portraits in the old, cramped flat in Malad, and
later in the office-sponsored bungalow in Goregaon, we seemed –
what's the word for it? – happy. Perhaps.

Yet, even now, when I think of it, think of those early years of advance
and optimism, of photographs and babble and intimacies, I perceive
collapse. Where was it then, the cataclysmic turning point, the shift
that marked the end of make-believe?

Was it when Mamma, now accustomed to Daddy's presence, emerged from the bathroom, her hair bunched into a clumsy knot, her footprints leaving a sodden trail on the floor? Was it when, post-Ranja, sleep-deprived and weary, she let her nightie hang loose, stained with baby burps and breast milk and carrot juice? Or was it when, after two daughters, and heavy with child once more, she let out a sob, then a mild expletive, *damn* – was it damn? – for reasons I will never know?

Or was it when Daddy, while filing a news story, unexpectedly saw the numbers blur, fat words mist up and vanish – so he returned to his now dowdy residence (early, too early) faint with nausea and fear and disbelief? Or was it when Daddy took a day off, squatted down, unrolled a sheet of canvas, and sniffed at it, insensible to Mamma, to the children around her, to the last child she was carrying –

Were these the awful crossroads?

I don't know. I don't think it's possible to know. For, I suspect, in relationships, there are rarely definite turning points, only long intervals of unknowing and neglect. Mamma oblivious to Daddy's dismay as she grew distant from the image he had built of her; Daddy immune to Mamma's anguish as he resisted the life she nudged him towards; Mamma and Daddy, both struggling, both unaware.

So, with time, disappointment overtook ardour.

I can hear Mamma's voice, hard, a thing of stone. 'You promised,' she'd say.

I can hear Daddy, feral, a creature trapped. 'Really!' he'd spit.

'You swore to the gods, to Appa. You said you'd look after a family.'

'I tried. Lord knows I'm still trying – '

'No, you aren't.'

'How much is enough?'

'You need to do better.'

'I need to go for a drive.'

'Don't you dare.'

'I must.'

'I will not let – '

'See you later.'

With each confrontation, Daddy's commitment to his trade waned a little. He came home too soon to broodingly watch a mess of oils and canvases. He came home too late after wandering the streets of that listless district of art.

'Where are you going?'

'Away.'

'Where?'

'Out.'

'Don't even – '

'Move.'

A door banging. A car screeching down a highway.

Vanishing.

If, during this period, my parents had been writing letters, these are the ones I'm convinced they'd dispatch. *Dear Vanna*, Daddy would scribble, blunt, high-pitched –

Dear Vanna,

I see two futures before me.

There's one that offers distinction and permanence, where I get to be a regular man. I go to work, complete assignments, return, ask after the children, soothe one, kiss you goodnight.

There's another future that I thought I had crushed, and it's resurfacing. It comes with flux and privation, few glories. And a lone consolation, seemingly trivial – knowing that I've kept alive a promise to myself.

Long years ago, when I was as old as Ranja, perhaps a little older, my mother would take me to wholesale markets in whichever town we found ourselves, Bhopal or Pondicherry or Bangalore, it doesn't matter. On one of these occasions, in one of these bazaars, I happened to stumble upon something sooty-dark. I grabbed a chunk of coal in my hands, and my skin was stained jet black. My palm was no longer my palm, my fingers ceased being familiar things. They were the branches of haunted trees, the limbs of the night. For a moment, I felt I could be anything – a superhero, a phantom, a chimney sweep. I was a blackbird resting on a tree.

As I morphed, became another, with wings, a beak, and clawed feet, everything around me stilled – the rush and push of vegetable vendors and sellers, spry women and nimble men, objects and people.

Vanna, I figured that if a stolen piece of charcoal could offer this, all of this, this sense of calm, blessed inertia, I needed little else. That day, I swore to the gods of the bazaar that I would pursue art.

Vanna, blind terror surrounds me now. I don't know what route I will take, which future I will opt for. But no matter the decision, I see behind me only a trail of waste.

I fear I will engage with art after all.

But then, what of you and my children? Will you stay with me, encourage me, while I chisel an errant image for months? Will you wait while I liaise with galleries and art fairs and exhibitors? Will you forgive me if I offer our children the smell of sodden paint and little else? Will you share this feeble existence?

Sometimes I think I know the answer, and this makes me even more afraid.

But look, Vanna, look what happens now. This clump of charcoal, this piece I had stolen as a child, it is painting giant wings on my body. It is leading me past this house, this road with trees and cosy restaurants, these families in slumber, this sky, to a place beyond my understanding.

Vanna, I am a blackbird vacating a tree. Stop me if you will.

Karthik

What would Mamma say to my father? How would she respond to his appeal? I believe like this, except now her tone would be halting, not with reserve and shy love, but with reined-in anger.

Dear Karthik,

I don't know what to say. You speak of promises. One was made in a bazaar. The other before a god. One is a childhood whim. The other a commitment altogether adult. For me the decision is obvious.

There was a time when roads could fork. When you could choose one or the other. That time has passed. You are married now. With three children. A family. A home to sustain.

Neither you nor I can grow wings. Such things are luxuries. Giddy indulgences. There are children to feed.

Unroll the canvases once you retire. For now, here is your bag. Your tiffin. Your pen. Go to work. You have your answer. You –

I get carried away.

I wish these letters had been exchanged, these truths exposed. But the fact is my parents weren't risking letters. They had learnt to seek cover behind cuss words and spats.

How long did it last, then – the savaging, the attempts at breaking and rebuilding, the reunions and withdrawals? Two years? Three? Five? Who is to tell?

All I know is this. That one day, suddenly, the tiffs ended.

*Many light years ago, when the Milky Way was only just arranging itself – this planet pinned here, that moon attached elsewhere – the sky and the earth, Rangi and Papa, got locked in a deep embrace. Within hours, they were wedded to one another.*

*It should have thrived, the first of marriages. But already the beings on Papa's body began griping – the trees, the fish, the flowers, and the birds. Already the breeze ruffling Rangi's hair was upset. For when Rangi kissed Papa, when Papa kissed him back, when the sky pressed against the waiting earth, and the earth clung on to an enormous sky, all things got enveloped in darkness.*

*And so, the creatures on Papa, the wind skimming across Rangi, they convened within the folds of gloom. They made a plan. The spirit in charge of the forests tore the tallest of trees, jabbed Rangi, propped him up with a trunk. The wind, puffing hard, blew the love-struck Papa far and away towards Venus. Rangi and Papa, the sky and the earth, the first of all married beings, split.*

*The precedent was set.*

Mamma.
Daddy.
Us.

*It's not like a tree where the roots have to end somewhere,*

# 1.

It was during a time of dissolution – when Mamma and Daddy's relationship faltered – that I laid claim to my first childhood memory.

The stars were countless that night. This is all I can tell.

We were in the hills, in Khandala. It would be our last holiday as a family, though at that time I didn't know it. If I had, I believe I would have held on to more substantial things – people, for instance, words, perhaps touch.

I must build memories around the little I have. The stars that were bright, large, and inexhaustible. They were blue, yellow, even rust red, and I know I tried counting them. I lay near the cottage we had rented in Khandala, raised an arm, and fixed every star with a number. 'Nine,' I began with my favourite integer, 'twelve', 'twenty', leapfrogging, 'thirty-three'.

Ranja must have been with Mamma, doing as she was instructed – changing into her nightclothes, muttering a Sanskrit prayer, kissing Tasha goodnight. Tasha, never one for bedtime rituals, likely sprinted, room to room, kitchen to hallway, till Mamma, at the end of her patience, would've scolded, 'Get out, Natasha, or go to bed!' So eventually, Tasha, reluctant to sleep, tumbled-skipped-hopped and joined me.

Yes, there we were, the two of us – I was counting awkwardly, and Tasha was trying to follow suit. Inside, Mamma was seated, wise and alert, studying the jungle produce before her.

There were things we had gathered that morning in the hills. The earth was moist; the barks of trees damp; their exposed roots slippery as wax.

'Careful,' Mamma warned us, even as we skidded down patches of deep green moss, puddles of monsoony water, the muck and slop of rain. Our clothes held splatters of mud, our nails carried sludge, our shoes had fierce streaks of gunk. On a normal day, Mamma would have shivered lightly, peeled the clothes off our grubby bodies, and ignoring our gripes, shoved us into the bathroom.

But that morning was far from ordinary. Mamma held a plaited rattan basket. Her sari was tied high, so we could see her calves, her socks, the soiled sneakers. Her hair was tousled and blossoms clung to the knots – frangipanis, jasmines, and (my favourite even now) deep purple passion flowers.

'What is that?' It was Ranja's subdued voice. On a decaying, mossy branch, my sister had spotted something. Brown, jelly-ish, a cluster of shiny lobes.

Mamma brandished a penknife, sliced one, brushed it clean, and studied it under her handglass. 'Judas's Ears,' my mother muttered and popped it into her basket. 'Good job, Ranja, good!'

After collecting a whole bunch, she told us about the mushroom. 'You see, Judas, he betrayed Jesus and died. And his spirit – '

'You mean his ghost?'

'Well, yes. His spirit returned, not in full human form, but as ears – clumps of them that sprouted on trees and waited for words of kindness, perhaps mercy.'

'Has anyone been nice to him – them?'

'I guess not. So, while he waits, it's said that he heals others. He cures sore throats and offers relief to those with achy necks.'

Susceptible even then to myths, I knelt low, patted the polished lot in my mother's basket, and said sotto-voce, 'I'm sorry, Judas. When I grow up, I'll forgive you.'

That was the last I saw of Judas's Ears. For we would never return to forage.

In the evening, after quick showers and nail-filing sessions, we joined Mamma in the kitchen. There were dozens of mushrooms in her pallu, and she emptied these on to a plate. A rapid wash, and Mamma produced a giant knife to shred each one. The slivers flopped like tongues. Ranja observed them intently. Tasha curved a piece into

a smiley. And I traced eyes with oil. 'Enough,' Mamma scolded her
two youngest daughters. We giggled.

My mother wiped a colossal pan, added a splotch of butter, and
began sautéing shallot leaves. Her breath turned soft, her lips quivered
at the edge of a song.

Maybe she sang and waited for us to join her. Perhaps we sang
as one.

As she splashed foul-smelling soy sauce and vinegar, she trilled,
'Not a cloud in the sky, got the sun in my eyes.'

And I won't be surprised if it's a dream.

I must be dreaming. I dream of the texture of mushrooms,
stretchy like India rubber. I dream of their flavour – sharp – after
soaking in the juice of the tender leaves. I dream of their scent –
sweet, delicate.

We queued up greedily for helpings – Ranja biding her time, Tasha
stealing shallots, someone (likely me) eating off the pan. Mamma
groaned and shooed us into the spare room. We were given plates
full of sautéed mushrooms and rice – supper at sharp variance with
the ghee-soaked dinners we were used to.

There we were, seated on the bare floor, the lights dim, the walls
dark and characterless. Mamma watched Ranja. Ranja clung to her
pallu's edge. Tasha stretched, bored. And I – where was I in this picture
of family life? I must have been in a corner of the room with Daddy,
my head on his lap, content, too content to eat.

Sometimes I try listening in on the conversations we had there.
But no matter how hard I try, I only hear pin-dropping quiet and
sounds that redouble the silence – the hum of a cricket, the shrill
drone of a loose-lipped mosquito.

'Speak!' Tasha must've finally ordered, for suddenly the
conference split. Daddy vanished through the back door. Mamma
jolted up, snatching her half-eaten meal. Ranja wiped her hands on a
napkin. And I scampered out, even as Tasha kept flitting, moth-like.

Later, after putting her oldest daughter to sleep, Mamma likely
entered her bedroom. She drew out a chair, sat by a dressing table,
and fished for a basket hidden in an alcove beneath. The light cast a
shallow pool of light, and Mamma's fingers glimmered.

Witch-like, my mother worked. She emptied out the basket, sifted through the contents, the morning's discoveries – intoxicating herbs, basil and parsley; pungent shoots, wild onion and meadow garlic; chickweed and cattail; acorns. She took in their scents, ran her hands over stalks and spores, milk and dew. She strung wild flowers through her hair, dabbed pollen on her neck, pressed bees' honey to her lips.

After these rituals, these long minutes of coquetting with herself, my mother glanced into a mirror. She smiled. How young she still was. Youngish. Not old.

Could Daddy tell?

As my mother studied the remains of the day, I stayed outside, prostrate, pinned to the lawn. There were tuberoses around me, thin and bloodless; night-blooming jasmines; evening primroses. There were bats swooping down, giddy with the scent of flowers. There were spiders spitting webs, fireflies pouring light.

But this, all of this, seemed finite, fixed in place, once I looked skyward. I can still see them, the stars, huddled together, light-filled. So many, so full, that I tried counting each one – 'Nine, twelve, twenty, thirty-three'. Tasha joining in – 'Thirty-four, thirty-five, thirty-six'. The numbers bourgeoned – ninety-seven, ninety-eight, ninety-nine –

Silence.

'What after?'

We looked at the earth for answers. I rolled over, lay flat on my belly, my chin cupped in my hands, my face scrunched up in confusion. Tasha followed, stretched, then gasped.

'Daddy?'

There he was, his hair windswept, his eyes half-hidden beneath his brows. He must have returned after a short walk through the woods. He sat down beside us, arranged Tasha on his lap, stroked my back.

'Daddy!'

'Yes, my Tashu?'

Tashu. My sister. The most beloved.

Quick, I rolled over, swung my arms around my father's neck, planted a kiss on his ear.

'Daddy – '

'Yes, my Deeba?'

Deeba, his.

'Daddy, what's after ninety-nine?' This must have been my sister, for the voice is sure, unwavering.

Daddy smiled, perhaps for the first time that week. He cleared his throat as though beginning a story. He started talking in a voice as deep as a trench. 'After ninety-nine? Well, a rule of thumb. When numbers cease making sense, there's infinity.'

Tasha and I tried the word for size, liked it, its four easy syllables. 'In-fi-ni-ty.'

'Precisely. Careful, though. The word can possess you.'

'How d'you mean, Daddy, *possess*?' That must have been me, for the voice is awe-filled, halting.

Daddy spoke like one who had considered the question, lugged it across states and dreams. He told us of the earliest of people – that they sought to know the infinite, touch it. So, one day, they said, let us build ourselves a tower stretching all the way to heaven. Upward, they constructed, and skyward – the spire of Babel kept growing – till the gods, shocked at their audacity, cursed them and sabotaged their hunt for the boundless.

Daddy told us that denied the infinite in the physical world, men pursued it by voyaging inward. He mentioned painters, the several he had read of, the few he knew. He cited Miró and his endless blue artworks, and Kusama and her unconfined polka-dotted fields. He must have touched upon Van Gogh, how finally he could see it – the most magnificent blue, endless like an azure sky – so he wrote in a letter to Theo, his brother, *I paint infinity*.

Daddy stopped, he must have. He held us in his arms and kissed us on our foreheads. He said, I do believe he said, 'Sometimes, Tashu–Deeba, I yearn for that. I yearn to know the infinite.'

The stars were countless that night. This is all I can tell.

# 2.

We returned to Bombay from the hills. We eased ourselves into a home.

For me, home was synonymous with an old open chest. I can still see it, made of oak or cedar or mahogany – expensive wood – buffed, lacquered, waxed. Inside, there were clothes – blue cardigans, black turtlenecks, a grey sweater – that Daddy wore during family breaks, those scrupulously planned trips to the hills.

When I was little, small enough to curl into a cannonball, I'd steal into this chest, belly first, drop in with a plop. It was like falling headlong into a pit, except instead of earth-damp-rot, there'd be mohair, smooth like Rapunzel's hair, and flannel, snug and floppy, and homespun wool, bristly to touch.

I recall the smells held within the garments – a faint mustiness; the pungency of mothballs; orange and nutmeg, perhaps Old Spice. And that scent, peculiar, eclipsing all else – oils off abandoned paintings, charcoal, ink – a scent of all-that-no-longer-was.

The chest had been placed in a tiny waiting room, so it looked out into our lawn, the street, a world of work. The waiting room in turn was a part of a larger structure, an isolated, single-storey bungalow in Goregaon.

In this space, Mamma fixed her family and the things she owned. The cabinets were nailed into the walls. The curtains, starched and taut, were pulled across the windows. The dining chairs were set, each for a designated member of the household – Daddy at the head of the table; Mamma, watchful, opposite; Ranja to her right; Tasha, as always, next to Daddy, cheek jammed against his elbow. Envious, I'd sit by his free arm. Here's where we'd share meals.

On Sundays, though, there'd be a shift – butter-smooth and timed. The chairs would slink into the well-tended lawn, the plates would line up on a bedspread, the fruits would start arranging themselves perfectly in bowls. We'd gather post-haste, feast, pose, slumber.

It must have been a Sunday, post-lunch, the three hours designated for play and rest and photographs. After staring self-consciously for a picture, I imagine I slid past the door, into the waiting room, and then towards the chest of woollies. I plopped in and pressed an eye against a wide crack.

The afternoon was dying, I could tell, for the light slipped in obliquely. Before me, there was the lawn, manicured and torpid. Tasha was there, all of four, studying-picking-chewing overripe plums. Ranja, ladylike, was dipping her spoon into a bowlful of purée. Mamma was, as always, a streak of colour, magenta or lilac or mauve, whizzing in-out, out-in, never still. And Daddy – Daddy was somewhere, in the garage or in the backyard or on the telephone, decidedly beyond the crack's purview. Unknowable.

I looked away from the scene before me and dived into the chest, so I was ensconced in clothes, warm, too warm to touch. There were lives to live within the folds of garments, secret ones, and these I had learnt to slip into. Wrapped in wool, I could be Gretel with green eyes, Goldilocks with untangled hair, even the Snow Queen studying sky atlases. But mostly I imagined I was in a space of harmony.

Such peace, touchable-close within the chest, had been absent outside for as long as I could recall.

It must have been a week prior to my swoop into the chest – and just days after our vacation in Khandala. To my five-year-old mind, much of the episode was unclear – there were no images. But I registered voices, those of my parents, denied kindness or pliancy, rough as burrs, as nothing I had ever known.

'Don't you dare.'

'I must.'

'I will not let – '

'See you later.' The jangle of keys.

'Where are you going?'

'Away.'

'Where?'

'Out.'

'Don't even – '

'Move.'

A door opening-slamming, a car screeching past the gate, a sob. And Mamma, now angry, stomping into the room Tasha and I were in, and accusing her youngest daughter.

'You're on your father's side, aren't you?'

'No.' A lie.

'Don't lie.'

'She isn't.' Always. Me. Springing to Tasha's defence.

'And you, too.'

Silence.

'Answer me.'

'What?'

'You think he is right.'

*Yes.*

'Don't you?'

'Yes.'

The hum of a hand swishing, hitting against skin. I don't think I sensed it, sensed anything.

I was collecting sound.

The week passed. It was Sunday.

I slipped deep into the chest, then peeked once more through the wide crack. The lawn outside, my sisters, their play, Mamma's haste – these were all at once obscured by a kneeling figure, tall (or not), lithe, with hair that was black and forest-dense.

Daddy.

I do not know how he got there – he just did, he slunk in, so now he was sitting, his body limp, his lips pursed, his skin luminous and wet. That's when I noticed his eyes hidden beneath his brows. Moist.

I had never seen Daddy cry. I didn't think he could summon up water, salt, sorrow.

I must have been concerned, for I stood up on unsteady feet on his clothes. They sank beneath my weight, and Daddy leapt, startled by the rustle. He saw me emerge, head first, and reached out for me. He must've sensed my fear – coarse, a tactile thing – for he asked soft, too soft, 'Deeba?'

It was the day I was the most beloved. Deeba. His.

Daddy pressed his cheek against my own, whispered, 'Is it nice in the box?'

I must have nodded, for Daddy went on, 'Tell me, Deeba. Tell me. Tell me it's in there. A life, a real one.'

I traced the trail of wet on Daddy's cheek. He smiled, murmured, 'It is raining somewhere.'

And I, half-child, I came to half-believe. 'Rain.'

Daddy stood up, wrapped his arms around my body, drew me out, so I smelt him everywhere – in the box that was, against his shirt, above. He threw me into the air, caught me twice, once, thrice. I laughed. My stomach lurched to my heart. My heart safe in his hands.

That night, Daddy left.

Onwards.
Three Generations.

*it's more like a song on a policeman's radio,*

# 1.

Tonight, I imagine Daddy's final moments at home – before his bag left a trail of dirt, before the door closed, before the key was tossed into the flower pot, before he conveyed that awful truth, *this life, it drops off me*. I imagine it, hoping to find a sentimental keepsake. Or, if nothing else, proof that my father valued the family he had built.

Did Daddy slide into the bedroom at midnight, touch Mamma's skin, defenceless in sleep, and kiss her toes, each one? Did he sneak into our beds and lie by our sides, snuggle up to Tasha or sing a lullaby to me? Did he scribble a *Dear Vanna* letter, seeking forgiveness and expressing regret? Did he?

Or did he call my mother from a phone booth down the road, like he had before marriage, his hand half-covering the mouthpiece, words tumbling over – 'Vanaja – ', 'Karthik – ', 'Yes – ', 'Karthik – '?

Yes, that must have been it. A call.

'Vanaja.'

'Yes. Karthik?'

'Yes, yes, Karthik. How are you?'

'Karthik – '

The morning after Daddy's midnight exit, Mamma was fish-eyed, inscrutable. She scrubbed more thoroughly than usual, dusted so vigorously that the chairs shivered. She polished and scoured and brushed and rubbed.

But beyond this, these accentuated rituals, everything remained the same. The snapshots remained clustered by an almirah – of Daddy feeding Mamma a roundish sweet, of Daddy with Mamma in an Ambassador, of Daddy holding Mamma's all-too-sure hands. My father's sun-dried shirts flapped on the clothes line. That awesome painting 'The Tired Flamingo' stayed perched above Mamma's bed. And the wooden chest stood in wait.

I must have crawled into the chest, looked desperately for an old world, for fragments of a personal Arcadia. My fingers must have sought lint and yarn, my nose must have tried sniffing out Old Spice and charcoal. They were still there, all there – the warp and the weave, the textures, the scents – more pronounced than ever before, as sharp as things on the brink of demise.

I didn't know it then, understand it, the principles dictating collapse. All I knew was that my child-body felt big, much too big. My arms hit the sides of the chest, my head bumped against a sharp corner. 'Daddy,' I whimpered, bruised, to no one in particular, to my father.

And Mamma heard. She gathered me in her arms and led me to the kitchen, to the dining table with three glasses of milk on it. On any other day, Daddy would have been there, pouring freshly brewed coffee into his cup, winking at Tasha, whistling for Ranja, blowing a kiss at me or drumming a note for Mamma. He'd offer little by way of words, but each of his gestures, his nods and shrugs, would knit us together.

That morning, when my sisters and I assembled, took our glasses, mumbled our thanks, waited, drank, we came unstitched. Mamma was a blur of colour, a spinning top. Ranja was ramrod straight, too straight to touch. I was big, adult too soon. And Tasha was a voice, a clanging voice in the distance. 'Where's Daddy?' she demanded, loud and shrill.

It was a question that hovered on all our lips, a question that made Mamma, the whirlwind of colour, stop. She glanced at her kitchen, at the cupboard my father would stand next to, at the mug he would sip noisily from. 'Drink your milk,' she scolded my sister. 'Don't slurp,' she ordered me.

The next thing I know, we were kept in the care of Mamma's friend, a woman I did not know well and recall only as a creature of enormity – enormous specs, enormous eyes, enormous hair done up in an enormous beehive. Enormous voice. Tasha, Ranja, and I would cower under its impact – 'Your Amma's taking a vacation'; 'Your Amma's busy'; 'Your Amma'll be back soon'.

'Soon'. My sisters and I, now bound to this word, grappled with it, its dimensions, night-shapes.

I can't remember the conversations I had with my sisters in darkness. At times, I'm convinced we did not talk at all. But when I try drawing out sentences, sounds from that time of unknowing, all I hear is Tasha's four-year-old voice whispering-whimpering with adult foresight, 'Gone.'

*Gone.*

Tonight, I look beyond these words. I build. This, for instance – I'm convinced Mamma learnt of my father's absence before he left.

It had been a Sunday afternoon of food and rest. The evening brought rain, then darkness.

In the veranda, in the midst of night-blooming jasmines, my mother was seated.

There was a power cut, and Daddy, restless in Bombay's moist heat, came out to join her. The moon was full, and Mamma, in a sari, shimmered like a sea-creature.

'You really are lovely,' Daddy whispered, not thinking.

Mamma smiled. 'I haven't heard that in a while.' A moth flitted near the hem of her petticoat, then vanished without warning. 'When did it end?'

'Vanna?'

'I try identifying the hour of change. But no – somehow I can't find it.'

'I'm sorry.'

'Yes.'

Daddy watched his wife – sleep lining her eyes, her lips dull with fatigue – still a picture of fidelity and comfort. 'We should make it work,' he said abruptly, his voice flustered.

Mamma breathed out, steady. 'How?'

'I don't know. But it is – it *must* be possible.'

'Perhaps.'

'We'll make it happen, Vanna. You know that, right?'

And Mamma knew.

She knew that this moment was no more than a glimmer from the past – the light, trapped in time, of a dead star. She knew from the frenzy in my father's voice that this was the last time she'd hear him speak. She knew with terrifying conviction that soon, all too soon, her marriage would end.

She knew that such are the laws of demise.

My mother took my father's hand in hers, and they tiptoed to the bedroom like first-time lovers. I do not know what followed, I do not want to know. The lovemaking of parents should be kept secret.

What I can speak of with greater conviction is the life my mother pieced together once she learnt of my father's exit. It's a story I have recovered in bits and pieces from sources close and distant – a mess of hearsay and fact.

Mamma learnt of Daddy's departure when he left a parting message – *this life, it drops off me.*

I don't know if it was written by hand on paper; typed on a sheet, the whited-out errors still visible; conveyed in an inaccessible and faraway voice; delivered by telegram; dispatched with a postman; or whispered under the cover of darkness.

I don't know if the message was a part of a longer note about the call of another existence and the pursuit of a dream, or if it was all that was offered.

I don't know if Daddy assured Mamma that he would be well or if he simply crossed over to a safer place.

All I know is that with those six words, and whatever else that preceded or followed them, Mamma learnt that Daddy had left for good.

If this were fiction, I'd have told my mother to find my father – comb the globe to trace his address, follow breadcrumbs to his door. But then, if this were fiction, I'd have also urged her to do the exact opposite – walk away.

As it stands, this isn't fiction, not wholly. And in life, there are no gallant acts, no heroic statements. Only bumbling attempts at survival.

Here is how my mother tried to survive. On the first day, once she left us with a distant friend for a week, she strained to respire.

Her lungs felt like they were choked with fluid; breath seemed to escape her air sacs. Like a baby newly birthed, she had to transit from foetal to adult suspiration, from shallow gasps to regular life-giving breath.

For the next two days, I imagine, the television, otherwise a strictly rationed luxury, flickered sounds and pictures. Doordarshan's swirls of orange, with the wailing shehnai in the background, kept spinning. Against this backdrop, my mother wandered. She moved from room to room, hallway to bedroom to lawn to kitchen, a feckless automaton. She looked, not knowing for what, under tables, beneath bedcovers, near cupboards –

Until she found it, the strangest thing of all, an apple.

She picked it up with unsteady fingers, rubbed it like a magic lamp, held it by her nose. Inhaling its scent, treacle-thick, she imagined that time of plenty when there were strains of fruit to discover, each unique, each with a biography of tang and scent. When there were tales to exchange in the garden patch, fruit-quips to laugh over, home-lives to relish.

My mother gasped. While there were flavours she would never recover, reflections she had been deprived of conclusively, there were moments still in her possession – the odd herb, the condiment, the myths hidden within each. This, she decided, at that precise point, this she could not mislay. Her legacy, her claim to memory. Her all.

At that moment, my mother decided to cook.

It didn't take her long to yoke her resolve to profit. There were office-goers, too busy to engage with the fine art of cookery. There were students hankering for meals with the aromas of home. There were housewives too weary to arrive at daily menus, and husbands too guarded to venture towards whisks and stoves. For them, Mamma decided, she'd pack three-tier tiffin boxes. Rice and breads, curries and yogurt, salads and pickles, she'd make them all.

For an instant, my mother's life acquired a kind of tepid joy. Just for an instant. Then it dispersed. That's the trouble with joy, it goes clear. And that's the trouble with grief, it won't recede, no, washing away, washing back, a wave.

By the fifth day of that week of recurrent despair, my mother arrived at a decision/non-decision – she would not file an FIR to find my father, she would not approach the police, she would not push to annul her marriage.

She would, however, note down the facts of significance. 'Yes,' she was told by her husband's colleagues and accountant, yes, Karthik has resigned from his job; yes, the house will be reclaimed by the office; yes, their joint bank account is still operational; yes, it has cash, substantial.

'No, it will not be enough.'

Sometime in that week of uncertainty and part resolve, my mother dialled a number, spoke to *her* mother.

'He has gone,' I believe she admitted to Amamma, her voice barely steady.

'So he has,' Amamma whispered to her daughter. Her fears had come to pass.

She had sensed it the day she had first seen my father. She had sensed it – in his gestures, his demeanour, his laugh, the way his voice glimmered, his eyes glowed, how he moved in flashes – that he was cursed to retreat.

She didn't know how this withdrawal would come about – if he'd grow faint in parts, bit by diminishing bit, or if he'd vanish, a sleight of hand, in minutes.

He had gone – *this* my grandmother understood – and she embraced her daughter with her voice. 'Have you eaten?' she asked.

'Yes. No.'

'I shall come.'

'It's okay – '

'I shall come.'

My mother wanted her mother. My mother didn't. What could Amamma offer, after all? Words conveying concern and sympathy, words of reassurance, words tired words? Mamma knew them all already, knew them from the marrow. Yes, life was unpredictable. Yes, this anguish would pass. Yes, hope would be within reach. Yes.

My mother, however, underestimated her mother. Amamma arrived with a steel trunk, a photo, a book, a closely held silk-sari-wrapped bundle, and asked as she entered, 'Is it true, this house will go?'

'Amma – '

'I thought as much. Here. A cheque. One lakh.'

'What?'

'I do have valuables, you know?'

'Like what?'

'Paintings. Art. Now listen. My neighbour Swami's friend, he said his brother Raghavan, yes, Raghavan is selling his house in Chembur. Going to America next week. Distress sale. One lakh should be enough?'

'Oh.'

'We should live there.'

'We?'

'What do you think? That I'll leave you alone?'

'But – '

'It's a two-bedroom flat. Plus storeroom. We can stay there quite easily. I shall sell my house in Madras. We will have savings.'

'Karthik – '

'Yes, about him. He must have left you something as well? Good. One can never have too much money with three children.'

'I thought I could cook. Earn something.'

'Even better. I'll help with the girls.'

'Amma – will it be okay?'

'Perhaps, kanna, perhaps.'

Yes, that must have been it, the general drift of the exchange. No empty commiseration, no patient bolstering. Amamma, true to character, took charge.

That very day, she caught an auto in a strange city and met Raghavan, a man I haven't met and have merely heard described in metaphors and hyperboles – as skinny as a toothpick, as kind as the sun in heaven.

At a bargain of eighty thousand rupees, Amamma secured his apartment, our new home.

Seven days after Daddy's departure, when my sisters and I were brought back to our childhood residence from Mamma's friend's home, we found our lives being dismantled.

Our neat piles of clothes, our books and dolls, our pencils and toothbrushes, these were sealed in cartons, carted off. Our beds and chairs and crayon-stained desks, these were whisked away in a truck. Our toy box was tied to a fast-retreating haath gaadi. A rocking horse was kept in a van.

Soon after Mamma had got us home, I had clambered into the chest. It would be the last plummet into, the final dip. Already the chest's edges were keeping me at bay. Worse, it smelt different, felt different, as though someone – Mamma, who else but Mamma? – had emptied it out, then crammed it with frivolities.

At that point more than ever, I wanted my father. I yearned for his scent. I longed to measure myself against his body. I wanted him to gift me tokens from an erstwhile life – the nosedive, the belly flop, the swing, the ascent, the plunge.

'Daddy?' I believe the word fell with a clang, for Mamma, the streak of pink, stopped, crouched.

'Deeya.'

'Yes.'

'Deeya, we must talk. Tasha and you and I.'

Tasha – I can't picture her, but she must have been there, mute. Mamma was with a pile of books on the lands Daddy had read about and mentioned in passing, Buenos Aires, Lapland, Tanzania, Scandinavia.

'Deeya–Tasha, I've told Ranja this already – '

'What?'

'Your father has gone.'

'Gone'. Suddenly, I *knew* the word – the syllable that had once been whispered in the dark, the one my mother now said aloud – knew it from the insides as a thing of absolutes, a thing denied reversals or hope.

Daddy – Daddy whose clothes held other lives, Daddy of mothballs and charcoal and Old Spice, Daddy who had caught my levitating body –

My Daddy wasn't.

'Gone.' My mother spoke, kept speaking. I watched her mouth move, swift, as though mirror-trained. 'He has a new job and will be working elsewhere, in another country. He says sorry, but he will write to – '

'When is he coming back?' This was Tasha, the first to interrupt.

'I don't know – when his office lets him. It might take a while. He's far away.'

'Far away?' This was me, holding on to words.

'Yes.'

'Where?'

Mamma frowned, confronted with a riddle she hadn't prepared for. She looked for answers in the books in her arms – South American cities, African nations, a land of persistent white, empty like a sheet –

'Norway,' Mamma said with baffling vehemence, with the certainty of a storyteller.

'Norway?' I asked

'Norway,' she asserted.

And Norway forever became a place holding lost people.

We did not ask Mamma about Daddy again. She did not let us. Her body resisted questions; it threatened to withdraw to a place as distant as our father's, as blank, if we pushed.

So my sisters and I, we spoke amongst ourselves of the world we had inherited. Sometimes, while speaking, our cheeks would grow moist. Sometimes, while speaking, much like Mamma, we'd only orbit pain.

What can one say of childhood grief? That it is lonely. That it is invisible. That it is denied the vocabulary granted to adult despair. That it shifts, mutates, but seldom vanishes. That it casts a mark.

My sisters and I, we were sorrow-stained.

# 2.
# *Amamma*

Amamma, as a sixteen-year-old at the threshold of marriage, knew something of childhood sorrow. There she sat in a bullock cart, in a rumpled dhavani three inches too short, about to be whisked away by a stranger / soon-to-be-spouse.

Not long after mouthing hymns and promises, tossing words into fire, treading rice – after completing the rituals that go with a wedding – Amamma was led through rain-damaged gullies, past potholes the size of moon craters, to a largish cottage. In it, deep inside, past twirling-twisting kolam patterns, a room, some room. Here, my grandmother was left, the door closing behind her.

For the first time since she crossed over, that life to this, Amamma was on her own. For an instant, she froze, unsure of herself, her body – where best to place her hand, which foot to cast forward, what to look at and how, towards or away from. Such things – once carried as muscle memory – such things my grandmother could no longer make sense of.

Uncertain, she stumbled to a window. Sat down. Breathed.

Slowly, she let it sink in, all of it – the tired palm leaves by the sill, the oppressive road beyond, the vanishing sky. How quickly the present had overtaken the past.

So this, Amamma realized, was what she had left behind – the school with English lessons; the deliberate long walk home; the interludes by paintings, full-bodied and unashamed; the view from treetops and from roofs; the house stuffed always like a dosa; a brother.

So this, Amamma realized, is what she had lost – her brother with a vocabulary now strong enough to challenge hers; her sisters,

younger, quieter, with bright blue ribbons and pale chokhas; her
father, surly but predictable; her mother, wide, soft-full lap, large
arms; the boy –

The boy –

My grandfather threw open the door, bolted it. Stomped in.

He was neither shy nor hesitant – for doubt is for novices or for
those who distinguish between body and body. My grandfather was
no neophyte nor was he a believer in subtle distinctions. Already
he knew the science of coition, and this mouth–that tongue, this
touch–that gesture, this knee–that foot, the shivers when touched,
these were all the same.

My grandfather approached the girl he had married. And my
grandmother lay down, an ensnared thing – her eyes still, pupils
stressed. Sixteen years had taught her persiflage and wordplay, but
the sport of limbs, of soles-and-fingertips, this was alien.

Or was it.

Was it.

And these, Amamma feared, were truths she'd never know. The
boy, the way he'd move beyond that early gesture, the brush of
forefinger-pinkie. The way he'd change, grow, as a lover is wont to
do, into a weaver knitting together wholes – her wrist–his hand, his
cheek–her nose, this tongue–that ear, there–here. His mouth, the way
it would taste if patient or hurried – tart, sweet or flickering with spice.

His mouth.

My grandfather, ever dismissive of kisses, dived in in haste. No
time for Tamil wordlings, those light sounds of affection – kutti,
chellam, kanna, kannamma. No time for rubs and caresses, for the
soft tickling of toes. No time for the ritual of coy undressing – the
drawing of curtains, a nervous lunge for cover, the heaping-discarding
of a cloth. No time.

Rather, my grandfather plunged into the act, the mechanics of it,
right there by the sun-warmed window. Hands drawn out, he reached
for Amamma's dhavani, pen-stained, rumpled, girlish. Next, he began
to undo his veshti, that tight silken knot. Lips pursed, he tried to bend
over her figure, a grown man with too much, too little know-how.

Amamma lay splayed, a cut open melon. Bewildered, she watched
the things that followed, the theatrics of the anatomy, how it puffed

up, bulged. His pupils ballooning ink blots. His member immense, no longer a shrivelled date. She learnt the facts, all of them – the spurt of white, hot and viscid; the dryness of skin, hers; the light flow of blood. Most of all, she gleaned what it was to sense another – inside her, probing like a trowel; inside her, pounding, insistent; inside her, still; and still –

Amamma half-closed her eyes, tried to blur the details, soften them. She clenched her fists, firm, gathering in them each twinge of pain. She held her breath, so all at once, she recalled what it felt like to respire – when the boy squabbled with her; when he let slip a no, *as if!*; when he yelled, *you're crazy* – why, then she knew what it was like to be bliss-filled, insane.

Amamma breathed out. And even as she did, something escaped her lips. A memory of rhapsody all but known. That memory of near-love. Almost-memory. A cry.

I can hear her now, my grandmother, her soft sob of grief. In her, briefly, I see myself a night into my marriage. She weeps as I did. I weep as she must have. We think of similar things. Of emptiness.

In the months to come, Amamma sorrowed over the abruptness with which things had ended – her mother's cooing on festive days, 'Chellam, kannamma'; her father's assertive call, 'Sarojaa'; the boy's horrified squeal, '*No, I am not!*'

She mourned over her separation from her strait-laced teachers, her feather-brained classmates, even the younger schoolgirls she had made it her mission to avoid.

Most of all, she rued the pressures she now confronted – of tolerating a dogged husband, of producing an heir, of enduring the post-mortems of nosy bystanders.

And, 'Good news yet, Anna? Good news?' the neighbours would ask. Except now, in their tone, one sensed not impatient concern, but mock sympathy and judgement.

'No,' Amamma'd hear her husband comment. 'New wife, she's shy. Too shy. Unable. Cannot yield.'

If you drop a statement often enough, drop it so it collides with the earth, it comes to be real. Amamma, it was agreed, was passionless. A prude.

# 3.

When Daddy left, my sisters and I began living in the apartment Amamma had procured in Chembur, then a drowsy suburb in Bombay. It was far removed from the neighbourhood we had spent our early years in, with construction and lights and that whisper of glamour.

Chembur was what Tasha, at the age of fourteen, irately called 'a retirement colony'. It had five distinct centres of activity – a temple where the hum of prayers mingled with the chit-chat of the devout; a station with shanty markets selling curry leaves and banana flowers; a garden with a battered 1971 Indo-Pak Gnat; a popular film studio with sensational Hindi movie posters; and a golf club for the idle moneyed.

These were the points of convergence in a suburb otherwise sliced along regional lines. The Tamilians clustered like territorial meerkats in apartments near the garden, the temple, and the station. The Sindhis – Partition refugees – set up 'camps' beyond the golf course. And the Maharashtrians built their homes around the Bollywood studio.

Three distinct languages coursed through our new suburb, and my sisters and I found ourselves plumb in the middle of the Tamilian pocket, by the garden, in one of Chembur's bosky avenues. Our apartment was on the second floor of a modest three-storeyed building with a terrace. Our neighbours included an irascible seventy-year-old Iyer (looked after by an equally irascible son); a god-fearing widow with six children; and a waspish lawyer with four impolite parrots.

Over time, as we grew older, my sisters and I gathered the gossipy details of their lives. The Iyer was a closet alcoholic. The widow had been a small-time Tollywood actress. And – this is what Tasha, all of nine, learnt when she clambered up a tree, slid down too fast, and crashed into a parrot-infested veranda – the lawyer had a bedroom full of pricey footwear.

Denied the excitement of a fast-blossoming suburb with ice cream parlours and tony boutiques, with girls in rapidly shrinking skirts or boys in tight-fitting pants, my sisters and I directed our attention building-ward, found diversion in the lives of its residents and amusement in their doings and misdoings. We jerry-built with the little we had – hearsay and clues and stumbled upon facts – and created juicy potboilers.

The Iyer, we decided, was more than a common alcoholic. He was a star-crossed Romeo, a jilted lover, a man pining for his long-lost beloved.

'Who do you think his mistress was?' This must've been Ranja, the first to get to the point.

We considered the question with due seriousness, ten-year-old Tasha and I. Tasha, halfway through reading an abridged edition of *Madame Bovary*, volunteered, 'A married woman.'

'No!'

'Of course. A married woman. Named Saraswati. Unbeknownst to Iyer, Saraswati had several suitors.'

'No!'

'Let's face it, Saraswati was *beautiful*. Iyer was setting himself up for disaster.'

'What happened next?' This must have been Ranja, aghast.

'What do you think? One day, Iyer saw Saraswati at the station. She was holding the hand of a much older man. Whispering to him. Playing with her plait. Iyer started walking up to her. Then he changed his mind, ran away – '

'And?'

'That day, he bought his first bottle of cognac.'

We could barely picture Iyer as a younger man, his chest bare, his veshti sweeping the streets, his hands clutching on to that bottle of brandy. But we believed Tasha, we wanted to. It was all the entertainment we could afford.

We believed her enough to shake our heads and *tch-tch* each time Iyer passed us by, up the staircase or down. Enough to leave him a card signed 'Saraswati' on his birthday. Enough to feel superior each time his name was mentioned.

So it came to be – we created biographies for all our neighbours. The widow, we agreed, had married a director, an ageing doyen of the South Indian film industry, who, after fathering six children with her, lost his money in a game of cards and succumbed to a heart attack. Ever since, the widow had been trying to appease the fickle gods of fortune.

The lawyer – we came to this conclusion after Tasha's narrow escape – was, in fact, a dancer. 'But men don't shimmy like Helen!' Ranja protested. Tasha snorted, tossed her head, and said, 'If only that were true, my child!'

If there was a thread binding our childhoods, it was the desire to reimagine. We fantasized about the lives of our friends, distant relations, and foes, even Mamma. We stole her love letters, read the stories she shared in them, made-believe –

'Look here,' Tasha would sometimes say, or Ranja, 'Mamma's letter. *"Padma asked, if 9 x 3 is 27, is 3 x 9 equal to 72?"* Who is Padma?'

'I bet her favourite student,' I'd proclaim.

'Yes.' The voice is Tasha's. 'And I bet Mamma would read Daddy's letters to her.'

'Yes.' The voice is mine. 'And I bet – I bet Padma suggested Daddy's Tamil pet name, so the letter would be romantic.'

'What makes you say so?' Of course, Ranja.

'Who doesn't want a teacher to fall in love?'

'I don't!'

'Sure. But Padma was different. She was the ad-hees-sive.' Tasha showing off. 'Fevicol, you know. Stuck our mother and father together.'

So, as children, we reimagined our absent father, too. Daddy was in Norway, we half-believed, earning money, stashing it away in a bank. Daddy was in Norway, a famous journalist or watercolourist. Daddy was in Norway – and we pictured that land –

First, as a country, altogether literal, that we studied for hours and scrutinized in books, on maps, in films, so we knew each cleft and corner of the fish bone nation –

Then, as an un-country, one that had been dreamt up by our mother – a lie, a white lie, no more –

And, finally, *finally*, as a place of myth, that held our pasts the way only stories can.

So, when we were older, old enough to inhabit this tale we had heard, Tasha and I travelled to Scandinavia.

But that – that came later.

First, we had to build.


When I study my childhood from a distance, analyse it, I see that myth-making was in fact Amamma's gift to us.

I still remember the day she entered the Chembur apartment with a large steel trunk – five saris, three blouses, two petticoats – and other odds and ends. Her hair even then was salt-and-pepper, her eyes rat-sharp, her dimples wise and deep. She turned to Mamma, announced, 'I chose well!', then staggered into the bedroom that held my things. She fished inside her blouse, drew out a piece of chalk, and etched a line across the length of the room.

'This is my turf,' my grandmother announced, 'and that, Deeya, is all yours.'

For the next two decades or so, Amamma and I would share a bedroom, her possessions stacked under her bed, the most precious in a cardboard carton, and mine littered across half a floor. The line dividing our room would be traced and retraced with chalk-crayon-paint; the division of space would be scrupulously observed. On the rare occasion that I'd trespass – leave a book or a toy or a sock in Amamma's territory – the errant item would be flung like a soccer ball, beyond the boundary line, out of my bedside window, into an unfortunate neighbour's kitchen.

There are three dominant memories I hold of sharing a room with my grandmother –

Of spending long hours trying to recover my goods that had wandered into her corner.

Of making nervous escapes at midnight when Amamma's steady sleep-breath would swell into a faint whistle, a skirl, then a high-pitched cry like that of a piccolo. Terrified, I'd tiptoe out, wander into Tasha's storeroom-bedchamber, or the bedroom Mamma and Ranja shared, and hide beneath their sheets.

And of waiting eagerly in my bed after dinner. Each night, Ranja and Tasha would join me, snuggle under a white sheet, and look out for our grandmother. I can see her even now tottering like a bobblehead, careening towards us, sending us scattering like so many pins. We'd rearrange ourselves around her body, crouch by her arms-feet-belly, and hold our breath.

We knew what would follow. Without any warning, without those familiar pre-speech conventions – the licking of lips, the clearing of the throat – Amamma would begin a story in medias res.

'So,' she'd say, 'so – Catherine was a sissy.'

'Who, Amamma?'

'Stop interrupting. Princess Catherine had been given a room in the neighbouring kingdom, pretty pink pyjamas, a bed with a fluffy mattress – not like this one, you know, this is lumpy, I must tell Vanaja. The princess ought to have slept well, don't you think?'

'But why was she in the neighbouring kingdom, Amamma?'

'I'll explain if you will let me! Now, like I was saying, Princess Catherine was in the neighbouring kingdom because Esmeralda, the maharani, had announced that she wanted her son to marry. All the world's princesses – old maids in flouncy dresses, sharp-nosed adolescents, little women with too much lipstick – made a beeline for the kingdom. Our dear Catherine was no exception.'

'What happened then?'

'Hush, Tasha, hush. Catherine, like I said, had been lodged in the lap of luxury. She should have been well rested. But she awoke with aches and pains. "My back is sore!" she cried. "My neck hurts. I think I have bruised myself." Then she screamed, "Look! Look at my tailbone – I believe it has a red spot!"'

'Wuss.'

'My view exactly, Tasha. Catherine wept before Esmeralda, "I think there was something under my mattress. I believe I slept on a pea!"'

'And?'

'If you'll let me continue – Esmeralda sighed. "The ninety-ninth princess to fret about a green pea. And the hundredth if we count

Andersen's girl. This is frightful, I say, just frightful." Then – "John!"
she called her son. "John!"'

  'Enter John.'

  'Hmm. Thank you for that, Deeya. Enter John. And exit Catherine.
Esmeralda spoke. "My son, my heir, here is my advice. Steer clear
of blue blood, upper-crusters, all princesses. Find yourself instead
an unaffected girl."'

  'Did John listen?'

  'Better than you do. The next day, he bumped into a working girl.
Her teeth were irregular, her hair was unruly. She painted by day
and taught children at night. Immersed in these pursuits, she missed
pods, peas, runner beans – you get the drift. For the first time, young
John truly fell in love.'

  'But our teacher told us something else!' This must have been
Ranja, paying heed in class.

  'Of course she did. But she's wrong. Prissy princesses, remember,
make boring subjects. The best books have women unafraid of peas.'

  Each night, Amamma would redraft a fairy story. She'd speak
of an adventurous Goldilocks, a misunderstood Rumpelstiltskin, a
kindly Snow Queen, a penitent witch.

  My sisters and I, we may have grown up in a suburb of
nothingness. But when I look back at our childhoods, I recall, not
indigent days and nights, but madness and possibility and stories.

Tonight, the childhood story I reach out for is one celebrating fool-
courage, gumption.

  I remember the night it was first narrated. My grandmother
produced a book, the one she had entered our apartment with, from
the cardboard carton under her bed. Its pages were dog-eared, its
binding was coming undone. Amamma held the book in her arms,
stroked its glossy images, paused, her eyes misting over, and smiled.

  'These are Titian's paintings. Aren't they incredible?'

  'Where did you find the book?' Tasha was quick to ask.

  'Stop probing!' Amamma said. 'And to answer your rather pert
question, someone left it for me. Look, here is Eve after scouring
all of Eden.'

  'Eve?'

'Such impatience! You see, God had blown an obedient man into existence, a woman, a heaven – a little world. "This is your garden," He had said. "Call it Eden. It has herbs and fronds of bracken, trees and precious fruit. Love these, my children. But – "'

'But what?'

'Nosy cats, aren't we? "But," God warned, "remember, there is one tree you cannot know. *You shall not eat of the fruit of the tree that is in the midst of the garden, neither shall you touch it, lest you die.*"'

'Oh no!'

'Shush! For a while, Adam – yes, that was the name of the young man – and Eve – yes, she was the first of all women – Adam and Eve were content. There were colours to identify, shapes to define, textures to learn and sink into. But – '

'But what?'

'If I hear that question once more! But in a bit, Eve grew tired of Eden. She had named each blossom, labelled every bush. There was but one spot left to explore, one tree with blood-rich fruit.'

'God – '

'Yes, God had told her to stay away. But Eve had to probe. She approached the tree – look, here's the painting – the tree bending over with ripeness, the tree of promise. She touched a branch. And even as she did, she rejected the changeless joys of Eden, the safe comfort of heaven. She plucked a fruit, the apple.'

'And?'

'Hush! And God, that all-seeing God, He whisked His children away, planted them on an imperfect earth with skittish soil and changeable skies.'

'Awful!'

'No, not really. Despite its surface failings, Earth was more beautiful than Eden. For on this planet of rough-hewn wonder, Adam and Eve loved.'

'Oh.'

'And a kindly God – He blessed His daughters. "May you hold within you Eve's courage, her thirst for wisdom, her lust for all things strange."'

'But our teacher – '

'She really didn't get Eve, did she?'

No.

# 4.
# *Amamma*

On getting married, Amamma became part of a household that comprised my grandfather Rangaa and the first wife Janaki.

What must this have been like, I ask myself. What negotiations were called for to carry on with everyday activities? How was it decided, for instance, who'd do what and when and for whom?

Here's what I imagine. Soon after the unprompted Madras wedding, Rangaa, alert to the possibility of domestic rows, promised Amamma he'd play a firm administrator – delineate roles, spell out each wife's household tasks, create a timetable of duties. Yet, such was the newness of the second marriage, so many were the queries – 'Who is this lady, Anna? Which father's daughter? Such a pretty girl, how was she found?' – that my chuffed grandfather clean forgot.

And by the time the more oppressive questions followed, there seemed to be no need for solid intervention. The chores of the house had arranged themselves soundlessly around the women.

The first wife Janaki came to clean and cook the rice and millet, polish utensils and wring dry the clothes, scrub off the courtyard's dirt and moss, and brush away the dust. Amamma's duties did not overlap. On busy days – a good many days – she'd pound spices at dawn. Then she'd cast lumbering kolam patterns, gather sweet-scented flowers, and play caretaker to an exacting spouse – she'd be head waitress at mealtimes, the custodian of his wardrobe, the fulfiller of his persistent nightly needs.

Amamma, resigned to her new life, decided to make what she could of it. She learnt to brew the finest coffee, tinkering with the proportion of freshly ground beans till the richness of the decoction was near-faultless. She found a kind of joy in arranging Rangaa's clothes, sometimes colour-coding the shirts, yellow-cream-white; sometimes piling up the veshtis, so the heap wobbled but never quite collapsed. In-between, she occupied herself by scouring the immaculate bedroom, pocketing careless annas, and hiding them in the kitchen.

Amamma, in her own way, learnt to cohabit with Rangaa. She tap-tapped his desk, made music while he slurped his morning coffee. She reimagined his wardrobe while he wolfed down his meals. She uncrossed her legs and dreamt of the sky while he probed her body. Sometimes, when she let her hands run over his clammy back, she thought, 'This is a cloud, this is how it feels when it's dark, rain-ful.' At times, she'd touch his pendulous belly and make-believe it was a puff of cotton. Now and then, she'd let her hands slide down his navel – this, the wing of a fledging bird.

Through it all, my grandfather remained a melancholic man. 'Good news yet, Anna? Good news?' He could hear the neighbours titter.

# 5.

In drowsy Chembur, my sisters and I were growing up and embracing the joys and follies of preadolescence. Amongst us, Tasha was the early bloomer. One afternoon, she traipsed into a room, hurled down her school bag, and with the gravitas only a twelve-year-old can exude, announced, 'To love is to be alive!'

Tasha had spent the past three weeks telling all of us about a boy – not unlike most of the schoolboys we were vaguely acquainted with – with 'black, deep black hair', 'black, deep black eyes'. Soon enough, she was sharing a desk with her beau – a direct consequence of her teacher's ill-judged attempts at confining the two class troublemakers to the first bench. Under the educator's watchful gaze, the lovebirds exchanged invisible ink notes, played footsie, tossed spitballs –

'We held hands!' Tasha sighed.

Ranja, still unresponsive to the opposite sex, rolled her eyes. 'And now, you'll get married. Yes, we get it.'

Tasha bristled. 'When did I say that?'

'Isn't that what wooing asks for?'

'Is it? And that worked brilliantly for Mamma, no?'

There it was, the writing on the wall – Tasha was nearly a teenager. We saw the signs, all of them – those sharp-edged comebacks, the bouts of ill-humour, that curious attachment to 'the truth'.

It was the truth. And no matter how much we made-believe, how many stories we told and untold, there were moments when facts leapt at us, when reality ceased being a fast-changing, a changeable thing.

Here were the facts, all of them – Daddy was gone, we didn't know where exactly. Mamma was in limbo. Amamma was losing her mind.

It was more than I could confront. 'Mamma's fine. Daddy's in Norway, that's all.'

Ranja must have been tuckered out, for she didn't protest. And Tasha, suitably preoccupied, persisted with her description of her school crush. It was sentimental, it was dippy, and it lacked the bite of fact.

Tonight, let me recover what was of my childhood, beyond myth and storytelling, whimsy and make-believe. Let me peel off the bubble wrap of fantasy. Let us, as a family, risk exposure.

Let's begin with Mamma.

When my father disappeared, here's what happened – my mother submerged in liquid grief many times over. In each instance, it seems, she got spat out like a cork.

To hold herself steady, even while being tossed about by pain, Mamma devoted herself to her vocation. From the break of dawn to full light, she chopped-stirred-fried for office-goers. It was the one occasion she seemed content. Sometimes she'd hum a tune, an old filmy number. Sometimes she'd watch her reflection on steel utensils – the full arc of her hips, the peppery sheen of her hair (now rolled into a bun), the moons under her eyes – and tut. And sometimes she'd rat-a-tat against watermelons and pumpkins, a happy drummer.

At such times, my sisters and I (especially when we were children) could approach her, talk of foolish, significant things – the ice cream sticks we had collected to raise a house, the skirt we had attached flags and buntings to, the cherry seeds we had planted in Diamond Garden. Mamma'd indulge us with a smile, tease us with questions, nudge us towards statements of full disclosure. 'Ranja cut her trousers,' we'd reveal, or 'Tasha spied on the neighbour-uncle downstairs.' A work-engrossed Mamma would never disapprove.

At all other times, our mother was remote, present but not touchable, the leftovers of a dream. So if we'd talk to her, try to, she'd watch us distantly, cut short our confessions, ask us about our homework, take notes.

On the face of it, even while detached, Mamma was everything a textbook mother had to be – concerned about PTA meetings, attentive to those scratches on our bodies, alert to the company we kept. No one could find fault with her nurturance, accuse her of a lapse of duty.

But somehow, her daily vigilance further distanced her. Her solicitude made her absence doubly palpable.

As children, we didn't yearn for matronly care. Rather, we wanted a mother who would befriend us, trust us with stories from her life, guard our trifling big-secrets. We wanted the mother we had lost in the hills, digging out mushrooms with dirt-streaked hands. We wanted the mother we sometimes had, humming songs, packing tiffin boxes. If only Mamma could see how much we wanted –

But she couldn't. She was otherwise occupied.

Besides seeking escape in work, my mother coped by arranging and rearranging the details of the past, tweaking elements that seemed discordant, adding flourishes.

Mamma and Daddy got married, not because of a scheming astrologer, but at the behest of her parents. Daddy hand-picked a stable vocation, not to satisfy Mamma, but to earn acclaim.

Scratch that out.

Mamma got married to Daddy, not to please her parents, but because my father relentlessly pursued her. Daddy became a reporter, not to earn acclaim, but for the love of storytelling.

Scratch that out.

Mamma got married to Daddy, not because my father relentlessly pursued her –

That was the beauty of the distant past – it offered room for make-believe.

It was the time beyond Daddy's departure that presented some difficulty for Mamma. There was little to build with, nothing to tweak – till my mother stumbled into a false assertion, that my father was in Norway.

Straight away, she clung to the statement. She repeated it to us, her friends, her neighbours – not just because it was clear-cut and acceptable but because it could be manipulated.

On some afternoons, when we'd return from school, we'd find

Mamma hunched near the dining table, a pen in her hand, a postcard before her. There'd be a dozen Gandhi stamps arranged in a row and one word for an address – Norway.

On these postcards, Mamma would tell our father about the routine happenings in our routine lives – those habitual dinners with two ghee-soaked curries and rotis; the bills that had to be paid; the clothes we had outgrown. *Is it cold?* She'd always ask. *Wish you were here*, she'd add.

*Dear Karthik*, she'd start, and proceed in staccato sentences –

*Dear Karthik,*
*I hope you are well. We are fine here. It is getting warm. It is 34 degrees centigrade. The Met says it will get hotter. I have two new clients. I now wake up at 3 a.m.*
*Ranja topped Physics. Dee liked reading Emma. Tasha used a bad word. I scolded her. She is getting to be difficult. I wish you were here.*
*But Norway must keep you busy. Is it cold?*
*Hope to see you soon in Bombay.*
*Vanaja*

Sometimes there'd be news conveyed like tickers on television screens.

*Dear Karthik,*
*I hope you are well. We are fine here. It is raining. The harbour line train services have stopped. Amma could not visit Sion.*
*Amma does not seem well. She forgets. Yesterday she lost her way home. This has never happened.*
*Dee thinks Amma has a problem. Alzheimer's she calls it. Tasha says it is senility. I don't like the words she chooses. Ranja seems worried.*
*I wish you were here. But Norway must keep you busy. Is it cold?*
*Hope to see you soon in Bombay.*
*Vanaja*

And sometimes there'd be confessions, timid and halting.

*Dear Karthik,*
*I hope you are well. We are fine here. It is winter. Any colder and I'll*
*need a shawl.*
    *Amma is asleep. Tasha is talking on the phone. I can hear her. Dee*
*is arranging books. Ranja is studying.*
    *I'm at a table. No one around.*
    *You could come. You could hold my hand. You could lift the edge of*
*my sari. And who would know.*
    *You see, don't you? I wish you were here. But Norway must keep*
*you busy. Is it cold?*
    *Hope to see you soon in Bombay.*
    *Vanaja*

So many words, such letters. If Mamma's postcards could be lined end to end, I am convinced they'd arch into a bridge, connect Bombay to Oslo.

Let's admit it – twelve-year-old Tasha had no patience for Mamma's postcards.

It must have been the day her first school crush ignored her, forgot to whisper sweet nothings, cringed when she held his hand – for Tasha came home and flung her school bag viciously. I can still hear it, that ugly satchel, crashing into Mamma's dining chair. My mother teetered.

'Natasha!'

Mamma must have been angry. Full names were reserved solely for moments of indignation.

'Natasha!' she repeated. 'Natasha, look what you've done, smudging my letter!'

That was it. Natasha erupted in rage. 'For god's sake, lady, for *god's* sake, get over those letters already!'

'Nat – '

'You think he cares? You think he reads about the food you cook or the goddamned boring lives we lead? You think he has received a single postcard?'

Tasha stomped out, stormed into Mamma's bedroom, yanked

open a cupboard, and pulled out three, four, five gunnysacks, crammed with *Norway, Norway, Norway, Dear Karthik, Is it cold.*

She hurled them in the drawing room, these sacks – the postcards spilling out across the dining table, the floor, before Mamma, Amamma, all of us. Then she yelled, 'Get it right! Daddy has left us. Your husband, our father, Dear Karthik, he is *not* coming home.'

I wanted to close my ears, close Mamma's ears, but I couldn't move.

And soon – soon, it was too late.

Mamma said nothing, not a word. No. Instead, she sank to the floor as though in worship. With hands that seemed slight, seemed vast, she reached out for the postcards, those strewn on the floor, those piled high like holy mountains.

She kissed them the way she would have kissed a beloved god.

Then she went to her bedroom, lowered a painting – the one with flamingos – and wrote carefully, much too carefully, about gods and retribution, perhaps karma, a sentence, no more.

Finally, she emerged. Hands outstretched, she approached Tasha, held her close, pressed her mouth to her ear, and said, 'I'm sorry. I'm sorry, baby. I'm sorry he doesn't write – '

Tasha shivered.

'But he wants to, you know? He does. He thinks of you every day.'

Suddenly, in Tasha's inward-looking world, the callous schoolboy seemed distant. The desk in school where they met, then parted, seemed distant. The trials of preadolescence seemed far away.

Tasha held Mamma, gentle, unsure, as if handling a being of glass, and said, 'Yes, I know, I know, yes, I'm sorry, I forgot.'

Yes.

If I could, I would revise the facts of the day – erase my sister's teenage outburst and place Mamma once more on a chair, the dining table before her, a row of Gandhi stamps, a postcard, and that line, so common, so sorrowful – *Is it cold?*

And, *Dear Vanna,* I would make Daddy write –

*Dear Vanna,*
*It is bloody cold.*

As it stands, I cannot redraft what happened. I can only report it.

Mamma never wrote another postcard. Or, if she did, she kept the act hidden from us, placed the letters in bags we would not recover. *Dear Karthik*, she must have written in the dark –

*Dear Karthik,*
*Come. Warm our world.*

# 6.
## *Amamma*

1947. It marked the fourth year of Amamma's marriage.

Outside, India was witnessing the rush and tumble of change. There was talk of Independence and Partition. Of Reddiyar becoming chief minister. Of Dalits storming into temples. Of victories and blood and suffering.

My grandmother oddly enough remained impervious to these churnings. The jabber of national history, the diatribes, the solemn boasts – these seemed hollow to her, as though emerging from a village well. Ensconced as she was in Rangaa's home, there was merely the gab prevalent around domestic chores.

Perhaps then it isn't wholly surprising that Amamma, when prodded, recalled but one event linked to the freedom thirst of 1947 – of being taken to the railway station on 14 August by Rangaa to meet an acquaintance. There were more people than she had anticipated, more bleary-eyed than ordinary travel-worn tourists. They did not hold polished tin cases. Rather, around them, in their grimy hands, by their calloused feet, there were cotton bags, sheets of paper, rags. They sat on floors, by doorways, near arches, and spoke softly in rasping foreign languages.

'Who are they?' my grandmother asked, trying to decode their tongue.

And Rangaa, pressing onwards, glowered, 'Northern folk. You know, Partition.'

My grandmother frowned. She had heard of it, the word, but she was unsure of its scope and compass, its ramifications. All she sensed as she rambled forward was that the term accommodated her. Her history of ruptures.

Amamma slipped out of Rangaa's field of vision and wandered past vendors and coolies to an emptied-out train. She surveyed a desolate compartment – till a man walked up to her. He was distinguished-looking, tall, rendered even taller by the turban riding on his head. He spoke to her, dropping sentences she could not puzzle out. But she gleaned that, in spirit, they were solicitous.

Amamma wasn't used to this – to syllables that fell low and gentle like early morning prayers, to a tone that nourished, to words that opened out as merciful arms – especially not in a man's voice, no. Something gathered in my grandmother's eyes, something like water. So the man in the turban lowered his head, muttered by way of introduction a name, almost alien – Colonel Gurdial Singh Gill – and served fistfuls of puffed rice. Amamma accepted the offering, nibbled on it, eating kindnesses.

Till Rangaa bumped into her.

'Where were you?' he asked, brusque and disapproving. 'What are you having?' And not waiting for a response, he grumbled, 'Bloody nuisance. This station has become a slum for refugees.'

'But – '

'And how is one to find Subramanian in this mess? I give up!'

'I – '

'And soon we'll have *colonies* of immigrants, what with the Punjab Association and Gill feeding and clothing and rehabilitating them. Colonies of *greedy* Partition immigrants.'

'Gill? Colonel Gurdial – '

Amamma would never know for certain. Rangaa whisked her off, past the homeless populace, past the bodies lying in wait, to their limewashed house.

In there, memories of the morning faded away – the teeming station, the estranged crowds, the loneliness of the cross-border train. Amamma was now only alert to the whisper of a broom, the clank of utensils, Janaki.

For my grandmother, Janaki's presence was germane; the world outside was textbook history.

Janaki and Amamma should have been adversaries – the first wife resentful of the second; the second wary of the first.

But from the outset, there was *something* about my grandmother – how she zigzagged like a sunstruck moth as a new bride in Rangaa's house; how she peeped into empty flowerpots as though they contained treasures; how she hiccupped and gasped fish-like for air when Janaki said, 'I'm *first wife*.' Despite the unity of her features, their adult symmetry, Amamma seemed thin-skinned, a little girl.

So after that first day of 'lovemaking' – when ravel-haired Amamma stumbled into the backyard, flopped down, looked skyward, and murmured, 'The clouds, they've stilled' – Janaki, instead of being dismissive or curt, squatted down beside her, swung a hand fan, and whispered, 'Not so, not any more.' The air rustled, the sky swayed. A blur of wispy blue.

After that, I believe, Amamma and Janaki looked out for one another. Janaki took on the more exacting chores to shield my grandmother from housekeeping's rigours. Amamma attended to Rangaa's demands to shelter Janaki from his gibes.

The two came to exchange confidences. Amamma told the first wife about the home she had lost, the trees she had loved, the argumentative brother, the guileless sisters. Janaki in turn told her of her short-tempered father, her dead mother, the villages she had been to, and the neighbours she had grown to like –

'Was there ever a *man* you really liked?' my grandmother must've asked.

And Janaki, startled, must've murmured, 'Liked? How do you mean?'

'I mean, someone who made you giddy-nervous-happy? Like a trapeze artist, flying?'

'Flying? No, I don't think so.'

'Never? Really?'

'I haven't been to school like you have, Ro. But I've learnt one truth.'

'What is that?'

'Such ascents – they're for another life.'

'Oh.'

'As for this one, it's all but done.'

Amamma studied Janaki as she cooled the milk, separated the cream, stored the whey, accomplished one chore, then another, with the detachment of a marionette. She observed herself, her own body, as she ground the cloves and pounded the chillies with similar aloofness. And she sensed more than ever the permanence of her situation, its irrevocability, and worse, the remoteness of all her early rebellions.

So when Janaki asked, 'Why don't you tell me – have you ever liked a man?', Amamma only shook her head. 'No – not even close. No.'

If there was one visible prospect for Amamma now, it was this – becoming a mother. My grandmother wasn't sure how she felt about it – the growth of a new being in her body, the cramps and the contractions, the fluid and the blood. A part of her wished to produce a baby, not out of a sense of maternal longing, but to escape the punishing queries of neighbours, the midnight jostling of an impatient husband.

'Do you ever wish you had a child?' one day, my grandmother probed.

And Janaki, half-smile in place, said, 'Yes. But look, I got a sister.'

'That is true,' my grandmother conceded in a whisper. 'But what if I bear a child?'

'What if you do?'

'Will it upset you?'

'No, not at all.'

'How come?'

'Because it's all the same. Don't you see?'

'How so, Akka?'

'It's like this. A man can plant a seed in this field or that or another. One brings in a harvest, another doesn't. The crop is what counts, isn't it? Not the land that yields.'

I'm trying to picture what followed – Amamma cringing, protesting, saying that she was more than fecund soil –

But no. I doubt she said that. Such pronouncements are for our generation, for those of us who open frayed books in libraries and read the assertions of first-wave feminist writers.

My grandmother, unembittered by theory, refused to stage a

revolt. Rather, she hugged the toiling first wife, told her once, then twice, slow or fast, 'Thank you, thank you.' *Thank you for not hating me.*

And Janaki hugged her back.


'So, why do people have babies, Akka?' In due course, my grandmother must've asked.

Janaki shrugged. 'To leave something of themselves behind, I suppose.'

'Do you worry you won't be able to?'

'I – Ro, can I tell you a secret? I've taken care of that.'

'You have?' Amamma's face, a knot of concern.

'Yes.' The voice low.

'How?'

'It's hard to explain. That tree outside – do you see it? – isn't it beautiful? Now watch its bark. Watch closely. That splotch?'

'I see it – '

'It's me, Ro.'

'It is?'

I don't know why some things speak to me. But they do – such as the tree outside. So I press my thumb – like now when it's red with beetroot – against it.'

'You do?'

'Yes. So the world carries something of my body.'


And then, one morning, it suddenly happened. Janaki, while peeling a beetroot, felt her breath grow faint. She called out to Rangaa. He rushed in. He found her lying prostrate. He reached for her wrist, for that dull throb of blood.

Janaki was dead.

Nobody quite knew the cause. A cardiac arrest? A case of premature ageing? The rigours of running a home? A broken heart?

'God's will,' my grandfather announced to his neighbours before he lit the pyre.


From this point, my grandmother was on her own.

For days after Janaki's demise, Amamma followed sound – a crunch, a whoosh, a rustle – hoping to find her soul-sister through these reverberations. But much like a cricket that chirps but can't be spotted, Janaki remained elusive.

Yes, that was it, Amamma told herself. Janaki was around – wasn't that the swish of her broom? – just hard to get hold of.

So sometimes, while attempting the chores that Janaki used to complete with ease, Amamma would, like in the old days, talk of things – of stray memories, ideas, a nagging doubt. She'd wait for a response – a sigh, a lament, a laugh – and on receiving none, invent answers of her own. But not one of these rejoinders carried Janaki's earthbound wisdom, her solidity. They floated away, soap bubbles.

Eventually, Amamma stopped talking to herself.

Too soon, the house mirrored her. There was stillness in all things, a kind of speechlessness.

Amamma wasn't used to this. As a schoolgirl, she had come to expect the prattle of giddy classmates, the chides of an overbearing teacher. As a wife, she had learnt to live with the easy idioms of Janaki. And now –

A week of silence passed. My grandmother was in her bedroom.

She opened and closed her almirah. Not a creak. She pushed a pile of folded saris. They toppled over, fell quietly on to the bed. She spoke, tried to, but it was futile. It was as though her lips could release only explosions of air.

Amamma staggered to the storeroom, hoping that here – in this space she rarely visited, in such uncharted territory – there'd be sound.

Through tongue-tied spiders and their close-mouthed webs, she made her way to an ancient cupboard. Before it, she squatted, opened one drawer, then another. There were discarded fountain pens, pamphlets advertising katcheris or protest marches, neglected envelopes and forgotten stamps, cowry shells, playing cards and chess pieces, a children's atlas – and beneath these bits and bobs of other lives, a book, one she hadn't seen earlier. Amamma gathered it in her arms, sniffed at it, read the black and yellow title – *Titian and Myth*.

Like a teenage shoplifter, my grandmother wrapped the book in her pallu, looked around, crept through the muddle of cobwebs, and snuck out into her room of summer. There she released the book, so it dropped bedward, flared. Pages rustled like notes of music. *Sa-re-ga-ma*. A-hint-of-sound.

Amamma observed an opened-out page. On it she saw a full-bosomed woman, her skin bare and unblemished, her legs splayed. Caressing her thighs were orbs of yellow. Coins. 'Danae,' Amamma read against the image, 'Danae and the golden shower'.

The air carried the ting-a-ling of money. The curtains plinked.

My grandmother was ravished by art. She watched, wide-eyed and open-mouthed – like she had in another life, in another place, as a schoolgirl studying paintings on the sly – the rape of Europa, the exertions of the soul-tired Sisyphus. Each image was committed to memory, each caption intoned, each myth by the margins repeated, till finally, she knew not just the chassis of the collection, but the vibrations it carried.

For the first time since Janaki's demise, Amamma sensed a kind of kinship. If the gods and their consorts knew of dejection, if the kings of distant lands encountered loss, perhaps *her* pain was merely a part of theirs, an extension.

Amamma closed the book, then opened it, this time seeking the title page. There, cancelled out, was an Englishman's note – Sir William's chaste message to Margaret. In its place, a whorl of deep red.

Amamma gasped. For a second, she was immobile.

Then, all at once, it returned – the movement of limbs, precious breath. Amamma, book in hand, tiptoed to the kitchen. Was this where Janaki had gone through it? *Like this?* Amamma squatted. Was this how she conversed with the paintings? *Like this?* Amamma raised an eyebrow at Danae. Was this how she preserved the book? *Like this –*

But why? And where had she found it? And when? And how?

Amamma pressed her thumb against the whorl, seeking answers –

And even as she did, for an instant, she was convinced she saw Janaki by her side. She believed she could hear her talk, not the way friends do or sisters, but like seamen navigating choppy waters, with clacks and clicks, dits and dahs, a kind of Morse.

What did Janaki tell her? Not what she hoped for – she seemed to ignore her probing questions. She described, instead, summer mangoes and lemons, bazaars and vegetable gardens – the non-stories that make a life.

With that – after bequeathing a part of herself – Janaki withdrew.

# 7.

In Chembur, Tasha wasn't the only one growing up too soon. She had friends – young girls who were equally impatient. One of them had become a temporary fixture in our lives (for reasons that would soon reveal themselves). I believe her name was Samhita. Sammy for short.

'This world is more than I can deal with!' Sammy barged in one day and declared melodramatically.

It was late in the evening, the birds had all but vanished, and the neighbourhood lights were turning on in succession, quick darts of colour, yellow-white-discoblue. Thirteen-year-old Sammy, her hair tousled, her face a draughtboard of emotions, whispered, 'Something bad has happened.' Then, wringing her hands, she revealed, 'I'm pregnant.'

My sisters and I were seated on my bed. Tasha was winning a game of Scrabble and did not take kindly to Sammy's intrusion. 'As if!' she said, disdain dripping from every word.

'Really, it *happened!*'

I, no longer a contender in the game, was happy to humour my sister's friend. 'Was it that Italian? Mario?'

'Carlo.'

Sammy had been having a love affair, not terribly discreet, with a friendless Italian who used to visit the adjoining building for English lessons. They'd meet each evening, the Italian at the edge of his teacher's terrace, Sammy at the edge of ours, strain themselves across the shared wall, and clasp each other like slipper snails.

'Carlo,' I repeated.

'Yes.'

'What happened?'

Sammy sobbed. 'I – we – we were on the terrace. And Carlo told me something I didn't understand. And – and he kissed me!'

The game ended. Tasha, Ranja, and I gathered around Sammy. 'Details!' Tasha insisted.

By now, Sammy was hiccupping and telling us between hurried, phlegm-filled breaths all that had transpired – the careless evening; the retreat of the birds; Carlo's lunatic attempt at following a flock to her side of the terrace; his proclamations as he leapt across the wall, a string of foreign words; Sammy's conviction that he was calling her beautiful –

Here's where the details got blurred, seemed to shift to suit the moral scale of every listener.

'Carlo curled my hair on his finger, came close, kissed me. Like they do on *Dynasty*.'

'You *let* him?' This was Ranja, aghast.

'I looked away, but he didn't get it.'

'That's so stupid. Why did you look away?' This was obviously Tasha.

'Well, actually, I didn't. I went to him and told him – I told him, *come closer*.'

'That's more like it!'

'So you *didn't* look away?' This was Ranja, a stickler for facts.

'I did, but not really, I mean, sort of, it all happened very quickly.'

'You *let* him!' Ranja repeated.

'But then I told him he was bad.'

'But he wasn't!' Tasha protested.

'He *was*! I'm pregnant now!' Sammy whined.

Tasha smirked. 'Listen, kid, you're fine.'

If Tasha could assume an air of authority regarding such matters, it was despite our mother.

Mamma had had 'the talk' with us on our respective eleventh birthdays.

Here's how it went. She nudged us awake, crammed our mouths with yogurt and sugar, and wished us with a hassled embrace. Then she dragged us to the kitchen. Here, she stuffed our mouths with another helping of yogurt (so, of course, we couldn't speak) and began her spiel. Her choice of words, her angle of attack, even her approach, sharp and lightning quick, remained identical.

She told us that we had blossomed into young women. That the world we had tumbled into was treacherous. That boys were singularly to blame for the end of innocence. That it was wisest to keep them far far away. There were consequences, she warned, if we rebelled. If we lay with boys, kissed them or even held their hands, we risked 'going the family way'. That was it. The verdict. Mamma shunted us off to school. No arguing. No more talk.

Happily for Mamma, she got to deliver her speech – smooth and uncontested – the first two times. Then there was Tasha. Disinclined to accept my mother's counsel, my sister had protested in my presence.

'But I've held hands, and I've hugged boys, and I don't have a baby.'

'Tasha – '

'Yours views are *unscientific*. Babies come from sex.'

After a minute of silence, Mamma muttered, 'Who told you that?'

'It's in *Lady Chatterley's Lover*.'

'Don't lie. There are no babies in the book!'

'So you've read it?'

'That's not the point! And stop corrupting your sister!' Mamma shot a glance at me.

'I'm not. Dee's older than me, for Chrissake. Anyway, Amamma told us the facts of life.'

'Amamma? Did Am – it doesn't matter. Not another word. You're late for school.'

Then Mamma turned to me and asked, 'Is this true?'

'About sex?'

'No, I – wait, you *know*?'

'Of course.'

'Who else knows? As for Amma, did she tell you something? *Anything*? About making babies?'

'Yes. And *everything*.'

'Like what?'

'Well, that when two people desire each other and make love, it may lead to – '

'When did she tell you this?'

'Two years ago maybe.'

When I was ten, and my mother was out somewhere, my grandmother led Ranja, Tasha, and me to her side of the room.

'We need to talk,' Amamma said.

'What about?' I recall Tasha asking.

'About birds, bees. Creation.'

'You're telling us a story?' I asked.

'Yes. Yes, I believe so. Though it's our secret.'

With that, Amamma began her Scandinavian tale – who knows where she sourced it from. She told us of the first man and the first woman, Askr and Embla. Of how their names sealed their fates – for 'askr' meant an ash tree reaching out for the skies, while 'embla' signified an earthen water pot. When Askr rained into Embla, shed dewdrops into her body, the earliest of beings was conceived.

'So all of life was created. And still is.'

'Wait a minute. A tree showers dew and there's a baby. You expect me to believe that?' Tasha asked, incredulous.

'Hush. How many times have I told you not to interrupt? And to answer your question – obviously, that *isn't* what I'm getting at.'

'Then what *are* you saying?'

Amamma proceeded to explain what she had come to learn and what she imagined. She spoke of Embla and Askr, of how they tumbled into one another, drawn by scent or sound or the sleek beauty of youth. She spoke of them, their bellies fused, their gasps learning to connect. She spoke of Embla, how she opened herself out, her vesseled body. Of Askr, how he plunged in, a mighty tree, the dew, the sweet rain of his being flooding into her. She spoke of ecstasy, then of a gradual quietening.

And she spoke of the moment after, when Embla and Askr, woman and man, moved apart, their imperfect bodies now distinct, so what remained was sorrow, the lingering ache of something ending. Thus, to recover the joy they once knew, they drew close again and mated. Kept mating. Maybe spawned.

'This is the dance of creation,' Amamma said, '*this*. When we try recovering the moment when Embla and Askr touched.'

My grandmother looked away, scanned the window, the world beyond, then muttered, 'Sometimes we find abundance in a stranger.

Sometimes in a woman, much like us. Sometimes, only sometimes, in the one we wed. And if we're lucky, in ourselves.'

We listened, rapt, uncertain. After a while, we scuttled to the library, borrowed *Don Quixote*, hid a pamphlet crammed with the facts of life within. We learnt other things – more concrete, less inventive – of how it all began a zillion years ago, when two single-celled organisms had an accidental one-night stand, swapped genes, bred. This was sex, we learnt, the sum of it. An instant all too brief.

'You're not pregnant,' Tasha told Sammy sagely.

'How d'you know?'

'Well, because, to stand a chance, you need to fuck.'

Ranja gasped, her voice a thin wire of distress.

Tasha kept speaking. 'If that happens, let's talk.'

In the years to come, my sisters and I, in our own ways, would try making sense of the coming together, the choreography of beings. Sometimes we'd inch close to that first instant when spore collided with spore, or when Embla and Askr played, their hearts full, beating like wings.

But soon, too soon, the moment would escape, and we'd land, mortal, still aching.

# 8.
## *Amamma*

1947 still – but the fag end of the year. A season had passed since Janaki's demise.

As long as the first wife had been alive, Amamma had had a bulwark. If Rangaa seemed disappointed with my grandmother, he expressed equal dissatisfaction with Janaki. If the neighbours tut-tutted about Amamma's aloofness, they appeared to, with equal gusto, sneer at Janaki's stodginess.

With Janaki gone, all eyes were on my grandmother.

Rangaa was not unaware of this shift in attention, and as a celebrated doctor of Ayurveda he felt compelled to do something. Why, if he could make colds flee and rashes disappear – why, then surely getting a woman to conceive wasn't impossible. There were answers hidden within common plants – wasn't this what the ancestors had said? Rangaa had devoted himself to their science, had practised it on ill-humoured patients. He had only to tap into the truths he knew.

So he began writing prescriptions for Amamma, tweaking potions, reimagining ancient tonics. He sourced deep purple velvet beans, mixed their paste with asphaltum, tinged this with strands of saffron. After making Amamma consume the viscous blend, he began in earnest the familiar routine of baby-making.

Twenty-eight days later, Amamma bled. Five days later, after she emerged from the outhouse, Rangaa started the ritual all over again – new herbs, a vile mixture, more careless, careworn lovemaking.

So it went. Days slipped into months into years.

In this time of aridity, my grandmother sought a sounding board, a neighbour, the one content with a child on her hip, another at her breast, and four trailing near her sari pallu.

'I worry, you know. Four years. No children,' so began Amamma's halting confession.

'I would, too,' Mrs Swami helpfully declared.

'It's not that I'm not trying. I am, believe me. But then, sometimes I have a thought – '

'What thought?'

'You know – whether this is what I want – babies. Tell me, how did you *know* you longed for children?'

Mrs Swami cocked her head, spaniel-like, and scowled. The doctor's second wife, she had always been a peculiar one. Cold as a fish, now a common idiot, too. 'Such a strange question to ask.'

'Well?'

'Well, what's there to *know*? I mean – it's what you do, no?'

'Is it?'

'Why else this body? A womb? Breasts? For what purpose? Tell me?'

So, all at once, Amamma was conscious of her breasts. She imagined Mrs Swami shaking her head, hissing – so much potential, a once gentle smoothness, gone to waste.

'You're right, of course,' Amamma muttered, half-convinced.

My grandmother's head whirled. She yearned for clarity, for a portent that could reveal the things to come. In truth, she wished to live backward – understand her future, then walk towards it.

So Amamma approached a common soothsayer. 'Tell me, Amma,' she quickly asked, pressing coins into her hand, 'tell me, will I ever conceive?'

The soothsayer studied the lines on Amamma's palm, a zigzagging mess, and frowned. 'Only you can answer that,' she rasped.

'What d'you mean?'

'I mean – it's up to you.'

'You make it sound easy.'

'It is.'

'I don't follow – '

'You must *want*.'

My grandmother bit her lip. Maybe she was to blame after all. How much she vacillated about childbearing. How reluctant she was to commit to a son. Why, if she absolutely *had* to have a child, she'd rather a girl who climbed trees and swam rivers. Of what use was a pliant mamma's boy?

Yes, clearly, she was at fault.

My grandmother felt a pang of guilt. She also smelt betrayal – that she was gloriously failing her end of a pact. If Rangaa could house her, offer currency and food, she was obliged to start a family – bear a boy, birth him, swaddle his wriggling body.

And yet – yet was she really obligated to do so?

Amamma's hair stood on end. Then, quickly, she smothered the questions that threatened to erupt, those that came without answers, those that would, like so much hot lava, raze all that had been precariously built.

Here were the facts, all of them. Amamma had to bear children. Amamma had failed to do so. Amamma had to persist with all attempts at baby-making.

Maybe it was my grandmother's resolve that did it.

Maybe she *wanted* sufficiently.

Or maybe – maybe it was something else, a secret yet to be disclosed.

At any rate, fourteen years after her confession to Mrs Swami, Amamma birthed my mother.

# 9.

My sisters and I may have inherited a fast-transforming world. But there remained a constant – Mamma's quiet ache.

Yet, not once did she confide in us – not even when we grew older and began making sense of the world; or came to understand the inevitability of grief and heartbreak; or approached her and asked, brusque, perhaps too brusque, 'Why don't you tell us *anything*?' To which Mamma responded, crisp and cool, her voice brooking no dissent, 'There's nothing to tell.'

Who, then, did my mother learn to confide in?

Not in Amamma, I know – my grandmother had no patience for phantoms and flimflam.

Not in her neighbours – Mamma ignored the pining Iyer, the god-fearing widow, and the shoe-obsessed lawyer.

Not in the lady who cared for us as terrified infants – she claimed to know too much.

And certainly not in her sundry clients – my mother was loath to mix gossip and commerce.

However, the last rule wasn't entirely watertight, and Mamma hesitantly made exceptions of two of her customers – Miss Mimmy who worked in a neighbourhood bank and asked for a Jain tiffin each morning, and Mani Murthy. In them, Mamma found easy acquaintances, if not friends.

Miss Mimmy (and for some reason we would always call her that, a title prefixing her name) had a voice that clanged like a bell and a gait that redoubled the impression – her body swayed like a bonsho suspended on ropes.

Mamma liked talking to Miss Mimmy, not least because she accepted the things she heard at face value and displayed no inclination to probe. When Mamma'd speak, she'd cock her head to one side, eyes unblinking-wide, then offer sentences that conveyed commiseration, if not curiosity. Even when Mamma revealed those staid untruths – that Daddy had stumbled upon a high-flying job in Norway; that the offer was simply too good to refuse; that he believed that more than his active presence, his children needed the opportunities money could buy – Miss Mimmy only sighed loudly, and announced, 'This is the way the world is, Vannu. You have to choose, always choose, between love and wealth, a career and friends and children.' Then, perceiving Mamma's silence, Miss Mimmy journeyed inward as best she could and added, 'Look at me now, Vannu, look. I became a bank manager and had no time for men! And then there was my sister – god bless her soul – she quit her job to raise a family. She was a doctor, you know. But before she could know the joys of a grandchild – first her husband died, then she – oh, Vannu, she's no more.'

Reaching for Mamma's hands, Miss Mimmy rapidly shook her head. From my spot in the kitchen, I could see her move from side to side. What I couldn't see, couldn't possibly know, was how she'd crash into my future and take charge – but such manoeuvrings were for later.

Miss Mimmy would visit our residence every Sunday, and with her Mamma would discuss some of her worries – workaday dilemmas and the problems that emerged while raising three daughters – Ranja's anguish when she scored a B in art class ('She didn't even eat her lunch, Miss Mimmy!'); Tasha's habitual disappearances ('Now, why must she borrow books in the evening?'); Amamma's fading memory ('She forgot Dee's name, Miss Mimmy!'). In each instance, Mamma's friend would submit platitudes and skirt analysis.

Miss Mimmy, however, did manage to surprise us – it happened once. It was the day my mother whispered my full name, unaware that I was eavesdropping. 'I worry for Deeya sometimes,' Mamma said, her voice trembling. 'Amma is so careless with the things she tells her. Yesterday, for example, Amma said – you know – that Deeya – that her breasts – ' My mother's voice softened. It must have. For

from my spot in the kitchen, I perceived a strange kind of quiet –
the occasional fricative, a burst of air, and then, once more, silence.
It was like listening to an obsolete audiocassette, its spool chewed.

Suddenly, there was sputter. A voice emerged, clear and sharp. It
was Miss Mimmy's. I'd recognize her bell-cry anywhere. 'Oh Vannu!
That's awful!'

Mamma must've been startled – I know I was – Miss Mimmy was
not one to express strong sentiments. 'What, my dear?'

'Your mother. How could she say that? Deeya – she's pretty, you
know!'

There. It was said. And yet –

Yet – what is it about praise – why does it sound insincere? Why
do the eulogies recede like light, and why does censure stick? I wish
I could tell.

What I do know is this. That that day, I wished to reach out to
Miss Mimmy, hug her, kiss her overfull cheeks, say, 'Thank you, thank
you, I'm grateful.'


Our next visitor likely was Mani – Mani of striped ironed shirts and
low-waisted trousers; Mani of slick gelled hair and over-white teeth;
Mani with a face that could have graced matrimonial adverts. Why
he was unmarried then remains a mystery – though Tasha was quick
to blame those trousers, they made a man in his forties look like a
tenderfoot boy.

Mani liked visiting Mamma. Every weekend, he'd ring our
doorbell and say, 'Vanaja, your Friday tiffin was super,' then smack
his lips to emphasize the point. Mamma in turn would grin widely,
feign surprise – 'Was it?' – and proceed to present a scrolling list of
questions – 'What did you like? Was the cauliflower soggy, you think?
And what of the beans? Could they have been crisper?' And no, Mani
would protest, no, of course not. And Mamma'd reveal, always in a
quiet voice, that she'd be attempting a new recipe on Monday.

Mamma and Mani would mostly share culinary talk. Mani
viewed himself as a food connoisseur – on the whole because his
great-grandfather, a former cook of the blue-blooded Wodeyars,
had invented the now popular bisi-bele-bhath. From him, Mamma
learnt of red chilli chutneys, steamed lentil dumplings that melted

like sugar cubes in the mouth, and the royal recipe for Mysuru paaka, which Mani claimed was his ancestor's second invention in the Mysore Palace.

'Tell me more,' Mamma begged him.

So Mani told her that when the great king Wodeyar happened to seat himself for his evening repast, the chief chef Madappa – Mani's ancient relative – found an item missing on the elaborate royal platter. There was no sweetmeat. Even as the king began wiping off the early courses, Madappa, in an attempt to salvage his reputation, tried to whip up the absent pudding. The chief chef stirred a thick, never-tried-before syrup – a blend of gram flour, ghee, cardamom, and sugar. By the time Wodeyar announced his desire for something sweet, Madappa's hurried concoction had settled into a cake. Nervous, the chief chef presented a soft gold slab. Intrigued, the king took a bite. Then six. 'What is this I eat?' Wodeyar asked between mouthfuls. And Madappa, confronted with the last challenge for the day, babbled, 'The city's sweet syrup. Or if you please, Mysuru paaka.' So it was that the king of southern sweets was born.

Mamma enjoyed Mani's story, and the following Friday, offered a lunch spread that the best chefs of Mysore would approve of – bisi-bele-bhath, hiccup-inducing red chutney, and butter-soft Mysuru paaka. Two days later, Mani could barely hold back the panegyrics extolling Mamma's cooking. 'Your Friday tiffin – ' he started, then fell short of words.

My sisters and I got used to Mani's visits, and Mani came to terms with our meddling ways. We were around, in and out of the room, when he narrated his ancestor's kitchen stories; when he shared with Mamma recipes from the Mysore Palace; when one Sunday, he asked if she'd accompany him to a spanking new Udupi restaurant the next evening. 'Yes,' Mamma said. *Yes.*

Soon after, my sisters and I gathered in Tasha's storeroom-bedchamber, closed the door, and discussed the implications of Mani's conversation with Mamma.

'Is it a date, you think?' I remember asking.

'Duh. I bet she's choosing an outfit as we speak!' The voice was brisk. Tasha.

'I don't like Mani,' someone whined. Ranja.

'And I don't want a stepfather,' I declared.

The last statement, which spelt out the world to come all too clearly, made us subside into quiet. We envisioned a future with Brylcreem-Mani, Mani of slipping trousers, Mani who (when compelled to acknowledge our presence) would address us as 'hello children'. We imagined school mornings with Mani at the breakfast table, occupying Daddy's chair. We conjured up evenings with Mani licking his lips and praising Mamma's bisi-bele-bhath. We could picture the nights even if we didn't want to; even though those moments were not for us to see.

'You know what will happen next, don't you?' Tasha whispered.

'What?' two sisters asked as one.

'We will be sent to boarding school,' Tasha said with a decisive nod. 'And Mamma and Mani, they will forget us.'

A collective gasp.

Till Ranja protested, 'That will never happen!'

Tasha shook her head and said – of course she did – 'It's all so bloody fucked up.' A second later, she added, 'There's only one thing to do. Go to Norway and find Daddy.'

'What?' Two voices.

'Let's start saving money *now*. So, as soon as we're older, we head there and make everything okay!'

'What?'

'Don't you see – Mamma needs company. Love. *Romantic* love. And we alone can make it happen.'

At that moment – and for years after – Tasha's proposal made sense. It was a plan we'd discuss, tear apart, fix with renewed enthusiasm, all along saving loose change like our grandmother. It was a plan we'd seek out when in despair. It was a plan we'd pursue because – because what else was there to run after?

'That's ridiculous!' Ranja yelled.

'I don't expect you to understand!' Tasha yelled back.

I couldn't take it any more. I walked out of one bedroom and into another, where Mamma now was. (Clearly, after asking her out, Mani had left.)

'Why?' I shouted. '*Why?*'

'I'm sorry?' Mamma asked, arranging her clothes in the cupboard as though this were just another evening, as though the conversation with Mani hadn't happened, as though Daddy –

I thought of Daddy and suddenly felt possessive of our shared histories, of our imagined histories, of that poor man struggling in Norway. I, at the very least, had to protect this family's non-inheritance.

So, full of misguided rage, I came right to the point. 'Your saris are ugly, and nobody will like them, and I thought you were taking us out for a movie tomorrow!'

Mamma turned around. She seemed genuinely hurt. 'My saris?' she asked. 'My saris – I thought you liked the red one?'

I said nothing.

'Oh. This? Do you at least like this?' She pointed to six yards of blue silk.

'No.'

'Oh Dee, I thought – '

'They are lousy, all lousy. Can we at least go for the film?'

'The film – which one? There was no plan, you know. But sure, we can go. And then do dinner at the new Udupi restaurant.'

I stared goggle-eyed at my mother. 'Tomorrow evening is good?' I double-checked.

'Of course, it is.'

'And – ?'

'Yes?'

'And you don't – no other plans?'

'No, though I did tell the vegetable vendor to deliver cabbages in the evening. I'll ask him to come in the morning.'

I left the room, found Ranja–Tasha, and relayed the entire conversation four times. 'It's all so bloody fucked up,' Tasha repeated.

The next evening, Mamma took Amamma and us for a Disney animation – one that even Tasha, after the preceding day's shocks, deigned to watch without an air of superciliousness. We chomped on popcorn, watched the credits roll, and went together to the new Udupi restaurant. There were mile-long paper dosas, steaming idlis, and scoops of vanilla ice cream on falooda.

There was no Mani Murthy.

All evening I worried over what had come to pass. Did Mani back out of Mamma's potential date with him? Did Mamma stand him up? Did they both decide, as consenting adults sometimes do, that they were better off exchanging stories?

The next weekend, Mani visited as always, his hair slick, his pants low. He praised Mamma's Friday tiffin, told her of a Mysore delicacy, and then, clearing his throat, announced that our suburb had a new Chinese restaurant.

'We should visit it soon,' he whispered with a coy smile.

'Yes, we should,' Mamma said.

It would never come to pass.

# 10.
## *Amamma*

Twenty-two years after Mamma's birth, Rangaa died.

My mother, at that point, was heavily pregnant with Ranja; she couldn't withstand the strain of long journeys. Daddy was holed up in Ranchi, beyond the reach of phone calls. My grandmother, therefore, was on her own.

It was a sunless February, and Amamma was standing at the threshold of her bungalow. Her hair was bunched up, the greys just beginning to show. Her feet were bare. Her skin sagged with exhaustion.

Just moments ago, Amamma's husband had been hoisted to a crematorium. She had had a final glimpse from the entrance of her house – a hurried sighting between male shoulders and arms. She had seen his eyes – too quiet for sleep; his mouth – limp and dismissive; his jaw – outlined by a ruff of flowers.

The chief mourner, the closest male relative, Rangaa's dead cousin's eighteen-year-old son Shrini had led the way, gripping the stretcher, trying hard to look sorrowful. A distant uncle had kept pace with the boy, and then an army of acquaintances.

Hours or perhaps minutes after Rangaa was taken away, my grandmother entered her house.

What did she know of her husband? What could she dredge up, what anecdote, what story, that would grant this man's demise significance? What could she claim to have shared with Rangaa – and thus, what could she claim to have lost?

After analysing her four-decade-long association with her

husband, Amamma saw that her most dominant memory was this – of being shunted into a bullock cart with my impatient grandfather; of hearing him announce with barely concealed triumph, 'Sarojaa! Hello! Hello, hello!'

Amamma tried summoning up other memories – the morning Rangaa half-smiled when she served him coffee; the afternoon he returned from work, waving two movie tickets; the day he discovered she was with child, and leapt to proclaim to all who would hear, '*Good news*, I say, good news!'

She remembered how he ordered his daughter – a disappointment – to sit ladylike, legs together; how he tinkled a bell when he prayed to a god; how he swaggered at dawn to the neighbourhood temple; how he scrubbed his feet before entering the house; how he sat cross-legged upon the floor and slurped when the sambhar was poured.

Yet, the first of all memories, the very start of their partnership, obscured every other remembrance. Let's freeze the day, as Amamma did, and observe it – the bumpy cart ride, the sun-warmed house, the closed door. That nervous wait within a bedroom. The awful transaction between bodies.

She could still smell it – the fear, the blood.

What was it about beginnings? What vital black magic did they possess that they eclipsed the episodes that followed? What rendered them inert when all else got reordered? Why did beginnings endure?

Amamma could not tell for certain, but she knew that her position was not unlike eighteen-year-old Shrini's. She was without lament.

A little over a week after Rangaa's cremation, a priest arrived at Amamma's doorstep. He was well fed and hungry. He looked at Amamma; looked at her glistening thali, her nose stud, her bangles – all proof of matrimony – her toe rings, earrings, brash diamonds.

'These things,' the Brahmin said, pointing, 'these things, not good for the deceased soul. Consider Rangaa-saar going upward, heavenward. He sees his wife, decked and nice-looking. Consider him please. He cannot leave her, not when she's well maintained, no. So his soul hovers forever and ever, neither of earth nor sky. Not good, Amma, no.'

Now the priest chanted words in a dead language, sing-song and severe. He blotted out the pottu on Amamma's forehead, cut her thali in two, put away her sun-dappled nose stud, slipped out the rings adorning her ears and toes. 'Wear a sari, Amma, white or pale. Then Rangaa-saar will look, spot something second-rate, and climb quickly to heaven. This is good.'

'Is it?'

'Amma, the books say this is good.'

'What else do the books say?'

'That if Rangaa-saar is in heaven, you will get a rightful seat up there by his side.'

Amamma nodded, said nothing. She paid the Brahmin. She slipped away into her bedroom.

The morning was streaming in. A shard of blinding yellow light. She followed this to the edge of the room, to a mirror. She peered into it as though it were an oracle and sighed.

How strange she looked, she thought, her face shorn of red and gold, of markings and ornaments, of the symbols she had carried turtle-like on her body. She couldn't recognize herself.

Then she looked closer, traced her reflection with steady fingers. There were no breaks, no odds and ends interfering with her profile. For the first time in years, she could tell that her nose was straight, her nostrils shaped like mango leaves. She could see her forehead, wide and smooth; her ears curled like shells; her neck, long and assertive. She could assess the brushstrokes that were clavicles; measure the length of her second toe; feel the pulse racing by her wrist.

Amamma was piqued by the wonders of her body. 'What all can it do?' she asked herself and watched spellbound as it responded. It glimmered in the morning sun, shivered when exposed to a slight draught, jumped through shifting shadows. Her nose quivered as it smelt the day's passage; her neck craned to catch street gossip; her toes, thus far tied to rings and riches, sped not knowing where to.

No, Amamma scolded herself, no, you can't spin like a chipper top, you're in mourning, halt. But her feet, her body could not be curtailed. For the first time in years, decades, Amamma felt like the girl she once was – tree-climber, milk-stealer, careless cloud-watcher – only freer, without an indignant father, a chiding mother. She could roll as a dog in the garden; laugh banshee-like in her room; tear the bedspread off the mattress; sleep till the sun disappeared; run –

Where could she run? Amamma skipped to the kitchen. Paused. By the window, she could see it, a lissom tree. And on it a whorl of red, lifting off, slowly vanishing.

*Janaki.*

Had Janaki grown wings?

And if she had, perhaps –

Over the next month, Amamma gathered several of her saris, those grand Kanjeevaram silks, the unworn nine yards in orange and green, and sold them at a wholesale market. She went to the goldsmith's and offered ornaments for money; walked to a merchant's and exchanged gems for cash. In thirty days, Amamma had gathered enough wealth to build an outhouse, propitiate a god or feed the entire district's children.

But my grandmother had other plans. On an ordinary March day, she went to George Town and ordered a travel agent to book her on a flight.

'Name, Madam?' he asked.

'Sarojaa.'

'Surname?'

My grandmother paused for a moment – did she dare disturb her husband's soul? – smiled wryly and invoked the name of a soul-sister. 'Janaki.'

'Madam?'

'Write *Janaki.*'

'Not possible, Madam, that is – '

'Write *Janaki.* Do I know my name or do you?'

The next hour proved to be uncomfortable.

'Where to, Madam?'

'New York.' After London (and she had no desire to visit London), it was the only foreign city that occurred to her – how often Mrs Swami had bragged about visiting it!

'Sorry, Madam?'

'New York. Need me to spell it out for you?'

'Yes. I mean, no. Travelling with, Madam?'

'One bag.'

'Who, Madam?'

'Object, not person. One bag.'

'Husband?'

'Since when did bags become husbands? Though god knows bags are more useful!'

'Oh.'

'I trust you have a flight you can book me on?'

'Yes. No. Yes. Payment made by?'

'Me.'

'You, Madam?'

'Yes, I believe so. Me.'

'Passport?'

'Here. You'll be pleased to know my husband gave this to me. His idea of an anniversary present.'

'Surname different, Madam.'

'Elizabeth Taylor changed names six times – six husbands, you know? Or was it seven? I'm like that.'

'What, Madam?'

'Smart boy. I need to leave two months later. May.'

'Where to, Madam?'

Eventually, after feigning impatience and putting on an act of peevishness, Sarojaa Janaki was booked on a Pan Am flight, India–Karachi–Frankfurt–New York.

It was a warm May evening when Amamma, in a nine-yard summer yellow sari, tumbled out of the airplane. She followed the crowds, imitated their gestures, carried with her the air of a disenchanted frequent traveller. She kept pace with a German gentleman, asked for a cab as he did, said 'Times Square' softly, cautiously, just like him.

So this was Amamma's first brush with the world, with streets outside Madras, beyond India. Around her, buildings rose and vanished behind clouds. People gathered like the pleats in a skirt, then blew away.

In a bit, the cab swerved into Times Square. Amamma peeled a bundle of currency off her sari pallu. She handed a fifty to the driver, accepted change, then slipped out.

The sun had dipped, and the streets were brash. There were flashing billboards, ads for Fuji Film, lights. And things my grandmother lacked a clear vocabulary for – peep shows, sex shops, back-room brothels, pimps, strippers. B-boys. Wrapped in silken yellow, Amamma ambled down 42nd Street, paused at an advert for Blondie, peered at a dimly lit arcade, and read open-mouthed as a banner screamed, 'Live Nude Girls: $3'.

So this was Manhattan, *this*, an island stripped of inhibition and reserve, a place without taboos. My grandmother, I imagine, was momentarily perturbed, unsure of the things before her – the brazen advance of the night, the smuttiness of the lanes, the gloss of bodies. Equally, she didn't know how best to respond. Was it right to be scandalized? Was she to stay nonchalant? Ought she to stare like the men before her? Or was it correct to turn away?

Suddenly – and I imagine Amamma watching with awe – a young boy gyred his gold-black body, windmilled his arms, spun backward. He glimmered like a river, twisted and turned with the ease of a runnel. He air-flared – a circus performer – then windmilled his arms once more.

My grandmother wanted to borrow the breakdancer's ease, his suppleness, his sheer riverine exuberance. Emboldened, she marched forward, tapped him, and whispered, 'Hello'. Asked, 'How is it done?'

The breakdancer, his body twinkling with sweat, drew out an arm, reached for my grandmother. His fingers locked in hers, he put one foot forward, then another, skipped lightly, and took Amamma along.

A throng gathered – moviegoers and out-of-work actors and waitresses – but my grandmother missed the inquisitive bystanders. Already she was travelling, time-travelling, beyond the strip of earth she had landed in, beyond the feathery shimmer of the night, beyond. She was sixteen, bounding past puddles of milk, scampering up trees, sliding down fences. The future could be anything she wanted it to be – dizzy and frivolous, a Ferris wheel spin. Such was the privilege of youth.

And that night, Amamma was young.

'Take this, lady,' the dancer told her, and he pinned a brooch shaped as a bird to her sari.

Moments or hours later, my grandmother found herself alone, without the breakdancer, the crowds, that imaginary spotlight. She shook her head, then looked skyward. There wasn't a star to be seen, only a mesh of smog and neon; no heaven watching over her, just audacious light.

This, too, was beautiful, this absence, this rash omission of right and wrong.

My grandmother was unrestrained.

Over the next fortnight, Amamma stayed in motels, tagged on with indulgent twenty-year-olds, hitched rides with college boys. She learnt of The Eagles, hummed to The Rolling Stones, danced one afternoon to 'Hey Jude'.

Alone, she walked through a sun-soaked Central Park, threw a coin into the Hudson, left a kiss on the Empire State Building. She bought discarded storybooks at the Strand, window-shopped along Fifth Avenue, waved out to the Statue of Liberty.

On some days, she'd have company. With Janaki, a shadow of Janaki, invisible to all except my grandmother, she'd visit museums – the MoMa, the Metropolitan, the Guggenheim or the Whitney. Together, they'd kneel before a Van Gogh, study a Picasso, weep noisily when confronted with a life-size Titian. Then they'd drift towards Times Square, comment on its sauciness, soak in its chutzpah.

'How do you like New York?' one of them would ask.

And the other would whisper, 'It's *alive*.'

I don't know how my grandmother did it – how she travelled solo through 1980s New York, through its brassy hovels and impertinent joints, in a sari, with loosely tied currency.

I don't know how she sought directions from tramps and scroungers, picked at meals alone outside subways, bargained for souvenirs and pretty trinkets, followed strangers through carefully numbered roads.

I will never know if she caught an X-rated film, made conversation with an opiate addict or wandered into a nightclub.

Most of all, I cannot tell how Amamma will respond to Times Square today, to its sterile marquees and vanilla stores and cheery streets in apple-pie order.

All I know for certain is this – that as a pigtailed schoolgirl, each time I'd ask her about New York, about that faraway city-country, she'd smile and drawl, 'It's *alive*.'

# 11.

Back in Bombay, while Tasha staggered from crush to crush, I waited. Sometimes, when I puzzled over love and what it meant, Tasha would smile and say, 'It's a warm feeling, hon.'

For most of my adolescence, I could only imagine what she meant. I'd wrap myself in Mamma's pashminas and believe – this is a body, this is how it feels, close-fitting, snug. I'd gulp down filter coffee and take in its heat – the fever of mouths. I'd switch off the fans, shut out the draught – sweat and ardour.

I wanted to know of love, experience it, its physical symptoms. I wanted to sense the pulse's quiver, that rush of blood, a tremor running like a spider down the back. I wanted love to descend on my skin.

And it didn't.

I kept waiting, lurching madly from patience to resignation to rage. I saw age crawl by – thirteen, fourteen, fifteen, sixteen – without markers, without men who'd act as bookmarks.

I was convinced I needed men.

'Why?' Ranja would ask, bewildered at my impatience. And I would offer a vague explanation. 'Because it would be nice. Well, I like the idea. Just – *because*.'

The truth, if only I could articulate it, was that I needed a man or *someone* not just to remind me of myself – who I was, what I could become – but also to confirm that I existed. In my house – with Mamma's coolness, my sisters' self-absorption, Amamma's growing obliviousness – it was easy to feel like a paper doll, frangible and unreal.

I needed a man also to hold on to friends – so I could enclose my biography within theirs. Unlike Tasha, I had but a fistful of acquaintances, and each time they'd refer to crushes and dalliances, I'd offer a sympathetic ear, a clichéd statement of fact, but little else – no lived anecdote, no wisdom distilled from experience, no half-true, sanctioned memory. If adolescence is marked by collective love-lamentation, I remained outside the circle of dismay; I could peek inside, slink in on occasion, but never actively participate.

I needed a man most of all to keep pace with my sisters, measure up. I had to contend with not just Tasha – a girl who had been wooed by at least half a dozen boys ('Eight,' she had said matter-of-factly when asked for a count at the age of sixteen) – but also Ranja, prissy Ranja, who had sprouted a temporary admirer.

It was more than I could endure. I remember approaching Mamma early one morning when she was chopping vegetables for office-goers. She was drunk on the aroma of onions-garlic-mustard and amenable to talk, all talk. 'Good morning!' she almost trilled, and I gathered the courage to pour out my heart.

Nobody loves me, I said, *nobody*, not one boy.

Mamma stopped chopping, looked away, far and away, beyond the horizon of antennae and buildings. 'Your father worshipped the ground beneath my feet.'

'Yes. But why – '

'I could have chosen anyone, Amma said so. But I married Karthik.'

'Yes – '

'He still loves me, you know? He does.'

I remember thinking – my mother can be startlingly self-obsessed.

I also remember thinking – I am alone in my misery.

Amamma, never one to mince words, reaffirmed the singularity of my condition.

'No boys?' she asked one evening, even as her memory slipped, played tricks.

'Well, I have friends. Boy – friends.'

'Tch. Useless. Girls your age hold hands.'

'Okay. Good.'

'It is good. You know your problem? Too small.'

'What?'

'Too small. Your breasts' – then flailing her arms – 'really, you should do something about them.'

I wanted to protest, register my displeasure, but the words iced over in my throat.

Amamma's comment – it seemed to clarify everything. It explained Jug's reluctance to call me despite my reckless attention-seeking gambits – leaving a thumbprint on his book, writing a 'D' under his desk, and (the most audacious of all moves) sneaking my number into his bag. It explained why Tasha's boyfriends always smiled at, even indulged me. It explained Ranja's high-handedness, Mamma's remoteness, and Amamma's vitriol.

I was poorly formed.

It explained Ravi's snigger when I wore an outfit I believed to be flattering – peach trousers, a peach T-shirt, two peach clips, a peach-shaped brooch. It explained Manjul's indifference when I read Rossetti in English class – *I loved you first: but afterwards your love,/ Outsoaring mine, sang such a loftier song* – look how he fidgeted and yawned. It explained Ashwin's shilly-shallying and Shashi's wariness when I suggested we form a study group and meet in the garden by my home.

*I was poorly formed.*

It explained the non-events that marked my teenage years – my drift towards men who did not exhilarate me, my fraught attempts at earning their esteem, my dismay when even they came to spurn my advances. It explained everything, but everything – the nights I spent alone playing Tasha's alibi, the nights I spent in silence envying Ranja her admirer. The nights, worst of all, the nights.

There was nothing to do about it. Nothing I hadn't tried – high heels, gloss, hair spray, mascara.

There was a party sixteen-year-old Tasha had taken me to after lying to Mamma. In the car – in her boyfriend's car – I awkwardly tried dressing up – rolling off my trousers, pulling up a skirt, revealing my thighs. Tasha sprayed glitter on my hair, painted my lips, plumped up my cheeks. I was supposed to be dancing with her friend Sammy's brother, a year older than I was, undoubtedly wiser. I got out of the car, my skin raw and freshly waxed. The evening pinched my knees.

'Where is he?' I asked Tasha. Her boyfriend. People I did not know.

Who.

Him. I must dance.

Who.

Friend. Boy. Boy – friend. Sammy's brother.

'Taken ill,' Tasha finally let slip, almost careless. 'Sammy says it's diarrhoea.'

That evening, as I danced alone, danced badly, didn't dance, I reimagined the treasure chest of my childhood, with mothballs and wool and Old Spice. I pictured my father walking up to it. I saw him reach out for my face, wipe my eyes.

Then, I imagined myself in the near future – flying past the Arabian Sea, the Mediterranean, northward to Norway. I saw myself in Oslo, Tasha by my side – the plans we had made-unmade-remade finally coming to pass. I pictured Daddy – there he was, greyer, kinder, right before us, opening his arms out. I heard him whisper in a voice I still know, 'Deeba, Dee? Deeba, you're beautiful.'

For a few moments, the evening – it proved to be tolerable. But then, as always, Amamma's voice intruded, chalk scraping against a board. *Too small, too small.*

And the past, future, all of time, got snuffed out like light.

For the most part, I spent my adolescence in darkness, hiding under bedcovers and between the pages of tattered books. There was so much to learn from poems and essays, myths and novels – from Heathcliff and Catherine, Vronsky and Anna, Farebrother and Mary Garth – about struggle and setbacks, about blasted hope and hopelessness, about the impossibility, total impossibility of love.

*There's a story of Clytie and Apollo – the former, an ordinary nymph; the latter, the god of light. How much Clytie loved Apollo, how hard she tried to secure his attention. Apollo, however, had other concerns – there were queens he wished to entice, princesses he hoped to seduce. Apollo had no time for unexceptional Clytie.*

*And Clytie pined.*

*Through the day, from morning to twilight, she turned her gaze skyward. Every hour, she called out to the unresponsive god of light. She dug in her tired heels and stretched out her aching arms. Her legs clung to the soil. Her hands swayed leaf-like against the sky. Her face, drained of blood, tanned a burnt umber.*

*Clytie, morphing into a sunflower, opened herself out to a careless Apollo. She leapt east as he rose, bowed west as he slept, wilted even as he dissolved to blue, then black. Embrace me, she'd tell the fading god of light. Her outspread arms would clutch nothing but air.*

As an adolescent, I'd extend my being like an ill-starred Clytie, hoping to lurch into affection. My arms would rise; my body would freeze in wait. For the most part, I'd grip emptiness.

If only I had understood Clytie better, I might've grasped how fortunate she was. She was fated to become, not someone's beloved, but a Van Gogh blossom, more luminous than the sun.

As it stands, I could not learn this – not then. Not at eighteen. I was destined by age, by my body, to look, fail, keep looking, fail –

And then, one day, he came.

# Many Loves.

*how we rolled up the carpet so we could dance, and the days were bright red,*

# 1.

It all began with a book – hardbound, with a grey dust jacket. There was a charcoal drawing across it, thick black strokes – never-ending fingers or strands of hair or wave after wave of seawater, who could tell. Hovering beneath, a string of letters – *The Shape of Grief.* I ran my hand across the upright stalk of the 'T', the whorled 'e', the blob of ink over the 'i' –

'Good choice,' someone whispered.

I was in a bookstore, waiting for Tasha. It must have been late in the afternoon. I must've skipped class. Quite possibly, I was hoping to find a new distraction – a poem, a statement of unflagging hope, *something* – so I squeezed past piles of bestselling titles, rows of thrillers ordered alphabetically, till I reached a corner dedicated to poetry and short stories and forgotten fiction. This was my most beloved space, my kingdom, where I claimed the rights of ownership. I ordered and reordered books, sometimes privileging the Hungarians – Krasznahorkai's 'vast black river of type'; at times foregrounding Kavan's dreamscapes; occasionally arranging the spines by colour, the reds following the greens and blues, a marching band of rainbow hues. Here, I could demand a floor cushion, squeeze myself against a wall, read aloud – or not.

It was while I was arranging the last of the spines, the greys and blacks, that I chanced upon a book I hadn't seen earlier, by an author I didn't know of. Sahil Vyas. *The Shape of Grief.* I turned to the last page. There were lines conveying withdrawals – a man was bidding a woman goodbye – so when I read them aloud, they sounded like a lament for the dead.

'Good choice,' I heard someone say, someone standing by my side. A man. He was talking to me. I started.

I tried to think of something glib in response, a statement Tasha would have thrown if confronted with a new voice. 'You think?' The question fell casually, the way it was meant to. Magic.

'Though the first page is my favourite. The rest falls short.'

'I see you've read the book.'

'All too often.'

'You like the author.'

A chuckle. 'I wouldn't say that.'

'Ah.'

'Perhaps on some days.'

'Why would you recommend this book?'

'I suppose – it tries. It isn't lazy.'

'You're generous when you praise.'

'And you – you've colour-coded these books?'

I flinched. My little country spanning six shelves, hitherto off the maps, had been exposed. 'I guess,' I murmured.

'I used to do that, too. A long time ago.'

'Really?'

'Mind if I join you here?'

'Yes. No. I mean, sure.'

The intruder sat right by my floor cushion. It occurred to me that I had barely noticed this stranger, so absorbed had I been with myself, my turn of phrase, my conduct. If this were a motion picture, I'd have been the sole focus of an all-seeing, all-knowing camera. As it happens, I was still watching myself, the way my skirt crowded around my ankles, my shirt and the creases by the hem, the light that fell on my hands, so they seemed like glass, transparent.

I forced myself to look away and observe the man, so that instant – when I registered the facts of his body for the first time – still endures. It's the clearest portrait I hold of him.

He was tall, this much was incontestable; and his body was wiry, all bone and skin, set off by a prominent Adam's apple that fluttered each time he spoke. In the days to come, I'd spend hours watching his neck, the half-apple snagged there. I'd touch it and feel its steady pulse, sense it hum as he whispered a poem, feel its seesaw tremor when he laughed.

But this was for later.

For now, I watched his face – the large eyes that became letterbox slits when he read; the single dimple hovering by his mouth; the nose, so straight that it seemed like a child's ruler-assisted line drawing. He didn't smile often, but when he did, he looked into the distance as though apprehending joys once known.

His hair was closely cut, pepper-and-salt. He wasn't young. This I could tell for certain. It wasn't just his hair and the unblack stubble he had missed over a morning shave. It was his skin – it seemed tired. His eyes – at times sneering, often cynical. His manner – generally wry. These weren't the currencies of youth.

'You've made yourself comfortable,' he commented, noting the splay-legged knapsack and my abandoned shoes.

'Well, this is my second home.'

'Is it? Is there a book you especially like here?'

'That one,' I said, pointing to *Nightwood* by Djuna Barnes. Almost invisible against a row of black-spined titles.

'Interesting. I used to have Barnes's poster up on my wall – coloured lips, the hat somewhat askew, a gentleman's coat, you know?'

'Yeah. Where's the poster now?'

He shrugged. 'We grow old. We move on.' He paused. 'But you're too young to know that.'

'I'm not. I understand.'

'Do you?'

'I used to love the Bee Gees. Back when I was twelve. I don't any longer.'

'It's something like that, yes.'

'Yes. Do you come here often?'

'Sometimes. On days when I'm reading.'

'Are there other kinds of days?'

'Sure. Those composed of empty hours. Those when I claim to work but do nothing.'

'Where do you work?'

'Mostly out of home.'

'Do – '

'It's my turn to ask questions. What do you do – apart from annexing bookstores?'

'Well, I'm a student. I'm practically done with the second year of my bachelor's degree. And then – in a week – I travel for a fortnight with my sister.'

'Where to?'

'Scandinavia. Norway actually.'

'You don't hear that often. Why Norway?'

'Well. It's a long story and – and I'm not wholly sure.'

'Love?'

'It's never that simple.'

'Spoken like a wise old soul. How old are you, anyway?'

'I'm older than I look. I'm nineteen, almost twenty.'

'It's a good age to be.'

'So I hear. How old are you? Or is that impolite?'

'I'm not one to conceal my age. Fifty-two.'

'Really?'

'Do you not want to talk to me now?'

I dithered, then chastised myself for my petty conservatism. 'No, it's just a number.'

'If you say so.'

'What's your name?'

'Let's start with yours. You are?'

'Deeya. Though everyone calls me Dee. Unless annoyed.'

'Well, since I'm not annoyed – Dee, I'm Sahil.'

'Oh! You're his namesake.' I flashed the book in my hands. 'Did you read him because you share his name – Sahil – what's your surname?'

'Vyas. I'm Sahil Vyas.'

'You – '

'I wasn't entirely forthright. That book – I wrote it.'

'You're a writer?'

'When I don't talk about writing – my favourite pastime – yes, I write.'

'Oh – '

'I'm actually flattered. You picked this book, you read a page – '

'Let me buy it.'

'Let me gift it to you.'

'Will you autograph it?'

'Sure. I have an extra copy at home, two streets away. Would you like to come with me?'

I considered his offer. Tasha was expected. We were meant to catch the long train home. She would tell me of the day's adventures, the men she had spoken to, those she had professed interest in, the dates and pretences and compassionate kisses. While I would listen, nod attentively, interject with a yes –

'Yes,' I heard myself say, almost blasé, as though this were a normal turn of events.

'Great,' Sahil said, equally blasé.

So we walked. This was a Bombay I knew, that I had wandered through for years. Yet, suddenly, it seemed alien, like a wedge off a tourist map. Was that a crumbling fort? Was this a promenade? Was that a jagged skyline with tiered hotels? What names did they hold? I opened atlases of the mind, tried identifying signposts and landmarks, looked to Sahil for clues.

'The city keeps changing,' I murmured.

'Does it? I fear it's stagnant.'

'Why do you say that?'

'Dig deep under the buildings in Churchgate, beneath Apollo Bunder and the Gateway of India. And you'll find a network of basement passages, perhaps cellars. They used to exist when this city was a fort, a thing of moats and ramparts. They still live. Nothing changes.'

'But everything does.'

'Only on the surface. Slick cars, roads. But scratch these off, and you'll see – change isn't the only constant in life. Inertia is.'

'That's awfully pessimistic.'

'So say the young.'

'You can't keep telling me that, you know. I'm being held to ransom by a birth certificate.'

'Let's talk twenty years from now. You might feel differently.'

'I won't.'

'We'll see.'

I looked away, and Sahil interrupted. 'On to cheerier subjects. Are you from Bombay?'

'I suppose. But I've spent much time dreaming of elsewheres, occupying other spaces.'

'Spaces like?'

'Norway, for one. Has your address always been Bombay?'

'No. In another life I inhabited Delhi. And London. And New York.'

'Do you miss them?'

'I miss the drift of seasons. Bombay doesn't have that. It rains, then it doesn't.'

'I suppose.'

'And here's my home.'

It was an unscrubbed building, grey and mossy, streaks of dirt running down its windows. We climbed up the stairs, past scenes of quiet domesticity – baby doodles on walls, hurried swirls of rangoli, a goddess, perhaps Lakshmi, pasted near an entrance – to reach the second floor. Sahil fiddled with his keys, led me in.

'Make yourself at home.'

I looked around and observed the room, a matchbox. Yet, like so many other tenements in the city, it was a carpetbag of tricks; the more I looked at it, the more it seemed to hold. There was a laptop in a corner, near a window, yellow Post-its with hurried notes dotting its screen; a sketch with bits of cross-hatching; an inscription on a block of wood – *it comes out of / your soul like a rocket*; a dhurrie with faded cushions; a folding table with two squat benches; a stereo. There was a bookshelf nailed to a wall, perhaps the most prominent fixture; it was chock-full of books. I went to it, tried gathering the details, the genre-wise assembly of titles – rare poetry anthologies, fiction, travel guides, cookbooks, so many.

'Can I get you anything?'

'No. No, thanks.'

'I can offer reasonably good black coffee. It's my favourite.'

'Not a big fan, I'm afraid. I need a dash of milk. And ideally some ice.'

'Ah.'

'But I'm fine, really. You collect cookbooks?'

'I do.'

'And *Lonely Planet* guides. Here's Norway.'

'Yes.'

'You've visited?'

'Years ago, Dee.'

'What took you there?'

'Well – I needed to get away. Go to a place without memories. I was in mourning.'

'Mourning?'

'I had lost my wife.'

'Oh.' Of course, I told myself, of course, he must've been married – he was past fifty. 'I'm sorry.'

'So am I. I was cheating on her even as the cancer spread.'

I didn't know what to say. 'I don't know what to say.'

'It's what it is.'

How do you move past a stranger's confession? By making an admission of your own as fair barter.

'I'm going to Scandinavia to find my father,' I said.

'He lives there?'

'No. Yes. He could be anywhere. But since, as a child, I thought he had moved to Norway, I'm willing to buy into the idea as an adult.'

'A word of warning – you could be setting yourself up for disappointment.'

'Nah. I'm taking a pilgrimage.'

'How does that make the journey less perilous?'

'Because Anne Carson says that a pilgrim is like a No play – his end is not the point.'

'Do you believe everything Anne Carson says?'

'I believe anything that's well-written.'

'As did I when – '

' – You were young, yes, I get it.' I smiled. 'Would you like a gift from Norway?'

'A postcard would be good.'

'It's yours.'

Sahil went to his bedroom to fish for his book, the one he was meant to present to me. I was alone in his drawing room. It struck me that we had submitted parts of our lives, entirely secret, to one another. That so far the revelations had been unthreatening – we knew too little to make weighty assessments or use disclosures as bargaining chips. We inhabited a territory free of serious consequences.

But already that was changing. As I looked around Sahil's crowded living space, I realized that I was learning of his inner life – the books he had thumbed through far too often (*Crime and Punishment, The Brothers Karamazov,* how worn the spines were); the Post-its that acted as reminders (*'call Sheena'; 'a bottle of wine'*). I knew far too much.

As did Sahil. He had gleaned truths about me beyond the half-specifics I had shared. He knew, for instance, that I was lonely (why else would I have followed him to his residence?); that I was foolish (it would explain my impending trip to the edge of the earth); that I was susceptible to those who read and remembered. That I was willing and young.

Suddenly, I was terrified. I found myself coasting down a space, altogether precarious, where conversations could be built on past exchanges, where promises could be made and kept.

'Here's your book,' Sahil said, emerging. 'It comes with a note.'

'What does it say?'

'To more todays.'

'Thank you.'

I left, perhaps too hastily, the book secure in my arms, my number on Sahil's Post-it. I skidded down the stairs, past the ordinary homes of people, through the gate, into the unquestioning streets of the city.

Eventually, I met Tasha at home. She was irate since she had had to wait, doubly irate since she had been unable to share her news. Once mollified, she told me, as she always did, her tales about too-many-men.

For once, I had a story to trade. But suddenly I didn't want to. Somehow, in the telling, too much would get defined, too many conjectures would turn to fact.

Besides, the more I considered it, the more I was overwhelmed by the events of the day – my discovery of a book as its author entered the store; his attentiveness as I read out an excerpt. The serendipity baffled.

And yet it shouldn't have. Because maybe, just maybe, all of life is no more than happenstance. Maybe, as people, we are not unlike strands of moss, Goblins' Gold found in grottos, the existence of each filament driven by a chain of daily coincidences – the sun positioning itself just so; a single ray of light piercing a cave; a mossy shoot eating a strand of illumination. The life of Goblins' Gold – a story of synchronicity.

That evening, as my phone rang, I sprang, ran with it to the terrace.

'It's me,' a voice said, smooth like the afternoon.

'How are you?'

'I'm well, Dee. I found a book you'd like.'

'Which one?'

'*Ryder*.'

'Djuna Barnes?'

'Exactly, yes.'

'I'd love to read it.'

'Why don't you come and take it? Saturday? Does that work?'

Yes.

# 2.
# *Amamma*

Let's go back in time – before my grandmother took a giddy flight to America, before Rangaa's demise, well before Mamma was even born –

October 1948. Already, in her fourteen-month life, independent India had witnessed the death of Gandhi, the surrender of Hyderabad's Nizam, and the accession of Kashmir to the Dominion. For Amamma, though, these rumblings must've seemed distant. I imagine she wept when Gandhi died, not because she knew the Mahatma, but because somehow when she heard Nehru's voice, a thin sputter on All India Radio – *the light has gone out of our lives* – she was reminded of her own bereavements – of the family she had been sundered from, of the soul-sister she had lost, of the children she hadn't been able to create.

It must have been a squally October afternoon, the rain falling as sheets of blue-grey. Amamma – for the first time since Janaki's demise, for the very first time since her wedding day – was on her way to her parents'. Her only brother was to get engaged, and her husband and she were invited. Rangaa, complaining of work and surly patients, excused himself from the family gathering, from the solicitous comments of his in-laws, from gratuitous questions that were bound to begin with 'Good news yet, Anna? Good news?'

Amamma was on her own. Unlike her journey so many years ago to her husband's – bumpy, with two indisposed bullocks – my grandmother's visit to her parents' proved to be undemanding. Rangaa, to assert his affluence, had arranged for a car, a borrowed Morris Oxford, with strict instructions that his wife conceal the precise details of ownership. Then he had ordered his apprentice to drive – no pit stops, no unreasonable diversions at his wife's behest – and take Amamma pell-mell to her parents'.

The driver was obedient. And Amamma was bored. To make the journey eventful, she began inventing games for entertainment. She burst into song with each clap of thunder, gave a round of applause to lightning bolts, blinked twice when the wind chose to holler. If the driver was baffled, he didn't make it obvious, focusing instead on the rain-drenched highway, blurred signposts, potholes. A little later, the road narrowed. And Amamma grew still. 'Slow down,' she told the apprentice-driver and craned her neck.

They were certain to appear any moment now – the milky puddles; the half-nude, if sodden, paintings; the measureless tamarind tree. That, there, was her school, its walls higher than she remembered, its students tumbling out, too busy for games. That, there, was the neighbouring garden, still in bloom. As for the tamarind tree – it was sure to come into sight now, a long trail of pods, calloused branches – where was it? There were houses, more than the six she had once counted with her brother; modish cycle-rickshaws; a new telegraph pole – was *that* where the tree had been?

Before Amamma could tell for certain – tell that the tree's branches had made way for looped wires, and the milky puddles had all but vanished, and the paintings had been washed away – her house drew close, or something like it, moss-free, the leaky roof patched up, a mailbox outside, compact and picture-book-red. No babies. Instead, girls, old enough to hide behind curtains. There were curtains with English flowers. And a spindly boy circling a banyan in worship – perhaps her brother? Her brother.

Suddenly, Amamma longed to return to Rangaa's house with the palm leaves outside and a hive for wasps and an east-rising sun. This – this place from her childhood – it was alien.

'Turn back, turn back,' Amamma commanded her apprentice-driver. But the man would not listen. Instead, he let the car sputter-cough-belch-wheeze, then halt – so my great-grandmother emerged, and her husband, and her son (the boy now touching the bonnet). There they were, a row of three calm and collected faces, maybe subdued into quiet by a polished fender, lights.

Amamma stumbled out, rearranged her sari – 'the best silk Madras has,' her husband had insisted – and as a matter of practice, ensured that her pottu wasn't smudged. The apprentice held an umbrella over her head while she studied the people gathered before her, her family – her mother, slighter, slimmer, as though her body had gently deflated once her children had outgrown her lap; her father, greyer, more imperious; her brother, no longer playing with words.

'You well,' my great-grandmother finally whispered, more a statement than a question, letting her fingers caress her daughter's face, this woman she had birthed.

My great-grandfather nodded from a distance, a silent 'hello', a tacit 'you look fine'.

His son half-smiled, then rushed back into the house.

Amamma considered chasing him the way she used to as a schoolgirl, her ribbons trailing, her feet too quick for his. But already she knew she couldn't. Her sari would unravel. Her bangles, when she'd be trying to outmanoeuvre him, would clang and reveal her whereabouts. It was pointless.

Amamma quietly walked into the house, and her mother followed, asking her the questions that needed asking – 'Is your husband fine? Are the neighbours nice? Shall I ask your driver to keep the bags in a bedroom?' – and Amamma said yes to each of them. She looked at her mother from the corner of her eye – this woman who had produced her; who had held her to her breasts; who had changed her diapers; who had attended to her instinctively like a bitch would a pup; who now acknowledged her from a distance.

My grandmother wanted to break the ice. She longed to hold her mother's hands and confide in her. She wished to hug her less-ample body. But then she realized that the gesture, *any* gesture, would provoke embarrassment. The two had seldom disclosed secrets. The two had hardly ever embraced.

So my grandmother left her mother – this woman she'd never know – and reacquainted herself with the house, touching the walls that had been newly painted, ruffling a curtain with trimmings, peeking into the room she used to sleep in, now spilling over with gifts for her brother. She walked through the kitchen, sticky with ghee and oil, into the backyard, seeking the trees she used to climb.

Most of them had vanished – the mango and guava and banana trees making way for a storehouse.

Amamma's brother was inside it, playing aimlessly with wood shavings. My grandmother waved, hoping to earn a reaction. She did.

'Go up the hill,' he quickly said.

'I'm sorry?'

'Go up the hill.'

'Why?'

'Because she's waiting there.'

'Who is?'

'Your best friend.'

'I don't have best friends.'

'Well, her brother disagrees. He said the girl you used to share a school desk with is in town. He said she wishes to speak to you in private. He said she is waiting on top of the hill.'

'Is this another prank you're – '

'I'm past that age,' her brother primly answered.

Amamma frowned. She realized that she didn't know her brother well enough – not any more – to confirm that he was lying. She also realized that her past was slipping away from her – who was her best friend, when had she shared a desk, hadn't she elbowed out all her classmates?

My grandmother could no longer tell.

'If you're lying, I swear – '

'Yes?'

'Well, I will hang you upside down, I will complain to your fiancée, I will – '

'Relax. I'm only the messenger.'

It was a lost cause. In her absence, Amamma's brother had become all too sage.

Abruptly, my grandmother excused herself, wandered out of the backyard, walked down a road she once knew. The morning shower had become a faint drizzle, and in the distance was the once familiar hillock. It had sprouted a village all around, a girdle of tin shacks. Amamma crossed this hub of commotion, trundled up – no longer the mountain goat she used to be – huffing lightly, clutching the sides of her belly, wiping a bead of sweat.

Soon, my grandmother found herself on the summit – grassy, with a dense cluster of bushes at one end – the only corner of her childhood township that hadn't been invaded by brick and steel. When was the last time she had conquered the knoll? When the stray cat led her a merry chase; the evening she had fought with a sister; the day she had left – no. No, that was the day she had wished to climb uphill, but –

*'You're such a coward!'*

*'No, I am not!'*

*'Then climb that mountain with me!'*

Amamma remembered the boy – unable to accept her challenge, unable to bolt. She shook her head. How silly that tryst seemed – his arguments, her rejoinders, their dilly-dallying and coquetry. How silly *everything* was when viewed from a hill!

My grandmother sighed dramatically and scanned the crest – nobody, not even an overreaching bird. She lay on a bed of grass and looked skyward – not a cloud. She rolled as well as she could in her sari – not even a whisper of air.

Now, my grandmother got up, paced, restless. Wherever was her supposed best friend? Why did she want to meet on a hill? And what could she possibly have to disclose? The misdoings of an ex-teacher? The flirtations of a classmate she barely knew? Perhaps a confession – that she had stolen her pencil – why, then my grandmother would send her packing!

'Hello?' Amamma hollered.

Not a sound in response, not even an echo.

'Hello?' my grandmother repeated, now feeling foolish. If her brother was pulling her leg, why, then she'd – she'd –

'Hello,' a faint voice answered. My grandmother jumped. The bushes rustled, and something emerged – an ironed red shirt, grey trousers – a *man*. An *unknown* man.

Amamma's jaw dropped. She retrieved a safety pin from her sari, brandished it as a sword. 'Who are you?' she yelled.

The man, his hair gummed to his scalp, cowered. 'I am – sorry?'

'Yes? Don't you dare come close! I will poke you till you wish you were stung by a thousand bees!'

'Well, actually, please, I – '

Amamma observed this man like she would a potentially venomous insect, up close and with extreme caution. She took in the specifics – colour, shape, size. Slowly, her fear dissipated and made way for curiosity. Why did this man suddenly seem familiar – like a creature from her past? When had she encountered this snivelling stranger? And *where*?

My grandmother was convinced that if she identified the space of their first interaction, the geographical specifics, she'd know the man. She looked back in time. Had she met him as a child at her parents' – was he a guest she had been forced to serve tumblers of coffee to? Had she seen him in her school – was he the delinquent son of a teacher? Had she chanced upon him on her way back home like she had the boy with a bouquet of flowers –

Amamma gasped.

'*You!*'

The man gawped, then spluttered, 'I guess.' Once more, I must call him Venu.

'You!' Amamma repeated.

'And you,' Venu said.

'Perhaps.'

'That girl – the pigtails have gone. But otherwise, yes, you are more or less the same.'

'You haven't aged too badly either.'

'What?'

'Nothing. I said you seem well. And get a grip. Stop trembling. Tell me, what on earth are you doing here?'

'Why – why, I *climbed* the mountain.'

A statement of fact. Yet, in all her life, Amamma hadn't heard a more ardent comment.

'So you did.'

'I heard, you know? They said that your brother – he is getting engaged.'

'So he is.'

'Yes. I thought – I thought you might visit. And I wanted to meet. So –'

'Wait – so – so, *you* lied to my brother –'

'Well. Yes. I suppose –'

'And to think that fool believed you!'

'I did make a convincing case. I told him of your views on mushrooms and Viking ships and the sea and whales – all – erm – factually incorrect, may I add. And he agreed that only your best friend could know such things.'

'Such an idiot!'

'In his defence – '

'What defence? And how did you find your way here anyway? Did he tell you? It isn't a straight path – '

'No, well – well, I thought of what you'd do. So I followed a cumulonimbus cloud and believed I'd reach the summit eventually.'

'Your combo-cloud got you here?'

'Apparently.'

'What is that anyway – combo – ?'

'Oh, *cumulo*nimbus – it's a dense vertical cloud associated with atmospheric instabil – '

'Sounds like a giant dinosaur. It must also be shaped like a giant dinosaur.'

'Well, actually, no, it's like a mushroom because of – '

'Once a dinosaur, always a dinosaur.'

Venu stared.

He hemmed and hawed.

So, suddenly, Amamma felt sorry for this man quaking like poorly set jelly.

What d'you do, my grandmother asked, holding out something of an olive branch.

'Well, I teach,' Venu replied, for once on solid ground. 'Though my school is not here, no. It must be, well, in my estimation, one kilometre away.'

'Oh. What subject?'

'Maths. To ten-year-old girls. They ask lots of questions.'

'And you mislead them with facts?' Amamma could broker peace for only so long.

Venu gulped, then muttered, 'Facts are important. It would interest you to know, for instance, that most storm cells in cumulonimbus clouds die in twenty minutes, which is why – '

'It has stopped raining dinosaurs, I can see that.'

'Yes, well, yes – I guess.' Venu scowled. My grandmother was more exasperating than all his students.

'Glad you agree.'

Venu didn't, but there were more pertinent matters to discuss. 'Tell me,' he said, 'tell me, are you fine since – '

'Since?'

'Since that day?'

'Which day? There are so many of them.'

'Well – *that* day. I don't know what happened. You were there, then you were in a bullock cart, a man was saying, "Hello, Hello," and I heard – though I am not sure – I heard you were getting married. Still, you could also have been sent off to your grandmother's home or your uncle's – I don't know.'

'Why don't you ask my brother? You seem to be quite pally with him.'

'I – I'm not. And I considered asking him – but I guess, I wanted to hear it from you.'

'Can't you tell what happened?' Amamma asked, pointing to her attire.

'Well – I – I frankly don't know. I've never been good with riddles. What are you saying?'

My grandmother looked at Venu, at this commonsensical man in perfectly ironed clothes. She ought to have disliked him – or if she were kindly disposed, pitied his blindness.

Instead, here she was trying to reach out, magick minutes into hours. Maybe it was because Venu accepted her slapdash remarks with sincerity. Maybe it was because he willingly staggered into spats, those that came without neat resolutions.

Or maybe it was quite simply because he said things she could not invent; he offered talk beyond the scope of her imagination.

'Look at me,' my grandmother said.

Venu quivered. 'I am looking.'

'And?'

'And – to get back to the main question – *what* happened that day?'

'Why do you care?' my grandmother yelled, peeved.

'Actually – I wish to know if you're well.'

'As well as I can be in a house with four walls.'

'There are worse things.'

Amamma smelt a cliché. She bristled. 'How is that any consolation?'

'I don't know. But it's meant to reassure.'

'Is it? *There are worse things.* Bah! Is that how you came to terms with the day I was married off?'

'So – so you did get married that day?'

'And to think that a word from you, just a word – *confirmation* that you would follow and – '

'You hold me responsible for the past?'

'You had the power to change the script.'

'No. Your parents did. And they weren't about to humour us.'

'That's an easy answer. But it's not the truth.'

Venu cleared his throat, for once with resolve. 'Listen. What are we arguing over anyway?'

Amamma looked away. 'I don't know.'

'What's done is done.'

'Perhaps. But I keep returning to that point in time when anything could have happened – that slim moment of possibility.'

'That moment did not exist. You're mistaken – *delusional* – if you think it did.'

'Then let me have my delusions. Let me also believe that you pined and never married.'

Venu baulked. His eyes ran over this woman – mage's skin and witch-like hair – though such beings weren't real, were they? No. They didn't exist. 'How do you know?'

'Know what?'

'That – that I didn't marry?'

It was Amamma's turn to look startled. 'So you didn't – ?'

'No.'

'Why not?'

'Because – because I was hard at work.'

'Yes.'

Yes. Amamma received the confirmation she needed. For all his faults, his hesitancy and reticence and pettifoggery and foolishness, Venu had been faithful to memory. He still hovered by the ghost of the tamarind tree, a young boy with young hands, his stubby fingers seeking hers. In the vicinity, Amamma imagined, her spirit lingered, hair ribbons undone. Her fingers touching his. Almost. Here was the story she wished to follow, the parallel one –

'It won't rain again today,' Venu interrupted, pulling her back to the present.

'No?'

'No. The clouds have passed.'

Amamma stuck out her tongue. No rain. Dry. She saw Venu fumbling, dusting some mud off his perfect red shirt, trying to take leave. 'Stop,' she wished to say.

But my grandmother couldn't. She observed herself – her bangles, her nose stud, that prominent pottu, possibly a wet streak. Her body declared that she was married. The rings around her toes – they bound her to Rangaa's house. Her thali confirmed her chastity.

But here she was coveting a stranger. What was she to do with this fact? For once, Amamma wasn't sure. For once, she felt compelled to seek direction from Venu. 'Yes. The clouds have passed. Now – what must we do?'

It was a poor question. It offered room for manoeuvre.

'Now that we agree it won't rain, you must do what you always do. And I – I must go home,' Venu answered, matter-of-fact, almost cold.

It was all Amamma needed – a sensible statement – to take charge. 'You don't have to.'

'My tiffin is waiting.'

'We can share the meal.'

'You're married.'

'Thanks for the reminder.'

'Well, you are.'

'If not a meal today, how about simply meeting next week? My home – it's just a car ride away.'

'I don't own a car. And, in any case, I won't be around.'

'Where are you going?'

'To England'

'To England? For how long?'

'I don't know. For a while. A few years.'

Amamma felt the ground shift beneath her. Faint, she clutched at questions to keep steady. 'When do you take off?'

'In two days.'

'How do you get to England?'

'By ship, then train.'

'Why are you going there?'

'It's a long story.'

'So what if it's long? I'm going nowhere.'

'I have a British friend. John. He left for England a year ago and started a school. He says I'm a good teacher, and he would like my help – '

'What will you be teaching?'

'The same. Maths.'

'What's wrong with your neighbourhood school?'

'Nothing really, but – well, I told John I'd come. So I should go.'

'Then why on earth did you try finding me?'

'To – I guess, so I'd know for certain – and then – as matters stand, to tell you I'm going.'

My grandmother could not allow it. She yielded to instinct – resisted, fought. Don't go, she said.

Why, Venu asked.

Because it's cold in England. Grey. I've read it rains.

I can get used to many things, Venu said.

But not the food. Potatoes every day. *Potatoes.*

I won't like it, but I'll live, Venu said.

Is living sufficient?

No, Venu guessed, but said nothing. Then, he whispered, 'These are our cards. There's nothing we can do.'

'If you say so.'

Amamma felt as though time had reeled backward – only now she didn't have the advantage of youth. She felt less able to recover.

Her features, always clear, seemed to dim.

And Venu, blind to most things, noticed. To him, it seemed like the headlights of a car had short-circuited. He had to act with the swiftness of a repairman. Yet, Amamma wasn't a thing made of cylinders and pistons. She was less banal, therefore less predictable.

Venu realized he had to move out of character, do the unexpected, if only to return my grandmother to herself.

'I'll write to you. You write to me,' he whispered.

'What about?'

'Tell me of the world within four walls. I shall tell you of the foreign city.'

'I'd like that.'

'Me too.'

'It will be less lonely.'

'Yes.'

My grandmother smiled.

I don't know what followed. I imagine Amamma disclosed her address. I imagine, moments later, Venu left.

The red scar that was his shirt became tiny, still tinier.

As Amamma watched him, the future – so far tightly sealed – seemed to snap open. A thin streak of light spilled in.

# 3.

While Tasha and I prepared in earnest for Norway, Ranja, too toffee-nosed to accompany us, participated by pouring scorn on our plans.

We had spent the past several years saving pennies – collecting spare change from Mamma for hand-delivering tiffins, asking Amamma for cash for massaging her feet, even earning prize money in college contests – I stood first in a handwriting competition, Tasha was awarded for playing a standout witch in *Macbeth*. We still fell short of our requirements, so our mother, in a weak moment, offered to cover the cost of our hostels and air tickets.

Even as we planned, Mamma remained a distant observer. She gathered the specifics of our itinerary – where we'd stay, when we'd return. She expressed concern for our safety. She made vague attempts at dissuading us from our chosen course – 'Eighteen- and nineteen-year-old girls travelling solo – it was unheard of in our times.' But she steadfastly avoided the more intrusive questions. She did not wish to know how we'd spend our time or confirm why we had chosen Scandinavian Europe – though minutes before we were to leave, she came to us, told us, 'Tell him – please say hello.' Then she kissed us goodbye so nervously that we couldn't probe.

It was as our cab hurtled down the road to the airport that Tasha and I paused to consider the big questions. What did Mamma mean? What were we going after? Really, *why* were we travelling so far?

*Hecataeus has written of that classical bird, the phoenix. Once every five hundred years she lays an egg and bursts into flames. And the egg, warmed by the parent's dying light, hatches to reveal a fully-grown offspring.*

*This revivified creature, born into mourning, scours all of Arabia, finds sacred myrrh, and rolls it into a hollow ball. With her wings at half-mast, she gathers what remains of her dead parent. Slowly, she secures this in the orb.*

*The young phoenix places the ball on her sorrowing body. Soaring high, still higher, she travels a distance of a thousand miles, past the sand and dust of Arabia, to Egypt, Heliopolis, the Temple of the Sun. Here, she plummets and uncovers what she holds. Quietly, she buries her parent. Then she returns to Arabia, her emptied-out home.*

Phoenix-like, we were carrying Daddy, east to west.

Sometimes physical journeys alone cover the scope and compass of loss.

Summer crept into Oslo as we reached.

Four months ago, darkness and ice-soil. Now, a yolk-like sun, quivering with life, all yellow. As we walked down the streets we had learnt by heart, we learnt of a Norway that lived beyond maps. We saw a nation of startling contrasts – tired buildings rubbed again palaces; bustling pubs faced lonesome piers.

For a fortnight, Tasha and I inhabited Oslo. Each place we went to, we asked, 'Does a famous Indian live here?' At every pit stop, we searched for a man with black hair and restless eyes. Across destinations, we tried identifying one voice – the rich baritone of childhood dreams – in the whoops of onlookers. We were tourists who studied faces rather than monuments; frequented neglected restaurants instead of popular bistros; sought post offices, banks, and grocery stores, not chic boutiques.

We caught a bus to Grønland, that rough-and-tumble hub of Asian immigrants, and tripped into colour – the alabaster hands and fair hair of the city centre making way for psychedelic shirts and Mohawks in dazzling rainbow hues. We watched the men in Turkish barber shops; the men next to women in floral headscarves; the men inside Jubba breaking bread with their hands; the men in shops selling exotic silks; the men in booths offering cheap calls to Bombay; the men, all the men, in narrow alleys thick with the scent of curry.

'I bet he's here,' Tasha hurriedly whispered as we walked through

the doors of the first Indian restaurant we came across, Punjab
Tandoori. We spoke to Harinder Singh, the owner, Kiran Jot, his chef-
wife. Over spoonfuls of palak paneer and glasses of mango lassi, we
asked of the man we had crossed countries to meet. Yet, even as we
spoke, I sensed the staleness of our recollections, the imprecision of
each memory – 'Black hair, he had black hair. But perhaps he's balding
now? Yes. Likely balding. He's tall. Though, actually, now that we're
adults, he might seem short. Medium build, I'd say. And he's an artist.
Or should be – unless he has given up that life. In which case, he's a
journalist. Or not.' Kiran Jot's face only scrunched up in confusion.

For the next hour, we watched the customers seated in Punjab
Tandoori – a Briton with skin the shade of walnuts, claiming to own
a house in Bathinda; a couple in love, the girl with red bangles, wrist
to elbow, the boy with dark glasses perched on his head. We observed
the brown-skinned men who entered – the portly gent tripping past
tables, his words a muddle of English and Hindi; the sightseer with a
point-and-shoot camera, capturing the cutlery on display; the man in
a bright blue turban, greeting everyone with folded hands. In them,
in all of them, these men we shared a homeland with, we found
intriguing portraits, little else.

So Tasha and I looked beyond these self-contained India
bubbles. We went to spaces associated with art – to Frognerparken
with a totem of entwined bodies; to Dronebrygg, that artist-run
microbrewery; to Lorry's where watercolourists could trade paintings
for beer. In the last place, we met a man – hooded eyes and burnished
lips, his breath stale with liquor. We told him of our quest, and he
offered a cold-grim smirk.

You aren't going to find him, he prophesied.

Why, we pestered.

Because, here – well, here, *our* gods rule.

The man proceeded to tell us of Baldr, the god of light, who by
the oddest turn of events was killed. The lord of the underworld
promised to grant him a second life if all things, living and dead, wept.

As though on cue, plants shed chlorophyll tears; crickets rubbed
their legs and bawled; winding rivers turned into oceans brimming
o'er with sorrow.

Baldr ought to have come alive.

And yet he didn't – for there was a giantess known to some as Þökk. She watched the sky blow his runny nose – a mighty sneeze into a tissue of cloud – and rolled over with laughter. Her belly jiggled, her breath grew quick, and in a world deep in mourning, her joy rang through –

'So that's that,' the man announced, slapping his thighs.

'What d'you mean?'

'Those gone, they aren't returning.' Then filling his glass, he slurred, 'Coz that giantess – can you hear her? – she still laughs.'

I wanted to dispute the claims of the drunken man, prove him wrong – and soon enough, this seemed possible.

Tasha and I were in a park. In front of us were children in starched shorts, old women engrossed in a game of checkers, and a lonely man on a lonely bench, asleep, his chin digging into his chest. His hair was a great mop of black, his cheeks were sunned brown, and his fingers were a mess of soot and colour. Beside him, a duffel bag, paintbrushes peeking through.

I froze. My body seemed to shrink in this stranger's presence. I was a child once more, crashing into some phantom from my head. Yet, unlike my childhood self, equipped with strategies to deal with it – I would regale the phantom with a song; I would win it over by offering it jam – I didn't have a plan of action for this man. It occurred to me that even while plotting to recover our father in Norway, neither my sister nor I had actually foreseen the possibility of meeting him.

'Is that Daddy?' I nudged Tasha. She looked at the bench. A shiver running through her body.

'Is it?' she whispered back.

I scrutinized the man's indeterminate body – neither short nor tall, neither old nor young. He could be anyone.

Therefore he could be – he *was* our father.

I considered placing my hand on Daddy's, saying hello, prodding him to wakefulness. I'd tell him – what would I tell him? – that I was small enough to squeeze into a chest, small enough to be thrown into the air. Still small.

I drew close so I could touch his fingers. Hidden in them – was that a picture of us, the one I knew? Ranja with pear purée, Tasha with those plums. I peered.

A receipt.

Deceived.

Suddenly, I was reluctant to offer kindnesses to this man. I longed to beat my fists against his chest, stamp the earth beneath his shoes, rage against his quiet retreat, his awful neglect, his self-absorbed pursuit of another life. I held him responsible for everything – for our mother's mania, Amamma's absent-mindedness, even my drift towards love, so late. I decided he deserved, not acceptance, but judgement, the most severe kind.

I'd tell him – what would I tell him? – that we didn't need him any more. No.

'Is it him?' Tasha's voice cut through.

I could not speak. I nodded.

Tasha came up to me. 'What do we say?'

*I don't know.*

'Let's say – let's tell him our names. That's a start.'

'And then?' I willed myself to say it.

'Then tell him Mamma is waiting.'

'And then?' Tears rolled down my cheeks. I could feel them.

'Then tell him to come home.'

'And then?'

'What else is there to say? Isn't this what we want?'

I was without words. But deep down I realized that we were so accustomed to arranging ourselves like moons around a ghost star – Daddy's eventual return – that if he *did* come back, we'd spin off axis.

'I don't know,' I whispered.

'Would you rather go away?'

'I want to,' I confessed. 'But I don't.'

So we stood rooted to the spot, for a minute, an hour, no, longer.

Suddenly, the man on the bench stirred, flicked a fly off his cheek, lifted his head up, and opened his eyes. We saw his face, for the first time whole; his forehead, a furrow in-between; his eyes – like a cat's – gemstone green, sap green. *Green.*

For an instant, I felt relief.

Then all I knew was anguish, heavier than any I had experienced. I could survive Daddy's desertion, his prolonged silence – but to find him, almost, and have him recede – this was more than I could endure.

I held my sister's hand, softer than my father's. I heard a long sob. It could be Tasha's. Or my own. 'Surely, this – this is more than all the world's weeping,' she said/I said. 'Surely, this will offset that giantess' mirth. Surely – '

Hush.

How could we have been so naïve? What were we thinking –

*The heart lies to itself because it must.* Remember?

Jack Gilbert. Our favourite poet. He knew –

Maybe he lost a father, too.

No. A woman.

All vanishings, they're equal.

I pushed my sister away. 'It's my fault,' I said.

'What is?'

'I will not tell Daddy off,' I promised, quick like a child bartering promises for stars. 'I will let him know he's loved. It's my mistake – '

'What is?'

'How could I think of nitpicking?'

'Shush,' Tasha said. 'Shush. Soon, we'll be in Bombay. Soon, this man, this park, everything will be far away. Right? Tell me I'm right.'

Tasha was right.

But we couldn't know it then – I mean, how could we? One mourns in the present tense.

Over the days that followed, I imagined my father, saw him – his every nuance, the gestures, what I could remember of them. I went to the opera house, pressed myself against its walls, and heard Daddy's voice, the inflections, *Deeba, Dee.* I walked into a gallery and saw him by my side, tall (or not), speaking of a Munch, a Tideman, a Dahl. I stumbled into a restaurant and heard him place an order – 'One cup of coffee, please.'

But mostly, I'd spot Daddy near Karl Johans where artists, old and young, would gather. Here, I would see him, not whole, but as a being of parts – in the fingers of a Turk as he measured a full length of canvas; in the hair of a Goth as he bent over a pencil sketch; in a painter's eyes, half-hidden beneath his brows, as he urged tourists to buy his works of art. If this, the sum of this, could be fused together –

But how does one solder body and body?

I would come to leave Norway without.

# 4.
## *Amamma*

After his abrupt promise on the hill, Venu did write to Amamma.

While I haven't seen the letters – the ones Venu would drop into the mouth of a London postbox; the ones Amamma would wait for (im)patiently – I can make-believe the things that were written –

Venu's first letter, for instance.

After catching an Italian liner from Cochin and seating himself in the lower deck with nine other Indians, Venu must have found himself in the ship's first port of call, Aden. Every passenger bought a postcard, or tore a ruled sheet from a diary, or stole stationery to reach out to a wife, a beloved, a daughter. Venu, a victim of peer pressure, must have followed suit – borrowed a notepad, an ink pen, an envelope, a stamp – and started his terse message to the only one waiting back home.

*Hello,* he must have begun, then crumpled the sheet of paper – it reminded him too much of the man in the bullock cart. *Good morning!* There, that was better.

Good morning! I write from Aden. The journey has been long. I was very seasick. My bile was liquid yellow, and my stomach churned –

– Ack, too much information. But what else was there to say? Still, he was overstepping the bounds of acceptable talk. Then, again, without these details, he'd be left with a four-sentence letter – how could he possibly dispatch that?

Eventually, Venu cancelled those offensive lines, kept the notepad away, promised to return the ink pen in Italy, and mulled over what else he could add in the next stop, Port Suez. There, he found a worthwhile story.

> After we traversed the Red Sea, I saw the pyramids of Egypt. They were nice, big, seemed to touch the sky, though, of course, this was an illusion. The Egyptians say the pyramids are meant to serve as gigantic stairways that lead a deceased pharaoh's soul to heaven. I must question the technical soundness of this theory. After all, there's no evidence that the soul exists or, for that matter, paradise. But I think, as a story, it is fine.

There, at least an argument of value. But the note was still too short to justify international postage charges. So Venu waited for Port Said, for yet another travel adventure, for ten more sentences – which, by his calculations, would make the letter-posting exercise somewhat reasonable.

> At Port Said, once the ship refuelled and was nearly sailing out, a few dhows (these are lateen-rigged ships) came along, selling shirts. The shirts were snow-white and excellently packed in cellophane. Best of all, they were cheap. The sellers assured us that they came at a 'Nehru Indian special price'. Since the ship was practically sailing, none of us had time to choose, and we bought the first shirts we saw. I purchased six for what I thought was a wonderful bargain. Once we were in the open seas, a friend and I tore open the cellophane wrappers to admire our foreign goods. It's shocking what we saw! The shirts were half-shirts, really, with cloth in the front and cardboard at the back! I've never been more miserably fooled!

Now, three concluding sentences –

> I hope you're fine in Madras. My highest regards to your family. I trust writing this letter isn't an affront or a crime.

No signature. After all, we've established, the correspondent was lily-livered. Besides, his identity was obvious.

By the time Amamma received this letter, I imagine Venu had travelled to Milan by ship; had caught a train from there to Calais, then a boat-train to Victoria Station; had been greeted in London by John, his British friend; and had been led to his accommodation – one that came without a latrine or a laundry room. So appalled was Venu that he began writing another note post-haste.

Amamma, in the meantime, must've been taken by surprise when the postman arrived to deliver the first letter addressed to *Mrs Rangaa* – had her brother told Venu her husband's name? Why, that blabbermouth!

After Venu's departure, Amamma had expected very little. Sure, he had vowed to keep in touch, but that was a promise rooted in Madras. In a new city, where words would assume fresh meanings, what significance would old guarantees hold?

Amamma realized that while life shunned pipe dreams, it didn't endorse cynicism either.

She grabbed the letter, guiltily paid the postman an anna, and ran inside, the envelope secure at her breast. In the kitchen – the room her husband rarely approached – she drew out the missive, opened it, hands trembling.

*Good morning* – was that the best Venu could do? How English he seemed already!

*I write from Aden* . . . Amamma, at this point, tiptoed to the storeroom, and drew out a book she had once spotted, a children's atlas. She ran her fingers across countries and continents, across states and rivers and cities, until she found that shoehorn world-village, the busy port. How far it seemed from Madras – the map-blue Arabian Sea stretching in-between.

*The journey has been long.* Then, lines hurriedly cancelled out. Amamma, ever-curious, held the page up, peered, deciphered letters, words. She grimaced. Venu was as bad as her husband, after all, describing bodily fluids with gusto.

In the lines that followed, she read of Egypt and the Red Sea – was it really red? Once more she looked up the atlas, which claimed that the sea housed a special kind of bacteria, sea sawdust, that shone crimson on certain days. She closed her eyes and pictured the waters, hibiscus flowers or the seeds of coral trees afloat. How much she loved those seeds – as a child, she'd collect them in her dhavani, boil them when her mother was away, and sow them in the garden. 'Why?' her younger brother had enquired. 'Because on normal days they go through the hot-hot milk-belly of a cow, and come out cooked, ready to be planted. I'm imitating that.' Yes, coral seeds. Egypt was just like India, after all.

How incredible the world seemed – yet how familiar.

Amamma must've scowled when she read Venu's analysis of the pyramids, laughed when she imagined his misadventures at Port Said, and been driven to fury when she scanned that last carefully scripted line.

*This isn't a crime* – here was Amamma's first sentence as soon as she was done with Venu's letter and found a pen and a loose page in the storeroom.

*No, it isn't*. And then, word after word, uninhibited, unmindful of punctuation or grammar.

So stupid to think such things, when two beings communicate it is natural, the way squirrels do, have you heard their metallic barks when they warn each other of trouble, or their low clicks when they say it's okay, everything's fine. When they talk why can't we? It's why we exist, have survived, are even born. Do you know, they say when the earth emerged, the grasshoppers sang, the crickets sang, the sparrows sang, and even the coral tree sang, and from the coral tree burst words, and from words we were born and

you're by the red sea which has coral seeds, and it is holy, and the pyramids too, they are holy, and I believe the Egyptians are right, that they're stairways leading to God, and how can they not be. when i picture them i see stone piled on stone, light on light and sunbeams must lead to whatever you view as a god

and don't question god, not when you're travelling, not good. I have also been travelling, first my husband surprised me by buying movie tickets, who'd have thought, he was very happy, apparently a patient recommended him to chief minister reddiyar, so to celebrate he took me to the theatre to watch *Gokuladasi*, it was okay

Then Mr Swami got a powder blue hillman and I saw it last week by his door, very grand with four wheels and two big headlights, and he invited us for a drive, so off we went, my husband and i, and it was one of the happiest days, the street was a grey pencil line, so straight, and marina beach road was blurry. we stopped at elphinstone theatre, have you been there, and i got the one foot tall glass of ice cream at jaffar's, without a spoon, instead an enormous ladle, and Mrs Swami got jaffar's special for 2.50 rupees, I think they are very wealthy, they even went to America, but it was nice of them to share that day with us. my husband said it's because he ensured the woman produced many children, I don't know if that's true, but I have revised my view of Mrs swami. She seemed haughty when I approached her once but i now think her husband and she are just generous neighbours

otherwise life has been the same cooking and cleaning and now waiting for letters, don't stop writing them and also oh I found many many annas in my husband's shirt today I. shouldn't tell you this but when he is careless with money I take it and hide it this I hid in the bin for chillies. Why I even got a painting recently with the money I had pinched though the transaction has left me poor. but never mind i will just steal some more

has your ship reached and how is london, is it like dickens said it was, you know, my teacher told me of the writer the day before i got married, and London, with factories and poor children and grey air, is it grey where you are, how so, and she spoke of gas lamps, are there gas lamps

There was no more space on the page, even the margins were taken, so Amamma ended her letter right there. Besides, she had asked the questions that had most troubled her about the English city.

When, after what seemed like an eternity, commonsensical Venu received a letter that ended with abruptness, he peered into the envelope to look for a missing sheet, found nothing, and decided that the evasive English postman, who ran each time Venu harangued him for mail, had spitefully stolen a page.

*I think half your letter has been stolen* – there, nothing quite like starting with a statement of fact.

But let me address the points you have made. First, it troubles me very much when you suggest that the Red Sea has coral seeds. It does not. Its name is actually meant to pin down its location relative to the ancient Mediterranean world. You see, back then, the colours black, red, green, and white referred to the north, south, east, and west respectively. The Red Sea, as you must now deduce, is a 'southern' water body.

I will not argue with you regarding your views on the pyramids or god because such arguments will take whole days to resolve. What I will say is that I like your story on the creation of language and people. I shall relay it to my students. I am sure they will find it entertaining.

Venu, now intrigued by the potential reaction of his students – who, so far, had responded to him with lukewarm interest and bare courtesy – decided to practise the story before a mirror. 'Boys, today I wish to tell you a tale.' Perhaps that was a tad stiff? 'Hello, do you know about the evolution of language?' No – or as the kids would say, 'Deathly dull!' 'Good morning, I have a message for you.' He could hear a snigger. Venu, clutching on to Amamma's letter, tried imagining what she'd do if confronted with a similar situation. How would she story-tell? Suddenly, he knew. 'Forget science, forget mathematics, forget everything you've learnt about amoebae and evolution. Nonsense things. We were born of words.' Silence. Then Venu bowed before a round of imaginary applause. After days, he felt content.

Yes, I think they'll like it. How did you know? And where do you find such stories?

Glad you had a pleasant time in Madras, first with your husband, then with your neighbours. I shall withhold my views on stealing money. It is not for me to comment on domestic matters.

I didn't know you liked Dickens, though I believe he described England accurately. Now that you mention it, it is rather grey.

How so? Well, the gaberdine trench coat of the banker is grey, the newspaper the clerk carries is a kind of grey, the bomb sites are blackish and greyish. Did Dickens speak of bomb sites? I imagine not. I see my schoolchildren going to such places, throwing bricks and stones at UXBs to see if they blow up. They don't seem to realize the danger, foolish boys, and I often have to chase them away with my umbrella. I complained to John last evening, and he simply said, 'Spare the rod and spoil the child.' I took him seriously at first, I thought I'd start bringing a cane to class, but then I imagined you would disapprove.

Yes, there still are gas lamps.

I haven't been to Elphinstone Theatre, but I am tempted to visit it. Perhaps when I come by next, we can ask your neighbour for another ride? With your husband, of course.

Amamma received this letter almost in conjunction with the previous one.

I have reached London at long last. Imagine my horror when John tells me I can wash myself and my clothes in the community bath once a week. Think of the germs! What if I die of disease? I have tried protesting, but John says this is the best he can do. A third of London's homes, he claims, have been destroyed or damaged during the war, there is some kind of accommodation drought, and rents have skyrocketed. A roof over one's head is a blessing, he says, and a bathroom is a complete luxury. I don't understand it. I also don't understand the food situation. The grocer I approached for twelve bananas seemed horrified, and then he spoke of 'rationing'.

I am still confused, but maybe in the weeks to come things will become clear.

Amamma was so ecstatic about the double bonanza – two letters across two consecutive days – that she was ready to overlook the last line in the half-your-letter-has-been-stolen missive, was willing to forget the slight about gods and pyramids, was even perfectly happy to excuse Venu's preoccupation with germs. Instead, she memorized his words on the monochromatic hues of London, wondered at wartime scarcity, looked up the meaning of 'gaberdine' – how peculiar it sounded. Then she wrote –

> Where do i gather my stories from, well, sometimes from the books in the houses of my neighbours. the Swamis with the blue hillman have an especially large collection, rumour has it mr swami inherited those books from his grandfather, who in turn had an English mistress, she left him her library when she died, no money, only books, and he was very sore, but everyone still guards her collection, after all, if neglected, the mistress' spirit could haunt the house. scary, yes. sometimes, i find stories in my husband's storeroom but, I rarely go there, too many spiders, though I wonder where he got those books from, and sometimes I hear them as gossip or on radio, find them in stores and libraries. and now and again to tell you the truth i make them up. I will never reveal the precise source but it could be any of these or something else
>
> i hope your students liked my story, you're right, I would not approve of them being beaten, that does not help. as a child, I used to climb down and up trees and my father would get annoyed and chase me with a stick, and i'd run and climb the tree again, such a waste
>
> you seem to have got my whole letter it was only one page, what got lost
>
> london sounds drab but i'm sure it is vibrant, all cities are, you just need to look in the right places, perhaps hunt for festivals or katcheris, did I tell you of the one I went to last week, the singer sounded just like MS
>
> you'll even get used to not bathing every day once you find friends who do not bathe. this is not a joke
>
> tell me more about london, and i'll tell you about madras and news from india, for instance, did you hear Sarojini Naidu has died

So I imagine the letters continued, Venu to Amamma to Venu. Non-events would be recorded, cities chronicled, and the distant stride of history registered. Venu got acquainted with news from the place of his birth. He learnt of the release of the film *Chandralekha* (*the flower girl told me there is a drum dance and a big sword fight and it sounds quite terrible but i want to see it*); of the Congress's meeting in Avadi (*nehru said people consume more sugar these days, but I don't know about that i'm only tempted by ice cream*); and of the introduction of decimal coins (*it's so confusing, twenty five new paise will now equal four annas, and the fruitsellers are rounding off prices to the closest new paises and we're all losing money, as if we had extra going around*).

Amamma, for her part, learnt about London – about the royal coronation of 1953 (*Interestingly, the Queen Mother had our Koh-i-noor on her crown, and the streets were lined with cheering, flag-waving onlookers*); about the publication of *Noblesse Oblige* (*Apparently it is rude to ask for the toilet; the word to use is 'lavatory'*); and about the escalating race riots (*Notting Hill is in trouble. Young boys say they want to keep Britain white. I want to leave. A year or two, and I must*).

Eventually, a note arrived on 31 October 1960: '*Meet me tomorrow at four in Chetpet.*'

Venu, true to his word, had returned.

# 5.

I returned to Bombay after my Norwegian pilgrimage.

I returned to Sahil.

'You've been away for much too long,' Sahil said the day I arrived.

'I know. It feels like forever.'

'Did you find your father?'

'No.' It was all I could recover, a word, the emptiest one.

'I'm sorry.'

'Don't be.' Notwithstanding the ache, Tasha was right. Already, Oslo, the almost-father, seemed distant. Already, life was reasserting itself, accustomed as it was to his absence. Already.

'Your mother must have missed you.'

'I guess. Though she says nothing – as though we hopped over to the next building, no further.'

'Your sister then – '

'Ranja? Not really.'

'Your neighbours?'

'Sure. And you?'

'What d'you think?'

'How would I know?'

'Well, here's a fact – your postcard kept me company.'

I had written to Sahil a few days into my Scandinavian sojourn – written various versions of the same letter across six Vigeland Park postcards. Finally, I couriered the one that seemed least compromising.

Tonight, years later, I barely recall the words I had so carefully hand-picked, the sentences I had stacked, precarious, like Jenga blocks. But I remember the tenor of the postcard – almost timid; its commitment to describing trees and meadows and midnight sunsets; the forced reference to a poem. And I recall the last sentence, taking stock – *Nothing retrieved, but nothing mislaid.*

I remember, too, writing a note to myself in Norway – a description of that unordinary Saturday before my flight to Europe, when Sahil and I were to meet, when we did meet.

I said, I must have said, with college-girl breathlessness –

As I sit by the Akerselva, the sun above, a yellow thumbprint that will not fade, I find myself travelling back in time to another city, to a weekend unlike any other, to the evening at your residence.

I must write of it – of your residence – of the gauzy curtains, the compact table for two, the stout candle placed emphatically in-between. So I watched the light as it flickered, spun patterns, first on the book lying by your elbow; then on your shirt, alive, breathing in-out, out-in; and finally, on your eyes, perceptive like a dolphin's, as beautiful. I must write of your eyes –

– And then of your hands, of their slow drift across the candle to snuff out that strident, all-too-brassy flame; across my neck; down the hurried arch of my back. So, all at once, I found my clothes unravelling, my breast by your tongue, my palm by your throat.

That's when I began withdrawing –

– Not because you were indelicate, not because you were ungenerous or inept or indifferent, not because you were a trespasser on a self I may have leased to a stranger or somebody else, but because as I unwound, lips-hands-fingertips, I staggered for the first time in my life towards extinction.

I couldn't risk that, not extinction, not yet. So I fled in medias res – hair undone, shirt open – saying, 'I'm sorry, I'm sorry, I must go.'

In retrospect, I wish I had returned, if only to grant the evening a denouement.

There's a future to repair past lapses. Wait for me.

Despite being unacquainted with the hastily written note, Sahil waited. I returned to a city with a man.

The months that followed were dizzy. Even now, when I picture them, I see scenes rush by as though captured through trick time-lapse photography. I watch myself with Sahil in coffee shops, run-of-the-mill Udupis, his apartment, sometimes exiting an auto, on occasion sharing a taxi, always talking. I hear snatches of conversation, brisk and, with time, more revelatory.

Here's a scene. Let's slow it down. It's Sahil's home – I can tell by the curtains – and he's reading something off his laptop, a sneak preview of a developing novel. He describes an airplane tobogganing down clouds, blundering-dipping-nosediving. Faces pressed against windows, flat as rice paper. Panic.

Sahil pauses, looks away. 'It's true – it's like that each time.'

'What is?'

'Each flight. As terrifying as the last.'

'What are you so scared of?'

He smiles, says nothing.

That the engines will fail? You'll die?

No.

Then what terrifies you?

Sahil takes my hand. 'That the plane will crash. And I'll live.'

I don't know what to say, not even here, now, after the passage of all these years. So I gather his man-body in my arms – in my dreams, in the flesh, for real.

Here's another episode. Still Sahil's house. This time, his kitchen. He's making me a drink, cold coffee; the blender whipping noise. My voice cuts through. 'He left,' I disclose. 'Daddy abandoned us as children.'

The blender goes silent. 'I know, yes.'

'And to think – to think he went just to pursue painting.'

Sahil tastes the coffee; a streak of froth on his left cheek. 'Well,' he says, distracted, 'it's the curse of Gauguin.'

'What?'

'"*I am more than ever tormented by art.*" Remember?'

'Yes.'

'He said that. Left his wife and children.'

'But this is different.'

'How so?'

'My father isn't Gauguin.'

'Ah. Then you speak of moral luck.'

I consider the statement – I can tell I'm thinking since I scratch my palm – it's a tic I still possess. 'You're right,' I admit, 'I'm no one to judge.'

'No, you get me wrong. *I* cannot judge. You must.'

'Really?'

'But of course. You should. You carry his absence.'

I stand on my toes, neither contesting nor accepting his verdict. I approach Sahil's cheek, lick off the froth. So easy.

Here, another incident, jaunty. We're playing with language, I can tell, because we're seated face to face, laughing.

'My favourite un-English word,' I say, 'let's see, tartle!'

'What's that?'

'That awkward moment when you know someone but can't recall her name. Especially a Scottish problem, I imagine – the word comes from Scotland.'

'The story of my life. Okay, my turn.'

'Go on.'

'Saudade.'

'Tell me more.'

'There is a word built of longing. Saudade, the Portuguese say. In the great age of discovery, there were those who sailed towards the unknown. And there were those who waited – women and children – seeking the return of those who had gone. That feeling, accessible only to those who linger – more than melancholy, more than even want – *that*. Saudade.'

'Lovely.'

Sahil, a half-smile, his eyes watching. 'Okay, your turn.'

I lean close. 'That's mamihlapinatapai.'

'What?'

*Mamihlapinatapai.*

I will not tell him what it means. I cannot.

Another time. I can't tell where we are. Not exactly. By the sea, that's for certain; the wind is lifting skirts. Sahil has taken to walking hand in hand – though only at night when it's too dark to tell if it's true. I'm saying something, I can't decipher what it is, but I imagine it is irrelevant since Sahil, not one to interrupt, cuts me short.

'This time, five years ago – or was it six? – I was married.'

'I'm sorry she is no more.'

'But she is.'

'I don't understand – '

'What don't you?'

I glower. Suddenly, I'm beside myself with rage. 'You told me – the day we met you told me – you declared *emphatically* that your wife is dead.'

'The first, yes. Then I married Maya – the other woman.'

'Oh,' I say, too quiet to be heard. 'I misunderstood.'

For the first time in our association, I realize I know nothing about this man – his pasts, his aspirations, his loves. But then, I remind myself, console myself, I know nothing about my family either, about Tasha or Mamma or Daddy. Maybe *not knowing* isn't really a big deal. Maybe if we strain relationships like hot tea, what we have left as solid residue is ignorance. Maybe –

'I'm sorry, Dee, I should be phrasing stuff better. But anniversaries remind you of your worst decisions.'

'Not always.'

'By the time you are my age – '

'Here we go again.'

A dull snicker.

'I assume the second marriage collapsed?'

'We divorced within months.'

'How come?'

'I don't know. Maybe it had been tainted. Or maybe, more likely, it was meant to be a fling, no more.'

'Yes.'

'Or maybe – let me admit it – I'm just no good with commitment.'

I say nothing. A vague sense of foreboding overcomes me – it must – but I shrug it off. Sahil is right. I am too young to grapple with these problems, comprehend the dimensions of great-big decisions.

I understand the sea, the wind playing with my skirt. I know desire.
I let go of my man's hand, kiss him whole, stop –

For all the talk, the adolescent kisses, the tight clasps, and the
coddling, Sahil and I, after that unwonted Saturday, had evaded
proximity, the real kind.

I could see why Sahil had turned inward, become cautious. After
my Saturday getaway – shirt buttons undone, my hair a mess – down
the stairs, out of the gate, across the road, my voice a thin, hassled
trail, *sorry, I must go,* he must have felt accountable, the way grown-
ups do when the young are left all evening in their custody.

And it's true, I was young, a girl, a neophyte, unclear, flustered,
alternating between want and panic. Each time I fled home to meet
Sahil, I was certain of my actions, their plain onward trajectory.
I'd sneak into his residence, plonk myself down on a couch, and
whisper the way some writer did, *I am so thirsty for the marvellous.*
Yet, even as I'd approached his dwelling, the words would hiccup-
sputter, transform into unadventurous reproof – 'He is as old as
your father. Leave.'

Leave. But how to carry the decision through – when now, Sahil
opened the door; when now, with a quick flick of his wrist, he drew
out a coin from my shoe; when now, he *tch-tch*ed, 'Wise girls don't
save money.'

When now, he tripped over a word – what was it? – *curmudgeonly;*
when now, I balanced the syllables on my tongue; when now, he
clasped my cheeks so he could feel the word explode, pop-pop-pop-
pop, a cherry bomb.

When now, he laughed, and I followed suit. How to carry it
through –

I couldn't abide by my resolutions. And Sahil was too apprehensive
to take a stand. So we skirted the issue of intimacy the way two full-
grown adults do. We went on dates that ended with goodbyes inside
waiting autos. I visited his home and found refuge, till sundown, in
books. He led me to pavement eateries known for raucous gatherings
and publicness. We could've sustained this forever –

No, we couldn't have. For he was old. And I was young. And
neither could wait indefinitely.

So now, I must hold the minutes against light. I'm in Sahil's house, seated on his dhurrie, a pile of books by my side, another heap on my lap. I seem to be reading. I look for Sahil, and I see he is right next to me, turning a page of a novel. We aren't talking, not yet, and the silence hangs easy. It must be five months into our first meeting, perhaps six. I imagine it's mid-afternoon since I'm visiting straight from college; besides, I can see the sun by the window, a garish yellow.

Sahil puts away his book. I watch him watching me read, and I stop following the words on the page.

'Show me your palm,' he says.

'What?'

'Here.' He opens out my fingers and draws close. His forefinger starts circling my wrist, my hand. What are you doing, I ask, trembling lightly as it tickles, scattering books. *Read*, is all he whispers.

So I read.

That's an 'e', I say. A 'v'? Yes, a 'v', an 'e' again.

Shh, just give me the word.

His fingers keep moving in loops and swirls, up my wrist, my elbow, a shoulder – *even this late* – a button undone, another, the length of my clavicle – *it happens* – my chest where a heart beats wildly – *the coming of love* – a swoop across a breast – *the coming* – more buttons, a belly, my belly, a navel – *of light* – legs parting –

> *Even this late it happens:*
> *the coming of love, the coming of light.*

His thumb, his pinkie, swoops, letters, code on skin. *Even*. Yes.

> *Even this late the bones of the body shine*
> *and tomorrow's dust flares into breath.*

*Breath.* A shout in my head, a shout in the room. Words whooshing past synapses, blood roaring. I am a being, not of contemplation, but of sound. It's like nothing I've known.

Hours, seconds, a margin of time passes. Quiet.

I recover. I return the offering.

What are you doing?

Read, I say.

How –

Hush.

My fingers are trained. They mimic, run across Sahil's body, his face – a strand of hair, the bridge of the nose, his philtrum, lips. A swift detour – down the chin, his neck, that throbbing Adam's apple – here, I must stop. Then, greedy, I speed down his chest, his belly –

*Tell me –*

Yes? I whisper.

*About the dream –*

Uh-huh.

*Where we pull the bodies –*

Go on.

*Out of –* I can't

Go on.

*The lake –*

*Tell me about the dream where we pull the bodies out of the lake*
                              *and dress them in warm clothes again.*

My hands cease being hands; they become torches that scan, circle, probe.

           *How it was late, and no one could sleep, the horses running*
*until they forget that they are horses.*

My hands, a flood of wet. I kiss him, pull away, then approach, say –

           *It's not like a tree where the roots have to end somewhere,*
        *it's more like a song on a policeman's radio,*
                *how we rolled up the carpet so we could dance, and the days*
        *were bright red, and every time we kissed there was another apple*
                                        *to slice into pieces.*

We lie together as one, on books, by them, spines pressing against our skins, pages rustling. Moments, half-hours, and he enters –

*Look at the light through the windowpane. That means it's noon, that means*
      *we're inconsolable.*
                    *Tell me how all this, and love too, will ruin us.*
*These, our bodies, possessed by light.*

– I close my eyes.

                        *Tell me we'll never get used to it.*

# 6.
## *Amamma*


It had been a few days since Venu's return to Madras, and Amamma, in a yellow sari, walked out of her house, down the road. This, and everything else that follows, has to be imagined – how she scanned her surroundings, left, then right (no cars, no neighbours, no tale-carrying urchins); how she scampered, fleet-footed, from tree-shadow to tree-shadow; how she paused to reorient herself.

Even as she studied an imaginary map, tried plotting the way forward, a flower-girl descended like a swooping bat, so my grandmother leapt. 'Akka, you going somewhere?' the flower-girl asked.

Amamma, caught off guard, muttered, 'Why, yes, yes. No.'

'Yes and no?'

'No.'

'Then why you are here?'

Amamma felt beads of sweat collect on her forehead. Why ever was she out? She considered the answers she could offer – I like taking a walk on scorching afternoons; I'm shopping for groceries on an empty road; I'm trying to identify the trees along these streets. The last response somehow seemed plausible, so Amamma articulated it.

'Ah, trees,' the flower-girl nodded, accepting the reply as wholly sound. 'Yes, that one is pu vakai, that, lya vakai – but this one, I don't know this.' It was a tall tree, its leaves narrowing at the tips, its bark gnarled like an old man's hand. Therefore, it could be anything. And Amamma named it ah-vakai.

'Really? I've never heard of that,' the flower-girl said, astonished.

'There's lots we've never heard of.'

'Is there?' The flower-girl seemed worried now. 'Will you teach me the names of trees?'

Amamma was at last treading on familiar ground. 'Yes. But to know them, you need to walk alone, speak to every sapling you spot, touch each full-grown branch.'

'And then?'

'And then the names will come to you.'

This, too, the flower-girl accepted. Amamma watched her drift away, down one road, then another, touching each half-tree, each full-sized one, a withering leaf, some frond, whispering mad nothings. The next day, she'd tell Amamma that not one of them had proffered a name and that her friends had laughed at her story. But that was for later. For now, Amamma was on her own again.

After the shock encounter, Amamma struggled to remember her exact mission. She recovered the two letters she had received the previous day, now hidden in her blouse, and studied them – *Meet me tomorrow at four in Chetpet*; and a second message with a more definite address. She reacquainted herself with the house's number, then squinted to read the etchings near each bungalow – some in gold, some engraved on marble and lost behind wild ivy, a few scribbled with chalk, erased, then replaced with a new set of digits.

Amamma had a hunch that the house she sought would have neatly carved numerals; that the number plate would be scrubbed clean, smelling of detergent; that the house itself would be a square block – none of those odd geometric shapes, trapeziums and rhombuses and parallelograms, no.

Amamma wasn't wrong. Even if she hadn't received the full address, she'd have known this was *it* – a gatepost with one clear numeral; the lawn mowed, each blade of grass of uniform length; the kolum sticker positioned in the middle of the porch; the door, a consistent brown. She knocked, too nervous to ring the bell.

And he appeared.

Travel changes most people. After months of wander, they return, displaying selves hitherto invisible.

The man in front of Amamma, however, wasn't most people. And after years abroad, in a land of bitter cold and wafer-crisp syllables, he seemed to have come back with nothing to show for his exile. He was still of medium build; his clothes were immaculately ironed; his movements were hesitant. If anything had changed, it was a function of age, not experience. His hair was somewhat thinner, so you could tell that at sixty he'd be partially bald. His skin was no longer supple. And his arms were speckled grey. Clearly, travel had done little to diminish or ennoble him

Amamma wondered if she, too, displayed stasis – but then she decided that couldn't be. While it was true that her body still came with its girlhood attributes – integrity and wholeness and startling abundance – my grandmother could tell that it had also begun to convey her disenchantment with Rangaa's house and her exhaustion with her husband's cold stabs at son-making.

'Hello,' the man said, his voice unaffected, still carrying a familiar, sing-song accent.

'Good afternoon, Venu,' Amamma replied carefully. Then, quickly, before some flower-girl could spot her, she let herself in and made herself comfortable on a couch in an otherwise bare room.

Amamma watched Venu – how he parked himself at the other end of the couch; how he sprang up altogether abruptly; how he scuttled to the kitchen and returned with a steel tumbler. Water, he said, and my grandmother whispered, thank you.

As she fiddled with the tumbler, it struck Amamma that now, without a sheet of paper before her, without a pen to read her thoughts, without an imperceptible Venu to whom she could assign token tics and traits, she was at a loss for words.

And yet, my grandmother reminded herself, here was the man she had had the longest association with. She had conversed with him for years, building story upon story. She had known him as a diffident boy reaching out for her hands, and later as a diffident adult seeking her out on a hill. He was no stranger. She had little reason to hesitate.

'So – how is it to be back?' Amamma said by way of starting a conversation.

'Not bad, it is good. There are things I don't like. The streets here are at least two feet narrower than those in London. And it is twenty degrees hotter. But food is cheaper by – '

'I get it. Madras is home.'

Amamma was now in her element. All it took was a fastidious

statement from Venu for my grandmother to recover wordplay. 'Show me your house. Surely there's more to it than a couch?'

Venu looked around, drew out a neatly folded handkerchief from his shirt pocket, wiped his forehead, then stuttered, 'Yes – I mean – not quite.'

Amamma was already walking through the door of the drawing room into the kitchen – it had one more steel tumbler, a porcelain plate, doubtless from England, and a saucepan. 'How do you cook?'

'I don't – I mean I do, but it asks for some manoeuvring. I need to wash the pan four times for an average meal – '

'And god forbid, what if you have guests? You could invest in utensils, you know? If you can buy a house, surely such expenses must seem insignificant?'

'The house is on mortgage.'

'So?'

Amamma walked into the next room with a wide-open window, a desk, and a pile of books. She opened a few hardbacks, scrutinized them, grumbled, 'No pictures!' Then, she tilted her head as though watching a windmill and commented, 'This room, it is shaped like a thengai burfi.'

'What?'

'You know, the sweet? It wants to be a square, but its edges are jagged.'

'That's an odd comparison. And I object. There's nothing uneven about my study.'

Amamma laughed, ventured into the next room, while Venu drew out a ruler to establish that his house was perfectly symmetrical.

My grandmother was now in what looked like Venu's bedroom. There was a slim divan on which the man presumably slept, a sideboard for clothes, and an iron. Amamma seated herself on the makeshift bed, even as Venu entered announcing, 'Nothing uneven at all.'

This is the moment I want to freeze. My grandmother in her yellow sari, the pallu gathering around her like a petal. Venu would not know it, but at that instant, my grandmother was akin to a Georgia O'Keeffe painting – a flower straining, in bloom, tumescent.

Venu floundered. As always, when flummoxed, he turned to the familiar – which in this case led him to natural history, to a time when water lilies and magnolias were the first of petalled things, luring honeybees with their white corollas. Soon, other flowers followed with brash purple petals, brazen red stigmas, each new blossom outfoxing the next, claiming the short-lived interest of bees. It was the golden blossom though that trounced all competitors – its yellow beating heart, nectar-ful mouth inviting pollinators, stirring in them desires previously unknown.

Amamma was in yellow like the most alluring of flowers – surely for a reason?

Venu walked up, sat right beside her, and my grandmother didn't pull away. Lightly, like the little boy he once was, Venu allowed his arm to stir. Her forefinger coiled around his pinkie.

What else can I say? I could describe what followed. How Amamma's sunlit sari slipped away. How the letters in her blouse took wing. How Venu discarded his clothes – they fell in a crumpled heap, and he didn't notice. I could tell you that the bed proved sufficient as the two let their bodies entwine like a braid. I could speak of so many things – Amamma's impatience, Venu's startling bravado, Amamma's girlish laughter ringing like a bell.

But I shouldn't – for where would such disclosures take us?

What I can tell you is that at the end of all that transpired, Amamma recovered one of the two letters she had carried. She walked down the streets of Chetpet whispering secrets to her friends, those trees.

# 7.

I returned to Sahil's a day after our lovemaking. And the day after –
I marked my time with him – a pencilled tally stick for every month, steady at first, assured like only new crushes can be; then each stroke nervy.

'Do you love me?' I asked Sahil a year into our association.

He laughed. 'Aren't you a child.'

'Stop calling me that.' I gathered my skirt and wrapped it around my waist, threw his shirt at him.

'Fine – '

'No, really, stop dismissing me. Tasha says her boyfriends, all of them, love her. You know, she's *convinced*. And I – '

'Yes?'

'I'm always uncertain – it's not fair.'

'So you want to tell Tasha, "Sahil loves me, too"?'

'Why must you make it sound silly?'

'Let's understand this. You want me to tell you you're loved because – you don't know it yet? Or do you want to relay my statement verbatim to your sister?'

'Really, why does *everything* have to be analysed threadbare?'

'It doesn't.'

Sahil drew close, unwrapped my skirt. It fell to my feet. His mouth hovered close to mine. I could feel his breath, warm and sweet with the scent of cherries; the pips scattered on a table, so many.

'Oh,' he said, his tongue flickering by mine. I caved. 'Are you fine, Dee?' he asked; he always asked, his hand against my mouth.

'Yes,' I whispered, 'yes.'

'Sweet.'

We were still new to each other – new enough to get waylaid by a scar on the skin, by a curious change in tenor, by the quivering jelly of breath, by cherry-breath. If we argued, it was easy to scotch words with touch.

It was easy. We didn't need to speak of love.

And yet – yet, tonight, as I watch us lunging at each other like animals in heat, I can spot the end right there. In the question – *do you love me?* In its vanishing.

Here's a fact – bodies entice only for so long. They say, when Hephaestus, the smithing god, approached two lovers as they lay together; when he offered to unite them (as only a master blacksmith could), their bodies fused in a passionate clinch – the lovers chose not to respond. One can assume that their silence spelt, not consent, but panic – for how long to revel in each other's bodies? What pleasure in eternal bondage? When scared or unsure or discontented, how to express their frustrations?

So it was – so it would always be – first, the dizziness of new intimacies. And then, *then* hesitation.

I hesitated.

It was the same room, always was, but another time, three months after I asked Sahil if he loved me. I was right by him, reading; my free arm around his waist; his fingers playing with my hair. Suddenly, he stopped, asked, 'Has there been another?'

'What?'

'Another man you've loved?'

'Why do you ask?'

'I wondered.'

'What do you think?'

'I don't know. At your age, there are only possibilities.'

'And at yours?'

'An aimless past.'

'Of course.'

'So tell me – '

'I did love once.' A lie. A half-truth – if one counted the men in books. Heathcliff. It was all the same.

'Who was he?'

'Doesn't matter.'

'What went wrong?'

'Nothing. I guess I grew up.

'Hmm.'

'In any case, I don't reveal secrets to men who don't proclaim their love.'

'Really, Dee? You know this is silly, don't you?'

'It isn't.'

Nine months later. I recall the afternoon, a dull smudge of light. Sahil at his laptop, typing. I knew better than to interrupt him at work, but left to myself, I began worrying. I had to speak.

'Talk to me – '

'Hmm?' The keyboard clattering.

'Tell me, Sahil, how long have we been together?'

'Hm?' Still distracted. 'I don't know. Do the math.'

'Two years? A little longer perhaps?'

'Okay.'

'Yes. You know so much about my life.'

'Hmm.'

'Sahil, I know *so* little about yours.'

'What's a synonym for cold?'

'Sorry?'

'I want another word for it. *Cold* – it's rather weak, isn't it?'

'Are you even listening to me?'

'Of course. You say you know nothing about my life.'

'And?'

'And I disagree.'

Sahil got up, walked to me, held my face in his palms. This time, I pushed him away. 'Stop it.' My voice trembled. 'I don't know if you love me, I barely know if we exist beyond this room.'

'What's got into – '

'Each time I try pinning things down, *each time*, you fob me off. I'm tired.'

'What do you want me to do?'

'For one, tell me that you love me.'

'I do.'

There. That easy.

I'm not sure what I had expected with the admission – drum rolls and paradiddles, roses and rain, perhaps with the naiveté of first love all the above, but especially, *especially* gravitas.

Sahil's statement, however, fell flat, assumed the significance of a weather forecast – today will be bright and clear. *I do.*

It seemed churlish to argue the point.

'You do?'

'Yes. And you don't need to respond. I *know* you do.'

'Great. Thank you.'

Sahil came close, ran his hand down my back. His fingers were the same, gentle and curious, but suddenly, they had nothing new to offer. I knew the path they'd take, the way they'd probe, rest. 'Wait,' I said.

'What now?'

'How do you plan to make this, *us*, real?'

'I'm not sure – '

'Two years, and I barely know your friends. You haven't even attempted meeting mine.'

'I don't need to.'

'Why not? Aren't you curious about my sisters – at least Tasha? Or my classmates?'

'No. You're sufficient. And what you carry of them is enough.'

'That's ridiculous.'

'Dee, I'm not at an age where I need to widen my world.'

'Fine, then factor in my age – '

'Okay. What would you like of me?'

I paused. Once more it had been too easy. I had expected, even wanted, struggle, opposition, charges of immaturity. Instead, here, I had asked, he had dodged, and then, without a murmur of dissent, had given.

What would I have liked of Sahil? The dramatic. But he seemed to reserve such frenzy for his art. So what else was there to ask of Sahil?

I tried arriving at something tangible.

'You and I, along with Tasha – she'll bring a date, of course – let's go out.'

'Go out?'

'Dinner maybe? Next week?'

'If that makes you happy – '

'Happier than happy.'

'Then yes.'

The week went by slowly. Then it moved much too fast.

I told Tasha about Sahil. She was the first to learn of the specifics, know him by name, profession, an address – by more than just a string of stale adjectives, 'gentle', 'wise', 'patient' – even by age. I expected her to be dismissive, at the very least surprised, but somehow she seemed to accept the details with the coolness of a fortune teller.

'I expected exactly this,' she said.

'What d'you mean?'

'You're an old soul, Dee. You couldn't possibly like a young boy. Except – '

'Yes?'

'I wish you had.'

'Why?'

'I guess – for sweetness and light.'

I didn't understand what she meant.

And then I did.

A few days after my admission to my sister, a group of us – Tasha and I, and a lithe boy with a name I can't recall and a voice I won't forget, hoarse and quick and young – found ourselves in his car outside a fast-food takeaway. Sahil was running late – he called to say – he was in the middle of writing something, unable to leave, but happy to come later, still later.

Close, trains chug-chugged to predictable stations. Beyond, the sea rose and fell, crashing and hissing and crashing again. Even the cars, streaks of yellow light, appeared to follow a set pattern, shimmering, then not.

I seemed to be an aberration in this land of certainties – flailing, unsure, now joyous, now crushed, stoic and not.

'Let it be,' Tasha said. 'It doesn't matter if Sahil's late. Here, a slice of pizza.'

'No. No, thank you. I'm not hungry.'

The boy lunged forward – 'I am!' – then kept talking. 'Oh man, remember the college prom? And the *mountains* of pizza? And how we broke into EJ's room and crouched there with boxes of food and torches? And the watchman – *that* was epic.'

It didn't take long for Tasha to get distracted, laugh, roll her eyes, 'Man, the *watchman!*'

I knew the story. I had been there at the college prom. I still remember. The many-many gangly boys; those drinks snuck in, in giant Pepsi bottles; the joints in forgotten corridors. Tasha and a boy hidden behind a tree. I was with a group of girls, all bitter after breakups.

Then rumours, Chinese whispers. Stout-hearted teenagers breaking into a teacher's empty room; the spinning of bottles, the pizzas, the pyjama party; the sleep-sodden watchman locked outside, snoring. Late night, couples skidding down moss-covered water pipes, their knees-knuckles-shins bruised, their heads giddy.

The catalogue of events was inane, frivolous. Yet, how much it amused us then, how it still captivated us. Perhaps because the evening was one of flippancy. Perhaps because we were being aimless dissenters. Perhaps because we knew this was the last sputter of recklessness before we'd settle into guarded adult routines.

Strangely, I hadn't shared this episode with Sahil, not because the evening had been forgotten, but because there had always been more pertinent things to discuss – things he and I enjoyed, things of mutual interest, books and writers and words.

Yet, that night, I was upset about Sahil's air of preoccupation, about his disregard for a scrupulously planned evening and the time of three twenty-somethings huddled together in a car. So when he did emerge two hours later, squeezed in, and drew out his wallet to pay for us – the ultimate act of grown-up chivalry – I began a slow narration of a story that would not fascinate him in the least, of the events surrounding that college prom – the dresses we wore, growing shorter as the night progressed; the scent of keen adolescent boys; the liquor, the smoke, the after-hours. Tasha chiming in, her friend as well.

'What d'you have to say?' I challenged Sahil.

Not much, he replied.

'You must think this stupid?'

No.

'So you find it funny.'

Hmm.

Tasha sensed the building of frost – my hostility, Sahil's growing irritation. So she changed the subject to one altogether indiscreet. 'Amamma, in a rare moment of lucidity, asked Mamma to end her marriage. Again. *In front of me.*'

'Okay then – '

'And Mamma said no. She asked, "What will my husband say when he returns?"' Tasha shook her head.

All of a sudden, Sahil interrupted, 'It's like Flaubert.'

'What?'

'When Flaubert lost his mother, he used to get his housekeeper to dress up in her old checked dress. Imagine that!'

'Eh?'

'Don't you see? The similarities? Call it myth-making, call it delusion. It's how we – all of us – carry on.'

'I guess – '

I watched my sister, her hair flying, suddenly almost-adult in her sombreness; her friend, no longer suppressing his laughter, pensive. Sahil, as always, severe. And I detested the scene – that this evening of flip jollity had become one of serious contemplation, of quiet.

For this, I blamed Sahil.

It was only later, still later, that I realized – I held him responsible not for the loss of a night's mirth but for something quite else – for being older.

This, I believe, was his greatest crime.

The night passed. I returned to Sahil's neighbourhood the next day – a matter of habit.

I should've expressed my dismay at his approach the preceding evening, railed against his grown-up crimes – and yet I did exactly the opposite. I sought cover behind niceties and silences.

Of what use were arguments anyhow, I reminded myself. Once the words that had to be traded were traded; when the tears and tirades were done – what then? Disingenuous appeals for forgiveness; a return to old selves and habits, only with more circumspection?

No, Sahil and I knew better than to fight. Instead we walked down Jogger's Park, so easy, his hand enclosing mine. How ordinary our conversation seemed, banal – his bad writing day, my run-of-the-mill morning devoted to arranging books in some library, our plans for the weekend – none really. We entered a restaurant, ordered one Greek salad, and arranged paper napkins on our laps. The waiter approached us with a bowl of fresh vegetables – tomatoes, cucumbers, onions, olives. Two forks.

I must've been on edge. The food, the servers running from kitchen to customer to kitchen, the whizzing cars – these, I realized, reminded me of the evening that had been. I felt my anger surface. Quickly, I smothered it.

No, I wasn't irritated. No, I was just fine. What plans for the weekend again?

Sahil didn't answer. I noticed the fork in his hand, how he attacked the very last of the olives, ate it.

'You could have left a few for me,' I muttered, then regretted the statement, its note of confrontation.

'What? The olives? You wanted them?'

'Well, yeah.'

'Why didn't you say so earlier?'

'You could've asked.'

'My bad.' Sahil shrugged his shoulders, the way he so often did when he had had his say – but that day, all it meant was that my love ~~for olives for him~~ for olives was irrelevant.

'*My bad?* The thing is you never ask. You think the olives are exclusively yours.'

'Well, the next time we order a meal, remind me to say, "Would you like the olives?"'

'Wonderful,' I spat. 'If only you had extended that courtesy to me yesterday. Asked me, "Would you mind if I came in late? Would you mind if I decided to pay for a meal I didn't order? Would you mind if I hijacked a conversation? Would you mind – "'

'Forgive me. And just to clarify, I didn't want to meet anyone, least of all a bunch of teenagers. You insisted, and I complied as best I could – '

'You *complied*? By almost missing dinner? And in case you've forgotten, the *bunch of teenagers* is my family. This is my world. It's a shame you're too old to fit in!'

Sahil glowered. 'I'm with a child. Yes. I ought to have missed your shindig completely.'

'Yes, you really should have. If all you wished to do was mark your presence, then mock me, my – '

'Mock you? I believe it's the other way around! And to think I left my work to be there!'

'I'm sorry to have disrupted your schedule of *barely* writing.'

'You know what? Fuck you. This is why I never wanted to be in a relationship. And this is *exactly* why I'll never marry again.'

'Good to know. I'm not begging you to make me your third wife. Go.'

'Excellent. I'm off. Enjoy your salad.'

'Like you've left me any. You stole the olives.'

'Really, Deeya? And when was it about the olives anyway?'

I paused. Then yelled, 'It's always about the fucking olives.'

Then I left before he could.

# Many Marriages.

*and every time we kissed there was another apple*
*to slice into pieces.*

# 1.

It's said that after the flip-flop of adolescence, life only knows inertia.

My sisters – the oldest a new employee of a PR agency; the youngest opting for a gap year, much to Mamma's chagrin – stumbled into and inhabited this truth. Ranja's remarks on returning home, 'Office, same old, same old'; Tasha's sighs, 'I'm bored of men' – these had become startlingly consistent.

While my life – despite the steady pursuit of a postgraduate degree in English – waxed and waned, the upheavals were such that they couldn't be disclosed. (No, I hadn't forgiven Sahil for his slight about my age; no, he'd never excuse me for calling him old; yes, we still conversed, but with far greater aloofness.)

So when Tasha'd ask, 'What's up?' I'd shrug and mutter, 'Same old, same old,' much like Ranja.

Just when we thought we could get used to a life fixed in space, we confronted change.

It all began with Ranja who told us, 'Two years, maybe three – then I'm out of here.'

'Where to?' I asked, not really curious.

'I don't know. It depends on the man I marry – on where he lives.'

'You're getting married?' I asked. I must have.

'Aren't we all?' Ranja shrugged.

'Speak for yourself.' This was Tasha, of course.

'Well, then fine. *I'll* get married; *I'll* leave. *You*, Tasha, can live here with Amamma and Mamma in the shoe cupboard you've been assigned.'

'Great.'

'Whatever happens, I vacate first.'

Ranja's comments must've thrummed at the back of Tasha's mind. She worried, not about the bare facts – that my older sister would get married and leave – but about the insinuation that she was doomed to inhabit a bedchamber that barely accommodated her body.

She pictured herself, older, bigger, her waist as wide as a hula hoop. She pictured how the bed would creak as she'd move in sleep; how she'd have to walk sideways out of a door; how, after these careful manoeuvrings, she'd trip over Mamma and Amamma. Each day, in her imagination, she grew just a little larger. So, finally, when her thoughts capsized, unable to support her girth, Tasha announced with unusual vehemence, 'I'm done living in a shoe cupboard.'

'What d'you mean?' Ranja and I asked, a Greek chorus.

'I've been thinking – enough of this storeroom-bedchamber. I'd like to move to Delhi.'

'*Delhi*?' Ranja almost shrieked.

'Yeah, *Delhi*? You won't like it. Nobody from *Bombay* does,' I asserted with the superior conviction of one who had never travelled to the city.

'Exactly. Every day, scores of women get raped. Every year, six thousand – ' Ranja rattled figures.

But Tasha had made up her mind. And therefore, Tasha repeated, 'I'm done living in a shoe cupboard.'

And there it was.

Soon after her announcement, my younger sister applied to a handful of colleges for a postgraduate degree. She received a letter from one. We suspected the news was good since there were side gallops and high-pitched whoops. Our suspicions were confirmed when Tasha jumped on her bed and squealed the name of that dodgy city. *Dilli*.

For once, Mamma heard. She came rushing into Tasha's room, a blur of blue cotton-silk. 'Delhi?' she asked when the bed threatened to collapse.

Tasha was good with confessing. 'Well, sort of, yeah.'

'What about Delhi?'

'Tasha has got admission in a university there and thinks her bedroom is tiny and is moving,' Ranja tattled.

'Thanks,' my younger sister hissed.

'You should tell her something, *stop* her,' Ranja yelled at my mother.

Mamma, assailed by sentence after sentence, reeled. Then she turned to her youngest daughter. 'You want a bigger room?'

Before Tasha could answer, Ranja interrupted, 'If she gets a bigger room, so do I!'

Loath to be left with the tiniest corner of a tiny home, I echoed Ranja's statement.

Cacophony is three sisters bargaining.

'Fine,' Mamma said, without debating the legitimacy of our demands. 'Fine.'

'I still go to Delhi,' Tasha said, her voice tense and unyielding.

'But I'll give you a bigger room,' Mamma replied.

'I don't want a bigger room.'

'But you said you did,' Mamma persisted.

'Ranja did.'

'Ranja lied?'

'That's not what I'm saying.'

'So it's sorted.'

'No, it's not!' Tasha shot back, each word a hurled rock. 'I want some goddamned *space*. And a room, hell, a *mansion* isn't enough!'

For an instant, our home knew absolute silence. We could hear a leaky faucet's tap-tap-tap; the whip of the fan's blades; the window, its hinges creaking. How old the apartment seemed, how much it complained.

Then the quiet shattered. All it took was a word. 'Fine,' Mamma said. She walked away.

With that, it was decided. Tasha would leave.

Ranja was noticeably discomfited by the turn of events. One could tell by the way she refused to engage with Tasha – she neither scoffed at her assertions nor offered brutal feedback. All she did was pace the room she shared with Mamma.

I should have tried asking after my older sister. But I had troubles of my own; I could not accommodate anybody else's worries.

At last, Ranja approached me, not with a question or an admission (that was unlike her), but with a comment – 'Tasha should wait.'

'Why?' I asked, distracted.

'Because I have first dibs on leaving.'

'Yeah,' I said because the word fell easy. Always a mistake.

'Yes. But since Tasha won't wait, I need to do everything quicker.'

'What?'

'Nothing.'

In the meantime, Mamma – concerned about future revolts, or worried that she'd inherit an empty nest, or prodded towards the realization that her daughters were private beings, too old for shared beds and minuscule rooms – decided to act.

'Amma, can I borrow some money?' she asked Amamma.

Amamma, still sharp when her belongings seemed imperilled, frowned. 'Money? Mine?'

'Yes.'

'Money?'

'Yes.'

'Money?'

'I need what's left. We need a bigger house. The girls need more room.'

'So do I!'

'Okay. Hence money.'

'Yes. The British headmaster is my friend. He can lend you some cash before he leaves.'

'The –'

'I'll talk to him.'

Mamma saw it all too clearly. Amamma – stubborn as a mule, even astute – yes, her personality remained undisturbed. But her inner world – that was rooted in the distant past, in a time of post-Independence newness, optimism and fear, goings and fresh comings.

'You will, of course,' Mamma whispered.

'Yes.'

'Who am I, Amma?' my mother suddenly asked, without meaning to.

'Why – well,' Amamma hesitated. Then my grandmother laughed and pinched Mamma's chin, 'Why, kutti, why, you're my old chum.'

Mamma nodded. Mamma smiled – grateful for a friend, if not a mother.

Mamma finally got Amamma to transfer cash to her account.

While she house-hunted and Tasha accumulated sweaters – 'It's *so* cold in Delhi, you can see your breath' – Ranja had an announcement of her own to make. And she chose the most opportune moment – exactly a fortnight after Tasha's disclosure, when Mamma was about to pick one of two apartments. (My mother seldom dawdled.)

'What have you selected?' Ranja asked, by way of opening a conversation. We had gathered for dinner.

'Well, one apartment is down the road. One is in Vashi. Three bedrooms. A study where I can sleep. I prefer – '

'You don't need to sleep in the study.'

'But I do, Ranja. Amma, that's one room. Deeya and you, that's two more gone. When Tasha visits, she can sleep – '

'Well, Tasha can take my room when she visits.'

Tasha snorted. 'Who says I'll visit!'

'Fine. Then keep my room locked,' Ranja said.

'But that makes no sense,' Mamma replied.

'I don't – really, why is it *so* hard to make a point here?'

'You're telling me!' Tasha snorted again.

'Does anyone wish to know why I *don't* need a room?' Ranja wailed.

'Why?' Mamma asked, obedient.

Ranja threw up her hands. 'Well, as it happens, I plan to leave.'

'What?' Tasha asked, at last curious.

'All thanks to you, by the way.'

'What?' Tasha repeated.

'I'm getting married.'

Mamma dropped her spoon. A shiver. Already she was growing distant – eyes dimming, her skin acquiring a dull patina.

Maybe our mother was time-travelling. There she was, by a temple, in a courtyard – when life had opened out with choices before her; when she had had the right to pick fictions; when she could have been anything, anyone – a content homemaker, a Mata Hari, the eternal spinster.

Now, her eldest daughter was in that courtyard. What advice to give? Wait? Don't hurry? Weigh your options with care? But Mamma knew such counsel was futile. For we don't choose the stories that frame our lives; stories sniff us out and claim us.

'You've found someone?' my mother finally whispered.

Amamma, ever tactful, harrumphed, 'As if!'

Ranja ignored my grandmother. Instead, in a disturbingly even voice, she said, 'No, I haven't. But that's what you're there for.'

Mamma blinked, wiped her face with the edge of her pallu. 'It's not right,' she said and shook her head. The more she wished away her past, the more it returned as her daughters.

But Ranja would brook no opposition. 'What do you mean *it's not right*? It's high time!'

Mamma nodded. 'I understand.'

Amamma didn't. 'Does this look like a matchmaking bureau to you?'

Mamma shushed her mother. 'You may not remember this, Amma, but long years ago, you had found Karthik for me.'

Amamma scoffed. 'And you may *choose* not to remember this but – but I bet it didn't end well.'

Mamma glared. 'You're mistaken.' Then she chose to focus on Ranja. 'I'll find you a husband. We can go to the temple – '

'Or online,' Tasha recommended.

'Whichever is quicker,' Ranja said. 'I *will* leave home before Tasha does.'

Mamma had six months.

What on earth had seized our sister, Tasha and I wondered. But not for very long. We could hazard a guess.

Ranja had been the first to claim our parents' attention; the first to answer questions in class; the first to polish off her breakfast and dinner; the first to spurn an admirer. The word 'first' defined her, made her aura of success seem indestructible.

While Tasha and I stumbled from experience to false experience, Ranja seemed to leapfrog past milestones. No speed bumps along her route, no potholes, no miscalculated dead ends. Every turn was clear. And the next goalpost was *leaving*.

She ought to have been first.

She would be, still. For that night, when Ranja looked at all of us – Mamma, Amamma, Tasha, and me – and announced 'I'm getting married', she took the lead.

I don't recall if we talked Ranja out of her resolution or advised her against making an exit her journey's end – we mustn't have. After all, what did we know at that time? Tasha was too capricious to take a stand. And I – I was confused, about Sahil, propositions, leave-takings. What could I say about wrong and right?

What can I still say?

Perhaps Mamma could have extended counsel. But how? Advice is offered by those who gain insight from the past. And my mother, it was clear, couldn't. She had to build histories layer by layer; construct her life, not actively learn from it. At best, Mamma could abide by Ranja's decision. And she did.

Besides, in the din for leaving-takings and unions, Mamma, I imagine, was reminded all too starkly of her own marriage. Things hadn't gone quite the way she had planned them – no wife would want her man to toil abroad. But such was the world of work and such was matrimony. All in all, she was happy, she consoled herself.

Somewhere in icy Europe, her husband was salting riches away for her. Somewhere he missed having his children around. Somewhere he was running his fingers across a picture – li'l Tasha, a pile of plums; Ranja, so prim; Dee, those eyes –

Somewhere he was booking his tickets back home.

Mamma flinched – *home* – and he was coming back. If she shifted apartments, he'd ring *this* bell and spot another household – stranger children, an unfamiliar wife, a different doting in-law.

'Amma,' Mamma said and reached for her mother, 'Amma, let's not move home.'

# 2.
## *Amamma*

Shortly after the burst of euphoria in Venu's house, the joy of giving and receiving, Amamma, I imagine, was left with this, only this – panic, animal fear that her transgressions were obvious. She worried about a crease in her sari; checked to see that her nose stud was intact; fiddled with a strand that had come undone, then curled it behind her ear.

As she entered her house, she poured a bucket of water over her clothed body, and washed away the afternoon that was – the scents; a bit of yarn, too white, too ordinary, to be hers. But no matter how hard she scrubbed, the afternoon would not wash away. It stuck to her skin like phosphoric ink, remained on her mouth as moisture, lingered in her very blood.

In a few hours, Rangaa would be walking back home. He'd ask to be served dinner and vaguely perceive a pair of hands – hers. Would he notice that they had memorized fresh sensations; that they moved without a stutter but with new-found ease; that they carried the perfume of another?

Amamma was convinced that he'd discern all of this. That like some sleuth he'd piece together the facts – that she had been a furtive dealer in letters; that she had intentionally visited another man's house; that she had chosen to lie down on his bed; that, worst of all, in this she had found pleasure.

What would he say when he learnt of such bliss? How would he respond?

A quiver ran down Amamma's body as she heard a voice, brusque – her mother's – narrating a morality tale. Of Ahalya, the young wife of a celibate sage. Of how, when Indra, the god of thunder, came disguised as her husband, Ahalya saw through his charade. Even so, she accepted his brash advances. In response, her husband turned her to stone.

Amamma felt her chest – it was still warm, beating, un-stone-like. For this, she was briefly grateful.

My grandmother, after her bath, walked to the kitchen window. She wondered what Janaki would have said had she been there – that Amamma hadn't really erred; that if she had been unfaithful, so had her husband. But my grandmother knew these truths already, was sympathetic to their logic.

Still, life wasn't meant to be a reasonable thing. In life, she'd suffer the aftershocks.

If Rangaa found out – and he likely would; her hands, they babbled – he'd dissolve their association, order her to leave. 'Be off,' he'd say. And where would she go? Her parents would disown her. Her neighbours would look away. And Venu – why, Venu, he was nice but delicate.

Amamma's hands grew cold.

Fear, it's said, paralyses. But fear also resists stillness. Impelled by two contradictory impulses, Amamma spun without direction. She laundered clean garments, turned over pots, pulled down fresh curtains and hung up soiled ones. She added red chillies to setting yogurt, kneaded rice to a pulp.

When Rangaa entered – and she could tell he did; his feet stomped dust – she had nothing to offer by way of a meal, by way of talk. But that night, as it happens, Rangaa had other plans.

'Hello!' Rangaa shouted minutes after he entered.

Amamma willed herself to walk, approach him.

'Hello! Hello!'

My grandmother hid in the shadows.

'Have this,' he said.

Amamma drew out her hands. Rangaa wasn't looking. She received a prescription – *1 November 1960. One tomato, two cashew nuts.*

'This,' he said, 'mix it with this drink' – now, a vile green potion – 'no dinner.'

Amamma did as she was told.

What followed was a re-enactment of the afternoon – if we were to define one episode, then the other, as no more than a transaction between bodies.

Amamma, still nervous, accepted Rangaa's dogged form. Any moment now, he'd know-feel-smell her betrayals. She hid her hands beneath a bedspread, curled her toes – but what to do with her mouth, her cheeks, her ears? These things – stained, touched, whispered into – were still visible.

'What's this?' Rangaa asked as he hovered over her body.

Amamma looked away. Here, now, she'd turn to stone.

'What's this?' Rangaa repeated.

What, Amamma asked, still able to.

This. Dirty curtains?

Amamma, she felt a tear, hot and merciful. It rolled down her cheek, her mouth, washed. 'Sorry.'

Minutes later, Rangaa and she were done. 'A boy,' Rangaa told her as he tied his veshti. 'Today we've made a boy.'

Amamma – she sensed he was partly right.

# 3.

After Ranja's announcement – *I'm getting married (in six months)* – Mamma diligently set to work, seeking a suitable groom for her eldest daughter. She went to the neighbourhood temple, let word spread from one tale-telling devotee to the next. But no matter what claims she made about her child, each temple-goer only asked, 'Vanna, can we meet the young girl's father?'

So Mamma waved a horoscope before a priest. But then, recalling her own misadventures, she swiftly hid behind a pushier-heftier mother, then walked away.

Dispirited, Mamma spoke to a puzzled Mani and a solicitous Miss Mimmy. 'How would we know anyone?' both complained. And Mamma reluctantly saw their point. Mani himself was on the prowl, and Miss Mimmy, confined all day within a bank, was the last woman to furnish someone with a list of grooms.

Desperate and without an update for her daughter – despite a long day of frantic people-meeting – Mamma considered Tasha's advice. She went online, posted a photograph of Ranja, an appropriate one – a sari, a shy smile, the hair pulled back – and wrote an unoriginal paragraph in praise of her daughter – *Very caring. Loyal. Homely but ambitious. College-topper seeking a well-behaved boy.*

Over the weeks that followed, young men with predictable degrees and equally predictable jobs responded to Ranja's profile picture. Some emailed their merits in bullet points; some sent college dissertations; several dispatched Photoshopped pictures with sundry relatives, nephews, and the neighbours' obliging babies. Almost everyone offered professionally tweaked marriage résumés in which – instead of exaggerated work accomplishments – personal achievements, those that underscored husbandly virtue, were emphasized. The contentions each time were the same – *I spend an hour each day in the local orphanage; I argued in favour of women's suffrage in school; I enjoy making the occasional omelette.*

The first recipient of these communiqués was inevitably Mamma, and she was nothing if not meticulous. She created an Excel sheet, listed each boy by surname, and added carefully titled rows – profile ID, location, height, weight, date of birth, degrees, salary, spoken languages, hobbies.

Each evening, Ranja would scan this honeycomb sheet and make quick calculations. A handsome pay cheque compensated for a somewhat dishevelled appearance. A hobby that highlighted pedigree, such as polo, made up for a lack of enterprise. A degree in business, always a mark of ambition, scored over all else. Based on their attributes, imagined or otherwise, the men were rated on a scale of one to ten. At the end of a day's work, no more than one suitor would emerge unscathed.

My sister would speak to her chosen men. She'd exchange letters with them, occasionally share her phone number, sometimes allow our mother to invite their parents home. At all times, she was ruthless. A single unseemly remark from a man, and she'd disappear from his life without a trace. A suggestion of a past, and she'd choose to pull away. A hint of preoccupation, and she'd play hard to get.

After much back and forth, Ranja pared down her list to ten eligible bachelors.

To us, hapless onlookers, Ranja's strategies at husband-winning seemed dreadfully technical.

'You can't find a man through Excel spreadsheets!' Tasha told Ranja, horrified.

'Really? And why not? Some find men across terrace walls. Some by sharing a class bench. And some by analysing columns of data.'

'But the magic – ' This was me, of course.

'What of it?'

'*What of it?*'

'It's Hollywood hokum.'

'Don't say that!'

'Fine. Let me rephrase it. *It's not true!'*

'That's bloody cynical.'

'It's realistic. I've done my research. And I know what I'm doing.'

Relying on the tabulated facts before her, my sister rejected the first three men on her scaled-down list – the founder of a flourishing start-up, a microbiologist pursuing a PhD, a sales manager for a pharmaceutical giant (though rebuffing him was especially tough).

Then, swiftly, Ranja turned her gaze towards those who remained – a motley group of seven – and demolished the award-winning horticulturalist, the Japanese interpreter for the government, the automotive engineer from Munich, the optometrist, the chiropractor, the homeopath – so she was left with the last man on her list.

Jay.

Jay was a corporate lawyer with an affiliate degree in business management. He practised in Dubai. He was devoted to golf. These facts Ranja had already established. The clincher was Jay's (presumably) innocent remark, 'I've already chosen a school for my children – its students always secure admission in the Ivies.'

Ranja's decision was easy. Jay, for his part, doubtless sensing the onslaught of age and the burden of professional success combined with skimpy personal triumph – and finding in Ranja a companion who was sympathetic to these pressures – decided to play along and visit us.

I remember the meeting all too clearly. There we were in the drawing room – Mamma with a string of jasmines pinned to her hair, Amamma with her prized American brooch holding her sari pallu in place, Tasha in a long skirt. I hovered close. We arranged ourselves on a woefully small sofa and stared at the boy and the mother before us.

Jay was exactly like the photograph he had sent us – unchanging. He rarely blinked, made no attempt to relax his face into a smile. Not a strand of hair was out of place. His bow tie had two precise diamond tipped ends. The aglets of his shoelaces were set evenly apart. The symmetry of this man was so distressing that Amamma, otherwise loath to excuse herself from a potentially action-packed affair, hurriedly left the room.

Mamma, entirely on her own with her daughters, did what she had mastered – she made polite conversation. She offered Jay biscuits (which he coolly refused), offered his mother sweets (which she grabbed by the fistful), and vaguely commented on the absence of their respective spouses.

'I'm sorry your husband is away,' Mamma muttered.

'Yes, what to do, that's the way the hospitality industry runs. He never gets to leave the Maldives.'

'Yes, I understand.'

'And your man?'

'Like your husband, he never gets time off. He's in Norway.'

'Ah, Jay told me he's a journalist?'

'Yes, a good one.'

'I'm sure. And he paints also?'

'Not badly. It's a hobby, nothing more.'

'Good, good. He'll come for his daughter's wedding obviously?'

'Perhaps. And your husband?'

'Perhaps.'

Mamma liked Jay's mother. She found in her a doppelgänger, someone who lurched from uncertainty to uncertainty, who answered questions, not with firmness, but with words that were double-edged, a no and a yes.

As Mamma mentally approved of Jay's family – and by extension, Jay – Ranja entered. She exhibited, much like the man before her, perfect harmony. Each pleat of her sari was a taut pencil stroke. Her bangles – a precise dozen on each arm. Her earrings fluttered as one.

When Ranja sat next to Jay, it was like watching two trees in a photograph set in South Korea – poised, shipshape, shunning eccentricity. It was almost sad.

And yet my oldest sister was anything but sorrowful. In Jay, it seemed she had found a twin soul – someone like her who valued order and uniformity; who cared, not for the unruliness of ardour, but for the discipline of hard work and achievement. Here was a man who had no interest in the vagaries of magic; he sought the steady pulse of fact.

Months later, Ranja would learn that Jay, too, had relied on the logic of Excel; that the spreadsheets that had led my sister to him had in tandem led him to my sister.

The day they met, Jay and Ranja were allowed to exchange secrets in a corner while all of us watched. They returned to announce a wedding date. They let their perfectly tapering fingers touch.

Well before her personal deadline, Ranja married Jay.

Theirs wasn't the perfect wedding – no wedding ever can be. The server tripped and spilled lemonade on the carpet. A colicky infant wept incessantly. A woman publicly fought with her husband. The photographer spent all his time flirting with the florist. And Mamma and Jay's mother remained preoccupied, making quick excuses for the absence of their partners.

In the midst of these all-too-human lapses and deceits, Ranja and Jay remained wax figurines – their smiles were inverted umbrellas; their bodies stayed ramrod straight.

Three weeks before Tasha's flight to Delhi, Ranja moved to Dubai with Jay.

# 4.

'I wish you had come for Ranja's wedding,' I told Sahil a day after Ranja left.

'I was busy.'

'Yes. I know.'

'And, in any case, it would have been awkward.'

'Yes.'

'Sorry.'

'It's what it is.'

'How was the wedding?'

'Good. The photographer and the flor – '

'Yes?'

'It doesn't matter.'

The incident that had amused Tasha and me no end, and that had upset Ranja in equal measure – of the cameraman who, in a bid to lure the florist, had photographed the dahlias to the exclusion of all else – suddenly seemed far too immature to relay. Sahil had larger concerns, grander narratives of love and loss, and stories like this one would only prove my own inexperience.

Ever since Sahil had accused me in the restaurant of being no more than a child, I had started ruthlessly blue-pencilling conversations, editing out talk that would be deemed flippant. I avoided comments that were fanciful, words made of gewgaws and tinsel. I cherry-picked the books I wished to discuss, the films I expressed interest in, the cuisines I referred to –

'I liked the lightly braised water chestnuts at the wedding.'

'Interesting.'

'How was your week?'

'Oh, the same. Slightly busy since Maya was in town' – his second wife – 'and she wanted to gallery hop.'

'I imagine she was better company than my family – '

'Oh, come on, Deeya, you know she's – '

'Of course. In any case, I've been busy, too. There was Gautam – '

'Hmm.'

'I met him at the wedding – my age, a lawyer in Dubai like Jay – and he wanted someone to play city guide. So, after the wedding, I led him through the streets of Bombay.'

'I hope you showed him this side of town?'

'Of course.'

I had also started embellishing the truth. Conscious, more than I ever had been, of Sahil's complex history – of his women and friends and temporary lovers, of those he had lost interest in, abandoned or divorced – I found my own stories of crushes and imaginary beaus and half-boyfriends wanting, devoid of gravitas and drama, *childish* – oh, that awful word. So I addressed the gaps in my life, dreamt up people and pasts with greater authority, more detachment –

If truth be told, I didn't know Gautam. If truth be told, during the wedding and after, I sat in a corner with my phone on my lap, waiting for a message from Sahil. A call.

'Great, Dee.'

'Yeah. How is Maya?'

'Good. She's more loquacious than I remember. She might be visiting again in a month or two.'

'Maybe we can all meet.'

'Maybe.'

'I'm sure she'd like to.'

'Well, I don't know. I haven't really spoken of us.'

'Oh?'

'I mean, it's not like I don't want to.'

'Good to know.'

'Really, Dee. It was just hard to get a word in edgeways while she spoke.'

'I understand.'

'You're sure?'

'Sure. It's not like I spoke to Gautam about you.'

'Ah.'

*We're square, we're good.*

If Sahil was sceptical, he didn't disclose it. If he was hurt, he didn't make it known. He merely shrugged off each of my confessions, those oddly structured semi-stories.

Today, when I look back, I know that Sahil was neither sceptical nor hurt. Merely tolerant, the way adults often are of adolescents going through an unfortunate phase.

Throughout those months marked by frantic catch-up and forbearance, there was something that glued Sahil and me together. Maybe it was the fact that Sahil knew that my aggressive attempts at keeping pace didn't define me. Maybe it was that, despite everything, I was convinced that Sahil was concerned.

Or maybe the reason was something quite else. We stayed together out of reverence for what had been sustained against all the odds. We watched with gentle awe.

# 5.

Tasha packed and left for Delhi.

Unlike Ranja who shipped everything she could to Dubai, my younger sister left behind her a trail of cheery, populated photographs ('They're so yesterday'); a poster of the Scissor Sisters, procured with some difficulty from an overseas acquaintance ('Seriously, I'm past them'); dated compact discs ('Who cares for them these days?'); a desk; a closet; a single bed.

For a year, I'd live alone with my mother and Amamma. I'd walk through a now immense, emptied-out house. Sometimes I'd feel like I was speeding down a wideopen freeway – no bends, no obstructions, just swathes, vast swathes of nothingness.

I considered moving from the room I shared with Amamma to Tasha's. It made complete sense. I'd no longer have to sneak out of bed, tiptoe through the door, and sprint to the terrace when Sahil called, or avoid the objects that came hurtling towards me (still) when they'd slip into my grandmother's dominion.

The day after Tasha left, I collected my clothes, piled my books in cartons, and flung them into my sister's bedroom. Yet, the moment I tried arranging my novels on her desk or my skirts in her closet, I felt no better than a marauder swooping in and nailing my nameplate on to somebody else's wall. Minutes later, I was collecting my belongings and shifting right back to my grandmother's. By way of greeting, Amamma lobbed a rolled-up sock at me.

In this time of moving and unmoving, if I had one consolation, it was this – that I had secured a job soon after completing my degree; that in a few days, I'd be a part of the workforce, teaching English in

a suburban school. Between rushing to a classroom before the clang
of a bell and travelling across town to Sahil's to make-believe we still
loved, I'd only have to visit home under cover of darkness, when its
barrenness would seem distant, dim; when its night-time silences
and sounds would be familiar.

If I coped by running away, Mamma survived by resurrecting her
missing daughters. Two days after Tasha left, Mamma knocked at
her door, waited for an answer, then crept in. She re-stuck the peeling
poster by her bed, rearranged the CDs near her desk. She changed
old sheets, ironed out the bedspread, and left a note for her daughter
– *dinner is in the fridge.*

The night I returned from my first day of work, Mamma told
me all about Tasha – that she had emailed; that she liked the classes
she attended; that she had cooked a meal for herself by following
Mamma's precise instructions. 'She's happy,' Mamma said, then
added, 'I'm sure she'll be home for dinner soon.'

'Unlikely,' I replied without feeling.

'True. Studying keeps her busy.'

'She's also far away.'

Mamma nodded abstractedly, then left the room. I'll never know
if she heard me.

Over the days that followed, as Tasha dispatched hurried emails and
Ranja made ecstatic Skype calls to Bombay, Mamma had plenty to tell
me about my sisters – Tasha likes her teachers; Ranja is holidaying
in Spain; Tasha made rajma-chawal; Ranja is now in Italy; Tasha has
opened a bank account; Ranja has bought a vibrant blue dinner set.
'I'm sure they'll be back soon,' my mother would add. 'And crows
will sing,' I'd retort.

'Any time now, your sisters will be sleeping in their beds,' Mamma
said one evening.

'Yes,' I replied, losing patience. 'Of course, they will. Really, it's
all about them, isn't it?'

'What, my dear?'

'I've started a new job, I have classes to take, I return late – would
you like to ask me about my day?'

Mamma watched me, wide-eyed, startled. 'Your day. Yes. Yes, tell me.'

I couldn't.

I stomped off to the terrace and looked into the far distance – the row of street lamps, the aircraft warning lights of a skyscraper, fireworks. As I watched the distant shimmer of yellow and red and green, it struck me what Mamma had done, was doing. Her gaze was directed, not at her immediate neighbourhood, but at everything that lay just beyond, out of reach.

No wonder Mamma looked past her mother and me – we were outside her visual field. Instead, she considered those barely perceptible, never there – Ranja, Tasha, Daddy – all inhabitants of the same region, a territory, not of solid departures, but of imagined homecomings.

Who was it who said, '*This is the mourner's secret position: I have to say this person is dead, but I don't have to believe it*'? The sentence framed my mother. To visitors she'd admit that Ranja was in Dubai, the good wife of an upstanding lawyer; that Tasha, always independent, was studying in New Delhi; that Daddy toiled in Norway. Yet, privately, she'd believe this was only a half-fact, Part One of an extensive novel. The absolute truth, which only she was privy to, was far simpler. That each of them, after completing the things they had to complete – family-making, an education, work – each of them would dream their way back to her.

That night, I returned from the terrace to my bare home and entered Mamma's bedroom. I could hazily perceive the double bed – Mamma, deep in sleep, curled like a foetus, occupying a tiny corner. The rest of the mattress remained vacant for Ranja.

I crept up to my mother, lay down by her body, held her hand.

She flinched lightly, turned, then let her arm wrap itself around my wrist. 'So you're back after all,' she whispered in sleep.

How beautiful, her smile.

# 6.

Even while sending Mamma those cautiously worded emails, Tasha (too busy to talk, too busy to craft cogent letters, *too busy*) chose to share with Ranja and me snippets from her diary.

Tonight, I wish I could retrieve the things Tasha had sent us, carry them – her voice, her turn of phrase – verbatim. But I cannot. I've misplaced her hasty dispatches. All I have with me are impressions – vague echoes of what she hoped to convey; recollections of a word here, a hurried sentence elsewhere; synopses. The sense, if not the sound.

**I** know that after spending a week in a Delhi hostel, Tasha decided to break free from restrictions, from curfews and prying wardens. I know that following a series of dead-end conversations with landlords about her marital status and her partiality for wayward boys, she finally found a home – a cramped set of rooms on a wideopen terrace – which could be hers, no questions asked, for a princely sum of ten thousand rupees. I know that to pay the rent and meet the expenses that go with being unattached in a city of plenty, she started working post-college in a neighbourhood cake shop, where for three hours each evening she'd record spoilt milk, recommend pastries, and ice muffins.

**I** also know of other things – of the men she sought. They were like garments, a new one for each season.

There was M., for instance, short for – I'll never know. He was an art gallery receptionist. She chanced upon him in the bakery, saying something ordinary, predictable, 'A cupcake, please.' So she scooped one out, laid it in a box, then dropped a sentence with ballerina-lightness. Disarmed, the young M. responded with a guffaw, then asked, 'What do you do? I mean, apart from selling cakes?'

'What do you think I do?'

'Are you a photographer?'

'Am I?'

'I feel like I've seen you elsewhere.'

'Perhaps you have.'

'Weren't you one of the young photographers at last week's workshop?'

'Quite likely I was.' And Tasha smiled.

For the next three weeks, Tasha played a recreational photographer, brandishing her phone each time she spotted something of value. She watched with attention, seeking the exceptional in the ordinary and the ordinary in things deemed exceptional – a dog by the obelisk in Coronation Park, clothes pinned for drying beside the Yamuna, the mole on the body of her lover.

Tasha mentioned M.'s mole – I remember this – how black it was, how it stood out on his neck, especially if he happened to be wearing a bright tee. She described other things, too, in words, with pictures – his palms, how they creased under water; and his arms, blue veins running like tributaries.

Till one day, she let slip that treacherous word – *ennui*.

*I'm consumed by a sense of ennui*, she must have said.

*I'm fast outgrowing the role of an observer making brisk choices about what to include and eliminate, what detail to emphasize. I'm tired of the language of contrast and balance, focus and depth. I guess, if truth be told, I'm wearying of this self I've assumed for M.*

*It was exciting to begin with – like somersaulting for the first time, but eventually, after the tenth tumble, once the body curls into a comma at will, it becomes mundane – this has become mundane. I have no more stories to offer. I have built what I can of this life – my first Kodak gifted by a loving father when I was no older than six; my careless loss of a prized camera while playing badminton with my girlfriends; my dreams of pursuing professional photography after earning a degree.*

*I'm done.*

*Tonight, when I trace M.'s mole, it will be for the last time. Already*
*I've moved on –*

M. stopped starring in Tasha's diary. He vanished, became a thing
of the past.

Soon after M., there was the Tibetan scholar R., short for – once more,
I'll never know. With him, in his company, Tasha was a hermit. She
was content with everyday rituals, with home-class-bakery-home,
shifting her fingers through one, then another, as though they were
the beads of a rosary. She found fulfilment in little things – deseeding
tomatoes, blood-red liquid staining her palms; watering the only plant
in her possession, so the buds blossomed into tuberoses; holding
hands with her boy.

Eventually, though, that word appeared – *ennui*. Or something
like it.

*I tire of this, of never seeking more or pushing harder, of being happy but*
*not happier. There is a world beyond the steady flatline of contentment,*
*where colours dazzle and gestures are dizzy. And I want that, the*
*intensity of variable delights.*

*But first, I must hold R., this time unsteadily, so he learns of the*
*impulses that course through my body.*

*And once he does, I must leave. I must claim the life that beckons.*

In more ways than I would like to concede, at that phase in our
lives, Tasha and I were dissimilar souls. There I was, holding on to
one man, hoping desperately that upon this still point I could pile
my tomorrows, build a future. And there was Tasha, letting names
pass through her –

Would that she stayed the same.

# 7.
## *Amamma*

Weeks after her meeting with Venu, and after consuming Rangaa's magic brew, Amamma learnt that she had nosedived into motherhood.

The day Amamma knew for certain – knew that she'd be the bearer of an offspring – she went up to her husband. There he was, seated on a chair, reading the morning papers. My grandmother, skulking outside the door, whispered, 'I have news to give.'

My grandfather lowered the papers. 'Yes, I know. Subramanian had been promoted. Head clerk. Bah. Like he's saving lives.'

'What? No.'

'No? Swami himself told me – '

'You'll be an Appa.'

'So everyone says, it's never – '

'I'm pregnant.'

The papers slid down my grandfather's lap. 'Repeat, I say!'

'I'm pregnant. I – '

My grandfather leapt up, sped. Recovering a self he had all but lost – almost becoming the man he had been when he had spotted Amamma as a schoolgirl – he yelled, 'Iyer! Good news, good news! Swami! G'news! Cheema! *Good* news, I say!'

Soon, the entire town had heard – Rangaa at last had something to broadcast – but what? An inheritance? An award? A new baby bride? 'Cheh!' Mrs Swami, son in tow, spat. 'Such rubbish you talk. For Rangaa, there's only one kind of news.'

And so, with that spelt out, whole families flocked to Rangaa's – the women to congratulate my grandmother, but really to relive their own days of childbearing ('How sick I was!' Mrs Swami complained. 'How much my stomach hurt!'); the men to rejoice with Rangaa, but in truth to learn how it had come to pass ('Cashews and tomatoes, really?' an incredulous Swami asked. 'Is that what women want?').

An hour after Rangaa's announcement, the suburb returned to a semblance of normality. Young men cycled to work; well-to-do lawyers zipped by in cars; mothers ignored headstrong toddlers demanding sweets in the market; flower-girls clambered up trees, fell. As he strode to his clinic, Rangaa tried rearranging the scenes before him – stopping the cyclist; shushing the toddler; strutting before a tumbling flower-girl so his deeds would go acknowledged. But nothing would shape up. The cyclist pedalled off; the infant's mother snarled; and the flower-girl quickly outstripped my grandfather, intent on scrambling up another plant.

Rangaa, he felt a hollow in his heart. He suffered the physical symptoms of a let-down. After decades of study, potion-making, and coition; after years of sidestepping sneers and jibes; after months of patient toil that had (at last!) borne fruit, my grandfather expected a long round of applause. Instead, all he got was Swami's hare-brained question and a neighbourhood too self-involved to stick around. It was as though the morning never was.

Rangaa told himself that such apathy was meant to be short-lived. That the world would take notice once his wife produced a boy. Quickly, he began gathering odds and ends in his office – six cloves, a green chilli, a touch of pepper –

– Cinnamon. He started pounding a mixture of sneeze-inducing spices. Provoked by an indifferent suburb, he vowed to fashion a torrid son.

My grandmother, in the meantime, sat alone at home. She considered the weeks that had passed – the letter and all that had followed – the long walk, the house, the prescription, Rangaa's attempts at baby-making. She dwelt on the chronology of events, how each overlapped with the next, how, at times, it was almost impossible to isolate the episodes.

Amamma tried finding her way through the fuzz to arrive at a firm sequence of occurrences – then stopped. What was she doing?

Somehow – and she didn't quite know how – she had to avoid thinking, calculating. She had to seek diversions.

My grandmother knocked at Mrs Swami's. There was no response. She searched for flower-girls, on trees, down below. They seemed to have retired for an early siesta. She tried following a scurrying wild cat. He proved to be too swift for her unsteady feet.

Finally, she returned to the kitchen. Terrified of mulling over the past, she imagined a future – a parallel one – in a square house with Venu; far from an airless suburb and its prying flower-girls; in London with her daughter.

Venu and she, they'd walk through the city, gauge the length of the tube lines, estimate the depth of some river – and then what? Somehow, the more Amamma considered it, the less solid her story seemed.

Already she could spot the chinks in the armour of her narrative. Venu's impatience with her impulsive claims – 'The tube lines are no longer than a bobcat's tail.' Her frustration with his cast-iron stances – 'This river is twelve metres deep.' Venu's growing irritation – 'Enough, a cat's tail can't measure seventy-one kilometres.' Her exasperation – 'Who cares about stupid numbers while admiring a waterbody?' Her daughter wrenched at once by fact and fancy.

This – the sum total of this – the future they'd fall heir to. Was this what she was reaching for?

After a day in Venu's house – unlike any she had known, with newness and yellow-enchantment – Amamma sensed that her story had spun into a denouement. There was no climax she could hope for now, no high-pitched culmination. From here, the liaison was fated to plummet.

There'd be quiet dialogues, tedious lovemaking, a morning voice saying hello-hello –

But Amamma knew these things already, knew them from the marrow of her bones. Of what use seeking them again?

My grandmother, quick with all decisions, tore a page from a notebook, wrote a letter, a sentence – *I come I go we cannot meet.* She dropped this by Venu's gate, into the open mouth of a mailbox.

An almost-tear.

Then nothing.

My grandmother came to swallow her grief whole.

# 8.

It was summer. Of this I'm certain. The light was a gaudy yellow. I made my way to Sahil's apartment. I rang the bell.

Sahil peeked through the peephole, I imagine – he always did – then slid the latch. It squeaked. 'Hey there,' he said, and I smiled. We were no longer close – it has been months since we had revealed snatches of our inner lives – yet we refused to pull away. Young as I was, I lacked the pluck for such finality, and Sahil, for all his age and experience, seemed to flounder. For him, every severance was the first.

I entered Sahil's apartment, slid out of my shoes, drifted off to his whitewashed bedroom. He followed. As always, we talked. I told him of a Ray film that lent itself to erudite chatter and of a Lispector novel he would approve of. Sahil smiled, but his eyes – they seemed plaintive. So I changed the subject, offered, as in the past, a word – a word I can't remember right now. Something in Japanese, something that meant – no, not adoration at first sight – rather, a strong hunch during an early meeting that the future will yield love.

'Did you feel that way when you met me?' I asked, then looked away, alert to the precariousness of the question.

Sahil said nothing. Then he said even less, 'You must know people who have lived the word.'

I played along. 'Well. Yeah.'

'Like?'

'Well, my mother claims that my father knew the moment they met that they'd build a future together, marry.'

'Claims? You find that hard to believe?'

'I suppose.'

'Hmm.'

'Somehow, when I think of Mamma, of the things she says, I see a magician's hat. There's *what is*, obvious, apparently stable. Yet, slide away the false bottom, and there's a whole other world.'

Sahil nodded. 'Your mother reminds me of a story I read on Moses.'

'What of it?'

'You know how it goes – that he smashed a stone tablet inscribed by god when the children of Israel disappointed him. Then he cut a second tablet, forty days later, with god's rewritten laws.'

'Yeah.'

'For a long time, people puzzled over the broken table – had it been destroyed or simply lost? Then they found the shattered pieces safe in the Ark of the Testimony. The broken tablet was right next to the intact slab. You see?'

'See what?'

'It's how it must be for each of us – for me, for your mother, for you. Two selves in a body, side by side – one broken, the other whole.'

'Yes.'

Yes. The statement, its matter-of-fact acknowledgement of our ruptured selves, made me yearn for something sated, complete.

I approached Sahil, took his hand in mine, claimed his face, his mouth, hoping that in this if nothing else, in this cloverleaf of bodies, we'd find cohesion. His hair, shorter, greyer, commingling with mine. His palms, rough, lightly creased, enfolding my own. His lashes closing the space, the hair-width cleft, between us.

'Are you fine, Dee? Are you sure?' His hand by my mouth.

'Yes.'

'Lovely.'

I drew Sahil in, barely conscious, impelled by a primeval urge – the need to exist in one piece. I annexed Sahil's body. He borrowed my skin. Two halves erasing whatever else may be shattered.

When we were done, when we had concluded our rushed attempts at wholeness, I looked away. From Sahil to the grilled window, from the grilled window to the low ceiling, to a mirror by the bed. It had always been there, the mirror. But for the first time, I watched us, two bodies close. Watched him, age casting an uneven shadow. Watched the loose skin around his neck; the veins, prominent, criss-crossing his hands; the hesitant swag by his elbows.

At length, I watched myself watching him. It was like sitting through a half-loved film; I could be Luisa Cortes or just about anyone, past the bloom of the twenties, past springtide and youth, past. How adult I seemed. My skin was opaque, less eager to absorb. My lips were thin, quiet. My eyes were small, no longer seeking this mysterious world. Here I was, canny and experienced. Here I was, a being of stories – and I could measure up to just about any fiction.

And, with this, I had lost something – something vital. Unknowing; openness; a casual past. The possibility of being twenty-plus, impossibly young.

I would've tried to recover the girl I once was – but where to search, which bend to investigate – she seemed lost, irrevocably. So, in that split second, I decided – if *this* girl, streetwise and sharp, was the person I had grown into, if she was the only self I possessed, I had to live her life to its logical end. I owed her, if nothing else, a conclusion.

I looked at Sahil, took his hand in mine, whispered, 'Marry me.'

Sahil escaped my clasp, got up, slipped into his trousers. I assumed he hadn't heard, so I said it again, this time louder. *Marry me.*

*No.*

There it was, an answer.

I took a shirt, his shirt, maybe mine, let it cover something, anything, my back. Sahil approached me, his hand gliding across my face. I allowed him to. Then didn't.

'Is this how it ends – is this it?' he asked.

I looked away, spoke to the grilled window. 'You never felt it, did you?'

'What?'

'The word, Japanese, koi no yokan?' – *that*.

'Dee – '

I did not wait. I ran down the stairs. I left.

# 9.

I darted across the road, past the trees of Sahil's neighbourhood. My cheeks wet. After the initial shock of grief, I only knew rage.

I was angry that I had exposed myself, but equally, I was angry that my disclosure had invited, not tenderness, but indifference. I was angry that while my sorrow had been a visible thing – messy and flailing – Sahil's pain had remained tucked beneath a question, altogether smooth, *'Is this how it ends – is this it?'* Most of all, I was angry that while I had paraded all the symptoms of a youth I thought had passed me by – paraded dreams and ambition and hope – Sahil had remained remote. Adult.

If rage is attached, not to hesitancy but to action, at that moment all I desired was to carry on. But how? I thought of the preceding hours – of the lovemaking, the distancing, the artless appeal – and suddenly the answer seemed obvious. I had to follow the statement *marry me* to its end.

It would show Sahil, I told myself. That without him, too, I'd live that life.

Buoyed up by what seemed like a decision, a plan of action, I caught an auto home. I rang the doorbell, wiped my cheeks, and rushed to my mother. 'I want to get married,' I announced.

'What?'

'I must. It's high time.'

Mamma had heard the words before –

'Do you have someone in mind?'

'Of course not,' I replied. 'But that's what you're here for.'

Mamma had learnt the chain of appropriate responses.

'Yes.'

'I must get married immediately.'

'All right. I'll go to the temple,' Mamma said.

'Or online.'

'Whichever is faster.'

Matters should have rested there. But no. Sooner than I had expected, than I had wanted – too soon – the future stirred.

It began with Miss Mimmy who arrived two days after my announcement to ask for an extra packed lunchbox for a fortnight. Then she volunteered the reason. 'You know, my nephew, he is in town. Now, you'd think American boys, they'd fend for themselves like they do on TV. But no, not my nephew.'

Mamma sighed. She offered the currency her friend accepted – clichés. 'Boys never grow up, do they, Miss Mimmy?'

Miss Mimmy appreciated the response; one could tell by the vigour of her head-jiggle. 'No. So here I am taking two weeks chhutti from the bank to feed the boy – poor child – and help him find a homely girl.'

'Ah – '

'You wouldn't know anyone, would you, Vannu?'

Mamma smiled. Ever the opportunist when it concerned her daughters, she pounced. 'Actually, Deeya, it's a coincidence, but she's – *we're* – looking.'

All it took was a hastily conveyed statement. And time, which generally lumbered, now hurtled forward with boomerang speed.

'Really?'

'Yes, Miss Mimmy. I even went to the temple last morning. But the boys – '

'Forget those boys!'

'You're right.'

'We should get your Deeya to meet my Dev.'

'Yes.'

She's – what – twenty-three or twenty-four? Just right for my Dev. He's twenty-nine.'

As I watched Mamma and Miss Mimmy hug, my anger collapsed and gave way to panic. What was I doing, I asked myself, and to what end? I wanted to rush to Sahil's, to the comfort of his voice, and

reveal the calamities of the past forty-eight hours. 'It's all so stupid!'
I longed to say –

But then I recalled our last meeting. *Marry me. MARRY ME. No.*
Suddenly, I wanted none of it to matter.

So in a bright sari that flashed and shimmied and drew attention, I
met Dev, I smiled at Dev, and I acquiesced when Dev suggested that
we 'go out'. There we were, walking within the building's compound
– I kept tripping over my sari; Dev, tall, brawny, kept rescuing me
with deadpan hands. My mother and Miss Mimmy watched from
Tasha's bedroom, their faces pressed against a window, their eyes
wide, nervously working out the things we were saying.

Their guess is as good as mine. For today, when I try recalling
that first conversation, all I remember are disjointed sentences, half-
hearted attempts at sustaining a dialogue.

'I like reading, I suppose. Or at least I did.' This is my voice, so
it must be me.

'Me too. These days especially I like sudoku.' The accent is
indecisive, so one must assume it is Dev.

'Ah.'

'And Paulo Coelho. Number one across the world. You like him?'

'I can't say. Though there was a point when I wanted to visit
Brazil.'

'Las Vegas is nicer. You'd like it.'

'I think I'd like a place that lets me cycle.'

'Really? I used to do that as a child. Now, I work on a ship.'

No, I'm being unfair to Dev. He tried communicating as well
as he could – pitching in with the names of books when I spoke of
a reading habit; offering local cities in exchange for foreign lands;
keeping pace with me each time I changed the subject, placing nouns
against nouns, a ship against a spindly cycle. I realize, in hindsight,
that I was being difficult – throwing a fresh dare even as he tried
making sense of an old challenge.

'Why did you choose your profession?'

'I don't know,' Dev shrugged. 'It just happened.'

'If not this?'

'I'd – well, I'd be an astronaut.'

'Hmm. I wanted to embrace – not professions, no – I wanted to be people. Anais Nin, Elizabeth – '

'Hurley!'

'Not really. Browning. Women who loved men-of-words.'

'Ah.'

'But then – they chose poorly, didn't they? They all do.'

'If you say so.'

'Maybe not Elizabeth Browning.'

Oddly, despite the non-talk, the exchanges working at cross purposes, we considered getting married. I know what convinced me to take the plunge – a lone, seemingly harmless comment, 'Deeya, I'm generally away on ship, y'know.' It was exactly what I needed – time alone to lurch from memory to memory; the faraway, non-interfering presence of a bona fide partner; in essence, a marriage without a man.

But what propelled Dev to view me as a wife? When I tried probing, all I could gather was that he disliked returning to an empty house. I suppose his reasons were not unlike my own – I chose Dev, a man in absentia; he chose me, the occasional wife.

After that, events unfurled rather quickly – our formal consent; Miss Mimmy's whistle, 'First time lucky!'; Mamma's question, 'What date to set?' Dev said he could return five months later; I said I hated to procrastinate; so finally, it was decided that the wedding would happen soon, too soon, in under one hundred and fifty days.

For the next ten days, Dev submitted himself to Miss Mimmy and Mamma, to their jabber, to their relentless attempts at henpecking – go to the tailor, eat a little more, you need a purple necktie, you don't!

For my part, I tried getting to know Dev in a cold, scientific manner – the way I'd try familiarizing myself with the map of a far-flung city, maybe Reykjavik – only with a little less interest, a little more persistence. We had established that our definitions of books and travel and dreams diverged – I had, in any case – so I asked of other things, those that came with answers I wasn't deeply invested in. What do you work as (first mate, he said, chuffed); what's your house like (small, three rooms, a garden); where do you stay (Providence, Rhode Island); did you grow up in America (yes, of course, and Papa, too – I'm American).

'Where are your parents?'

'Papa died some years ago in an accident.'

'I'm sorry.'

'Ma didn't survive his demise.'

'That's tragic. Siblings?'

'None.'

'Hmm. Why didn't you find yourself a girl independently?'

'Why didn't you find yourself a man?'

I smiled at his presumption, then laughed silently at my own. I tried picturing Dev's boyhood in the States, the girls he might have asked out – those with electric blue hair, those popping giant gum bubbles, those blowing raspberries – but no, that wasn't like him at all. So I tried picturing other girls – those with pleated grey skirts, perfectly ironed black shirts, poker straight hair – but no, I couldn't see him approaching them either. No matter how hard I tried imagining his other lives, I found him a thousand miles away from land, alone, rocked by a ship; the foghorn blowing.

Perhaps I seemed equally prosaic to him – a girl with a day job in a school, teaching English to disinterested, hiccuping boys. What did I have to look forward to, who could I possibly date – divorced fathers, aged authors? Unlikely –

– Or not.

Perhaps I had been woefully rash with my assumptions. Perhaps Dev's past was populated with girls – brash, red-lipped, tattooed wives; students with quiet, manicured fingernails; the ones walking out of Bloomingdale's in stilettos with overstuffed bags. A lady in every port.

'I like it on ship,' he said all at once, so I abandoned my attempts at playing detective.

'What do you like?'

'Lots of things. The stuff I get to see. Such as – when we were crossing the South China Sea, it must have been early in the morning. The sea was covered with fire.'

'Really?'

Dev laughed. 'Got you. Squid fishermen. And electric lights. Squid find those impossible to resist.'

I looked at Dev, into his eyes, tried tracing oceans in them, deep seas speckled with fire. Instead all I found were irises, empty.

So I tried seeking reassurance in other things, his fingers, his hair, his mouth – I wished to touch his mouth and almost did. But Dev made me conscious of my own desire – not for him but *it*, that unknown quantity that makes relationships unpredictable and ungainly, corporeal.

Besides, I knew I was lying to myself, shadow-boxing with pronouns. I wanted fingers, hair, mouth, yes – but not Dev's, not his.

The closest I got to knowing Dev before marriage as a being beyond indifferent words and handshakes was on the final night of his visit, when Mamma and Miss Mimmy suggested I drop him at the airport. The cab sped down back alleys, poorly lit lanes, and we careened into each other, his face on my lap. He got up, barely, and let his hand enclose my own, not by accident. Then, shuffling, he leaned forward. His mouth pressed against my chin, slobbery like a schoolboy's. I sobbed.

'Don't worry,' he said.

'What?'

'Don't worry. It will be okay.'

'What will?'

'I'll be back.'

This is where I'd like the story to end – the non-kiss, an empty promise, the flight taxiing down the runway.

But then I'd be straying from the whole-entire story –

# Dev.
# And.

*Look at the light through the windowpane.*

# 1.

Dev returned to the States. Steadfast, he kept in touch, calling four times a day while he remained land-bound. It would be over a month before he'd be summoned to the seas.

Each time Dev and I would talk, Amamma would rush out of the room or press a pillow against her ears – 'I haven't met a more boring pair,' she'd complain long and loud.

My first Skype conversation with Dev (one that led to Amamma's pointed observation) revolved around vessels – giant machines rumbling in their bellies, spitting heat; the sharp smell of oil. Even as he spoke, I found myself imagining birds, the cry of an albatross; sea-creatures; the streamlined bodies of flying fish breaking through the water's surface, soaring, their forked tails slicing the air in half. Sahil would have loved to hear of this.

Dev interrupted, 'The worst weather conditions, I guess, are in the Med. You know? One day, the water is as flat as your palm. The next day, 90 miles per hour gusts and 15-foot breakers.'

'Have you experienced a storm?'

'Well, yeah, sort of. But it was nothing.'

'Hmm. There's a writer. Jean-Claude Izzo. Anyway, he says that sailors never speak of storms, not to their families, not at home, not even in letters. After all, what can they say? How can they describe the ferocity of wind and water?'

'I'm not sure – '

'"Storms," he said, "*don't exist. Any more than sailors do, when they're at sea. Men are only real when they're on land.*"'

'Deeya?'

'Yes?'

'That's true, you know.'

'I thought so.'

'Deeya, I – '

'Yeah?'

'I love you.'

I started. Then 'yes,' I spat out, 'yes', upset that an ordinary conversation had yielded sentiment; upset that such sentiment, unprovoked and wholly unjustified, had been expressed; upset that it had eroded the uncomplicatedness of our lives. And upset, *especially* upset, that I'd have to scrounge around for a response.

Then, stubbornly, I decided I would not. 'Yes,' I repeated, but this time softly. And Dev – he accepted the word.

All I hear now is Dev's voice – it surrounds me – how he spoke to me from America, kept speaking, of his job, his US relations, his friends.

'I love my friends,' Dev said.

'Nice,' I replied, conscious still of Sahil, of how our relationship had shrunk my world, so I no longer had acquaintances to call my own.

'I have – not many close friends – but three or four,' Dev continued.

'Good.'

'There's Yuvraj, he's Punjabi, and Mahesh, he's from LA – both colleagues. Sometimes Yuvi's wife joins us, too – the family stays close, a ten-minute drive away. I'll introduce you to them.'

'Great,' I replied, exhausting all the bald adjectives I knew.

'Yeah. Who are your friends? I barely had time to meet any of them.'

'I – well, I have too many to list,' I said, easy.

'Okay. No best friends?'

'No.'

'Ex-boyfriends?'

'What?'

'I'm sorry, I didn't mean to – '

'Okay.'

'I just wondered, you know – '

I wanted the call to end; I still want it to. But there was Dev, inert, watching. I had to respond. But what could I say? That I had had a lover; that he was un-young; that I had needed him in another life; that I still did?

'I – ' Tell him, I told myself, tell him; it's only right to come clean. 'I actually – '

'You know, it doesn't matter. Such talk is silly.'

So now, I was angry.

I am angry – that Dev can so simply ask, so simply dismiss; that he can reject a past, call it *silly*. More than ever, I want to tell him – this is who I am, here are the histories I bring, these selves, you will not wish them away.

But such assertion – my family isn't known for it. And in any case, before I could say anything, Dev muttered, 'I love you, Dee.'

'Yes.'

'Why don't we speak of your father instead?' Dev continued. He never stopped.

'What of him?'

'He's in Norway?'

'Yes, he is. A journalist by day. An artist by night. Busy.'

'Ah.'

'Quite simple.'

So four days passed, six, eight –

'The countdown has begun,' Dev said one evening.

'Has it?' And then, in an attempt to be polite, I asked, 'Has it begun for you?'

'A hundred and twenty-five days for our wedding. So I guess it has, yeah.'

'How many hours is that?'

'Well, let's see, over two thousand.'

'Is it? Sometimes I can't make sense of time.'

'Well, then try living on a ship!'

'Yes. Yes, so I read. Steinbeck spoke of this, I think. He said that things are far more complex by the sea, that besides the usual measures of time – the sun's passage or seasons – there are the rolling waves and *"the tides rise and fall as a great clepsydra."*'

'Hmm. You like quoting from books, don't you?'

'Some.'

'And these writers, they are always so – so *intellectual*.'

I laughed. 'Sometimes.'

'And I like hearing you speak of them, because then – you smile. You have a dimple.'

I looked away. 'I have a long day tomorrow.'

'Okay.'

'School.'

'Yes. Would you – I want to see more of you.'

'More?'

'Show me – I feel like I haven't seen enough – your knees – '

'There's time enough for that, Dev.' My voice. Ice.

'I'm sorry. Sorry. I didn't mean to offend.'

'You haven't.'

'I'm impatient. It's stupid.'

'See you soon.'

'Okay – okay. Buh-bye'

Dev waved and, ever obedient, disappeared.

The next morning, as Dev spoke, I watched my corner of the room, the rows of shelves, books. I read their spines, heard a rustle.

Bodies.

More books.

What are you looking at, Dev asked, and I shifted my gaze and said, a restless bird, an overreaching tree, a moth. And he laughed and muttered, you are a strange one.

I concealed my hands beneath a bedspread, clenched my fists, livid that despite everything I seemed unable to move past that distant afternoon or the ones that followed – the last especially, with its plea *marry me*, the rebuff.

What's up, Dev asked, and I lied – a veteran now – Ranja and I fought; Tasha forgot to call; what can I tell you, I live with Mamma.

And Dev, sweet, too sweet, whispered, 'Don't worry, once we're married, it will all be fine.'

# 2.

The truth is that it was all too much – Dev Sahil America Bombay books marriage the voice –

'I need to get away,' I told Tasha.

'Why don't you visit me?' she suggested.

It was just like my sister to overlook the precariousness of flight. It was just like me to yield to suggestion.

Spurred on by Tasha, I made my way from Bombay Central to New Delhi, and from there to my sister's home in Nizamuddin. Balancing my measly possessions in my hands, I walked past a corridor, up three flights of stairs, to a dull pink entrance.

I can see it even now, unlocked, half-open.

I snuck in and watched an immodest terrace before me. In a corner, two rooms. The first had been freshly painted; by its door, wind chimes tinkled and prayer flags flapped in the wind. The other was moss-stained, closed – windows shut, curtains drawn tight.

I called out to Tasha. She wasn't there. Typical. So I dropped my bags and rambled to the edge of her rooftop residence.

From there, I could watch the play of two metropolises, peculiar neighbours. There was a Delhi of commotion and bustle – parrot green and canary yellow autos, each carrying the babble of households; narrow lanes with bazaars, haggling merchants, and bargain hunters; a metro station swallowing queues of tourists; hoardings reaching out for the sky. And then there was a Delhi of stillness – old tombs, crumbling minarets, mosques that had given up on prayer. There were two cities – one living, one dead – so, all at once, I felt that this was a place that understood me.

Delhi – and I'd have never thought it possible – it felt like home.

As I waited on Tasha's terrace, I imagined I heard the creak of a door, an intimation of approaching footsteps, unfamiliar ones. Startled, I turned around. And I saw a boy with a cigarette.

Perhaps it was this that drew me to him – the tip glowing like an exposed heart.

'Sorry – oh, I'm sorry – I didn't know there was someone here,' he said.

'Yes?'

'Had been asleep – was shattered. Only just woke up.'

'What?'

'Jeez, I should introduce myself – I'm staying there – that room, the old one. There. Next to Tasha's?'

'Oh?'

'I was travelling through the city and bumped into her yesterday. She told me that if I needed a place, I could stop by for a day. I leave in a bit. A couple of hours actually.'

'Really.'

'You know Tasha, too?'

'Sometimes.'

'Ah. Cigarette?'

'No.'

'A drink then? There's some in the room – '

'I don't know – '

'Scotch?'

I flinched. If Hans Sperber was right – if the earliest of human languages were no more than mating calls, a string of hurried utterances meant to signify coition – the query, 'Scotch?', was talk at its most primal.

I thought of the interactions I had had just weeks prior, maybe days –

The discussions with Sahil, elevated, always grand – a comment, a rejoinder, a volley of speech, then as though inevitable, contact –

The conversations with Dev, decorous at all times, agreeable, too timid to approach the subject of lovemaking, too eager not to, so eventually there'd be a sense of thwarted potential, not even that, *nothing* –

And then there was the boy on the terrace with a name I can't recall, perhaps because he hadn't disclosed it, never would, saying 'Scotch', *Scotch*, like a caveman's chant, a potent Cuban wail – *let's*.

'Yes.'

'Excellent.'

'Yes.'

I don't know how it happens, how the flesh learns to yield to another. After every split, there seems to be an interlude – a year, a minute, a phase of quiet – when the body lies fallow, neither opening out nor taking in.

I had had my time of stillness – when I had closed the door to Sahil's house; when I had wept, then wiped those tears away; when I had met Dev and had thought that by holding on to him, I'd find a way to carry on.

I hadn't. And I wanted the hush to end.

So, there on the terrace, far from the men I knew, close to a stranger with tobacco breath, it all seemed exceptionally easy – the submission, the dance of body and body, the eventual withdrawal, the solitude.

'What brings you here?' I remember the boy asking.

I shrugged. 'I don't know.'

'Work?' he pressed.

No, I conceded.

'Close friends?'

'If only.'

'Sightseeing?'

'Not quite.'

He smiled. 'I think I know what it is like.'

'Do you?' I questioned, baffled at his presumption.

'Sometimes you're on an escalator. Y'know? And then there's no turning back.'

I nodded.

I don't recall what followed – if I gulped down the Scotch, spoke of things inconsequential and predictable, posed the question, 'Do we go inside?' or acquiesced when he made the proposal. All I know is that ten minutes later, I was in a room with the stranger-boy who was no more than twenty years of age.

He was young, and therefore he was exquisite – this I can tell for certain. But as little as I remember of him, his features, I recall the space we occupied, its flourishes – the sap green curtains drawn across the windows; the faded painting nailed into the wall, a vague impression of a Monet; the scarred lamp throwing a dull shadow; the unironed clothes littered by the mirror; the stained concrete floor; the patternless bedspread.

We were together, the boy and I, and sometimes, when I try, I can picture the scene second by poised second – as though it were a trailer from a movie – as though this wasn't me letting my lips brush against another's, but an artiste with easy hair and watchful eyes and a body of absences conducting an orchestra of tongues and fingertips.

How uncomplicated it was, all of it, the play of two beings. The deliberate shedding of clothes, blouse and skirt, shirt and trousers; the chest of the boy, bare as the wing of a moth, leaning over; the girl's body, near-luminous, exposed beneath – breasts firm, thighs parted.

I thought of things, several things, that day as the boy drew close. I thought of Sahil, of how he'd ask at such times, almost paternal, if I was okay – *'Are you fine, Dee? Are you sure?'* Of how his hand would press against my mouth, trying to seize the response, as though it were animate, precious. Of how he'd smile when I'd mumble *'yes'*, then offer a word in return, *'lovely'* or *'sweet'*.

I thought of Dev, of how he'd linger close – to catch a whiff of the day's scent on my body or for something more obvious, to feel the pressure of skin. Of how he'd hold back as though terrified of transgressing some unwritten social law.

I thought of how this, all of this, had disappeared or would change – how Sahil's voice had turned silent; how this vague yearning that Dev felt for me would dull. If this, the sum of this, signified love –

All at once, I felt the need for words, for their comfort, their wild assurance. 'Talk to me,' I urged the boy, the way I'd have implored Sahil on finding him apart, separate, after an evening of tenderness. The boy paused, mumbled, 'What?', then said fast, too fast, 'Your eyes are lovely.'

I nodded, conscious that this is what he had, this is all I'd get – a sentence that been offered earlier by this boy to other girls, by a billion men to their lovers – so I held on to the next best thing, the only thing, a body, and sensed the boy's blank mouth hover near my nipples, his heedless being plunge into my own. Bereft of sentiment, panic, the self-consciousness that comes with imagining a future, I pulled him into me, held him, counted each second rhythmically like an expert metronome – three, six, seven –

– Till each muscle in my body turned taut, hummed like frenzied bees, and the boy's back became fluid, a wave of minor spasms. And as he moaned and his eyes closed and his fingers doubled into his palm, I thought, surely, surely, this nothing-moment is grander than all the lovesick hours I've known.

Fifteen minutes later, we were naked on the bed, the boy and I, neither ashamed nor anxious, a distinct gap between us, his fingers clutching my fingers as though we were old friends. He fished for a matchbox in the clothes he had surrendered, recovered a cigarette, took a drag, then passed it on to me.

There, in the room, while smoking my first cigarette, I thought of the mundane, the ordinary – the unoccupied cobwebs by the ceiling, wisps of dirty grey; the stained spot on the floor; the mirror tilting as though bewildered by what had come to be, by what may have been once.

So I thought of the start, the beginning of all beginnings – of the very first man making peace with the body of another. I thought of Adam and Lilith. Once they had solved the riddle of copulation, Lilith, full and whole, left the Garden of Eden. This – this was how it was meant to happen – a thin, taut wire of delight, almost divine, and leave-taking.

Till Adam, dissatisfied with what he had got, reached for something ordinary – a lasting presence – volunteered a rib, and got Eve in return.

This is what he bequeathed, what we had come to inherit – the blessing of time without end. And un-feeling.

An hour later, the boy was gone.

# 3.

I barely spent any time with Tasha in Delhi. She had been nurturing a fledgling romance, the kind she was known for, one that dazzled like a firecracker before abruptly softening. She was distracted. I was distracted.

I returned to Bombay in less than a week, promising to catch up later. Besides, there was nothing to discuss, I told my sister, told myself. Nothing of consequence.

'I missed you, Dee,' Dev said, the night I returned. Then he added, 'How was the capital? Tell me everything.'

'It was – it was absolutely fine.'

'I get that. But tell me more. How is Tasha?'

'She forgot I was arriving. And was busy after. But otherwise she's fine.'

'Good. Who all did you meet?'

'Meet?'

'Go on, confess.' Dev threw back his head, laughed.

As I watched him watch me, I felt as though I was made of cellophane. My thoughts were obvious, my lapses all too clear. 'There's nothing to confess,' I muttered defensively.

'No?'

'No. Really, Dev. *No*. Is this your idea of an inquisition?'

'I'm sorry. I was only kidding. We don't have to speak of Delhi. We don't have to speak of anything.'

'Thank you.'

Dev smiled. 'As long as you are happy, that's all I need to know.'

I looked at Dev, possibly for the first time that night – his face was soap-scrubbed; his teeth were toothpaste-white. He was easy like a billboard, obvious, broadcasting amity and goodwill. I despised myself just then for not responding with equal affability, for holding back. I was unworthy of anything clean and placid, I told myself; undeserving of a man not completely ruined.

'What's up?' I heard Dev say, and I shook my head. *Nothing*.

The next thing I heard was Dev's voice again, whispering factoids about America and how I'd like it more than Delhi or Bombay or any other place I may have known. I saw his camera swivel and reveal a room, a door, lights. This is your place, he said, *home*.

Something about the word, its simplicity, something about the voice that offered it, so gentle, made me yearn to trade in kindnesses. But how? I came with truths, rough and calloused, little else.

Then again, the truth, no matter its texture, must be worth something.

Dev, I wanted to say, Dev, I slept with a boy. Dev, his body was impossibly young. Dev, you asked how Delhi was? One past slid under another.

'Dev.'

'Yes?'

'I –'

I couldn't. So reminded now of the flimsiness of my resolutions, made aware, all too keenly, of my failings and faults, I did the one thing, the only thing that could bolster my sagging morale. 'America,' I said. 'I'm sorry, Dev. I cannot call it home.' There. I rejected his offer.

And yet Dev, dear Dev, he didn't get it. 'Oh, it will be,' he said with a nod. 'It will be.'

So this is how the days went by. Fuelled by Dev's convictions.

'You know. I'm off,' he said one day. 'Three months at sea. Unreachable. So there's some respite from my calls.' An awkward laugh. 'And then we all know what follows.'

'Yes?'

'Our wedding, of course.'

'Yes.'

# 4.

For the next three months, I was well. I went to work. I did what I was told to do – shopped, dressed up, hand-delivered invites. Yet all along I told myself that I was living someone else's life. This was play-acting. None of it was real.

And when my sisters arrived – first Tasha, then Ranja, giddy with joy – there was so much to listen to, so much sound, that it was easy to block out memories of Dev's voice, his persistent I love yous, his buh-byes.

'How has marriage treated you?' I asked Ranja the day she arrived.

She smiled, 'It's everything they say it is.'

'And what is that?'

'Perfect.'

'Tell me more.'

'You'll find out for yourself,' she said, every word a secret.

'That's helpful.'

'No, really. You'll experience – what's the word for it? – well, let's just say, *stillness*.'

It was the sort of answer one could expect from Ranja – glib and easy – and that day, it *especially* irked. To me, marriage hardly seemed synonymous with 'stillness'. For overnight, it aimed to catapult me from a space of hazy alliances to one of firm, statutory ties; from unknowing to definitude; from possibility to a kind of closure.

On the eve of my wedding, this especially terrified me – the end. I realized that I had staggered towards marriage trusting in a past, in its capacity to reassert itself. And yet there I was, confronting, not the resurrections I had bargained for, but a slipping away.

'That's bullshit,' I told Ranja. She clicked her tongue, then smiled patronizingly. Such outbursts, she must've thought, were to be expected from an overwrought bride.

'Look, did I show you my new dinner set?' my sister clumsily changed the subject.

'What?'

'See!' She pulled out four blue plates from a bag. 'I told Mamma – she didn't mention it to you? Bone china. I got these from Italy.'

'Okay.'

'I was telling Jay we'll preserve these for our children. When we have two, a boy and a girl, we'll arrange the plates on the table, a neat circle, and – '

'Ranja, please – '

'Anyway – how silly of me. Let's talk about you.'

'Let's not.'

I couldn't say what was worse – being subjected to Ranja's plans, all revolving around crockery, or having her aim her attention at me. I left.

I drifted towards Tasha who was concluding a protracted conversation with a boy – perhaps the one who had preoccupied her during my Delhi visit.

'Insufferable,' I said, drawing a chair, still reeling from the aftershocks of my conversation with Ranja.

'I agree. He is.'

'No. Not your guy. *Her.*'

'Her?'

'Ranja.'

'Ah, her. Yes.' Tasha smiled. Then quickly, she whispered, 'Listen, I shouldn't tell you this, not now, but – '

'Yeah?'

'Sahil called.'

*What?* My heart, I could feel it pound. *When?* I could barely hear above the blood's commotion.

'It was a few hours ago.'

*And?*

'And he said that he had tried calling you. That your phone was switched off.'

*It was.*

'It doesn't matter, Dee. Anyway, he traced my number, called me, said he wanted to speak to you, could I help – I obviously refused to comply. I asked him what the hell he wanted. He was very evasive, you know? He claimed he longed to make amends – he wished he had phrased his hesitation better. That's what he said. I told him off, don't worry. I told him you had better things to do than care about – '

'How could you?' I recovered my voice. The wrong pitch. Too loud. I clambered to my feet. 'I must call.'

Tasha pulled me back. 'Why? So he can tell you *no* once more – but with greater smoothness?'

'He won't.'

'But he will – '

'How d'you know?'

'Isn't it obvious?'

*Not to me.*

'I spoke to him, remember?'

'Then why would he call?'

'I don't know – or I do. Dee, he's a writer, don't you see? He has to end things well.'

I sat down. Palms damp.

Tasha's voice changed, became kind, 'How're you doing?'

'How do you think?'

Tasha held me. 'You're strong, Dee. You'll be fine. Though you shouldn't have rushed things with the wedding.'

'I didn't plan to.'

'Then what happened?'

'I released a statement. And the time was ripe. And it came to be.'

'That has been known to happen.'

'Yes. And then I think – if that instant was hexed, if only I had known – what all I could've asked for, so many things.'

'Like?'

'Like redrafting that day – the day I lost Sahil.'

It's something I had often considered at night while curled alone on a bed – that I could use a second chance. If I had it – if I could recover that late afternoon – I'd be glad for Sahil's breath on my shoulder, the familiar shape of his hands, the intimacy of his fingers.

I'd be glad for cold coffee and the spine of books and a man tap-tapping at a keyboard. I'd be glad, so glad, that I wouldn't have to ask.

And yet – yet a part of me knew that if I relived the instant, I'd ask, then respond exactly the way I had. I would likely shift the angle of the light, phrase my offence differently, be more fluent about my leave-taking – but I'd leave.

'You know, you'd still have left,' Tasha read my mind.

'You think?'

'Maybe here's why there are no second chances – we do what we were meant to the first time.'

I circled the floor with my toes. 'Yes.'

I can't remember what followed. If Tasha received another call or if I left her room because what else was there to do? But I do recall standing outside the kitchen, hearing a voice quivering at the edge of a sob – 'Okay, but why?' – then changing in texture, becoming a stern hiss like a cat's. 'Enough! I don't want to know about you and her, okay? I just don't – '

My shadow must have announced my arrival, for suddenly, the voice turned quiet, then became exuberant. 'Oh, I'm glad, so glad. Get well, honey.' Ranja spun around, looked at me, her eyes crinkling into a smile. 'I didn't know you were here. All well?'

I nodded.

Ranja continued, 'Jay unfortunately must skip your wedding because he's unwell. He says he will miss being around. Jay says he gives his regards – '

'Okay. Though frankly – '

'Did I show you my new dinner set?' Ranja rushed out, returned, 'Look, isn't this gorgeous?' My sister pulled out a plate, held it against the window so it shone blue. 'It's perfect. See. A full circle.'

'Yes.'

Ranja got hyperbolic about the plate, and I stopped paying attention. I briefly considered Jay and her and, on the face of it, their perfectly rounded lives in Dubai – there they were, their moon-plates before them, and their future children.

And then I thought of kintsugi – of the Japanese tradition of valuing artefacts not entirely whole, so the artists of this island-nation highlighted all the fault lines on ceramic objects in shimmering metal.

Evidently, Ranja did not care for the Japanese school of thought. She wanted completion. She wanted jejune excellence. She wanted a dinner plate, not a splintering-rejuvenating universe.

'Oh, Dee, if only – ' Ranja's voice, a quiver.

'Yes?'

My sister's hands trembled, so suddenly, the plate wobbled, slipped. It crashed.

The moment remains suspended in time, so even now I can see it. The giant window. The light rushing in and outlining the fragments strewn on the floor, shards of tear-blue china. Ranja standing over the debris, her eyes conveying neither sorrow nor surprise. A gasp, probably mine.

'No!' I hollered, and stooped, attempting to collect what remained of the day, of the dinner plate for a family yet to be born. I tried piecing together what was broken – only, unlike those Japanese artists, my aim was to conceal the afternoon's catastrophes.

It was futile, the whole exercise. 'I'm sorry,' I said.

Ranja did not respond. Instead, quiet, she collected the shards – each piece placed delicately on her opened-out pallu – leaned over the windowsill, let them go. Then she turned to me, her mouth curving into a smile, and asked, 'Did I show you my new dinner set?'

I looked at my sister, shook my head, mystified.

'Here, isn't it lovely? I was telling Jay, we'll preserve these for our child. When we have one, a girl, we'll arrange the three plates on the table, a neat semicircle, and – it will be – '

'Perfect.'

'Exactly. It will be perfect.'

'Yes.'

# 5.

Soon after my sisters' arrival, Dev reached Bombay.

Too soon, the wedding day followed.

It was an unusually blustery morning – trees swaying, shedding leaves; sari pallus billowing like fishing nets; a woman's neatly braided hair escaping those bobby pins, flying.

Miss Mimmy, overseeing all formalities – the display of flowers, tubby marigolds ('Why is this one wilting? What will people say?'); the arrangement of chairs ('I want the front seat, okay?'); the food and the drinks ('No whisky, no marriage!') – seemed most flustered about the weather. 'The canopy will fall on people's heads, I tell you. It will be like – what's that movie? *Twelve Weddings and a Funeral* – only here there'll be many-many funerals and no wedding!'

As the make-up artist slapped on layers of pink glop on my cheeks, I wanted the prediction to come to pass. I wanted a thunderstorm, great, fat drops of rain, a flood that would wash away the chairs and tumid marigolds and sweep me back to a place that I missed.

I missed Sahil. I missed him enough to send him an invite – drop it outside his door, then flee – in the slim hope that he'd read it, make it to the wedding, and claim me back. I was relying on Hollywood dreamscape, on happenstance and joyous endings, and especially on a gallant lover who'd publicly seek my love. But when I paused, as I was compelled to in the make-up room, I saw the past and future all too distinctly – Sahil's likely failure to have spotted the invite and his impassiveness even if he had read it. He was the last person to make dazzling overtures of love.

'Stop squinting,' the make-up artist brusquely ordered, drawing from her purse a fat stump of kohl. Mamma appeared out of nowhere – as always, a streak of colour – and rearranged a pleat on a misbehaving pallu. Miss Mimmy fluttered close, pinched my chin, teased, 'What's this, my dear? Lost in thoughts about your man?'

I must've been peeved, for the make-up artist scolded, 'No scowling, please!' I erased the grimace, unflexed a raised eyebrow, forced myself to look indifferent.

I wasn't indifferent.

'Look at that, tears in your eyes!' Miss Mimmy cooed. 'Every bride feels this, beta. But then – then it always gets better, no?'

The make-up artist nodded, repainted my eyes, told me, 'It's okay, the liner is waterproof,' then led me to Mamma who hurried me out. The wind still blowing.

And so the wedding – with chatter and baby wails and the boom of barrel-shaped drums.

The priest, as master of ceremonies, commanded, cast your right foot forward; bow before the fire; place a hundred-rupee note in my palms.

Commanded, feed her milk; feed her sugar; be provider, man.

Commanded, still commanded – Dev, always Dev – take this girl as you would barren land; grant her the richness of soil, a good yield.

Yes.

Take this girl, wipe away her past, write what you will on the blank slate that is her body.

Yes.

Take this girl.

Yes.

Take.

Yes.

After this, I focused not on the event itself, not on the smiles on the faces of unknown relatives, not even on the seven giddy circles around the fire, but on stray things, irrelevant, relevant. I thought about a film I loved. *Her*. In it, when Theodore asked his incorporeal lover, a computer-generated voice, '*Do you talk to someone else while we are talking?*' the voice, smooth as brandy, said, '*Yes*'; said, '*To 8,316 others*'; said, '*Of these I love 641*'.

I remembered, too, something else, a fact disclosed by Tasha –

where did she read it? I cannot say – of a faraway community where every woman was urged to have numerous lovers – storytellers and mathematicians and weavers and magicians – so each whit of semen would contribute to her yet-to-be-formed foetus, every touch would chisel a step in the twisted ladder of her future baby's DNA. If a woman were to forget the men she made love to, obliterate them from her memory, her baby would be half-formed, never whole enough for birth.

Who forgot to tell those OS voices, those women in far-flung worlds, to erase their histories; who encouraged their men to write on bodies brimming over with experience; who –

That night, the first of our marriage, I was vacant. Dev and I were ushered into a hotel room – one that tried desperately to look ritzy, with chandeliers dripping crystals and wallpapered walls and faux marble flooring.

I went to the bathroom, locked myself in, removed whatever needed removing, the anklets and the nose ring and the beads crowding around my neck. The armlets and the bright red bangles. The safety pins and my grandmother's brooch.

Then I walked up to Dev. I'm yours, I said.

I had no time for preciousness and pretence – for coyness, for an anxious pulling away, for a 'no' that really meant 'maybe', 'yes', or perhaps, after all, 'no'. A pause, the tiniest break in proceedings, and I would have to wrestle with second thoughts.

That night, I did not want to deal with second thoughts – of what use were they anyhow? – Sahil hadn't –

I stopped myself. I made my pallu slip, my hair come undone, the sari unravel. I lay down and let Dev claim me as was his wont. He lunged, schoolboyish – his mouth wet, a cod out of water; his hips flailing; his fingers hungry, irresolute, fumbling with loose ends, a bra strap, a knot in a drawstring, a body separate from his own.

That night I learnt of another kind of lovemaking – without cadence, without sound, neither hesitant nor engrossed. *Write what you will on the blank slate that is my body.*

# Abroad.

*That means it's noon, that means we're inconsolable.*

# 1.

Three days later, after those mandatory farewells and a host of hurried comments – after Mamma's 'eat well' and Amamma's curt 'where's my brooch?' – my body travelled to Dev's country.

There I was in a driveway of rain-drenched Providence, America, jet-lagged, an overlarge suitcase by my shoes. I heard a key turning. I saw Dev step in, turn around, come back to get me. I felt his fingers wrapped around my hand, still strange. I followed him and walked through the house like I would any other place – a cheap restaurant, a motel, a government building, they were all the same, walls, windows, a ceiling too close. Dev kept talking, throwing words – kitchen, saucepans, bathroom, towel, balcony, lock, bedroom – a smile here, his. I nodded, comprehending nothing at all.

Then, clumsily, Dev scooped me up in his arms, let me drop on to his bed as he would an ungainly supermarket bag, and dived in. I let him, sensing the import of this ritual, this claiming of my body in his native country, these kisses on a familiar bed. Minutes later, Dev was asleep, his arm splayed across my torso. Then he woke up, mumbled, 'Is there tea?'

I collected my clothes, said neither a no nor a yes, walked away.

Dev was with me for two months. For sixty nights, we shared a bed; for sixty mornings, we made polite conversation over breakfast. Some afternoons were a haze of paperwork involving banks and credit cards; evenings were devoted to dinner, reticent tea lights placed between us.

And then there were those nights when Dev tried introducing me to the friends he had spoken of – the static group that included the middle-aged Yuvraj, his garrulous wife, and Mahesh, several years his senior, mostly silent. The first time we met, Dev introduced me as 'the missus', told them I had a 'book habit', and after that, since there was little else to append, the conversation swerved towards simpler subjects – sports, a new restaurant, the latest car. I held on to my glass of wine, twirled it, asked for a refill. Suddenly, the garrulous wife – who had introduced herself as Nina – leaned forward, whispered, 'Don't drink so much. No good if you're having a baby.'

I started. 'Sorry?'

'My advice? Be done with it.'

'What?'

'Two sons in two years. Now, *that's* off my list.'

I was at the edge of judgement – when it struck me, I couldn't act as an arbiter. I daren't. In any case, Nina was willing to take me under her wing, and god knows I was happy to consent to all benevolent offers.

Hours later, when Dev asked if I liked his friends, I evaded the question, claimed I liked him more. I was learning the art of obfuscation.

I was also learning the art of looking the other way.

I came to ignore Dev's half-hour ritual of trimming his toenails before bed (sending the clippings flying, then scrupulously gathering each one); his mortal fear of tea and coffee stains, so he'd strew coasters across the house; his desire to create neat piles of objects – clothes, napkins, plates, cups; his fondness for to-do lists and receipts and itineraries; and his need to schedule everything by the hour – 9 a.m. breakfasts, a 10 a.m. shave, 11 a.m. and a hurried attempt at lovemaking, often aborted.

I believe Dev had to make his share of adjustments, too, and when troubled beyond measure, he'd quietly try addressing my sins of omission. He'd rearrange the clothes I may have flung across the bathroom; wipe the cold coffee rings near the bed; rescue the receipts I may have tossed into a dustbin –

Besides, Dev seemed sufficiently absorbed by the newness of matrimony – by hormones and breath, cohabitation and sharing – so my daily slip-ups didn't overwhelm him, not completely.

For sixty days, my disorderliness remained 'cute'. On the sixty-first day, after scrubbing the last of the coffee splotches on a table, Dev let his bag roll out of the house. Before leaving for five months, he asked if I'd miss him. I tossed my head back, laughed, said, 'You're silly, aren't you – '

He believed – he must have – that the statement meant a yes.

# 2.

After Dev left, I studied his house for the first time. Walls that were a grubby brown. Photographs – who were these recurring figures? – an anxious woman and a chubby boy, his front teeth missing. Old trophies – whose? – cleaned till the letters had all but faded. Antique furniture with ornate whorls – look how the dust collects!

So, for a week, with an old sock and a brush, I scrubbed each awful curl on the sofa. I hid away the India souvenirs, so carefully displayed, so passé – Sanskrit chants on plastic strips; Hindu calendar art; elephants, tens of them, their mirrored bodies reflecting the wall. I approached the curtains, grey and opaque and inconsolable. I drew them back, and pale streaks of light flooded in. How much I had missed this – sunshine.

I walked out, down the road. I realized that in Dev's company I had raised a picket fence between myself and all else – a husband, a country, people – and had barred one from knowing the other. Suddenly, the fences were gone, and Providence rushed towards me – tall trees, a slate-blue sky, flowers, frail and soft to the touch. Everything seemed predictable.

Yet, in truth, nothing was. The houses were squat and natty; the gardens with their trellises, proper. Besides there was not a soul on the road, not even a sleeping dog.

I soon found myself approaching an outlet with bric-a-brac haphazardly displayed – embroidered tops and glossy lamps and candelabra and a poster announcing that Jesus loves me. I entered the Salvation Army store, walked past stacks of used books and keeling-over piles of cushions. I peered into a showcase displaying Venetian glass, rummaged through cartons of old skirts and strappy

shoes, tried on a scarf and preened before a mirror. At one end of the
store, I saw rolled-up blinds. 'Are these for sale?' I asked. An attendant
responded, his voice soft, 'Yes, pretty, aren't they? What's the word
for them – *ethnic*, yes, ethnic. You must be from – '

He kept talking as I unrolled the blinds. Slivers of light snuck in
through bamboo slats – a dance of shadow and gold. I could spend
hours watching this, I thought, such play. This could be the rest of
my life. 'I'll buy them,' I said, 'and this too,' grabbing a pair of shoes.
I collected two wrapped bundles, the man still talking softly.

My first purchase, I thought, and easy, thirty dollars. I ran to Dev's
house, my slippers kicking dust, nobody looking. I entered, drew
out a chair, stood on it, still panting, pulled down the grey curtains,
opened a bundle, and held a blind across a window. The pane popped
out at either end, but this only made the room more luminous. That
morning, after dressing all the windows in second-hand blinds, I sat
before one of them.

Another day was done.

Daily, Providence flaunted something – a shop of curios; a pool that
had turned a mossy green; a Chinese lantern; tents offering free drinks
(pitchers and stacked paper cups); the WaterFire Festival –

But soon, all too soon, such sights lost their novelty. I needed a
voice, a comment, a solicitous question. I longed to respond.

I knocked at a neighbour's door, but nobody was home. I rang
a doorbell the next day, and a cat hissed; I fled. I walked back to the
Salvation Army store, but the gabby attendant was missing; the
cashier refused to speak. Desperate, I called Nina, the garrulous wife.
Driven by a sense of national duty – the lone Indian needs help –
she met me. But after a hurried chat, during which time she shared
photographs of her children, she left to be with them.

So, finally, I caught a bus and decided to find my way to a
supermarket. I was wearing a new dress and Salvation Army's
matching shoes that went click-click-click whenever I walked.

On the road, I imagined my day out. I'd talk to the grocery
attendant, say how-do-you-do, invite her home for a meal of rice
and dal or vatha kuzhambu. I didn't know how to cook, not much
anyway. So perhaps I'd tweak the menu, offer Maggi noodles and
ketchup. Indian spaghetti with sauce, I'd call it.

At the supermarket, I approached an aisle, held on to a basket, filled it with tomatoes, milk, cereal bars, pasta, whatever seemed commonplace. I hunted for a checkout attendant, a woman I could bribe – dinner in exchange for conversation. I looked around, but there was no one in uniform, just rows of machines and queues of housewives talking on cell phones. I learnt that, out here, there was nobody to weigh the carrots, comment on the ripeness of bananas, *tch-tch* over the rising cost of beans, recommend a fresh bundle of spinach, or say 'good day, goodbye'. Instead, there were machines that bleep-bleeped when a barcode was scanned or pinged when items were inputted.

I fiddled with my groceries, conscious of the people behind me in line, patient-fidgety-impatient. I tried scanning the tomatoes, but the machine refused to acknowledge them. Someone drew close, a strawberry blonde, her teeth nicotine-stained, her eyes lost behind giant Ray-Bans – 'Need help, hon?' I nodded. Bleeps-pings-bleeps-pings, cash inserted. And my basket was emptied. The provisions – none of which I needed – were bagged. 'There you go, hon.'

Here was the moment I had been waiting for, a chance meeting with a stranger. Now I could ask – what could I ask? – I jumped straight to the point. 'Dinner?'

'I'm sorry?'

'I will cook.'

'What?'

'Company.'

The woman hurried away, and I followed her, abandoning a day's worth of shopping. 'Deeya, Dee for short,' I added by way of an introduction, then shouted before she could vanish, 'New. India. *Talk.*'

I was alone.

I retrieved my bag, took a cab home and had a candlelit dinner. Exactly as I had planned it, Maggi (all the way from India) and ketchup. But all alone.

In the days to come, I actively sought noise and companionship in Saturday bazaars, in plush cinemas, in the pubs frequented by RISD graduates –

– In these watering holes, I made some progress. A young girl, too drunk to discriminate between friends and strangers, took me by the hand and disclosed a past of frivolous liaisons. Then she said, holding her swooning head in her hands, 'I'm tired of it, bloody tired – you know what I'm talkin' about?'

I shrugged. 'I'm married, what would I know?'

Even as I said it, I sensed I had erred – that I had, by way of a statement, sliced a chasm between the two of us; that by flaunting my imagined certainties, I had poured scorn on her narratives of flux. She tottered to her feet. I apologized, 'I've been there, too, you know. I have.' But she laughed, and I knew it was too late to make amends.

Then there was the professor. Higgins was his name or something just as reminiscent of *My Fair Lady*. I must have told him I had a crush on Rex Harrison, mentioned that he looked like the actor, and he must have thought me a flirt – for, all at once, he told me he could get accustomed to the Indian Eliza's face. I smiled, thought I'd play along. Sit in his car and go some place, a whirlwind of city lights receding.

But suddenly I feared my capacity to follow through and let this lie pile on a litany of falsehoods. So I showed Higgins my ring, said, 'I am sorry, I must go.'

In the weeks that followed such pub crawls, I tried reading – but stories reminded me of my loneliness. I attempted writing – but I had nothing to tell.

I'd frequent Panera, the closest coffee shop, order an iced coffee, connect to free Wi-Fi, and wait for my sisters. Sometimes Ranja would pop up, a steady green dot on Skype, her voice high-pitched and pleased – 'Jay has planned a *fab* holiday in the Maldives!'; 'I'm knitting the most *stunning* sweater for Mamma!'; 'We're done painting the apartment – I can't tell you how *gorgeous* it is!' Talking to Ranja meant attending to a monologue, one studded with exclamations and superlatives. I couldn't cut in with my ennui.

So I'd wait for Mamma. Each time she'd call, she'd ask of the WaterFire Festival in Providence. She'd seek the details like a child angling for reassurance – 'Tell me the same story,' the little girl says, 'tell me it's whole.' So I'd speak of the downtown waterfront as it would appear on certain Fridays – a fading blue river with a never-ending row of floating lumber – and of the abrupt appearance of fire tenders. They'd hold torches, these beings slipping by in vessels, stoop over, retreat as each plank of wood would erupt into light. One hundred floating bonfires. The air would be thick with the scent of wood-smoke, the water warmed by fire. On such evenings, I'd tell Mamma, on such evenings, it felt like the night would never descend.

But it was Tasha I longed to speak to most, and she'd listen, patient, while I'd tell her nothing significant. Daily, she'd call with minor stories – the classes she skipped, the ripe guavas she purchased, the room that had sprung a leak. These morsels – they were enough to engross me for a day, mitigate my solitude.

I must have been especially lonesome one morning, and Tasha, the sorceress, could tell. Her voice filled the coffee shop. 'Do you remember the story Amamma told us as children?'

*Which story,* I wondered, listless. *There were so many.*

'Of Ilmatar?'

*No, not really.*

Tasha – in a tone akin to one employed by my grandmother, brusque and intolerant of questions – began her narration.

*Once upon a time, there was only a flat surface of wetness. Then, above it, there came a vast, wideopen sky. On this was born a girl, Ilmatar.*

*One day, Ilmatar sought the world below – those mysterious blue waters. She rolled over, descended. River-sea-lake surrounded her body, rain drenched her skin. Ilmatar was unable to rise, make her way back to her sky dwelling.*

*For seven centuries, Ilmatar floated on water; for seven centuries, she waited –*

*– Till, one day, a bluebird, seeking a place of rest, perched on her knees, laid a golden egg, and warmed it with its puffed-up belly. The egg ripened.*

*But no birdling would emerge from its yellow eye. Rather, one half of the hatching egg would form land and the other half would become air. The whites would turn into the moon and the yolk would be the sun.*

*All things – from the earth to the stars – are born in times of aloneness and quiet.*

Yet, marooned as I was in wet-wet Providence, I knew no such certainty. All I could see was a girl like Ilmatar – me – submerging, then bobbing, sinking, and rising, for months, decades, *seven hundred years –*

There were no bluebirds here.

# 3.

One month passed. Then three. And a succession of Skype chats at Panera with Tasha, Ranja, Mamma.

Each day, Mamma followed the same timetable, pinging Ranja, then me, then Tasha. In order of birthdate, no favourites – now that everyone was alike, remote. She rarely had anything of import to say. But hers was a voice, and that had value.

One morning, Mamma's whoop cut through the murmur of customers. 'A letter, Dee!'

'A letter?'

'Your father – he sent me a letter.'

'He did?'

'It was by the door. An aerogramme. Blank.'

'Blank?'

'Blank. Nothing on it. Who else would do that?'

'Well – '

'Don't you see? He's coming home.'

I watched my mother, her face soft, gentle furrows between her brows, a dull crease by her mouth. Suddenly, Mamma seemed old. Age had crept up on her while she was – doing what? – letter-hunting. I had always imagined that the process of ageing was leisurely, even polite – one wrinkle, a long pause, then another. But no, all at once, it seemed spur-of-the-moment, business-like, intent on getting a thankless job done.

I tried ignoring its onslaught and clutching on to a more restful past. I failed.

It's strange how swiftly new memories supplant the old. As I sat in the coffee shop and tried picturing the Mamma I once knew – that

streak of colour spinning from room to room; the intrepid surveyor
of mushrooms, sari hoisted, sneakers muddied; the one in the kitchen
stirring sambhar and humming distractedly – I realized that I could
not reclaim my mother, not entirely. The moments were there, but
the person inhabiting them was now frailer, older, similar to the one
chattering on Skype, saying, a letter, your father, home.

How is one to respond to age? Perhaps with kindness.

So I told my mother, maybe you're right, maybe it's happening,
maybe Daddy, at last, is on his way home.

Mamma smiled. 'I knew you'd see it one day.' Her tone grateful.
And I smiled back.

It surprised me that I had begun caring a lot less for the truth.

'Do you wish you could live your life again with today's wisdom?'
I asked my mother.

'I no longer have use for such wishes.'

'No?'

'No. You're not listening. Your Daddy, he's coming home!'

I thought about how an earlier self might have responded – a
rolling of the eyes, snide asides to the sisters. Now, I was just happy to
know Mamma's voice, hear it tripping o'er with joy. Now, there were
things more important than facts – hope, for instance, or camaraderie.

I wish my mother had flung my question back at me, asked if I
would've liked to live again with today's wisdom. For in response, I'd
have said yes. In response, I'd have admitted that I'd have done things
differently – wrestled with the details of my father's whereabouts a lot
less; studied Mamma's private life more gently; devoted fewer hours
to Sahil's past, to his women, to his bona fide histories –

'Tell me about the WaterFire Festival!' Mamma interrupted.

So I repeated what I recalled of it.

'How are you?' she asked abruptly, not expecting a reply.

I offered one because there was no one else to share my day with.
'I met Nina last evening – she is Dev's colleague's wife, remember?
And she told me we could meet again in a fortnight.'

'Oh, good, so you have friends.'

'I wouldn't call Nina that – but a presence, yes. And I met a man
while going to Cumberland by bus, and he gifted me the Bible. And
I bumped into a girl somewhere, and we shared a meal and talked

of people – how they're never as simple as they appear. You know?'

As always, Mamma, on being attacked with fiddly questions, ducked for cover. 'Here, speak to Amamma!' she said, and withdrew.

Slowly, like a gathering shadow, my grandmother appeared – face, neck, torso. 'You're going to school regularly?' she asked.

I nodded, 'Yes, I try. Yes.'

'Good. Break some heads.'

'Hearts?'

'Yes.'

'I plan to.'

'And wear push-up bras.'

I heard Mamma gasp, scold, 'Enough, Amma!' Like her, I ought to have been cross – but somehow, that day, I wasn't. Maybe without being wholly aware, I, too, was ageing – if ageing means being less conscious of the body's let-downs. For the first time, I let Amamma's statement go.

'You should visit, you know? Ranja and you and Tasha. Once your father is here,' Mamma said, elbowing her way back to the screen.

'Yes.'

'It will be just like old times.'

'Will it?'

'Of course.'

'I believe you.'

After my mother disconnected, I imagined the tomorrows she spoke of. I thought of her and Daddy – wrinkled – and of my sisters, perhaps fuller, their first greys showing. I imagined us at that dining table – Daddy at the head; Mamma, watchful, opposite; Ranja to her right; Tasha, as always, next to Daddy, cheek jammed against his elbow; somebody, perhaps me, envious, by his free arm.

There we were. Together at last.

Yet, as I pictured the family portrait, pictured the smiles stitched on to our faces, it all seemed inadequate. Unsatisfactory.

Perhaps this, too, is a sign of growing older – family is not enough.

# 4.

When Dev had said 'I'll be back in five months', I had smiled, relieved. Twenty weeks. Two seasons. Yes, much could happen in the interval.

Nothing did.

Instead – a creature of habit – I found myself in one of four places. In Panera where I'd reach out to a family that would answer Skype calls. In a bus orbiting Providence or travelling slightly beyond to Cumberland or Barrington or Greenville. In a pub where I'd speak to professors, Nina or to students who can break the hush settled over my mind. Or at Dev's where I'd tell myself, this is life *forever*.

But it wasn't.

And soon, Dev was expected back.

I wanted to count down the days to Dev's arrival, eagerly anticipate the doorbell's ring, be glad for his companionship, if nothing else. Yet the very idea of his return made me want to break away.

Maybe the reason was altogether simple. Dev left before I could weave my life with his, make him part of the quotidian, the everyday. He remained strange even as he withdrew. And, like most things unfamiliar, he provoked fear or at the very least unease.

But no, I knew such explanations were facile. That even if Dev had chosen to stay, even if we had shared meals and conversations and a house for years, he'd have remained distant, a speck on the horizon that could mean anything or nothing at all.

So what explained my anxiety? Maybe it was that finally my life in the States was acquiring a pattern of sorts. I knew how I'd spend my day – hours at a coffee shop, the occasional drink in a pub, dinner at Dev's house, an uninspired meal, the television flashing images of places I had only read of – Alabama and Arkansas and Delaware. It was all so easy, predictable. Dev's presence then would disrupt the snug schedule of my mornings, upset the numbness of sundown's routines, demand shake-ups, spontaneous responses, originality. This, above all else, ought to have explained my reluctance to have him back.

But no, the argument was convenient, a half-truth. I realized that, if I dared admit it, my unease was linked to the stiff framework circumscribing my association with Dev. That I was married to him. That the word 'marriage' signified more than an oversimple definition from a dictionary – *'the formally recognized union of two people as partners in a personal relationship'*. Rather, the term was burdened with presumption. To have a conjugal relationship meant to love, ask after, give, seek, know steadfastness, be faithful. To look out for, protect, swap life stories, be accommodating, forgiving, well-intentioned. To live with, make love to. To joyfully share a name, a bedroom, a bank account, friends, relatives, itineraries, conversations, dreams.

But in my most honest hour, I reminded myself that my anxiety wasn't linked to marriage or what it implied – for meanings can always be nudged, words can be prodded and reshaped – but that I was married to a man I didn't love.

Even as I rolled that truth in my mouth, tasted it, came to terms with its sharpness, it was time for Dev to return.


The doorbell rang persistently.

I forced myself to leave my spot by the window. I opened the door. I saw a man. The kind one runs into everywhere – in gas stations and supermarkets and offices. The kind one makes polite conversation with – good morning and excuse me and please go ahead. The kind one forgets.

On this man, I searched for a feature I could hold on to, a mole or a cleft chin or a bruise on the forehead. Finally, I spotted something – what was that? – blue lint on black hair. This – this I could use to mark him out.

As I stood there observing the speck, I realized I was watching Dev. Equally, it struck me that I recalled nothing of my husband. For almost half a year, I had been aware of his presence the way one knows the sun's heat at the nape of the neck – real but intangible. Now, suddenly, my husband had assumed a form. He was solid. He needed acknowledgement. I found myself scrimmaging for an appropriate response.

Fortunately, Dev recovered before I could. He hugged me at the doorstep, asked if I was well, proclaimed that he had missed me and had returned with gifts.

I opened a loosely tied brown paper package and found two books. 'Tortilla Flat by John Steinbeck? And The Lost Sailors by Jean-Claude Izzo?'

'Yes.'

'How come?'

'You mentioned them, remember? Before we got married?'

'Oh – '

'And then I googled the authors and the quotes – and presto, I found the books.'

I looked at Dev and was tormented once more by opposing feelings. For an instant, I was overwrought. Books were the nation states I had inhabited with someone else. What was Dev doing trespassing?

Yet my more rational self saw the absurdity of this stance. Dev wasn't encroaching; he was reaching out. I had to, at the very least, react with the warmth the gesture deserved.

And so I tried. 'Thank you,' I said. 'I want to hear all about your time on ship.'

Dev laughed. 'Oh, there's time enough for that.'

He fumbled. Then didn't. As he undressed himself, undressed me, I watched the fleck on his hair, watched it tumble down, a blue blur, watched as it skimmed across the carpet. I stooped, picked it up, pressed it to his hair.

'What are you doing?' Dev muttered.

'Nothing,' I said, then confessed, 'I'm annotating your body.'

Dev laughed, 'Yes, I forgot you're odd.'

What does it feel like to make love to a household stranger? That afternoon, I knew. There were glimmers of remembrance – the way Dev lunged while making the first move; his mouth, overeager; his fingers fiddling with a buttonhole – which made him seem familiar, even trusty. But then there was his voice, the texture of his palms – things which should have been intimate, but weren't, rendered new by time.

I didn't know who I reached out to. I knew even less what to expect of my body – if it would curl into an open quote and accept this man's weight; or lie prone and motionless; or mimic, hip swaying against hip. With a lover, the body is instinctive, responding like a sitar to the gliding of fingers. With a stranger, the body is performative, keenly aware of its range, amplifying strengths, making light of each failing. But with the household stranger – at such times the body is reticent, folding into itself.

After half a year of nullity though, this, too, suffices, leaden hands and restrained breath.

Later, when we were done, Dev, only half-awake, told me about the games he played with fellow sailors, of deck quoits and the balls made of masking tape.

'Did you see anything special?' I asked him.

'Actually, yes. *Ace Ventura: Pet Detective*. I liked it.'

'The film? But what about places? You must've got shore leave?'

'Well. We stopped at Zeebrugge for twelve hours, during which time the cranes and carriers did their job.'

'Ah. And you hopped ashore?'

'No. Not really. Terminals these days are built for deep water – it's rare to find your way to land.'

'Really?' I frowned.

Suddenly, I felt betrayed. Instead of being offered stories about olive green seas; or giant gulls swooping to snatch food from cormorants; or spinning ice circles; or cities with gypsies and mendicants and palm readers – I was being told of portainer cranes and straddle carriers.

'So – I asked if you could travel with me next time,' Dev's voice cut through.

'What?'

'I don't want to raise your hopes. But if it happens, it could – '

That was all I heard. I imagined myself on board – land no more than a pencil-drawn line; the ocean before me, a world unto itself;

Dev by my side, telling me of the laps he planned to run around the deck, or the gossip in the wheelhouse, or a Jim Carrey film.

'I'm fine here.'

'Are you sure?'

'Yes.'

'That's strange. What do you do when I'm away?'

'I don't know. Scrub furniture. Put up blinds.'

'I noticed.'

'And?'

'Well. It's your home, too.'

Something about the statement pleased me – its evasiveness, the fact that it dissembled. That I wasn't the only one creating smokescreens.

I reached for Dev, kissed his ear, ruffled his hair – blue lint no more. I observed him, so ordinary.

'Is there tea?' he drawled.

'I don't know,' I whispered, gathering my clothes, closing a door.

For three months, my husband was with me in America.

I tolerated Dev's love for spit and polish. Dev gave my mess and clutter a wide berth.

We did not fight, not once.

On the few occasions when Dev conveyed his impatience with the pans heaped on the kitchen ledge or the books scattered by the window, I went for a walk, unwilling to defend these signs of disorder or explain my need for chaos or chide him for his fastidiousness. Any response – censure or confutation – required investment, a giving of words, and thus a giving of self.

All at once, I felt impoverished.

Sometimes, when I look back, I can account for the three months with Dev in bullet points –

- Twenty days in San Francisco, a delayed honeymoon
- One week gardening and mending the old house
- A month of doing nothing really, eating and sleeping and cooking badly
- Three days in New York for bragging rights
- Four weeks devoted to three soaps on Netflix

In between, I'd make plans for evenings at the pub and for Skype calls, brusque and arbitrary. 'Don't forget me!' I'd beseech a flummoxed Tasha each time we'd speak. 'Wait for me!' I'd tell Ranja. I'd hope desperately that this corralled virtual-town wouldn't splinter in my absence.

My strongest memory of this period is a re-memory – a recollection piled upon a recollection. I can't confirm the date, but it was late in the evening, the sky opaque and mackintosh-grey. I was by the Moshassuck, the river winding across the city, more sound than image – a gurgling, a ripple, the swash of something. Oars.

And once more it transformed, the river bursting like a star, a shiver of reds and golds. Everything visible – the piles of wood floating on the water's surface, erupting into flames; the boatmen leaning over, torches in their hands, lighting, still lighting.

'Isn't it gorgeous?' I said, but I don't know to whom. Was it to Dev? No – it couldn't be.

That summer, Dev left once more, this time for two months. As always, he asked if I'd miss him. I tossed my head, smiled, said, 'You're silly, aren't you?'

# 5.

After Dev's second departure, I gathered the courage to venture beyond Panera, beyond Cumberland and Barrington and Greenville.

Now, I was headed to Boston – a city I had visited four times already in six weeks.

The train halted.

I can picture everything that followed – how I disembarked; how I moved with the poise of a native to the Red Line; how I found myself in Harvard Square, in a street with painters, pot-smoking students, panhandlers, and punks.

I wasn't sure why I was there – certainly not to attend a university lecture or cycle by the glass-blue Charles or get photographed by the mock-Flemish Lampoon Castle.

I was there because I had tired of Providence. By that yardstick, I could be just about anywhere – Phoenix or Newcastle or Berlin or Perth. Since it was easy to punch a ticket and catch a train to Boston, I found myself in the student city.

I was in a pinafore, too grey for a morning as bright as this. I smelt of breakfast – coffee and perhaps a dash of wine (of late, a guilty indulgence). I peered at my reflection in a salon door's mirror – my legs had tanned in the New England sun; my arms, formerly lean, had developed little pads of flesh; and my hair spilled below my shoulders. Somewhere between leave-takings and arrivals, my body had acquired a will of its own, had grown in shape, colour, and dimension without my consent.

I wanted to claim my body back, make it submit to my impulses. I walked into the salon, past rows of shampoos and serums, past airbrushed photographs of those with cascading hair, of those without faces. 'No appointment,' I told to the first stylist who'd listen. 'Take it all,' I said. What I heard next was the snip of scissors. The whisper of something falling.

I looked into a mirror. My hair barely reached my shoulders. It fell in rebellious layers across my face. A short fringe like lace trimming touched my forehead. I was meeting the girl I had left behind in Bombay, a former self. Whole years had dropped off, entire histories, the people-cities-things that had made me less sure, even older – Sahil, Dev, the nameless boy, Providence, that house.

With a dishevelled gamine crop, I walked down lanes and by-lanes – Holyoke Street, Auburn Street, Linden Street – wide roads intersecting narrow ones, narrow avenues spinning into dead ends. I did not know where I was going, what for, alert only distantly to signposts and pedestrians and automobiles and drivers.

Eventually, my shoes found themselves outside a bookshop. Inside, there were people, twinkling glasses of wine, stacks of books, prose – Woolf, Nin, Joyce, Carter – and poetry – Yeats, Akhmatova, Heaney, Olds. Instinctively, I squeezed through the door, made my way to the last row of people, an old gentleman making space for me, a young girl softly complaining. I couldn't see far ahead, could perceive only a voice.

'There is a word built of longing. Saudade, the Portuguese say. In the great age of discovery, there were those who sailed towards the unknown. And there were those who waited – women and children – seeking the return of those who had gone. That feeling, accessible only to those who linger – more than melancholy, more than even want – I understand that. Here, by the river, I wait for your return, your absence your most authentic presence. Saudade – '

I stopped listening. I knew that voice. I knew it from another time, its bourbon smoothness. I knew the words, their precise sequence, the build-up. I made my way forward, past reef knots of people, to the front.

The voice died.

Now, the clang of glasses. Gossip and chatter.

'Hello stranger.'

I froze.

'Fancy meeting you here.'

The voice clanged in my head. I was convinced I was in a dream. And yet I couldn't be. My dreams were never set in America, only Bombay. Besides, of late, they had been silent, so when I'd wake up, the ticking of the clock would seem awfully loud.

No, this was real. And I had to do what real people did. Speak.

'Sahil,' I said.

Sahil smiled. If nothing else, I had to mimic his response. I smiled back.

I watched myself being watched by him. How did I appear? Grey, all grey, my hair too short, my arms sunburnt. And then there was him, exactly the way he had been left so many months or years ago – frozen, a photograph – the colour, the texture of skin, untouched by time. I wanted to smudge the impression, make him even older, less brilliant. I wanted to see him stained by my absence.

But no. He remained before me, the same.

'What are you doing here?'

I forced myself to offer answers, reasonable ones. 'I'm – I live close.'

'I see. And soon you'll be a Harvard grad.'

'No. Not Harvard.'

'Tufts?'

'No.' I had to steer the conversation towards easier subjects, those involving others. Him. 'What are you doing here?'

'Well, I was asked to read from my manuscript – '

'The one you had been working on?'

'Yes, that. Did I mention it found a publisher? It happened – '

'Yes?'

'Nothing – well, it happened a week after you left. I didn't get to tell you.'

'No, you didn't.'

'Well, I'm glad you know now. Listen, let me meet some guys here, and then perhaps we could grab a coffee? Actually, let's walk the city.'

'I don't – '

'No is not an option. Just give me five minutes. Ten. Grab a drink.'

And just like that, he went, sometimes lost within a loop of people, sometimes clear. I watched the way he threw his head back and laughed, how he raised his eyebrows when puzzled, the way he waved his hand and smiled while making light of praise. His gestures, the sum of them, were very much the same. They conveyed his alertness to his own beauty.

He was beautiful from a distance. And he was beautiful even as he came near, spoke.

'Sorry, that took longer than I thought. But I'm done – and now, I must learn of Boston from you.'

'I barely know the city.'

'But I thought you studied here?'

'You assume that. You assume too much.'

'I'm chastised. Well, then let's wander the streets as only newcomers can.'

'I really should – '

'Please. For old times' sake.'

So we walked down streets I did not know, past shops I will never remember. Unlike me, Sahil was responsive to everything – to trees ('Red oaks – and here, a future giant, an acorn'), to stores ('My first Graham Greene was apparently from Raven; it carried his signature, the G a streak of lightning'), to people ('Is there anything sadder than a woman alone by a river?'). While the city remained inaccessible to me, even remote, Boston came to Sahil in quick breaths as flowers, as puddles, as a sky that changed, sun-yellow to grey to a hazy blue.

'If you don't like the weather here, an acquaintance said, wait a minute.'

'Ah.'

I envied Sahil. I envied the ease with which he walked, spoke, laughed, as though he were on a field trip with a casual friend. I envied his air of self-possession, his composure. Most of all, I envied the fact that he could shrug off the past, distance it from those hours in Boston.

Unlike him, I found allusions to our history in all things. Where he saw galleries, I heard snatches of our conversation on Gauguin. If he spotted a church, I pictured Moses, the tablet, those remains. When he rescued *Three Tales* from a basement bookstore, I recalled Flaubert and the dress. Our past lay scattered across Boston – who'd have thought? – in its lanes and cafés.

'Let's do coffee at Darwin's. It comes highly recommended.'

'Okay.'

'I still want updates from your life.'

'What's there to tell?'

'Everything.'

When we reached the café, I sat, not opposite, but next to Sahil – like I used to in Bombay. I'm not sure why I planted myself there. It wasn't to reclaim a time that had passed. More likely, I hoped that by restoring something physical – a place, a site – I'd understand the dimensions of our history.

'I've missed sitting with you like this,' Sahil's voice interrupted.

'Oh. I – maybe I should move.' I got up awkwardly.

'Don't be silly. You're fine here.'

I sat by Sahil's side again. We placed our orders.

'Black coffee,' he said and smiled. 'Some things don't change.'

'Yes.'

'And you'll have a cold coffee?'

'No.'

'Then some things do change.'

'Two black coffees.'

'I never thought I'd hear that.' Sahil's tone teased even as my struggle persisted. I longed to find the right quality of voice – easy, dismissive.

'How do you do it, Sahil?'

'Do what?'

'Talk. So careless.'

'What would you have me do?'

'I don't know. *Not* talk.'

'And?'

'And – and pay homage. *Quietly*. To the past.'

'And what would that achieve?'

'Make it seem worthwhile perhaps. Real.'

For the first time that day, Sahil hesitated, measured his comeback. 'You need confirmation that our past is real.'

'Don't you? Sometimes I'm convinced I dreamt it up. Or that I granted it more importance than it deserved.'

'Really? How do you measure such things? Measure *importance*?'

'I don't – Sahil, why are we here?'

Our orders were ready. Two black coffees were placed side by side. I held my cup. It was warm. It consoled.

'Let's start this meeting afresh, Dee. Let me also add that you matter to me. More than you know.'

'Do I? Then why didn't you say *yes* in Bombay?'

'I couldn't back then – though I wanted to explain my stance.'

'You could've called.'

'I did – and your sister wasn't pleased.'

'You could've persisted.'

'You think I didn't? Though, now, it all makes sense – you had left the country. I couldn't reach you.'

'Couldn't reach me? In the age of emails – '

'Fine – fine. I withdrew. Because as much as I wanted you back, I was constrained. I felt I couldn't give you what you needed.'

'You *presumed* you knew what I needed. And then you *presumed* that it was best to retreat.'

'You moved away, too, didn't you? And so far. Continents away.'

'I had no option.'

'And I did?'

'You were always the one with choices.'

Sahil looked away, and I followed his gaze. In the distance, giant oaks shed leaves, shadows slipped away, old lovers sought new diversions – life endured in flux. Yet neither Sahil nor I could star in this forward push, in this dance from old to new to new. We had to reel backward instead – broken spools – spin against time.

'What if I hadn't stumbled into the bookstore, Sahil? Would you have tried finding me?'

'I – I don't know. Maybe, all along, I was relying on a fluke occurrence.'

'How convenient – '

'It's how we met, isn't it?'

'Sahil – why are you even here?'

'To read. To read of the things we touched. Perhaps to record our lives in the city we knew.'

'Saudade. A favourite word. You had told me of it.'

'And so much else. Much that I can't remember.'

I gulped the coffee, the decoction bitter, sharp.

'Sahil – what has changed since I left?'

'I thought we had agreed a long time ago – nothing ever changes.'

'No, we hadn't agreed. You claimed that all things were static, I protested, and you called me young and naïve.'

'Are you still young and naïve?'

'I feel old. And sometimes cynical.'

'Is that so?'

'You haven't answered my question. What has changed since I left?'

'Well, I don't know. I sleep, I wake up, I write, delete, rewrite. Sometimes I read. Or take a walk. It's exactly how it used to be.'

'I see.'

'In any case, that's how it is when you lose someone, no? Nothing gets dismantled. Only now, each day is without heft.'

'I know what you mean.'

'Do you?'

Sahil reached for my hand. It still fit me like a mitt, soft and secure. 'I have a flight to Chicago tonight. I leave for Bombay in three days. I could postpone the future. Stay in America.'

'And do what?'

'Recover what has been lost. Deeya, let me earn you back.'

I heard, couldn't listen. Sahil must've sensed my inability to comprehend.

'Remember koi no yokan, Deeya? I should've told you. I felt it, felt the word, felt that the future *would* yield love the day I saw you doubled up in that bookshop.'

I started. My cup toppled over. I withdrew my hand from Sahil's, rubbed the stain on my dress with bare hands. The smudge blotted, became a foreign country, a continent, refused to disappear.

I thought of Sahil's proposal to be with me in the States for however long it took, to release me from my seclusion, to surround our lives with books, dialogue, camaraderie. I could picture the home we would build together – yellow walls, shelves slumped with novels and poetry, money plants in Mason jars by the window. I'd be lying on a bed, the *New Yorker* by my side; close, the tapping of keys, the sprint of a mouse, click-click-click. How close happiness seemed, how tangible. So, all at once, I wanted to take Sahil up on his offer, plunge, leave Dev and our pretences.

'Sahil.'

'Yes?'

But then it all came back – those last days in Bombay, the whitewashed bedroom, the grilled window. Cramped. Sahil's struggle to accommodate my hurried attempts at growing older, my refusal to be hedged in by his all-too-adult equivocations.

Back then, I thought that permanence, vows, a stolid marriage would heal the breach. But now, I arrived at two realizations – that for Sahil, my absence was a more potent force than my assured presence; and that no formal pact could overcome the impasse our association had reached.

'I live in Providence, Sahil.'

'That's close enough.'

'My husband lives there, too.'

Sahil flinched, held his cup so tight that I feared it would splinter. 'The coffee is good.'

'Yes.'

'I like it.'

'Yes.'

'I –'

'Sahil, his name is Dev.'

Sahil nodded. I couldn't read his expression. His eyes were quiet, his lips pressed close. It was as though he had vacated his body, had travelled a long way, to a place I could not reach. Then, suddenly, he returned, asked, 'When did this happen?'

'The wedding? Last year. I guess – you missed the invite? I had left it for you. Outside your door.'

'I didn't see it. No – no.'

'Oh. I'm sorry.'

'When did you meet him?'

'Dev? Shortly after I left you.'

'How long did you date him?'

'Date?'

'Yes.'

'We got to know each other a few months before the wedding.'

'Why didn't you call to tell me?'

'And what would that have achieved?'

Sahil produced his wallet, drew out ten dollars, maybe more.

'Let me pay,' I protested.

'No, Dee, grant me this privilege. And for once – don't misconstrue the gesture.'

'Sahil – '

'Yes?'

'Why?'

'I don't understand.'

'Why didn't you give us a chance a year ago?'

Sahil smiled the saddest smile I have known. 'Back then, Dee, I thought it was too soon to commit. And now – '

'Yes?'

'And now, it seems I'm much too late.'

Sahil reached for my face, held it in his palms as though it were a thing of glass, and continued, 'There is a moment, there always is in every relationship, when the asking and the giving coincide.'

'What was our moment?'

'I don't know. I thought it was now. But it isn't.'

'No.'

'It escaped when we weren't looking, Dee. It's gone.'

I pulled back, swallowed the tears threatening to surface. We got up as one.

'I want to go to the harbour, Dee.'

'Why?'

'A friend, he told me something. I must see it. Deeya?'

'Yes?'

'Do me this last favour. Accompany me.'

So we caught a cab and went seaward. Boston passed by as wisps of blue – sky, river, a common grackle, glass. I wanted to reach out and trap the colour, make it stick, pin it to my dress, a cheery brooch. But no, it fled like so much else. This time around, while I acknowledged the city's short-lived mementos – the blue-grey rain, those ultramarine shops – Sahil retreated, barely alert to the shape-shifting world outside.

In a while, the cab slowed down, stopped. I could smell the sea, its salt-breath; spot the foremasts of docked boats; hear the voices of tourists exclaiming in foreign dialects. Water shimmered before me and stretched all the way to the sky. We were walking within a blue orb.

'She's somewhere here,' Sahil said.

'Who?'

'At the wharf. Each evening. By the flags.'

'I don't understand.'

'That must be her. The brown dress, a hat, the drooping feather. Yes.'

'Who is she?'

'Saudade.'

'Tell me more.'

So Sahil told me of the mad woman by the wharf. Of how, long years ago, she had fallen in love. He was a sailor – a man who could navigate deep seas by observing the stars, who could predict the approach of storms by watching the flight of birds, who could tell the proximity of islands by looking at a horizon glimmering like tinfoil. He was someone who knew the ways, not of land, but of water.

The sailor planned to cross the rim of the world, study the things that lay outside it. He asked his lady to join him, to be his compass. When asked thus how could she refuse?

On the sailor's last evening in Boston, the lovers were meant to meet by the city's harbour, then sail outwards, beyond.

Even as the woman packed her belongings, she had misgivings. Once she set sail, would she ever find land? What if all the birds vanished? Could the stars get blown out on windy nights? Nothing was certain, all was fickle at sea. Paralysed, the woman clung to things that were familiar, rooted in land – windows, walls, a floor.

The night grew dark, still darker, a messy black, and the woman couldn't bring herself to move. Eventually, there was a flicker of light. Dawn.

That morning, the sea was clear, almost translucent. There was not one ship docked at the harbour. It was as though the preceding evening with sailors and boats and quivering flags had been swallowed up whole by water.

The woman, buoyed up by daylight, walked to the quayside.

'Henry,' she called, for that was the sailor's name. 'Henry, I'm late – but I'm here.'

There was not a sound in response.

'Henry.'

*Silence.*

It's said, since then, every evening, the woman has come to the wharf to find Henry, the ship she missed, the life she almost had. Sometimes she watches boats held fast by anchors. Sometimes she runs, convinced that if she is fast enough, faster than time, she will upend the laws of physics and meet her sailor at the port. And sometimes she catches an early star and tosses it seaward – 'Henry, your compass.'

'Will she find him?' I asked Sahil.

'Do moments ripe for the picking ever return?'

Sahil and I walked hand in hand down the wharf. We could almost have been mistaken for sweethearts.

'Do you love him, Dee?'

'I thought you'd never ask.'

'Well?'

'What do you think?'

Sahil paused, kissed my forehead. 'Promise me this. When the ship arrives, jump on.'

That was the last I heard of Sahil.

I imagine we said our goodbyes – he must've whispered *auf Wiedersehen*; I must've hugged him, sibling-like. I can't confirm these gestures, the parting.

What I do know is this – that at night, as an airplane skidded across the Providence sky, I bolted out of the house, jumped, tried leaping on. But no. It was too high, too far. Gone.

The moment lost.

# 6.

A day after Sahil left, I wanted nothing more than to forget my conversation with him, his offer, my refusal.

Here's what I did. I poured myself a glass of wine, then another. I tried stunning the mind with daytime soaps. I even attempted gardening, mowing at once weeds and rose bushes.

It was no good. Each time a plane flew overhead, I froze.

In a more lucid moment, I decided I needed company, one person to fill the breach left by another. For the first time since Dev left, I counted down the days to his return. I recovered a number that belonged to the distant future – twelve.

Suddenly, I found I missed Dev. Or, perhaps, not him, but what he could offer – a body, a mouth – to make me a being of sensation, no more.

Then again I chastised myself for seeking Dev like I would a spin in a carousel – as a short-lived diversion, blank and feckless.

No, I told myself, not Dev. Not again.

So I sought companionship that was less fraught with self-judgement. I strayed into my regular pub – that refuge where talk came cheap and easy. It struck me that, so far, I had missed learning it by day, knowing it as more than a place of gentle shadows.

That morning, as the pub balanced itself on daylight, its colours shone gaudily, no longer blunted by Edison bulbs and booze. In this deep sea of kitsch, I spotted, not students and professors, but workers – those grabbing lunch or shirking office duty – and a lone figure in a corner, reading – what was that book?

I tried drawing close to it. I stood by the side of a startlingly

young girl. I studied the page she had opened, the words. I knew
them from another time –

*Look at the light through the windowpane. That means it's noon, that means*
    *we're inconsolable.*

'Lovely,' the girl said.
'Excuse me?'
'The lines – you said them so well.'
'I said them?'
'And then, it goes – *Tell me how all this, and love too, will ruin us.*
*These –* '
I didn't wait to listen. I couldn't.
I ran out of the pub, lurched homeward, dodging Sahil, his fingers,
dodging him near red lights, in parking lots, by street lamps, in planes
hovering against giant skies.
Hastily, I called Nina. 'You're free?' I asked. '*Now*?'
'You're okay, Deeya?'
'Yes. I just – '
'You're panting.'
'I know – I mean, I've been busy. You're free?'
'Yeah, I suppose, Sid and Som are sleeping, and Ma's in town. I
could come over for a sec. Better than you taking a cab, no?'
'Thank you.'
Soon, Nina came. She offered cake ('I baked this myself!') and
spoke of Sid ('He's walking, that brat.'). But before she could tell
me of her mother or Som or her husband, I heard myself sobbing.
Fat tears.
'There, there,' Nina patted me gently-awkwardly. 'I knew something
was wrong.'
'Sorry.'
'It's hard, I know, this life we've chosen. But he'll come back.'
'What?'
'Believe me, he will.'
'Thank you,' I whispered. Thank you. Grateful for her voice. And
for a beautiful noun substitute.

# Memory.

*Tell me how all this, and love too, will ruin us.*

# 1.
# *Amamma*

Amamma seemed to have lost Venu. It happened after she dropped off the letter – *I come I go we cannot meet.* Venu did not write back with a plodding come-back-soon; Amamma did not spot him on her street. When she asked a flower-girl, asked about the house that was a perfect square, she was told that it was now an ageing widower's.

Venu had disappeared.

And in the days to come, more of him would peter out. His eyes, for instance, black like squid ink. His build, the lightness of his bones. And last, his pinkie – it was impossible to recall its length, its feel.

And yet Venu hadn't really vanished.

Soon after dropping off the letter, when my grandmother sensed the quiver of a butterfly's wing in her belly, she thought of Venu, of his whereabouts – that he was likely in London, possibly content. As her foetus grew – she could tell, her skin stretched like canvas – she imagined Venu with a wife, with someone who could measure the world with him. When her body suffered a paroxysm of cramps – well, she couldn't think of Venu right then, but she did soon after, when the midwife said, 'I have bad news' – that's when she thought of her lover. And that baby had slipped away like him. A sob. 'I'm sorry,' the midwife commiserated, 'I'm sorry that it's a girl.' Amamma stopped. Her eyes lit up. 'Of course,' she said and reached for her daughter. She named her child something akin to Venu – Vanaja.

For the next four decades, my grandmother thought of Venu – not every day, but often – as being witness to her life and her daughter's. He was there when my mother helped my grandmother make vatha kuzhambu – 'So yum,' Mamma said, and Amamma was convinced that she could spot Venu assessing its viscosity. He was around when mother and daughter made an impromptu trip to Gemini Studio – he measured the breadth of the cherubs' wings. He was an eyewitness to the placid adventures of the household – to the tending of vegetables, to the beach getaways, to the afternoons devoted to story-sharing and ice creams.

He was a presence the day Amamma visited the temple and heard that Daddy was an artist. There he was, Venu, studying the width of the flamingoed canvas while my grandmother spoke to the joshiar; commenting on the thickness of each brushstroke while Amamma and Rangaa sparred; quibbling about the colour of the feathers – 'Yellow, simply yellow,' Venu maintained, while Amamma thought, 'Carroty-gingery-red.'

He was in attendance the morning Rangaa died, counting the number of mourners, counting the ornaments my grandmother was forced to surrender, counting her toes as she studied her reflection.

'*You're such a coward!*'

'*No, I am not!*'

'*Then climb that mountain with me!*'

Venu was a bystander to my grandmother's negotiations at the ticket agent's. That day, Amamma considered catching a flight to London. But then she dismissed the idea. Not because she doubted Venu's presence in the city, but because, all at once, she was apprehensive about the meeting and what it would yield. The first time she had spotted Venu, my grandmother had found him wavering, unable to fulfil the tacit commitment of a knotted forefinger and pinkie; the next time he had appeared only to take leave and scramble on to a faraway vessel; and the third time he had offered so lavishly that there was little to reach out for in the future. Amamma wasn't sure she could live past another washout – watch Venu with wife and child make polite conversation over lunch.

So my grandmother booked a ticket to New York City.

While in Manhattan, in a bookshop (likely the Strand), Amamma came across a story. Of Niu Lang and Zhi Nu.

*Niu Lang was a man like any other who was in love with Zhi Nu, a woman who had descended from a celestial bloodline. When Zhi*

*Nu's mother learnt of their relationship, she dragged her daughter
heavenward, and with one stroke of her golden hairpin, scratched a river
between the lovers. Before Niu Lang could cross it, he was transformed
into the bright star Altair, and Zhi Nu, her hands outstretched, waiting
at the other end, became Vega, the luminous one.*

*For a year, the lovers shone, sending torch signals to one another –*

*– Till it was the seventh day of the seventh lunar month. Suddenly,
thousands upon thousands of magpies appeared, their wings linked like
laced fingers. They formed a bridge of feathers to connect the stars.*

In light-spangled Manhattan, by the bookshop, Amamma asked a
passing stranger if, as with Niu Lang and Zhi Nu, a bridge would
emerge between Venu and her.

In the days to come, it was a thought that often occurred to my
grandmother – when she abruptly caught a train to Bombay from
Madras, or committed to a tense flat-share with her granddaughters,
or gifted her family the stories she had found – that even though she
had chosen not to actively pursue Venu, the heavens would conspire
to make them connect.

How, she'd sometimes wonder, how was that even possible? And
always, in response, she'd go back to the myth of the magpies. She'd
imagine tunnels being hollowed out from clouds, or trees bending
over and becoming solid gangplanks, or crows flying at once to build
a walkway of feathers. Somehow a bridge would emerge.

Years later, the bridge my grandmother had been waiting for
appeared, but under circumstances that were less than magical.

I must picture this like so much else. My grandmother was in the
kitchen, hiding petty change inside a teapot, when she noticed my
mother's copy of the day's newspaper. After reading the headlines,
Amamma decided to skim through the obituaries – a habit she
had acquired after watching a neighbour's skin pucker with age;
after hearing of Mrs Swami's demise; after sensing her own body's
reluctance to obey her commands. Suddenly, death seemed to stalk,
not anonymous beings, but those with names.

There they were, the people whose lives had been snuffed out.
Mrs Kamath, aged sixty, 'deeply missed by her grandson'. Ms Tagore,

nineteen, 'mourned by her mother and brothers'. Jenny, ninety-three, 'in Jesus's loving arms'. Venu –

Amamma, she felt her breath still. 'Venu, 1925–1997. Resident of Hounslow, London. Deeply missed by John and his students.' Against this, a hazy picture of a man – bald, bespectacled, wiry – enclosed within an all-too-square box.

My grandmother found herself at the edge of a bridge of print.

For a long time, she didn't know how to respond – how to move-speak-act when iced-up.

Then, suddenly, she could feel pinpricks. Of anger – at herself for erecting scenes of domestic comity; at Venu for not. Of remorse – for what wasn't, for what had become. Of nostalgia, most persistent. Nostalgia –

Who was it who claimed, *'The people we most love become a physical part of us, ingrained in our synapses, in the pathways where memories are created?'* Venu – the man who had united Amamma's reckless adolescence, those gaunt years of making home and childbearing, the brief moments of flight – was intertwined with my grandmother's neurons.

Now, with him gone – with the vanishing of the being who had run through her life like a thread, in and out – everything risked coming undone. My grandmother was unstitched.

Her startlingly complete face – her eyes which led easily to the bridge of her nose, her nose which dipped into a plump upper lip – collapsed momentarily. Every feature discrete.

Our bodies hold our stories.

As her body gave way, the narratives that were a part of Amamma's inner life began mouldering, too. The strands detached. The mother-source wiped away.

*Aethalides – let's return to him – is seated by the edge of the mighty Lethe, the river that erases all recollection. Her waters cannot sever him from his past.*

*Hypsipyle, the woman he loves, is a pin holding together all his memories.*

*Suddenly, Lethe develops ripples. She hisses, carries semi-stories. She speaks of an abducted Hypsipyle; of her body tied to a stake; of a raging fire that –*

*Lethe stops. Her voice becomes a murmur, not even. Her waters become skin-smooth, hiding within them a beating heart, the truth – Hypsipyle's escape.*

*After decades of waiting, Aethalides is a man in a hurry to resolve half-tales. He leans close. 'Hypsipyle,' he says, 'Hypsipyle, are you gone?' even as he imagines the fire ravaging her body.*

*Silence.*

*She's gone. He is convinced.*

*Hypsipyle is unpinned from Aethalides's memory.*

*And with that, his body, his past, and all things sublime – love and faith and especially hope – come apart.*

*Aethalides, now pellucid, slips into the raging Lethe.*

To forget is to come unbound.

# 2.

**I** struggled to forget my meeting with Sahil. I held it close, telling nobody, not even Tasha, hoping that my silence would erase all thoughts about our encounter.

It was just as well that I had chosen quiet. For Tasha had news of her own to convey.

'I must talk,' she began a couple of days after my trip to Boston. I was seated with a cup of cold coffee at Panera.

'Sure. What about?' I asked, certain that I knew the answer already – she'd tell me of a truncated love affair or of a boy who had stayed too long.

'Well – ' Tasha hesitated.

'You may as well come out with it.'

'Dee – ' Tasha paused. I had seldom seen her prevaricate.

'Seriously. Get it over and done with already.'

'Dee, I plan to get married.'

Even as my sister enunciated the words, Panera turned quiet. The schoolgirl asking for coffee, the middle-aged father teaching his son the rules of addition with teacups, the women sharing memories of a Spanish holiday – they became performers of mime.

'I know, I know, it's sudden, but what can I say? I met someone. And he seems – ' Tasha shrugged her shoulders.

'He seems?'

'Sufficient.'

Tasha's love affair began in the wetlands of Bharatpur – not far from the noise and dust and squalor of Delhi.

Bharatpur's sky is seldom a fluent grey; it is punctuated with painted storks and warblers and hawks. Its treetops bend over with nests and hatchlings. Its horizon is composed of feathers.

But why do I tell you this? To explain Tasha's preoccupation with the sky. Like so many tourists, Tasha hired a bicycle and looked cloudward to name the creatures she spotted. 'Grey lost soul' she called a crane that flew aimlessly; 'blue glutton' she named the kingfisher that dived towards a fish.

Suddenly, Tasha paused. Before her was a man, but he seemed to scan, not the overcast sky above her, but the ground beneath. He bent low, produced a pocketknife, and gently dug the soil.

'What're you doing?' Tasha could not help asking.

'Ah. Nothing really,' the man replied, evasive.

'You know, everything is up there,' she said, pointing skyward.

The man smiled. 'And sometimes not.'

Soon enough, Tasha was being told about the countries beneath her shoes, populated with pot-bellied worms and slugs and snails and scurrying beetles and, most significantly, mould and toadstools. She was regaled with trivia about the macrocosm of fungi. She was informed of Tippler's Bane, an edible mushroom that when mixed with liquor made the guzzler's body violently convulse, and of False Morels that when parboiled released 'rocket fuel'.

Tasha listened with rapt attention. 'Look at that,' she suddenly said.

The man drew close, observed the fruiting body before him – floppy, almost like jello, a lump on a decaying log of wood.

'Judas's Ears,' Tasha said with authority.

'Excuse me?'

'That's its name.'

'I'm aware of that. Yes. But how do you know?'

Tasha parted her lips to say something – that she was a student of science, that she hoped to grow into a biologist, that she had written peer-reviewed papers on the wood-wide web. It was simplicity itself – conveying fictions that seemed as ordinary as fact; projecting selves that weren't but could be in parallel worlds.

Yet, at that moment, Tasha was unable to invent untruths. It was as though the term Judas's Ears was the beating heart of a larger memory. So if the heart got stilled, not only would the recollection collapse but also everything associated with it – Mamma, her animal-nose sniffing the soil, her hands finding their way through fungal filaments, her mouth curving into a gentle smile; Ranja breathlessly following Mamma as she fixed a mushroom on wax paper; Tasha watching as Mamma cooked the forest discoveries; Daddy, a real presence, joining us – the scene shifting to a secret garden that held my body –

The weight of all this slipping beneath a meshwork of deceit.

Tasha couldn't let that happen.

So she told the man, 'It's a long story.'

'I have time to listen,' he replied.

'Do you?'

Over cups of oversweetened tea, my sister told the man of the woods of her past.

He smiled. 'You know, for a second I thought you were a fellow mycologist.'

'I'm sorry to disappoint you.'

'Hell, no! I meet mycologists every day. You are so much more – well – '

'Yes?'

'Interesting.'

This was how Tasha's association with Mikhail began.

In the days to come, they'd crouch like cats, scrutinizing the soil, digging into the fissures of the earth, rescuing plump or soft or fleshy or tissue-thin or grey or chocolate brown wild fungi. Sometimes, they'd walk to her place or his – not far from her residence – with handfuls of mushrooms and gently brush and clean them. They'd slice off the caps, upturned like paper boats, and stuff them with cream cheese.

'We used to sauté these with Mamma,' Tasha would remember.

'Is that so?'

'Yes – we'd add butter, shallot leaves.'

'Why don't we try that next time?'

'I'd like to.'

With Tasha, Mikhail learnt of a world beyond textbook science, learnt of its interactions with the tongue. After his initial horror ('You need

to study things, for god's sake!'), he accepted the joys of mushroom
sap intermingling with oil-herb-salt – this, too, a science.

As for Tasha, with Mikhail, she became more than a 'pothunter'
– a forager claiming mushrooms as food. She came to see them as
agents that decontaminated the environment. So when she followed
Mikhail on field trips with a pocketknife, a brush, and wax paper,
or shadowed him to libraries, she learnt of Oyster Mushrooms
that gobbled up forest waste or of Slimy Spike-caps that absorbed
radioactive caesium.

For Tasha, admittedly, such learning came to be of secondary
relevance. What mattered, truly mattered, was observing Pinwheel
Mushrooms, cheery and pink; or collecting Brittle-gills, like coloured
glass; or, on a most propitious day, stumbling upon Judas's Ears –

And each time that happened, it was as though Tasha diminished
in size like Wonderland's Alice, found herself in Matheran or
Khandala or Mahabaleshwar – those distant hill stations – her infant-
shoes conquering territory.

Each time she followed mycological paths, it was as though she
could hear the chime of numbers – *nine, thirty-four, ninety-eight, ninety-
nine* – 'What after?' – and Daddy's voice saying *Tashu*, saying *infinity*.

*In-fi-ni-ty.*

*Precisely. Careful though. The word can possess you.*

Each time she watched those floppy brown mushrooms, it was
as if the past had never vanished. As if Daddy were still touchable,
conveying truths about Van Gogh and Babel and who-knows-what.

'I suppose, this is as good a reason as any other to marry Mikhail,'
Tasha told me over Skype.

'What is?'

'*This.*'

Later, in the silence of Dev's house, I tried making sense of
Tasha's monosyllable – what did she mean? – and for an instant, I
believe I understood.

There is a moment we wish to crawl into, occupy everlastingly.
There is *one* recollection we wish to cultivate. There is a fragment
from the past that we long for all our lives until someone offers us
access to it.

Maybe, for Tasha, that fragment was Khandala. When Mamma foraged and Daddy dined with us. When we still had a family to turn to.

Maybe, for my sister, time was meant to stop here.

There are so many reasons to commit to a person. Love, some people call it, or attraction or desire. But perhaps these are surface words for the same thing. We yoke ourselves to those who ferret out our happiest recollections. Who then build with us, not something new, but old and half-forgotten.

'**I**'m happy for you, Tasha.'

'I'm happy, too.'

'Who would've guessed this is where your adventures would get you – does Mikhail know of them?'

'Well – '

'The time you were with the art gallery receptionist, for example – what was his name? You rushed pell-mell across Delhi playing a photographer. And with that Tibetan scholar – you learnt about tuberoses. And – '

'Dee – stop.' Tasha opened out her closed fists – fists that had held within them moles, lovers. 'I've released them, don't you see?'

'I'm not sure – '

'They're gone. They don't matter.'

'Tasha?'

'*This* does. This alone. And what it takes me to. What it brings.'

# 3.

It was early, the light gentle. I must have called Mamma a day after Tasha's confession. I imagine she was unavailable. So, finally, I reached out to Ranja.

She spoke, her pitch shrill, puffs of squeaky delight, each word dipped in helium. 'Oh, hello,' she started. 'I'm in the middle of packing – Germany, you know – Jay is there already, and I plan to surprise him. He'll be happy to see me.'

The statement, with its rising inflection, was not unlike a question. And I – alarmed by Ranja's voice, its glass-like thinness, its susceptibility to damage – said yes. In any case, what did I know? Maybe Jay would be happy to see her.

I had to speak before Ranja rattled off an overlong itinerary. 'Tasha is getting married,' I said, hoping that with this enunciation the statement would become real.

'I heard. Mamma told me. It's good!'

'Is it?'

'Of course. About time.'

'I hope Tasha is happy,' I continued, more to wish away Ranja's voice than anything else. 'God knows our family seems to fall headlong into vexing marriages – '

'What d'you mean?' Words about to shatter. It made me want to retreat.

'Nothing.'

'Mamma says she has known a happy marriage. You're content, too. I've been blessed. What d'you mean when you say – '

'I was thinking of Amamma, of course,' I interrupted, alluding to the one person whose past seemed distant.

'Amamma?'

I wish I hadn't mentioned my grandmother. But since I had, I had to hold on to the comment, follow it to its logical end. Ranja wouldn't have it otherwise.

'Well, you know,' I tried sounding nonchalant, 'she married Thatha and wasn't exactly happy. That's what I meant.'

'Who says she wasn't happy?'

'How could she be? Thatha was, well, Thatha. And Amamma loved Venu.'

'Venu?'

But, of course, Ranja wouldn't know him, not by that name. The moniker is mine alone.

'The one who wrote the letter,' I said.

'What letter?'

'In Amamma's box of belongings. *"Meet me tomorrow at 4 in Chetpet".*'

'Ah. That.'

'Yes.'

'What of it? It was unsigned. It could be a friend, a relation, a fruit vendor – '

'A vendor? Really? Then why would she preserve it?'

'I don't know. What are you saying?'

'Remember what people would tell us as children? Of sixteen-year-old Amamma being whisked off in a bullock cart by Thatha? And of a timid boy who watched in the far distance? Let's call the boy Venu. Let's imagine he resurfaced. Let's assume that he moved to Chetpet. He sent a letter, and Amamma, driven to despair by Thatha and his demands, met him. And one thing led to another – '

'Impossible.'

'Consider the date: *31 October 1960.*'

'What of it?'

'Nine months later – Mamma born.'

'This is ridiculous! Really, Dee, you know what you're saying?'

'I do. Haven't you even once considered the possibility?'

'No, of course not!'

'Then how do you think Mamma was born – and years after Amamma's marriage?'

'Who knows – timing, a herb that worked – if I recall correctly, Thatha's prescription, too, was dated end-1960. Or maybe it was just luck – '

'Or another man.'

'You're wide of the mark, really – '

'Why? Because you'd rather not face up to facts? Because you're exactly like Mamma?'

Ranja baulked. Then her voice – it was no longer friable – it turned firm, of metal. 'Let's assume the boy – Venu, is that what you call him? – wrote to Amamma, sought an appointment. Amamma would never have responded whole.'

'Why not?'

'For all her faults, our grandmother is bound by a sense of duty.'

'Nonsense – '

'It's true. She married Thatha, made a promise. Her integrity would override her passion – '

'I disagree.'

'It's a fact, Dee. Our dispositions dictate our lives.'

'But no – '

'We're like planets, don't you see? We think we are free to do what we like, go where we please, but we're curtailed by our orbits.'

This is all I recall of my conversation with Ranja. All at once, the tales I had woven about Amamma's life began unspooling.

The more I considered it, the more I realized that Ranja's claims were not without substance. And *if* she was right, this, too, could be my grandmother's story. This especially.

I must go back to the morning when Amamma walked down the road, the letters from Venu hidden within her blouse. One sought a rendezvous, another carried an address.

This, at the very least, seems probable. She would have dignified the letters with an attempted meeting.

Let's assume that while on the road she bumped into the precocious flower-girl – who, in turn, demanded, 'Akka, you going somewhere?'

What would my grandmother say? I imagine something akin

to the truth because there was little to conceal. She was meeting a penfriend.

'An acquaintance is in town. I'm just saying hello.'

'Acquaintance? What acquaintance?'

'He's someone I knew in school.'

'He? Boys came to your school, Akka?'

'Not quite – '

'So how do you know him?'

No – there were still things to conceal.

So it's only right to assume that Amamma waylaid the flower-girl with un-facts – 'I'm trying to identify the trees along these streets' – a reply that both thought was wholly sound. Next, my grandmother added, 'To know trees, you need to walk alone, speak to every sapling you spot, touch each full-grown branch.'

'And then?'

'And then the names will come to you.'

This, too, the flower-girl accepted and drifted away. Amamma was on her own again.

Until this point, the narrative holds.

Now, my grandmother studied the numbers of the houses that went by. Suddenly, she stopped. This was the house she sought, that displayed all the signs of a fastidious owner. Amamma entered, the gate swinging open with well-oiled ease. She approached the door. She placed a finger on the bell –

– Then she stopped herself.

What was she doing? And to what end?

Why, she was only saying hello to Venu – as she would to Mrs Swami.

But was that all she was doing?

Amamma could tell that she was flirting with something that could devour her whole.

The moment she'd ring the doorbell, Venu would appear. He'd be much the same – interested in facts and numbers, yet desirous of engaging with Amamma's numinous world. He'd let slip a statement about lilies being no more than five inches wide – and Amamma would argue that beauty, by its very nature, was immeasurable.

And that's when she'd be unable to restrain herself. She'd follow

Venu indoors, one stark room leading to the next. She'd arrange herself on a bed, her sari gathering around her, yellow and honeyed. She'd invite him over –

– And it would be the collapse of everything she knew.

Amamma considered her life thus far – the abrupt belly-flop into marriage, the nights with her husband's nagging body, the mornings devoted to Janaki or Mrs Swami. Could she let this, all of this – this inherited world – rupture in pursuit of a kind of love?

Yes, Amamma flippantly thought, yes. Yes, she could.

Then she scolded herself – no, she couldn't.

Amamma realized that even when she transgressed – when she dared being so bold as to write to a man or rebel over everyday matters – she operated within the hedged boundaries of what she thought was fair, what she believed would allow her to remain true to her word.

The day she had been shunted off in a bullock cart – the day Venu had stayed behind and watched – she had promised to stand by another. If she renounced a vow she had aligned herself with, would she be renouncing a part of herself?

Yes, my grandmother was forced to concede. Yes, she would.

It wasn't a happy admission. Amamma wanted desperately to break the confines of her personality. She longed to slink into another body, know metamorphosis, so she could be easy with matters of love and honour.

More than anything else, Amamma, not for the first time, wished to belong to another era. For stories of longing, they exist – but not in dreamworlds. They are shaped by the mores of an age.

Sadly, time travel and magic transmutation – these remained beyond my grandmother's ken.

Amamma dipped a finger into a pool by a birdhouse, then into brown-red soil. In the colour of dry blood, she wrote behind one of Venu's letters – *I come I go we cannot meet*. This – she left in his mailbox.

My grandmother would not see her childhood beloved.

If Ranja is right, this is where Amamma's story with Venu ends.

# Secret.

*These, our bodies, possessed by light.*

# 1.

If Amamma is the beginning, this story is the end. And like all endings, it must be held close.

It happened soon after meeting Sahil, after my conversation with Tasha, after Amamma's secret life collapsed. Two nights ago.

I must have been at the local pub – yes, that was it – because it was dark, smoky, loud with chit-chat against television commentary; besides, I was nursing a drink, a tart gin and tonic. Around me were people invested in a game of soccer or in a lover or in talk about stock markets and office politics. I remained crimped within myself. Any moment now, Nina would appear, tell me of her kids, her life, complete with babble and baby-words. She'd complain of the strain of muchness. I would empathize, of course, but always I'd wish to borrow her day, a few paltry minutes, know what it was like to be tired with too much loving.

Nina arrived, but this time she wasn't alone. 'Here's Neil,' she said with a wave. A man in his early thirties drew close, close enough to be observed. I watched his hair, slick, maybe damp; his eyes, blue, each iris an ocean. 'Hello,' he said, his voice liquid. So it struck me that if some people are made of fire – bellowing and ardent; and some of air – will-o'-the wisp; this man was all water.

'Hi,' I muttered.

'Hey.'

'Hi.'

And so it would have gone on – hellos in exchange for hellos – but Nina took over.

'Neil, this is the woman I told you of, Deeya. My friend's friend – so, of course, my friend, too.'

'I see.'

'Deeya, Neil is, well, he's half-Indian – is your mum French, Neil? Yes, I thought so. And he's a photographer. His pictures have been displayed somewhere – Neil, help me here – in a hall?'

'You could say that.'

'Wait, in a gallery down the road, I now remember. I visited. It was nice.'

Neil accepted the statement with a nod.

I felt I had to say something, a full sentence, so I muttered the banal, the predictable – how do you know each other?

Nina believed she was good with answers. 'Well, it so happens that Neil photographs boats, so my husband is good friends with him. Or is it because my husband and Neil went to school together? Anyway, Dev has met Neil, too. Neil, Deeya is married to Dev.'

I recoiled. How odd it is to be told something true and yet not feel it in your bones. Always it took me a while to admit that I was someone's spouse.

Neil baulked, too. Maybe he took offence at Nina's callow precis of his vocation. Or perhaps – I'd like to believe in this outside chance – he was surprised by the offhand reference to a husband. Either way, Neil and I found ourselves no better off than we had been on first getting introduced. We were strangers without talk.

'I don't know Dev,' Neil finally muttered.

'Ah, really? He's away at the moment. On some ship. I'm sure you've met Dev.'

'Sorry. The name doesn't ring a bell.'

'Odd. I could wager that we were in that gallery, all of us – not you, Dee, this was an earlier time – and were discussing the Oscars.'

'Unlikely. I don't follow the Oscars.'

'No? Shame.' Nina took a sip of my drink. 'Anyhow, Dee,' she turned to me, 'Neil should've been out with my husband – it's his last night in the city and all – Neil's off in a few hours. But my husband is away. And I'm no fun with two babies. So when Neil dropped in, I asked myself, "Nina, who can entertain him? You have no single friends, hell, no friends at all, where's the time – " That's when I got an answer, inner voice and all. "Who better than Dee – ?"'

'Thanks,' I said. I should have been annoyed. I wasn't.

'Well, I have to leave, you know. Sid drives my mother mad. Neil, this is Deeya. Dee, Neil – but I've introduced you already, no? Neil, don't take three years to return. Dee, see you soonish.'

So now I was alone with Neil.

He looked at me, possibly seeking a question, something that would yield a conversation. But I found myself floundering. In this space I visited almost every night, where I let strangers speak of things that didn't matter, where I offered idle chatter in exchange for kind farewells, I felt unable to pull together a sentence that probed.

'Would you like to go out,' I mumbled, 'for air.'

'Sure. And, really, I don't wish to impose. It all happened very fast, you know? Visiting the Singhs, being shepherded by Nina. I can return to my hotel.'

'No, it's fine.' I shrugged.

We walked out, down a road, then another, the air growing wet, still. 'We're approaching the river, aren't we?'

Yes, I nodded.

'I can tell. The quality of air shifts. It's as though with the suggestion of water, everything slips into a state of suspended animation.'

Something about the comment moved me, maybe its unordinariness. 'What day is it?' I asked.

'I don't know. Friday?'

'I'm glad.'

'You are?'

'Come. We're late, but it's fine.'

Neil walked by my side, obedient. He seemed startlingly young in the dark, his body lithe, his gait sprightly. And yet those eyes, they held experience, which is a genteel way of saying that they carried the weight of age. How strange for a body to hold contradictions. I had forgotten that was possible.

We made our way through a crowd, stood by the tidal river. 'This helps me survive Providence,' I said.

'The river?'

'Look ahead.'

A hand brushed against mine, warm. 'My god.'

Before us, bonfires skimming lightly over the water's surface. The air hot. The scent of moisture mixed with that of cedar.

'This is exquisite.'

'Isn't it?'

'Who is that?' Neil asked, pointing.

'Oh, those? Fire tenders. They'll guard this until the end of the night.'

'I refuse to leave. Can we sit somewhere for a bit?'

We found a tetrapod and clambered up. I could feel the clamminess of the sky above us. I could feel the warmth of that scratch across the river. I could feel Neil by my side, his breath easy. I could feel.

For the first time since Sahil – this. In its allness.

Can a moment change an association? It has been known to. Suddenly, Neil was no longer a stranger. He was privy to a thing I loved. Therefore, he was known to me.

And yet the truth also was that he was unknown.

All at once, I wished to change that. And the questions, they surfaced.

'Nina says you're a photographer?'

'I am.'

'And of boats?'

He cringed. 'That wouldn't be incorrect.'

'But it's not the whole truth?'

'It isn't – '

'In that case, how would you describe what you do?'

'I don't know. That's always a tough one.'

'Boats, hmm?'

He laughed. 'I photograph the afterlife of ships. Where they go when sea travel forsakes them. But, really, I should stop. This must bore you. Your husband must've mentioned these things a hundred times over.'

'No. He hasn't.

'No?'

'Though he did tell me of squid fishermen with their electric lights – '

'And the ocean as though a field of poppies.'

'Dev didn't quite use that metaphor. I think he thought it cool. He may have even used that word. Or not. You've seen it?'

'Yup, taken photos, too. Though that was random. I was travelling somewhere, and then – well, the electric lights happened.'

'Tell me more about your photographs.'

'Why don't I send you an invite for my next exhibition?'

'Do. But first speak. Words create their own pictures.'

'Where do I begin?'

'How about with the exhibition Nina visited?'

So Neil told me that he had been trailing a navy ship – old and cantankerous but still a fierce beauty. One day, she was decommissioned. And his camera paid a final tribute. Here's what it caught – a flag at half mast thrashing as though beating its fists in sorrow; a thickly veined hand tying a pink 'friends forever' ribbon around a handrail; a captain watching the vast seas through a crack in the bullseye.

Soon, the mighty ship would be stripped, drained of her lifeblood – oil and fuel – and towed away. Soon, she'd be used for target practice. Soon, she'd blow up, sink.

'As she sank, the pink ribbon against the handrail bobbed for a bit. I don't know how I caught it – an impression of it – because I'm sure my hands trembled.' Neil paused. 'Some day I'll show you the photograph.'

I didn't want this voice to turn silent. 'Are there other ships you've followed to the end?'

'So many, I may have lost count. Have you heard of the SS *United States*?'

'No, I don't think so.'

Neil told me of her maiden voyage – how she broke a transatlantic speed record. But then, our raring-to-go vessel became listless. She burned out. Barely seventeen years after her star performance, she was withdrawn from service, then packed off to Philadelphia. When Neil visited her, he found her body pockmarked, her paint peeling.

'That's tragic,' I said.

'I know.'

In silence, we watched a fire tender row towards a bonfire, the oars splashing. Slowly, he retreated. He dissolved to black.

'It must be disheartening to confront demise every day. To know, even as you pursue an afterlife, that it doesn't exist.'

'Doesn't it? I think it does.' Neil looked at me. 'I was in India in a fishing village. A forgotten boat lay by the shore. I thought her sorrowful at first, this mottled green thing keeling over. But then – '

Neil told me that she had slipped into another life. Where once she had sallied forth, dazzling with her exploits at sea, now she was content encouraging the land-bound conquests of friends and strangers. Sometimes, she'd offer shelter to girls dodging household chores and gossiping about film stars. One day, she hid a little boy as he painted his toenails with his mother's lipstick. Then there was the night when she gently tipped over to make room for impatient lovers.

So this is what Neil's camera caught – the lovers' clasped hands near the starboard; the boy by the cleat, his fingers smudged pink; and those girls squatted on their haunches, exchanging Bollywood cut-outs.

'See, it's not all dismal.'

'Perhaps.'

'I guess the best of vessels know how to start afresh.'

I looked at Neil. He shrugged as though articulating something obvious.

At that moment, I longed to refute his certainties, tell him that things were never that simple. Here I was with a past I had all but outgrown, in a marriage that would never fulfil. And this was it – no matter how much I wished otherwise, for me there was no afterlife.

But confessing is hard work. It is also risky business. It is easier to ask. 'What made you follow dying vessels?'

Neil laughed, 'Do you want to know everything about me tonight? What's left for tomorrow?'

'There's no tomorrow. You leave a few hours from now.'

'Yes. Yes, I suppose.' He paused, then started speaking in a voice altogether flat as though repeating a story he had read to himself every night. 'Ma caught a ferry with a bunch of friends, and neither the vessel nor she returned. Newspapers reported that the ferry had carried too many people. It capsized.'

'I'm so sorry.'

'I was eleven, a kid. And I spent days, maybe years, perched on my tree house, wondering if somehow the ferry could be resuscitated – and with it Ma.' Neil rubbed his eyes. Dry. 'And so ships. And the pursuit of an afterlife.'

'We're doomed to spend our adult lives recovering from our childhoods.'

Neil laughed. 'And I thought you'd call my story clichéd.'

'Aren't clichés the greatest truths?'

'Well. So what traumatized the eleven-year-old you?'

I looked away. I didn't want to answer. Then I did. 'In short, father goes. Disappears. Sometimes I fear every decision I've ever taken is linked to the moment when he walked out of our house.'

'Is Providence connected with his departure?'

'I know it is. I just – I'm not sure I want to join the dots, you know? The picture will not be pretty.'

'Yes.' His hand holding mine.

By eleven o'clock, the flare across the river had dimmed. Now only the stars for light. A busker approached us, his mouth organ playing an easy tune, almost mushy. 'You must miss your spouse at such times,' Neil commented, tossing bills with his free hand into an upturned hat.

Yes, I was about to say, trained as I was in that response. But it was dark, and the truth felt close. 'No,' I admitted. Then, without wishing to, I whispered, 'But you must miss yours.'

Neil laughed. 'When you spend days and nights following ships, travelling, you lose certain privileges. Such as having relationships.'

'But travelling or staying put – these have little to do with cultivating relationships, no? Sometimes I'm convinced it's a matter of chance.'

'It's also about acknowledging the moment.'

'Yes.'

Neil let go of my hand, looked at me. 'So what do we do?'

# Epilogue.

*Tell me we'll never get used to it.*

Here is what I do.

I think.

Ever since Neil posed his question, I have been tracing the tangled lines of the past.

If what mathematicians say is true – if the mere flap of a butterfly's wings can set off a torrent of atmospheric events that, weeks later, produce a tornado in a distant continent – surely, surely, the actions of our forebears and contemporaries must create a series of ripples across time that impinge upon our selves.

Each decision we take must in some way – no matter how tenuous – be linked to the revolts and trade-offs of our relations.

I reach for clarity.

And here is what I know.

That after Neil asked, '*So what do we do?*' we hopped off the tetrapod we were perched on, walked hand in hand, refusing to address the question. Neil shared with me his itinerary – that he'd be going to New York; that he'd spend two nights in the city, then travel to Boston; that from this port city, he'd sail to another stalled vessel.

'What's her story?' I asked.

'Well,' he said, 'she's an old passenger ship biding her time in a scrapyard. But hers is a tale of rebirth. I'm told that she's all dressed up in graffiti. Apparently – '

I know that as Neil spoke, I wanted nothing more than to live such stories, inhabit renewals and second chances. I know that even as I yearned for this, I stopped walking, turned, stood on my toes. I know that I kissed Neil, that he kissed me back.

Here's what I don't know – how we negotiated the next moment. I don't know if we feigned indifference or laughed awkwardly or tried reinstating an easier past by walking hand in hand. I don't know if

Neil spoke of his mother, if I discussed Daddy, or if we simply, silently, studied a river. I don't know how long we spent talking, not talking.

What I do know is this. That we lost all track of time. Because, at some point, we sprinted to his hotel, and Neil grabbed his bag and hailed a taxi.

'Dee,' he said before leaving.

'Yes?'

'Meet me in Boston. At the harbour.'

'When?'

'First thing in the morning after two more nights pass.'

'And then?'

'I don't know. Let's travel. There are oceans to cross.'

I drew close to him; his hand running over my own.

'You'll be there?' he asked.

I said nothing, watched him enter the taxi, watched its retreat. And soon, he was a speck. Almost a dream.

I walked home. Poured myself a glass of wine. Didn't sleep.

That night passed. And another. The last is nearly done. Two hours, and dawn will break.

So now, I consider all the fragments I have gathered; hold them in my palms and watch –

Mamma seated, writing to Daddy, another postcard, *is it cold, Dear Karthik*. The ring of a doorbell, and Mani's voice announcing a new restaurant, Japanese or Korean – our suburb is changing – and Mamma feigning interest, saying yes, let us go. Really saying no.

Ranja, ~~visiting~~ not visiting Jay in Europe and waiting in an aseptic apartment in Dubai. There she is, arranging three plates on three table mats. Let us eat, my child, she says, but after praying.

Tasha by a tree, studying a cluster of mushroom-ears. 'I forgive you', she says, 'it's not your fault.' Who are you talking to, he asks. But Tasha, she can't be reached, she's counting, can't you tell – *thirty-four, thirty-five, thirty-six*. Around the corner, it's there – all that's limitless.

Amamma at Venu's gate. She has a letter, one conveying a pulling away (after lovemaking or before, it doesn't matter). Here's where she can take her story anywhere – tear up the letter, write another one, confess *I want you*. She doesn't tear up the letter. She drops it instead into the mailbox – *I come I go we cannot meet.* She returns home to Rangaa.

I lie on a bed, the one Dev shares with me from time to time. In a week, he'll be home. I can see him enter as he did the last time, ordinary, without distinguishing attributes, without Sahil's jouncing Adam's apple or the unnamed boy's youthful beauty or Neil's ocean-eyes. I accept him nonetheless, his wanting body. I imagine it ship-soiled. I imagine it's a ship. I make love to his scuttle-eyes; his frame, bow to stern. And when I hear something – murmurs, a deep low frequency – I tell myself it's those spinning propellers. Slow, I will myself to hear the lash of the waves, the squawking of gulls, maybe whale-song.

This can be my life, my forevers. Dissembling.

And yet I know that I don't want this to be my story. I don't want to mirror the narratives of my household. I don't wish to play-act like Mamma–Ranja or rein in my impulses like Amamma–Tasha.

I want to – let me admit it – I want to *know*. But what?

I open a book – it has been so long since I've attempted to read – and recover a story of cobra-courtesans. These are women who, from infancy, have been offered the venom of snakes. So now their bodies can destroy. Their blood and sweat and tears are laced with poison.

The story goes that a poet falls in love with a cobra-courtesan, and she with him. After days of coquetry – stolen glances, shy whispers – they arrive at a moment that asks for confessions. He speaks of desire, and she of something more terrifying – 'My body is toxic.'

She tells him that they cannot carry on as lovers – if lovers must reach out for each other's bodies – for if they do, they'll only know destruction. The suitor hears her out, then says that he's willing to risk death.

And sure enough, he dies.

But not before full moments of discovery, mad-sweetness, delight.

Not before living.

I don't know what I expect from Neil. I can't say what direction our future will take – if our tomorrows will know tedium; or if, as in the tale of the cobra-courtesan, they will bear witness to our delirious collapse.

What I do know is this – one must aspire to sweetness. Like the suitor in the story, I reach for knowledge.

It's this that drives me – this seeking – as I retrieve a bag, grab dresses, throw them in. I tear a sheet of paper, write *Dear Dev*; write *some day, I'll explain myself*; write *for now, I must go*.

Then I feel the urge to rewrite, to clarify my motivations, not later, but here. I want to go against my family's grain – make an honest offering of pasts. So I tell Dev everything – about the men who were, about the one who is, about Sahil, the-boy-what-is-his-name, Neil.

Unlike Amamma, I cannot play moral arbitrator. Rights and wrongs, good and bad, these aren't things I'm able to assess.

I flounder for a light switch, pause, watch the house as though for the final time. For the final time. The dirt-free sofa, the second-hand blinds –

There's comfort here, in this house, where the wine waits in the fridge, the glass by a mirror, the corkscrew in a drawer below. In less than a year, this space has wrapped itself around me like a stranger's duvet; I'm snug.

I pour myself a glass of wine, another, a third, and imagine I now inhabit the body of the mad lady near Boston's harbour. This is where she was so many years ago, in some such house, holding on.

I hold on – I don't know to what – to a prosaic curio, to a rock-solid table, to that familiar flicker of light. Dawn.

'Will I find him?' I ask.

*'Do moments, ripe for the picking, ever return?'*

I start.

I should reach for my bag. I should seal the note for Dev. I should approach the mirror and leave behind my glass.

I switch off the lights. *'Too small,'* I hear a voice.

I laugh.

I raise my glass of wine and propose a toast to my grandmother. 'To you,' I say. And sit on the floor.

I close my eyes.

Don't sleep, she whispers in the dark. Don't –

# References

The title of the book draws from the poem 'Scheherazade' by Richard Siken. On pages 173–74, Deeya inscribes this poem on Sahil's body. And on page 281, Deeya spots a girl reading it. Fragments of the poem appear across each of this novel's section breaks. 'Scheherazade', among several other poems – all equally remarkable – can be found in Richard Siken's *Crush* (Connecticut: Yale University Press, 2005).

On page 55, the song Mamma sings – 'Not a cloud in the sky, got the sun in my eyes' – is, of course, 'Top of the World' by The Carpenters.

On page 57, Daddy mentions the myth of the Tower of Babel (the Book of Genesis). His reference to Vincent Van Gogh on the same page draws from the artist's letter to his brother Theo on 11 August 1888.

On page 83, Amamma reinterprets the story of Adam and Eve. The sentence – 'You shall not eat of the fruit of the tree that is in the midst of the garden, neither shall you touch it, lest you die' – is from the Book of Genesis.

On page 94, the reference to Gurdial Singh Gill draws from Venkatesh Ramakrishnan's 'Those Were the Days: When Punjabis Made Madras Their Home', Daily Thanthi Next. In <https://www.dtnext.in/News/City/2018/04/29022930/1070700/Those-were-the-days-When-Punjabis-made-Madras-their-.vpf>.

On page 111, Mani's anecdote detailing the origins of Mysuru paaka has its origins in Radhika Iyer's 'How the Famous Mysore Pak Was Invented', NDTV. In <https://www.ndtv.com/south/how-the-famous-mysore-pak-was-invented-674512>.

On page 124, the lines by Christina Rossetti are from her sonnet sequence *Monna Innominata*.

On page 129, the reference to László Krasznahorkai's 'vast black river of type' is a fragment of poet and translator George Szirtes's description of his prose as 'a slow lava-flow of narrative, a vast black river of type'. In James Wood, 'Madness and Civilization: The Very Strange Fiction of László Krasznahorkai', *The New Yorker*, 4 July 2011.

On page 134, 'it comes out of / your soul like a rocket' is a fragment of a poem by Charles Bukowski, 'So You Want to be a Writer?' In *Sifting Through the Madness for the Word, the Line, the Way: New Poems* (New York: HarperCollins, 2004).

On page 135, Deeya paraphrases Anne Carson when she says that 'a pilgrim is like a No play – his end is not the point.' The original reads – 'How is a pilgrim like a No play? His end is not the point.' Excerpted from a book that can't be recommended strongly enough – *Plainwater: Essays and Poetry* (New York: Vintage, 2000). Incidentally, the Anne Carson quote that opens his novel – 'What makes life life and not a simple story? Jagged bits moving never still, all along the wall' – is also from this book. (The second quote opening this novel – 'You remember too much . . .' – is from Anne Carson's *Glass Irony and God*, New York: New Directions, 1996.)

On page 137, the reference to Goblins' Gold borrows from Robin Wall Kimmerer's *Gathering Moss: The Natural and Cultural History of Mosses* (Oregon: Oregon State University, 2003).

On page 138, Prime Minister Jawaharlal Nehru's statement, 'The light has gone out of our lives', is part of a speech delivered extempore by him on 30 January 1948 after the assassination of Mahatma Gandhi.

The myth of the phoenix across pages 150–51 also features in Anne Carson's devastatingly beautiful *Nox* (New York: New Directions, 2010). In it, she says, 'The phoenix mourns by shaping, weighing, testing, hollowing, plugging and carrying towards the light.'

On page 155, Deeya–Tasha quote the one and only Jack Gilbert when they say, 'The heart lies to itself because it must.' In 'Naked Except for the Jewelry', *Collected Poems* (New York: Knopf, 2012).

On page 168, Sahil's reference to Paul Gauguin's comment – 'I am more than ever tormented by art' – is from a January 1885 letter he wrote to artist Émile Shuffenecker.

On page 169 (and again on page 270), the history of the word 'saudade' draws from Barry Hatton's *The Portuguese: A Modern History* (Massachusetts: Interlink, 2011). The meanings of the other words detailed in this chapter and elsewhere – mamihlapinatapai, tartle, koi no yokan – have been derived from a range of online sources.

On page 171, the writer who said 'I am so thirsty for the marvellous', is the irrepressible Anais Nin. In *The Delta of Venus* (Boston: Mariner Books, 2004).

On page 172, the poem Sahil inscribes on Deeya's body ('Even this late it happens: / the coming of love, the coming of light') is 'The Coming of Light' by Mark Strand. In *Collected Poems* (New York: Knopf, 2014).

On page 181, the myth of Hephaestus has been inspired by an observation in Anne Carson's *Eros the Bittersweet* (Illinois: Dalkey, 1998).

On page 186, Sahil's comment that Flaubert made his housekeeper dress up in his dead mother's old checked dress draws from Julian Barnes's *Flaubert's Parrot* (New York: Vintage, 1990).

On page 211, the writer who, in fact, wrote, 'This is the mourner's secret position: I have to say this person is dead, but I don't have to believe it,' is Meghan O'Rourke. So, too, on page 288. The statement 'The people we most love become a physical part of us, ingrained in our synapses, in the pathways where memories are created', can be attributed to Meghan O'Rourke. In the heartbreaking *The Long Goodbye* (New York: Riverhead Books, 2012).

On Page 219, Sahil's reference to Moses draws from Marguerite Theophil's editorial 'The Broken and the Whole' in *The Speaking Tree*, 12 March 2014.

On page 229, Deeya's Jean-Claude Izzo quote – 'Storms don't exist. Any more than sailors do, when they're at sea. Men are only real when they're on land' – is from *The Lost Sailors* (New York: Europa Editions, 2007).

On page 231, Deeya refers to an observation by John Steinbeck – 'Time is more complex near the sea than in any other place, for in addition to the circling of the sun and the turning of the seasons, the waves beat out the passage of time on the rocks and the tides rise and fall as a great clepsydra.' In *Tortilla Flat* (New York: Penguin, 1977).

On page 234, the reference to linguist Hans Sperber draws from a note in Sigmund Freud's *The Interpretation of Dreams* where he confirms that 'Sperber believes that primitive words denoted sexual things exclusively' (translated by A.A. Brill).

On page 246, Deeya recalls a conversation between a lonely Theodore Twombly and Samantha, the female virtual assistant he develops feelings for; she tells him that she converses with '8,316 others' while engaging with him, and of these she loves '641'. In *Her* (film), directed by Spike Jonze.

On page 247, the fact disclosed by Tasha to Deeya (that certain tribes encourage women to have numerous lovers) borrows from a fascinating anecdote by anthropologists Stephen Beckerman and Paul Valentine. They say that in certain communities in the Amazon, pregnancy 'is viewed as a matter of degree, not clearly distinguished from gestation [. . .] semen accumulates in the womb, a fetus is formed, further acts of intercourse follow, and additional semen causes the fetus to grow more.' In Christopher Ryan and Cacilda Jetha's meticulously researched and compellingly argued *Sex at Dawn: The Prehistoric Origins of Modern Sexuality* (New York: HarperCollins, 2010).

On page 264, the definition of 'marriage' as 'the [legally or] formally recognized union of two people as partners in a personal relationship' is from the Oxford English Dictionary.

On page 313, the reference to tiny forces leading to drastic weather conditions – also known as the 'Butterfly Effect' – borrows from a paper presented by Edward Lorenz, an MIT professor studying climate through a mathematical model of air currents in the atmosphere. The title of his 1972 paper – presented at the annual meeting of the American Association for the Advancement of Science, Washington, DC – was 'Predictability: Does the Flap of a Butterfly's Wing in Brazil Set Off a Tornado in Texas?'

On page 315, the story of the cobra-courtesan has been powerfully described by Illiya Troyanov in *The Collector of Worlds: A Novel of Sir Richard Francis Burton* (New York: HarperCollins, 2010).

On pages 16–17 and 288–89, the story of Aethalides and Hypsipyle has, in parts, been borrowed from Greek mythology.

On pages 49, 125–26, 258–59, and 286–87, the stories of Rangi and Papa, Clytie and Apollo, Ilmatar, and Niu Lang and Zhi Nu draw from Maori, Greek, Finnish, and Chinese mythology respectively.

# Acknowledgements

This novel owes its life to Mamma who gifted me the most valuable thing in the world – words.

And to Daddy who gifted me travel.

I must thank –

Kushagr for the space and encouragement and gentle prodding; for asking me each day, relentlessly, 'Are you done yet?' and for never giving up on me.

Jeffrey Carson, my mentor, for the workshops. I imagine myself in your class in Paros every time I write.

Richard Siken whose poems have taught me how words can build a world, then break it down. Without 'Scheherazade' and Richard's immense kindness, this book would never have had a name.

Keki Daruwalla, one of the giants in the pantheon of writers I admire, whose endorsement stands testimony to his warmth and abiding support to new writing.

Gieve Patel, whose poems I have pored over, for reading this manuscript and blessing it with his words.

Sumana Roy – a writer who marries prose and poetry with effortless ease – for gifting this novel a most lyrical endorsement. Suddenly, this book is all music, it sings.

Chandrahas Choudhury, an author and a critic I have admired for years, for defining the contours of this book better than I ever could. For being a remarkable writer, a friend, a generous host – thank you.

Jessica Woollard, my agent, for the conversations in Bombay and the feedback.

Harshad Marathe, an artist unlike any other, for working tirelessly to make the cover art sing. Bhavi Mehta, a designer par excellence, for weaving in a set of disparate elements, so the cover design stands out.

*Caravan* for selecting me for the Writers of India Festival, Paris, in 2014.

The Writer's Game that first embraced me – Sheece, Ishita, Ashok, Roselyn.

Altaf for being friend, family, anchor, a man for all seasons.

Anindita for being a source of optimism and hope and wisdom; for simply being.

Riyaz, and especially Mridula Koshy and Abha Iyengar, for all the nurturance.

St Xavier's, Bombay, and specifically Shefali Balsari-Shah and Niti Sampat-Patel, for instilling in me a love for literature. The University of Leeds and Ananya Jahanara Kabir for teaching me new ways of seeing text and subtext. The University of Sheffield where it all began.

The Aegean Center for the Fine Arts, my Greek family. John Pack for bringing beauty into my life. Joshuah for Scorpio moons. Eleni for being a Greek goddess. Jun, Adrian, Betsy Bonner, Stella, John Van Buren, and everyone else who made an island a refuge.

Eliza, for reading an early draft of this manuscript. Without you, whole cities, entire books, would be incomplete. (Without you, there'd be no Jaffa cake.)

Yamini, Aditi, Vishakh – for never being too far away.

Abhishek – 'The world was never meant for one as beautiful as you.'

Those who helped me keep body and soul together while I attended to two babies – my son and this book – Seema Kazi-Rangnekar, Sanam Motwani, Natasha Badhwar, Sneha Gusain, Shreya Sridharan-Mhatre, and parents I have yet to meet but who have guided me with attachment parenting through the *Continuum Concept* network, among several others.

Sangeeta Mehta-Bhansali for giving me the time, the space, and the means to write when I first began. I'm eternally indebted.

My friends and colleagues in publishing – Sayantan Ghosh, Amrita

Mukerji, Sohini Pal, Gunjan Ahlawat (among so many others) – from whom I have learnt. The authors and agents, typesetters and artists, publishers and sales managers, booksellers and printers, I have had the privilege of working with while I was a full-time editor. The list is long, and you know who you are. I cherish our association.

The publishing groups that have nurtured me – Vakils, Feffer & Simons, Westland, Rupa, Simon & Schuster.

And especially, Hachette India, for offering this book a home. Poulomi Chatterjee, my editor, for her warmth, gentleness, incisive edits, and keen eye for detail. Prerna Vohra for holding this manuscript's hand as it took its first tentative steps into the world. Ronjini Bora and Aditi Nichani for granting books wings through enthusiastic marketing plans.

R. Ajith Kumar for the meticulous typesetting and Shyama Warner for the careful proofreading.

All the dogs who came and went. Frolic, the first. We'll meet at the rainbow bridge.

My family in Arizona, in Bombay, Paati, Thatha, my cousins, my in-laws, for being there when I most needed you.

Aayansh, my son, my world, who emerged before this manuscript could. For teaching me what wonder and faith and unadulterated joy and love truly mean.

Finally, Partho, the better craftsman – editor, counsellor, poet, soothsayer. You'll always be my first reader.